The Asylum Soul

Mal Foster

Published by: PublishNation

© Copyright 2015 by Mal Foster

ISBN: 978-1-326-26219-8

Brookwood Lunatic Asylum

A PATIENT'S DIARY

1929–1931

ABOUT THE AUTHOR

The Asylum Soul is the debut novel by Mal Foster. Born in Farnham, Surrey in 1956, he is already an accomplished poet and renowned local historian. In May 2014 he took early retirement from a successful thirty-year railway career to concentrate on his writing and other publishing interests. He currently lives in Knaphill near Woking in Surrey, and just a stone's throw from what remains of the old asylum. He is a great fan of progressive rock music although he turns to the Canadian singer/songwriter and poet Leonard Cohen when pressed about who and what inspires him. He has already started work on a second novel.

www.malfoster.co.uk

ACKNOWLEDGEMENTS

A number of people have assisted me with this project and I would like to thank Lesley Bowdidge, Karolyne Foster and Lee Heather especially. I would also like to mention the staff at the Surrey History Centre for their kind assistance.

A special thank you also to Julie Grenham.

When I first started writing this book at the beginning of July 2014 I asked a few friends and acquaintances to suggest some possible character names. The response was fantastic. Whilst I regret that I have not been able to use them all, I would however like to thank all the following for their input and encouragement, it is greatly appreciated: John Abbott, John Allen, Melissa Anderson, Simon Atkinson, Damiena Ballerini, Matt Bentley, Mick Berg, Nick Bloggs, Martyn Buzzing, Suzanna Calhoun, Andy Carless, Danny Carlisle, Paul Cooper, Pat D'Arcy, Conny Eley, Jan Ford, Ian Gabriel, Jeremy Goodwin, Emma Gray, Brian Jones, Graham Kennerson, Mick Lancaster, Chris Lloyd, Mary MacClellan-Buzzing, Sarah Nubeebuckus-Jones, Debbie Orbell, Tim Penycate, Emma Richardson, Aaron Sadeki, Linda Thorning, Jeff Towse, Clare Vodden, Chrissy Wilson and Mikey Woodland.

'Pack up your Troubles' lyric written by George Powell.
Originally published in 1915

Cover design: spiffingcovers.com

To whom it may concern...

AUTHOR'S NOTE

A revelation that a rusty old tin had been discovered by a workman felling a tree whilst clearing part of the former Brookwood Hospital grounds during redevelopment in 1994 has always intrigued me. Amongst other things the tin contained a dictionary, family letters, a lock of red hair and, most importantly, some small leather-bound books filled with the scribbled diary notes of a young male patient who resided at the asylum as far back as 1929. Sadly, there wasn't enough substance to simply reproduce what had been written. Entries were often indecipherable and random pages had been torn out. Essentially though, somewhere between the lines and within the surviving script there was a unique and harrowing story waiting to be told. This is that story...

BOOK ONE

29 July 1929

Why is everything taking so long? Today is my seventh day. Seven blasted days. It's been a week. I bang on the door, KNOCK, KNOCK! – But no-one comes. They've put me in this room until I'm examined by someone called the Admissions Doctor. He'll decide if I need to stay in isolation or go to a dormitory on one of the wards. The lady in the reception has told Uncle Charlie that everything will depend on a medical examination.

I've spent the whole week just staring at the ceiling and reading the writing on the walls and I've not really done anything else. I can't. The walls in this room are a horrid pale green colour. There's someone's name scratched on the wall by the door, Robert Caesar. Who was he? Why was he here? There are other names and dates etched into the wall but they're too hard to read. There are many drawings as well, some rude. There are two metal bars across the window. All I can see from the window is the tops of trees and what looks like a water tower. There are birds circling around in the sky, crows I think. They cackle and squawk.

The chaplain is a vicar called Parson Jaggs. He met me outside the reception yesterday morning and gave me a bible, a pencil, some notebooks and a small book about the asylum – it's a sort of rule book for inmates. The clothes they've given me are too big and don't fit properly. They make me itch.

I can hear footsteps walking up and down in the corridor outside my room. Up and down, up and down, but still no-one comes. There's a strong smell of gas. I can hear water running. There are voices but still, no-one. I'm getting hungry now, very hungry!

~~Dear Mother, Why?~~

Mother, why? Why have you sent me here?

1

30 July 1929

Today I met the Admissions Doctor. He's called Dr Carlisle; he was wearing horn-rimmed spectacles which he kept taking off and putting back on. He was dressed in a long white coat and stank of pipe tobacco. He looked into my ears and then flicked my hair about. He pulled it very hard and said that it needs a cut and a wash. He told me that he was looking for lice. He said that he's going to see me again tomorrow.

'You must come back for a proper examination,' he said.

He told me not to be afraid. What does he mean? I worry. I worry!

I can hear someone crying outside my room, a man I think. There's a thud, then nothing, just the sound of something or someone being dragged away along the corridor, and now there's silence, just silence!

31 July 1929

A woman in a grey uniform called Nurse Applejack came for me this morning. She grabbed me by the collar and took me along the corridor and down the stairs and out into another building to see Dr Carlisle. She told me that she will look after me until they decide what to do, but expects that I'll be sent to her ward. Dr Carlisle was standing in a big room by a window which overlooks a huge lawn with flowerbeds. There were some strange medical instruments and lots of electrical wires hanging down from the ceiling and off one of the walls. There were some leather straps on the bed. He told me to strip down to my waist. The examination took about an hour. He prodded and poked things into my head and neck and kept touching my leg. He then told me to take my trousers down and looked at my private parts with a magnifying glass, and then slapped my bottom when he'd finished.

I think Nurse Applejack comes from somewhere in Africa. She has very black skin. She is fat and has big white bulging eyes and pink lips. She carries a willow copper-stick just like the one Nanny used to have in her scullery to spin the washing.

Later, a rather pretty lady called Mrs Blenheim came to see me and said that she was very sorry that I'd been left alone for so long without being spoken to properly. She told me that her Christian name is Fiona and that she works in the Medical Superintendent's office and sometimes in the reception. She gave me my bootlaces and braces back. She said that I can call her Fiona, but only when no-one else is listening. It's her job to tell my mother how I am. She's writing to her next week and will expect Mother to reply. I told her that Mother can't read or write, although Uncle Charlie can. I told her that Mother lives with Uncle Charlie in Raynes Park. Fiona seems to be a soft and tender lady who understands what I'm trying to say despite the way I talk. She told me that her husband, Isaac, was blown up and died at Gallipoli in the Great War.

'He was a fine young man,' she said.

I like Fiona. She told me that Mother can visit in three weeks time. After four weeks I'll be allowed out for treats, but I must be in company. Mr Randall, one of the attendants, is in charge of days out.

4 August 1929

I was woken up at six o'clock. There was a bell ringing but I don't know where from. I was allowed to go for a walk in the grounds today. Mr Randall watched from a bench and told me not to leave his sight. He gave me a new pencil. Just outside the airing court there was a girl sitting under a tree. She was very pretty but she had a sad face. We didn't talk but Mr Randall told me that her name was Maisie Albright.

'She helps out a lot around the grounds, usually with the Percherons. They're horses,' he said.

I also met a boy, he's about twelve and he's called Master Jack Juett. He lives just outside the grounds in a beer house called the Nag's Head Inn. He comes over to help feed the pigs at the farm by the North Lodge gate which is where the chief fireman lives. Jack said that he would take me over there one day. He told me that there are over thirty pigs including one pot-bellied pig which they keep as a pet.

This evening I had roast chicken and potatoes with vegetables and onion gravy. A few other men were there and we had baked apples and syrup for afters. No-one talked except for when we said 'grace'. Parson Jaggs was sitting at the top table with the attendants and Nurse Applejack.

Outside the weather is very cloudy. The sky is looking dark and I think it might rain. There may be thunder. The whole place begins to feel even more cold and sinister when evening falls.

5 August 1929

Today I was allowed to walk around the grounds on my own beyond the airing court for a while.

'All the fences have been broken since we had strong winds in March,' Mr Randall said.

There's a pond which has a small island in the middle on the other side of the woods by a hedge. There are some big fish in there, and there are lots of ducks. The hedge is a mixture of holly and ivy and privet, and there are some railings. On the other side of the hedge there's a canal. I saw a barge being pulled along by two black and white ponies which were being led by a man along the towpath.

I know how to find out the time now. On one of the buildings there's a clock tower which has a clock face on four sides, but one has stopped at ten past ten.

I saw Maisie again. This time she said 'Hello' and asked me my name. I had to write some things down for her because of how I talk, but she said that she prefers to listen to me.

'Just say whatever it is you want to say, I'll try and understand,' she said.

I liked that!

I talked to a man called Royston Melledew. He always sits by me at breakfast and is near my age. He doesn't know why he's here either. He told me that he goes to the beer house once a week, usually on a Saturday afternoon with Mr Randall. He told me that I should go too one day, but he thinks that Mr Randall is a bit of a rogue. He told me to be careful what I say to him and to watch my money!

Another man called Colonel Peter just walks round and round in circles in the same place every day. He's very thin and even though it's hot weather he wears a long black winter coat. He just smiles and mumbles things and then pulls faces at the sky. I like him though, he always seems very friendly.

8 August 1929

Nurse Applejack came over to me yesterday and started shouting. She hit me on the back of my head and slapped my face. She said that I must not talk to Maisie and not cavort.

'Male and female inmates must not talk to each other,' she said.

I think Mr Randall must have told her.

There's no mirror in here but I think I've got a swollen eye. It's hard to see. Apart from at meal times I have not been allowed to leave the room today.

I think that they might move me into a dormitory in one of the male wards next week.

9 August 1929

Today I'm twenty-four. No-one knows and I didn't think that anyone would care, but Fiona came and saw me at breakfast.

'I wish you a very happy birthday, Thomas,' she said.

I wonder if Mother or Uncle Charlie has remembered. I want to tell Maisie that it's my birthday but I may not see her today. It's difficult.

Tomorrow I have got to go and see Dr Carlisle. I wonder what he'll say about my eye.

10 August 1929

Dr Carlisle asked me how I got my swollen eye and I told him what Nurse Applejack had done. He called me 'impertinent' and told me not to tell lies. He said that I must have done it to myself to seek attention. He flicked the back of my left ear and told me to be on my way. I don't know why I had to see him. There was no examination like last time. What does 'impertinent' mean? I think that Nurse Applejack was listening from behind the door.

19 August 1929

Today is visiting day. I waited in the patients' area in reception for two hours where the visitors come in. No-one came.

~~Dear Mother,~~

22 August 1929

Colonel Peter died last night. He'd been ill for a few days. I saw them taking him from the dormitory to the mortuary just before breakfast. James Dorey is one of the men who have been here for a long time and he said that it might be typhoid again. He told me that a few years ago the water was bad and that many patients and a doctor had died. He told me never to drink water from the stream or the canal. James told me that Colonel Peter's real name was Peter Ulysses De Havilland, and that he was never a Colonel.

Fiona said that she wants to talk to me about something serious tomorrow. I worry.

23 August 1929

Fiona told me that a policeman had visited from Woking. Mother was in hospital. There had been a fracas on Saturday night, 17 August, last in London, north of the river in a place called Berwick Street. Mother had been attacked by a man with a pocket knife and was found bleeding outside a drinking house early on Sunday morning. Fiona asked me why my mother should be in that part of London doing business in the early hours. I didn't know. Fiona said that the policeman had told her that Uncle Charlie would send for me when Mother was a bit better, and she'll tell me more when she can.

24 August 1929

Today I told Mr Randall about what had happened to Mother. He laughed and told me what he thought 'business' was.

I still think that it was him who told Nurse Applejack that I had talked to Maisie – now I'm not sure whether to trust him!

Tomorrow is Sunday. It's a church day. There's a chapel here. It has no tower or spire but it has a bell. It's a cold and eerie place with lots of echoes.

27 August 1929

Royston left today. A man in a brown bowler hat came for him and they went on the omnibus to Woking. The busman is called Albert. He's a portly, cheery chap.

Later the coalman came. His cart was pulled by a big old white horse. I saw Maisie stroking its mane. She told me that she loves horses and that she has her own pony at home which is kept in a field with some other horses.

28 August 1929

There are twelve cuts on my left arm now. My piece of metal is getting rusty with the blood. No-one has said anything. There are many other people here doing the same thing to themselves. Lionel Breavman, whose bed is next to mine, has very deep cuts to both his arms and legs. Some of the women across the way are even worse. One lady has even got cuts across one side of her face. One of my cuts is deeper than the rest. Nurse Applejack swabbed it with iodine and wrapped it with a bandage. It stung and I yelled. She just rolled her eyes and laughed and called me 'stupid'. My arm has turned a horrible violet colour and it still stings.

31 August 1929

It's harder to write since I've moved into the dormitory. Everyone wants to enquire why I write and what I'm writing. There are lots of nosy parkers in here. There's nowhere to keep my book and other things. I don't want other people seeing it, but I've found a hiding place for it now in the woods just outside the airing court. There's a hollow in a tree. I can keep it dry in an old tin, so I shall come here to write when I can. I hope no-one finds it!

Because I have trouble with my speech, Uncle Charlie once told me to always write things down.

'It's good for the memory too,' he said. He's right!

I have collected eight pencils now.

Today is Saturday. There are some boys from the village playing football on the cricket field near the chapel.

4 September 1929

It's rained for three days without stopping. Last night there was a big storm with lots of lightning and thunder. Some people were howling. Lionel jumped out of bed and started running up and down the dormitory. Mrs Meredith, the night nurse hid under her table and knocked a lantern over. There was nearly a fire.

5 September 1929

Today everyone had to be checked for tuberculosis. Mr Randall told me that it's a kind of cough which can kill people. The women were checked first and then the men this afternoon. Two doctors had come from Farnham. I was nearly last in the queue. They're coming back again tomorrow. Mr Randall said that he thinks tuberculosis is what killed Colonel Peter and not the typhoid which is what everyone was saying.

Tomorrow I'm going with Jack to feed the pigs.

6 September 1929

Today I fed the pigs. It was very hot and sunny. I counted thirty-three Middle White pigs. There's also a pot-bellied sow called Gertrude which is a slightly different shape.

'It's our pet piggy,' Jack said.

None of the other pigs have names. Jack told me that each pig has forty-four teeth and that they need at least two gallons of water each to drink a day! He told me that once a month one of the pigs is chosen to go off to one of the slaughterhouses in the village, usually Grimditch's where it's killed. They have two slaughterhouses in the High Street, one is for sheep and pigs and the other for cattle and horses. He mentioned that his father once told him that there used to be four slaughterhouses in Knaphill, but two of them closed and are now used for storing coal. There's a slaughterhouse here but it's not used very much.

'Other pigs are bought or sold to market.'

Harry Horlock the fireman came over to watch us while we worked.

'I don't think that he likes anybody, and because of that nobody really likes him either,' Jack whispered. I laughed.

8 September 1929

Today is Sunday. I left the asylum for the first time to go to a fuchsia show at a house called Almond Villa which is just outside the grounds. It's where the farm bailiff lives. There were eight of us and we went for nearly two hours. The show was in the garden and there was a big white tent. Mr Randall was in charge and he kept calling us a 'platoon' as we walked through the gate by the fireman's lodge.

'Right, right turn!' he ordered.

Mr Randall was a soldier in the Great War, but Lionel told me that he never got any further than Kent. A lady in the garden gave us some of her home-made parsnip wine. It was delicious. Mr Randall frowned and then drank most of what was left in the bottle himself and then went and got some more. Bertie Blackmore, one of my new friends, got a bit tipsy and I think Mr Randall did too.

Later, we had to go to the chapel to say prayers and we sang a hymn at evensong. We then had high tea and Parson Jaggs was sitting at the top table. He's quite a tall man and has a big Adam's apple which bounces up and down a lot when he talks.

9 September 1929

I saw Maisie today. We spoke for a while underneath the tree. Maisie thinks that I'm probably only here because of the way I talk. She said that she doesn't think there's anything really wrong with me. She advised that I should go and talk to Fiona. I asked Maisie why she was here. She told me that she has never told anyone.

'It's a secret, a very big secret and it must always stay that way!' she whispered.

She told me that she's been here for nearly a year now. She is lovely and she always twiddles her long red hair into ringlets with her finger when she talks, but her beautiful dark green eyes always look so sad. She is very sincere but something really haunts her, upsets her. I can almost hear that in her voice when she speaks.

13 September 1929

Nurse Applejack came into the dormitory at seven o'clock this morning. She banged the bottom of all the beds with her copper-stick. Lionel took a long time to wake up. Mrs Meredith who was just about to go home said that some important men were coming from Kingston. They were from the council's visiting committee.

Later this afternoon Mr Randall told us that the men had gone. Albert had come to collect them with his omnibus. They had left word that there had to be some big changes. And very quickly! With immediate effect, no-one is allowed to use the words asylum, lunatic or inmate anymore.

'This is a hospital and you will all be called patients. This should have all happened ten years ago,' he said.

14 September 1929

Today we went out of the grounds and walked up into the village again. There was no sun. We then walked down a hill to a garden nursery near a place called Whitfield at the bottom of Knaphill, behind a big field called Bluegates. We passed a blacksmith's shed and I saw some horses tethered outside. I must tell Maisie. There are many greenhouses at the nursery. Most have flowers but some have tomatoes. A lady called Mrs Bundy showed us around. She showed us a big weeping beech tree and said that it was 'one of the biggest in England'. She kept talking about azaleas and America. Just before we left, Bertie went off with a nursery worker called Joseph to a smaller greenhouse in the corner behind the bigger ones. On the way back up the hill Bertie told me that some 'naughty plants' were being grown in there. They looked like poppies with big pods, and he urged me not to tell anyone. At the top of the hill Mr Randall went into a beer house and we had to wait outside. A cart full of dead goats went by. There were lots of flies. We got back to the asylum just in time for tea.

17 September 1929

Today Mr Randall allowed five of us to go with him to Brookwood Cemetery to 'see' Colonel Peter. We walked along the canal towpath and then went through a little tunnel under the railway station. Mr Randall said that the asylum had its own pauper's place in the cemetery. We walked past lots of graves and then came to a road called Cemetery Pales. When we crossed the road there were more graves and a chapel. Mr Randall stopped.

'This is it, this is the place,' he said pointing at the ground.

Most of the graves did not have memorial stones but had wooden markers instead. Colonel Peter's grave was still very fresh, and the top was covered with sand. I noticed that the name on one of the wooden markers was Robert Caesar. I saw his name scratched on the wall of the isolation room in the reception when I first arrived.

On the way back we were allowed to stand on the station platform and wave at the trains. Some engines did not stop at the station and there was lots of steam.

18 September 1929

Today we went to pick blackberries for the scullery maid. Her name is Sarah. She needed four sieve loads to make some jam. I went with Bertie out into the grounds behind the trees towards the canal. There are many blackberry and loganberry bushes there. We found a dead adder which looked like it had choked to death on a field mouse. The mouse was still in its mouth. Bertie picked it up and wrapped it in a rag. He said that he was going to sneak it into Nurse Applejack's utility bag.

'That should be very funny!' He said laughing.

I laughed too. I think Nurse Applejack is scared of snakes.

19 September 1929

Last night Nurse Applejack came into the ward just before lights out. She was very angry and was rolling her eyes around a lot. It was about the snake. I don't know if it frightened her, but luckily she didn't know who had put it in her bag. She was still trying to find out and was shouting at everyone. Bertie was shaking and I had to stop him from telling her.

This afternoon there's a concert in the Recreation Hall. I think it's the choir of the Women's Institute from Bisley. Mr Randall said that it should be 'enjoyable entertainment'.

I learnt a new word today: 'Abundance'. It means lots of things!

20 September 1929

Lots of people were howling last night, mostly women in the female blocks. 'Oh, that's usual when we have a full moon,' Mrs Meredith said.

There was a full moon last night. I thought I heard foxes howling too.

21 September 1929

It's Saturday. The barber came today and all the men from our ward had haircuts. The barber is called Mr Cohen and he was born somewhere in Europe, but he is not German. He lives in Woking now. Yesterday he was at Inkerman Barracks, 'doing the soldiers'. He was very jolly but he chopped too much hair off and I now wonder what Maisie will say!

Some of the ladies have been doing crafts and making baskets in the Recreation Hall. I saw Maisie walking back with them but we couldn't talk.

This afternoon I've been out in the field playing football with Lionel and my new friend who's called Maurice, and some of the others. The boys from the village poked fun at us and tried to take our ball. Mr Randall chased them off.

There are two rainbows in the sky side by side, and I can smell autumn in the air. It gets dark at teatime now.

23 September 1929

This morning I got four big iced buns from Embleton's in Knaphill for a penny. I have saved one for Maisie. I have another penny left and I will get some more next Monday. The bakery in the asylum doesn't make iced buns, just bread.

Tomorrow, I have to go for 'therapy', the same thing Lionel had. Lionel told me that he was given electric shocks and was forced into a cold bath by Nurse Applejack and Dr Carlisle. He told me that they pushed his head under the water for a long time and then he panicked. He also told me that he had something stuck up him.

'It wasn't nice and it hurt,' he said.

He thinks that it might have been her copper-stick. A man called Derek Hogarth from another ward said that the same things had been done to him. Now I worry.

25 September 1929

I tried to run away yesterday before breakfast, but Albert the busman saw me near the blacksmith's shed. He reckoned that he knew where I was from because of my grey shirt and jacket, and brought me back. He said that he's always bringing people back and told me that because we all seem to walk the same it was easy to tell that I was from the asylum. He thinks it's something to do with us all being given the same sort of medicines.

Later yesterday I had my treatment. Lionel was right. Everything they did to him they did to me. Nurse Applejack held me down and tied and bound me up. A new doctor, I've forgotten his name, put a metal thing around my head. He told me that it was my 'crown of thorns'. There were lots of wires and some rubber things. He put metal clasps on both my eyes so that they wouldn't close. A huge bright light was shone into my face. I was dazzled. Suddenly there were three big pushes into my head and I jumped and squeezed my fists. I squeezed them hard. When it was over he told me that I needed to be washed. Nurse Applejack took me through to another room where Dr Carlisle was waiting. He told me to strip. I cannot say the rest.

27 September 1929

I'm not allowed to leave the grounds. Mr Randall said that he has been told by the Medical Superintendent to keep his eye on me because I ran off on Tuesday. He says that I will only make things worse for myself if I do it again.

I have not seen Maisie to give her the bun I got for her on Monday. It's stale now.

There's a black crow on the ground outside which cannot fly. I've called it Archie and put it in a box on a window sill. I gave it the bun and it seemed happy.

Sarah is working in the scullery again today. She told me that we're all having baked apples with cloves and demerara sugar for tea. She's cooking them herself. There might be custard too!

28 September 1929

Samuel Mycroft is an old man who lives in the gasworks' cottages. He's seventy-eight years old and told me that he used to work at Inkerman Barracks as a warder when it was still a prison. He has no teeth and is nearly always smoking a pipe with a long crooked stem. I think he chews his tobacco as well. He told me about a time in 1904 when a lady drowned in the lake. He said that it was when all the typhoid was about. It was all a big secret at the time and the visiting committee from the council didn't want news of the fever to get out.

'No-one was allowed to leave the place for three months, not even the people in the village knew about it at the time,' he said.

He told me that on clear moonlit nights the ghost of a 'grey lady' can be seen walking out of the lake towards the asylum buildings.

29 September 1929

Last night Mr Randall had all the tools pinched from his shed. He's blaming the gypsies from the camp at a place called Sheets Heath. He told us that there's always trouble when they're about and pointed to the west.

'You can see a spiral of acrid smoke in the sky when they're in the vicinity, and it never smells like normal bonfire smoke,' he said.

He's very angry and is waiting for the constable to come over from the police station which is just outside the grounds in the Bagshot Road.

30 September 1929

Today is Monday and it was my turn to help in the scullery. I peeled over a hundred King Edward potatoes that had been brought in from Johnson's, the greengrocers in the village. My fingers are red and feel raw.

Sarah gave me lots of treats, one was a nectarine – it was very sweet and juicy. I had never eaten one before.

I may be allowed out with some of the others tomorrow but I will have to wait and see what Fiona says.

Tomorrow there's going to be a big parade through the village.

1 October 1929

This morning, the soldiers from Inkerman Barracks marched down to Brookwood Station. We all stood in a line along the Broadway and waved our hankies. There was a band and over a hundred soldiers marching by. It was a grand sight! Mr Randall told us that it was a battalion of the Royal Warwickshire Regiment and that they were all off to catch a troop train to Aldershot.

'Another battalion of the same regiment is moving into the barracks soon,' he said.

2 October 1929

Today a new man called Norbert (Nobby) Hatch moved into our ward from isolation. He's been transferred from the refractory, and before that he was at Broadmoor. I'm sure I've heard of that place. Lionel thinks that he's the man who raped and murdered his own mother when he was just thirteen years old.

'It was in all the newspapers at the time,' he said.

I saw Maisie this afternoon. She's been helping with the new sheep and cattle that arrived from Guildford today. The animals are needed for grazing out in the field and will help keep the grass down.

'The sheep will be moved to the empty pens near the piggery, and the cows will probably go down to the Sparvell fields,' she said.

Mr Mycroft has informed Maisie that next week some Shire horses are coming. She told me that Mr Mycroft knows everything and that he's always the right gentleman to ask for news. I told Maisie about the crow and the bun I bought for her from Embleton's. She smiled and laughed.

5 October 1929

I've sent a letter to Mother with Aunt Betty in Camberley. Aunt Betty has been to visit me today from her new house in Watchetts Road. She came over in a Ford motor vehicle which was driven by Cousin Clifford. His wife Gloria also came. He scraped the car on a pillar box on the corner of a wall near Bagshot on the way. A big dog that was in the road had caused him to swerve. There's a bit of a dent and lots of missing paint on the passenger side. Gloria was very shaken up and Clifford wasn't happy. The motor vehicle is very expensive and is his pride and joy. Aunt Betty told me that she will read my letter to Mother when she goes to see her at Uncle Charlie's house in Raynes Park on Sunday 13th October. I have written it all over again:

Dear Mother,

I'm glad that you are now out of hospital after your accident. Did they catch the man who hurt you?

I'm still not happy that you had me sent here and that you did not come on the last visiting day. I now understand why you didn't come but I'm not a lunatic. Everyone here must be called a patient now.

There's a nurse here called Nurse Applejack who is black and fat. She keeps hitting me and touching me. She told me to stop telling lies about what she and a man called Dr Carlisle have been doing but I'm not telling lies. Mother, you must help me!

I have a dear friend called Maisie. She is very lovely. She loves horses. She listens to me like you used to when I was younger.

How is Uncle Charlie? When can I please come home?

I love you, Mother, Your loving son,

Tommy xxx

It was a nice surprise to see Aunt Betty today. I think that she cares.

6 October 1929

All the leaves on the trees are starting to turn brown and yellow now. Today I think and reflect. I must get out of here. If Mother doesn't help me I think Aunt Betty might, so I hope. I hope!

8 October 1929

It rained all day yesterday, so I couldn't come up to the woods.

Later, I have to see the bedsore nurse. Some older people have died at the asylum from bedsores.

Lionel has caught a fever. He's been shaking and was sick all over his bed. Last night he struggled to catch his breath. Mrs Meredith had to fetch the attendants about an hour before dawn. Everyone was woken up and then Nobby Hatch started swearing and messing around. The attendants had to come back and they restrained him and took him to the side room.

Today I must find Maisie. I haven't seen her for nearly a week. I worry.

9 October 1929

At last, I saw Maisie just before tea yesterday. She told me that she'd been suffering from the bad stomach cramps that women get. She told me not to worry and that she's fine. She still hasn't told me why she's here but I don't want to upset her by always asking. Perhaps one day she'll tell me.

Four new horses came today so that will make Maisie very happy. They've been put out to graze in the bottom field.

10 October 1929

Today has been quite cold. After breakfast I met Mr Mycroft and we spoke for a long time. He always tries hard to understand me because of how I talk and I have to keep repeating myself. He told me about all the reasons why people are sent to the asylum. He said that he can remember a time when people were sent here just because they used their left hand instead of their right.

'They had to walk around with their left arm strapped behind their back until they learnt how to use their right hand. When they did, they could go home,' he said. I wondered if he was telling me the truth!

He told me that most of the women only stay for about a year, although about forty have been here for over ten years.

'They're the ones who are the most disturbed. Men always seem to stay longer. Many of those still here are soldiers who came back from the Great War with shell shock. There have also been lots of suicides at the asylum.'

He told me that there's a long list dating from 1889 up on the wall in the reception which displays all the reasons why people are treated as lunatics.

I am NOT a lunatic!

Mr Mycroft said that he thinks that things have been a bit harsh on me.

11 October 1929

Today is Friday. This morning we went to Guildford in Albert's omnibus. We went to the cattle market and then ate our sandwiches by the river. It was very windy. There were sixteen of us as well as Jack from the beer house. He was allowed to come because he helps at the piggery. Mr Randall brought his friend called Silas Greenwood. Silas is a barrel man at the Anchor Hotel. When Mr Randall went to feed the ducks, Silas told us that Mr Randall's Christian name is Algernon. He never uses it because when he was at school and in the army all his friends would call him 'Algae'. This made Mr Randall very, very angry. Silas then told us that Algae is something that grows in a pond. We all laughed. On the way back to the asylum the omnibus nearly hit a deer.

12 October 1929

Today, I met Maisie near the water tower. She was on her way to do some crafts in the Recreation Hall but walked the long way round. She told me that she had been looking for me. She gave me a parcel wrapped in hessian and string and told me to shush! When I opened it, it was a dictionary. It was published in 1920. Inside Maisie has written:

Dear Tommy,

"Without tears, the soul would have no rainbow."

Your friend,

Maisie X

I will use it and treasure it forever, but now I must find somewhere safe to keep it.

15 October 1929

There's been bad weather since Sunday, but today, at last, the sun is shining.

This morning all men under thirty had to assemble in the Recreation Hall. We were warned that there should not be any physical contact with females. There's been a big row because one of the women patients has been put in the family way, and it's all happened since she's been here. Her father has been to collect her. My friend Bertie is getting the blame.

16 October 1929

The smell in the ward always makes me feel sick. In the mornings it smells of pee. Later it smells of iodine and disinfectant, and at night it smells of paraffin from the lamps.

Lionel came back from the infirmary today. He's better now and is very cheery.

17 October 1929

On Saturday all the doctors and nurses and ancillary staff are to stage a grand concert, and people from the village will be coming. In the morning we will all be allowed to watch their last dress rehearsal. They will all be wearing costumes I think. Sarah in the scullery told me that it's a show called *Yeoman of the Guard,* and that she's playing a character called Elsie.

19 October 1929

Today we went into the Main Hall and saw the dress rehearsal. It was a grand affair and was very good. Sarah sang and danced and was my favourite. Some of the men in the ward are marching up and down still singing one of the songs.

Tomorrow is church day. I'm beginning to hate church.

20 October 1929

'We plough the fields and scatter'...

After church, Reginald Smythe, the quiet man from the other end of our ward, and Lionel and I went with ~~Algae~~ Mr Randall to the Nag's Head Inn where Jack lives. Bertie wasn't allowed to come. The room there was very smokey. There were lots of old men smoking their pipes. There was a lady working on the ale pumps who had had long yellow hair which was tied in plaits. She had very big bosoms and smiled at us. We smiled too. Today is pocket money day so I drank cider. Mr Randall said that the lady is Jack's mother, and that she and Jack's father, Mr Juett, are the ones in charge. He told us that it gets very rowdy in there some nights and that there are lots of fights, usually between soldiers from different regiments. Mr Randall told us about another beer house on the other side of Knaphill which closed a few years ago.

'A soldier was murdered there, had his head chopped off,' he said.

It's nearly tea time now, High Tea. We have tea at 4 o'clock on most Sundays. Parson Jaggs told us that he'll be sitting at the top table again tonight. So that means 'grace!'

22 October 1929

Just after breakfast I watched Maisie in the bottom field with one of the horses. She didn't see me. I could hear a skylark singing. There was a low hazy sun. There was no-one else around. It looked like Maisie was dancing around the horse. It was a beautiful moment. I watched as the wind ruffled through her long red hair. It looked like she was smiling up at the sky and then the wind stopped and Maisie knelt to the ground. I think she was praying for something. She stood up again and it looked like she blew a kiss to the sun. Oh Maisie, my beautiful Maisie!

24 October 1929

This morning Nurse Applejack took me back to the reception to see Dr Carlisle. She told me that today was my review date. There was a burning pipe in a silver ash tray and a big bottle of black navy rum on his desk. He told me that it was time to talk to me about my case. He asked me if I was 'alright?' He then told me that he thinks I have a speech defect, probably caused by a stammer and showed me his notes. Idiot! – I've known that all my life, I rage!

25 October 1929

Sarah told me that she's leaving the scullery next week. She has a new position in the big kitchen where she will be cooking all the time. She told me that she will get sixpence more a week. Unless they work in there, patients aren't allowed in the big kitchen. I will miss her. She doesn't know who will replace her yet. I hope whoever it is will be as nice as her.

Tomorrow is Saturday.

26 October 1929

Yesterday I stayed in the woods too long. It was nearly dark and I could hear Mr Randall calling my name. As it grew darker it seemed like all the tree trunks were growing faces. I could hear them whispering at me but now I think that it was only really the wind playing tricks with my mind. It was very eerie. I ran as fast as I could and fell over.

On Monday I have an appointment with Fiona.

28 October 1929

In the office with Fiona today there was an old lady called Mrs Evenden. She had one blue eye and one brown eye and had steely grey hair. She asked me to say a few words then gave me a book and told me to try and read part of the story out loud. I then had to sit outside and wait to be called back in. I could hear them talking but I couldn't make out what they were saying. The door was closed. When I was called back in Mrs Evenden asked me if I liked music and singing. I do. She thought that if I learned to sing it could help me to talk better. She said that she has done this before with some other patients and that they could all talk much clearer now. She asked me to think about it and that she will talk to me again in three weeks time. Fiona smiled.

Because I had to meet Mrs Evenden I wasn't able to go to the village with the others today.

30 October 1929

The new scullery maid is called Missy Hope. Sarah was showing her how to bag and drain beetroot this morning. Hope used to be an ~~inmate~~ patient here but now lives with a family in Queens Road. I laughed as I thought to myself - where there's Hope, there's hope. I suppose.

I must get used to this: asylum is now hospital but everyone still calls it 'The Asylum'. Inmates or lunatics are now to be called patients. Harry Horlock, the fireman calls us all loonies or imbeciles. I think that he's an imbecile!

31 October 1929

Today a letter came from Aunt Betty in Camberley. She's been to see Mother in Raynes Park and is arranging for her to go and stay with them. They're making room downstairs. Mother is using an invalid chair now. She's been having trouble breathing and walking since her attack. Uncle Charlie has been finding it hard to look after her and cannot cope. Aunt Betty said in the letter that a lady called Mrs Evenden is coming to see me. She did, the other day. Mrs Evenden once taught Aunt Betty at school and they still know each other. Aunt Betty said that this should help. I must write back.

Tonight it's the witching hour. I worry.

1 November 1929

Last night there was a fire and we all had to leave the ward. A klaxon was going and the fire engine came. It was Harry Horlock and another man who I have seen in the village before. Mrs Meredith and the night attendants took us to the Main Hall. Nobby Hatch had been smoking under the blankets and had set fire to his bed. He was taken to the side room again. We were allowed back when the smoke had cleared and after the attendants had taken the bed away.

This morning there was a lot of fuss outside. One of the women had been found dead. She had committed suicide. A constable came before they took her dead body to the mortuary. The other women think that she had taken some poison. Her name was Pamela Gray. Mr Mycroft told me that a few years ago her sister threw a baby into the canal at St John's. The baby was rescued by two men and survived and is now growing up with its father in America. The father was a soldier who was serving at Inkerman Barracks just after the Great War. Pamela's sister had later killed herself in a grand mansion over in Worplesdon. Pamela had been mourning the loss of her sister ever since.

2 November 1929

Today there's been much excitement in the airing court. An airship flew over, it was very low and for a minute I thought it was going to crash into the water tower. I could see faces looking down from the cabin. The people were waving. The airship was making a strange whirring sound. I've never heard that sound before! Next, some Sopwith Camel aeroplanes flew over. They were not flying as low but I could see the pilots waving down at us. I counted twelve aeroplanes altogether. It was a grand sight. Mr Randall reckoned that they were on their way back to Farnborough.

'There's an aerodrome there,' he said.

I saw Maisie today. We couldn't talk properly because Nurse Applejack was watching and I didn't want to get into any more trouble.

3 November 1929

Today is Sunday. This morning we had church. Parson Jaggs was shouting out something about sinners.

'You are all sinners,' he shouted.

Reginald, the quiet man, moved towards him waving his fist and had to be held back by Mr Randall. He was taken away from the chapel by another attendant just before the service finished. I don't think that Reginald liked being called a sinner. I didn't either!

After dinner eight of us went for a short walk along the canal with Mr Randall. It was cold and it started to drizzle with rain. We didn't have time to go to the beer house.

Mr Randall told us that tomorrow some lumbermen are coming to build some new pens and a chicken shed near the piggery.

'The farmers need to get it ready so that they can bring in more birds in time for Christmas,' he said.

4 November 1929

I like Mr Mycroft. Today he gave me a big raspberry pie from Embleton's. I told him what happened yesterday in the chapel and he told me about Reginald. Reginald was one of the many soldiers who came back from the Great War with shell shock and has not uttered a word since. Reginald has been here since 1918 and is thirty-two years old now. He always carries a dented toy tin soldier under his left arm and marches instead of just walking.

Mr Mycroft also told me about the new chicken houses and pens that the lumbermen are putting up.

'The kitchen needs more eggs. The farm at Stafford Lake doesn't supply enough and their eggs are becoming far too expensive, it's best if we can produce more of our own eggs here,' he said.

Tomorrow, it's my turn to help in the laundry.

6 November 1929

Yesterday I was in the laundry all day. It was very hot in there and I had to wear some special dungarees and boots. There were lots and lots of towels and sheets and table cloths. A lady called Mrs Skilton is in charge and she just sang all the time. She told me about Nurse Applejack. Last year Nurse Applejack went into a Post Office in Knaphill and a man who worked in there called her a baboon.

'Theodora doesn't like to leave the grounds anymore because of that,' she said. I laughed. We both laughed.

I think that Theodora must be Nurse Applejack's Christian name.

Last night was Guy Fawkes Night and there was a big bonfire in the bottom field. We were all given potatoes and skewers so that we could roast them in the fire. One of the women caught her clothes alight and had to be rolled over by an attendant. He then threw water at her from a pail that was on the ground. Everything then stopped and we all had to go back inside.

7 November 1929

Mr Randall said that no-one will be allowed out in the grounds tomorrow. Mr Drake, the gamekeeper and two shooting men from Bisley will be out killing pheasants and rabbits. They also hope to shoot a deer. Mr Randall told me that the pheasants need about a week to 'bleed' after they've been shot but rabbits can usually be cooked and eaten straight away.

There's a Grand Annual Ball next Saturday and the men from the Surrey County Council are coming from Kingston. Members of the Visiting Committee will also be here.

On Saturday we're going on a trip, but Mr Randall couldn't remember where to. I would like to go to Guildford again.

9 November 1929

Today Albert came with his omnibus and picked us up. There were sixteen of us. Mr Randall now has a few days leave of absence and one of the other attendants Mr Elliott came with us. He's bald and has a long black beard and told us that he used to work on the ships. We went to Aldershot to see a big parade. There were lots of bands and soldiers. Mr Elliott told us that it was our treat for being 'good and well behaved.' As well as myself there was Lionel and Maurice. Most of the rest I didn't know except by their faces.

Mr Elliott told us that there had been three deaths during the night and that there was a problem because there were too many dead bodies in the mortuary. An undertaker from Woking was helping out. He told us that the asylum's mortuary only has room for eight bodies at a time.

'It's a bit over crowded in there just lately,' he said.

Lionel asked who they were and how they died but Mr Elliott wouldn't tell us.

Tomorrow is a church day. Again!

10 November 1929

After church I saw Mr Mycroft. I told him about what Mr Elliott had said yesterday about all the dead bodies when we were out on our trip. Mr Mycroft told me that it's always a big problem when people die at around the same time. He said that two of the three who died on Friday night had something called colitis and another was a lady who had bedsores. She'd been here ever since her husband accused her of having an affair in 1912. The mortuary has to keep the dead bodies until all the family have been informed. This takes quite a few days and has to be done because the family of the dead may wish to make their own burial arrangements.

Mr Mycroft told me that on Friday Mr Drake and the men from Bisley killed a total of forty-seven rabbits and twelve pheasants.

'They didn't get the deer they were hoping for,' he said. I smiled.

11 November 1929

Today Nurse Applejack took me and some others from our ward to be measured and weighed. I don't remember being weighed before. I am five feet and eleven inches tall and I weigh nine stone and seven pounds without my boots on. I now have a new shirt, coat and trousers. They all fit better and I fidget less.

It's the Armistice today and it's very cold.

16 November 1929

It has rained a lot over the last few days and it's been harder to get out.

Yesterday I did some odd jobs and helped out in the electrical store. It's a very dangerous room and the attendant there showed me all the switches and told me about volts and when the lights can be turned on and off. There's a big leak in the roof which he's worried about. My job was cutting rubber cable covers into equal lengths.

Tonight it's the Grand Annual Ball. We're not allowed to go because it's only for the staff and guests from the village. All the important men from the council and Visiting Committee will also be there again with their wives.

Next Saturday there's a Fancy Dress Ball for staff and patients. Mr Mycroft told me that last year he dressed up as Humpty Dumpty. I don't like dressing up!

17 November 1929

'In the bleak mid-winter frosty wind made moan'...

Church again. Parson Jaggs said that he wants us all to learn some carols in time for Christmas. He wants everyone to sing out loud.

'The people from the village will be coming for a special service and they will be singing with us,' he exclaimed.

After church we went to the Recreation Hall to do some crafts. There was a lady from the village there called Mrs Woolston and she showed me how to make a jaw harp with a small horseshoe from the blacksmith's and some wire. I twanged it in my mouth a few times and now I have a cut lip and another broken tooth.

18 November 1929

It's getting harder to see Maisie. The attendants have been told to make sure that we all stay in the airing courts. Most of the fences have been fixed now. It's ever since that female patient fell in the family way and had to be sent home in October. Bertie is still getting the blame for it by all the staff but another man from the village who's not a patient is also a suspect.

Last night someone I didn't really know died in our ward. Mrs Meredith tried to save him but he choked on his own sick. The porters took him away as quickly as they could but most of us were woken up when all the lights came on.

19 November 1929

Today when we woke up Reginald was missing from his bed. His tin soldier was left on his pillow. Mrs Meredith was worried and called the attendants. One of the night porters told her that he had seen Reginald going to the ablutions at about 5 o'clock. I've never heard Reginald speak and he's very mysterious. I know that he doesn't like church and he found it very hard to go back there on Sunday after what had happened the week before. After breakfast we were all called in from the airing court early. A constable came. Mr Randall, Mr Elliott and some other attendants and the constable have been out searching the grounds for Reginald. I've seen them in the woods and down by the oil screening tank.

There's a new nurse on our ward today who's been helping Nurse Applejack. A lot of men have been cutting themselves again. I've learnt not to do that anymore!

20 November 1929

Reginald is still missing. Some of the attendants and farmhands are now out looking for him up in the village. Others have gone down to the railway station in case he's tried to catch a train from Brookwood. Albert has come in his omnibus to help with the search and is driving the attendants around. We have all been told to keep an eye out. It's very cold and it will soon be dark. I hope they find him. I really do hope that they find him!

21 November 1929

Reginald has still not been found. There's a new man in his bed already. Lionel thinks that Reginald might have to go into isolation for awhile when he comes back. Everyone is still talking about him. I wonder where he's gone - I worry.

Later Nurse Applejack told us that Mrs Meredith had just been dismissed for 'failing to conduct her statutory duties'.

'Tonight a new nurse will be in charge,' she said.

Nurse Applejack seemed very happy about it. I liked Mrs Meredith.

There was a fight out in the airing court today. Nobby attacked Bertie and his face got badly bruised. They had been joking and laughing together but Nobby didn`t like something Bertie had said and just went mad. He hit him with his fist three times. An attendant came along at the end of the fight and Bertie got the blame for everything. Nobby just sat in the shelter laughing. I find at times that Nobby can be quite unsettling.

22 November 1929

The new night nurse is called Miss Montague; I think her Christian name is Mary. She's been transferred over from one of the female wards where she has worked for over ten years. She's the nurse who helped Nurse Applejack in the ward on Tuesday.

There are some peacocks up by the farm, they are very noisy things and have been brought here from Hilltop Place where Mrs Woolston lives. Mrs Woolston is one of the art and craft helpers and is quite a noble lady. Mr Randall told me that Mr Woolston is an important man at the Woking Council and that the peacocks have been brought here to be fattened up.

'Many well off people still prefer them to turkey or goose at Christmas,' he said. I don't believe him!

There's still no news about Reginald.

24 November 1929

This morning before church there was a lot of fuss. A dead body has been found in the one of the water wells. No-one has said who it is yet but it must be Reginald. Two police constables were talking quite loudly to Mr Randall, Mr Elliott and some other the men outside. The Medical Superintendent was also there. One of the farmhands told us that the dead body is that of a man. He had some sort of mask over his face. Some big stones were found tucked inside his clothes with more, smaller stones in his coat pockets. He was found head down. Lionel asked the farmhand if it was Reginald but he didn't know. He couldn't describe the body as it was already covered in sacking by the time he saw it. Dear Reginald, if it's you, Rest in Peace my friend.

Last night I went to the Fancy Dress Ball. I went dressed as Robin Hood but I didn't have time to make a bow and arrow. Maisie wasn't there.

25 November 1929

Miss Montague asked me if I would like to look after Reginald's tin soldier.

'He has no family,' she said. Of course, I agreed.

Later Mr Randall took some of us to the village and I was able to go into Embleton's. They didn't have any iced buns this time but were selling lardy cake today. It was still hot. We all bought some and sat on a rickety bench outside the Crown Inn and ate it before it all got cold. It was very nice and spicy. We saw Mr Randall's friend Silas. He was on a bicycle. He asked if we would like to go to Guildford again one day. We said 'Yes'. I was the only one to say 'yes please'. I think Silas liked that. Mr Randall told us that he would speak to Albert the busman but warned that we probably wouldn't be able to go until the spring.

'The weather can get very bad around these parts during the winter,' he said.

On the way back to the asylum I saw Maisie on the other side of the road. She was walking with a matron, an attendant and some other women from her ward. She waved and smiled. I smiled too. I feel happy now.

27 November 1929

Today is Mother's birthday. It's sunny but also very cold.

Poor James Dorey died last night from something called general paralysis. He was fifty-two years old. Mr Mycroft told me that a lot of men suffer from the same disease or have syphilis but most of them are in a special ward. He told me that it was a lot worse a few years ago but treatment for it is supposed to be much better now.

No-one has said any more about Reginald yet.

28 November 1929

Mr Randall told us that the body found in the well on Sunday is definitely that of Reginald Smythe. He's being buried at Brookwood Cemetery tomorrow and his brother Sydney will be there.

'The Constabulary have contacted his family and confirmed to them that is was a suicide,' he said.

We will not be allowed to go.

Fiona came into the ward this morning and told us that she will be leaving service tomorrow. She has a new post in Camberley and will be working as a bookkeeper at Herbert Solomon's.

'They sell very posh motor cars,' she said.

She told me that Mrs Evenden is coming to see me tomorrow. I will miss Fiona. She's always been very kind and has a friendly face.

29 November 1929

Mrs Evenden came at half past ten. We went to the Main Hall where there's a grand piano. Two other patients, Edward Leigh and a lady called Linda Spooner from one of the female wards were also there. Mrs Evenden said that we all have a similar condition and thinks that we will benefit from learning together. One of the servants brought in a big pot of tea.

'How now brown cow, how now brown cow, how now brown cow'...

Mrs Evenden asked us all to say *'How now brown cow'* a hundred times. One of the attendants was counting. Mrs Evenden then started playing the piano. She said that she would like us to learn at least one carol and one other song and asked us to read the words. I wanted to try *'In the bleak mid winter'* but she gave us *'Once, in Royal David's City'* instead. Mrs Evenden said that this will be the patient's carol for the Christmas service in the chapel. The other song is called *'Pack up Your Troubles in Your Old Kit-Bag, and Smile, Smile, Smile'.* 'It's a good song and will help you all with accentuation,' she said.

Mrs Evenden told us that it's a marching song that British soldiers sang in the Great War. She thinks we will all be talking a lot better in just a few weeks time.

Today I have prayed for Reginald.

30 November 1929

Today it's Saturday and there's a football match out on the field this afternoon. A team of doctors and staff are playing a team of soldiers from Pirbright Camp in the English Cup. Mr Randall thinks that the soldiers will win.

'They always do,' he said.

Before the football Mr Randall has promised to take some of us out to the Nag's Head Inn. I wonder if Mrs Juett will be there.

1 December 1929

Yesterday at the football match there was a big fight on the pitch and Mr Elliott was punched on the nose. He thinks it's broken. The soldiers won by scoring 14 goals. The staff team didn't score any but Lionel said that he thought they did get at least one. He might be right – it was getting very foggy!

Archie the injured crow is dead. It was found by Jack who thinks that it was killed by the engineer's cat. I mourn.

Today is another church day. This morning in the chapel Parson Jaggs said a prayer for Reginald and we all said Amen. It didn't feel right. Parson Jaggs kept shouting... 'Repent, repent, repent!' I wasn't sure what he meant but I remembered that Reginald hated church. I think that he felt that God had let him down. Parson Jaggs is such a hypocrite. He angers me!

6 December 1929

There's been snow on the ground since Tuesday but it's thawing now. Mr Randall thinks that it has come early this winter.

On Wednesday I was called to see Miss Rance. She's the new lady who has taken Fiona's position. I cannot go home for Christmas. Mother has moved to Camberley and is being looked after by Aunt Betty. There's no room for me at Aunt Betty's house. Uncle Charlie is not well, so I cannot go home to Raynes Park and stay with him. Miss Rance told me that Uncle Charlie is very ill and so I worry.

I saw Maisie yesterday. She told me that she's being collected on the day before Christmas Eve. She's going to stay at her father's house in Tilford Green. She's looking forward to seeing her pony.

Tomorrow there's a Christmas Ball and a party and the men from the village will be coming with their wives to dance.

9 December 1929

The Christmas Ball was great fun. Silas came and he was showing us some tricks and magic. Maisie and I danced. It was nice to hold her in my arms. Her hair was tied up on top of her head. I had never seen her like that before. She smelled as sweet as a rose. We didn't talk very much because Nurse Applejack was watching us again. I'm going to try and see Maisie again before Christmas.

This morning in the chapel we all had to sing *'Once, in Royal David's City'* three times. It was a practice for the Christmas Carol Service. Parson Jaggs was shouting at everyone again. Not many people were singing.

10 December 1929

There's a new man in our ward. He keeps slapping himself on the face and scratching his head. His head is closely shaven. I think he must have had lice. He won't tell us his name. He's about forty years old and has a tattoo of a naked lady on his left arm. He chain smokes and has already caught his bed alight. Lionel put the fire out before it got too big.

Miss Montague the night nurse has gone back to work on the day shift in the female block. Mr Randall told us that it's always difficult to keep night staff.

'They either stay for a long, long time or don't stay for long at all,' he said.

He told me that many are intimidated, not by the patients, but by other staff, often the senior ones who should know better.

'A lot of bad things can happen in here at night.'

Nurse Applejack told me that tomorrow I have to go for electrocution. I worry.

11 December 1929

The new man in our ward is called Raymond. He's been moved from another ward because he's a troublemaker. He's already made friends with Nobby Hatch, so there are now two troublemakers in our ward!

I didn't sleep at all last night because of what Nurse Applejack had said yesterday. All night I had laid awake thinking that I was in trouble for dancing with Maisie at the Christmas Ball. I didn't want to get beaten again.

Today Mrs Evenden came. I went to the hall with Edward. Mrs Evenden told us that Linda had died from asthma last week. We said a prayer.

'There are only the two of you for elocution now,' she said.

I think Nurse Applejack might be playing games with me. I told Mrs Evenden what she had said. She told me that I should wash my ears out and laughed quite loudly.

'Electrocution and elocution are two VERY DIFFERENT things.' She shouted.

I know that but I also know what I heard!

12 December 1929

This morning I helped Jack with the pigs. There was a cold and bitter wind. One of the pigs was being sent to Grimditch's for slaughter in time for Christmas and Cyril Luscombe, the Farm Bailiff asked me to choose which one to send. I felt like an executioner so I asked Jack to choose instead. It was sad to see the pig go. It looked like it knew its fate.

Mrs Woolston was passing by. She had been talking across the way with Harry Horlock's wife. Jack asked her if it was true that she was having a peacock for her Christmas dinner. She said she was.

'It's a family tradition up at Hilltop Place,' she said.

Mrs Woolston told us that peacocks have their own special taste and that the meat is very tender if cooked well. It seems that Mr Randall wasn't lying after all.

14 December 1929

Today is Saturday and I went out in the grounds with Lionel and Maurice to get some holly branches so that we could help make the Christmas decorations. It was cold but Missy Hope who works in the scullery kept the door open and she gave us some of her homemade mushroom soup to keep warm.

There was a smell of roasted chestnuts coming from the kitchen. Nanny used to roast chestnuts in the fireplace at Christmas so it reminded me of her and a happy time when I was young.

I wonder how Uncle Charlie is. I want to tell him that I have started shaving now.

'At last,' he'd say. I do hope he will be proud of me.

15 December 1929

I saw Maisie today. We had time to talk and she told me that it's her birthday on the day after next. She's eager to get home and ride her pony but she has fears about her uncle. She wouldn't say why but said that she will tell me one day. 'There's a lot to tell but for now I just can't say it,' she said.

Maisie told me that she thinks I'm talking much better. I sang her a verse of *'Once, in Royal David's City'* and she liked it. She said that I should sing a special song for her one day – how on earth?

Nobby and Raymond were causing mischief again last night and Mrs Eley, the new night nurse, had to call for the attendants. No-one got much sleep. The lights were going on and off all night and the klaxon went off twice. I think Raymond might get taken back to the refractory because he got into bed with Maurice. Maurice told me that Raymond played with his private parts but Nurse Applejack didn't believe him when he tried to tell her this morning.

17 December 1929

Today is Maisie's birthday. She's twenty-five years old. I haven't been able to see her yet. I so want to wish her many happy returns. I've made a gift card for her. On the front I have painted a galloping horse jumping over a big red rose. She loves horses and roses. On the inside there's a drawing of another rose and some holly because it's nearly Christmas. I do hope that she will like it!

Maurice left our ward this morning. He's been taken to the senile block. I think it's because he keeps forgetting things. On Sunday he couldn't remember his own name and wept when Nurse Applejack kept asking him. What happened with Raymond didn't help. When people go to the senile wards we don't usually see them again. Poor Maurice – I worry!

18 December 1929

One week to go until Christmas Day. Last year I was at Uncle Charlie's house with Mother. We had a goose for our dinner. There were lots of oranges and Uncle Charlie let me drink some rum. A man called Rufus called at the house after dinner and I didn't see Mother for the rest of the day.

Today I have been practicing singing. It's the Christmas Carol Service on Sunday.

I still haven't seen Maisie to give her the gift card I made. It's very cold and people are not coming out into the airing courts and grounds as much, perhaps that's why!

Tomorrow some of us are going to Woking in Albert's omnibus to do some shopping. Mr Elliot and another attendant will be in charge. It will be a bit strange going on a trip without Maurice. I haven't got much pocket money left so I'm not sure what to buy Mother and Uncle Charlie for Christmas.

20 December 1929

At last I saw Maisie today. I think she liked the gift card. It had become crumpled around the edge because I've been carrying it inside my coat in case I saw her. Nurse Applejack and a nurse from Maisie's ward were watching us so we couldn't talk for long.

Yesterday I bought Mother and Uncle Charlie each a tin of Mackintosh's De Luxe toffees. I only just had enough money. Miss

Rance is arranging for them to be sent with a letter to Aunt Betty in Camberley for me. I do hope the parcel arrives in time.

In Woking, Nobby was caught stealing some confectionary and cigars from a shop near the railway station and a policeman came. Mr Elliot had to sort things out. I don't think Nobby will be allowed to come out shopping with us anymore.

21 December 1929

Today is Saturday. I like Saturdays. There's a Grand Dance and the asylum's own band will be playing music this afternoon. A guest soprano singer is coming here by train from London to perform and Mrs Evenden is already here to play the piano.

I saw Mr Mycroft this morning. He's going to Cornwall today where his brother lives. He told me that his brother is a fisherman and lives in a house on a cliff by the sea. He told me that he plans to be back before the year ends. He gave me some chocolate. I think that I shall save it for Christmas Day.

22 December 1929

'Once, in Royal David's City'...

This morning it was the Christmas Carol Service in the chapel. Lots of people from the village were there. A minister from the Wesleyan Church came to read a lesson. Parson Jaggs was very quiet today. I heard Nurse Applejack sing, she was very loud and everyone was looking at her. Maisie was on the other side of the aisle with all the other ladies. The people from the village were all dressed up in their Sunday best and they sat in the pews at the front. Afterwards Mrs Evenden said that she had been listening to me. She said that she was 'very pleased'.

I kept thinking about Reginald.

23 December 1929

Today Maisie was collected by a man in a black motor car. I was watching from near the road. It must have been her father or uncle. He was wearing a flat grey cap. Maisie didn't tell me when she is coming back. I will miss her.

Some new cows and sheep came today. Donald, one of the farmhands told me that the farm had been struggling to build up the livestock since the Great War.

'It's all just about back to normal now,' he said.

I helped swill the pigs. Donald told me that he doesn't like working with the pigs. Sometimes they are fed organs and body parts from the mortuary and it makes him feel sick and all creepy. Now I wonder?

Jack wasn't with us today. Donald told me that he's helping out in the beer house.

'It's very busy this time of year, being Christmas and all that,' he said.

24 December 1929

Today Mr Elliott and Mr Drake, the gamekeeper took four of us out on a brisk walk to Bisley Church and back. It was very cold but there was a bright blue sky. We walked along a road until we came to a beer house called The Fox Inn. We then walked along a bridleway, which was to the side. We could hear a bell ringing from behind the trees. Mr Drake said that the bridleway is the end of Knaphill and the start of Bisley.

'It's the border between two villages,' he said.

Along the bridleway he showed us a couple of graves set back beneath a holly tree. He told us that it's believed that they are the graves of two highwaymen.

'They've been here since around 1665,' he said.

Mr Elliott laughed, but I don't know why.

When we got back I went to the scullery. Sarah was there and she gave me some soup. Missy Hope was preparing a dead peacock for Mrs Woolston to collect. Sarah told me that the farmhands are bringing some live chickens in later, so she had come out of the big kitchen to help.

'We've still got to kill them yet and pull their innards out,' she said.

25 December 1929

Merry Christmas, Mother.
Merry Christmas, Uncle Charlie.
Merry Christmas, Aunt Betty, Cousin Clifford and Gloria.
Merry Christmas, Maisie. X
Merry Christmas, Lionel, Maurice, Reginald – poor Reginald.

Today we had dinner. It was a fine affair. People from a church in the village came to help serve and brought presents. I now have a new fountain pen. Mr Elliott put flour in his beard and dressed up as Santa Claus. Now that it's all over I think of home. I don't want to be here. I want to go home. But where is home now? I worry. Why do I worry? Lionel calls it insecurity.

26 December 1929

There has not been many staff about today. Nurse Applejack is on a day off and has gone somewhere to meet her uncle from Africa. There's another nurse on our ward and the porters and attendants are showing her where everything is. She's already pulled an emergency chord by mistake. That was funny because it made her jump!

Some of the attendants and porters have gone in Albert's omnibus to watch a Boxing Day foxhunt near Bagshot Green. I think Mr Elliott must have gone as well. One of the nurses told us that each year they all come back very drunk and cheery.

'Mr Elliott is always worse for wear but don't worry, Mr Randall is back tomorrow,' she said.

I wonder when Maisie is coming back.

28 December 1929

Today is Saturday. This morning I was taken to see Mr Stevenson. He's a professor from London. He asked me if I felt like a true human-being. I am a true human-being! He asked me if I slept at night. I sleep! He asked me to tell him my story from boyhood for his 'case notes'. He said that he wanted to rid me of the unhealthy section of my mind and steer me on a course of fulfilment away from the institution. He told me that he was looking at new methods of psychiatry and that a patient's narrative might help.

'What's that?' I thought.

He kept writing things down but I don't think that he was really listening. Most people keep saying 'what' or 'pardon' when I talk, but he didn't say it once. I'll never forget the things he said to me. I hurt.

29 December 1929

I spent all night awake and thinking about what Mr Stevenson had said. This place is still an asylum - it's not a hospital. I fear that I may be here forever. I should never have been sent here! It's only Maisie who is stopping me from going really mad. I have to tell somebody but I don't know who can help. Miss Rance is not the same as Fiona; she's flighty and two-faced and only thinks about herself. She doesn't care like Fiona did.

Last night Parson Jaggs came and did his bedside rounds. He told me that he's here to listen but I don't like him and after what happened to Reginald I don't want to be a Christian anymore. I don't really know what to do. I despair.

30 December 1929

Bertie Blackmore has returned to the ward. It's good to see him back after he was blamed for putting that female patient in the family way. He told me that a man from the village had owned up after being seen lying down in a field with her by one of the farmhands.

Today is a very mild and warm day. I don't need a coat even though it's December. Mr Randall is taking some of us to the Nag's Head Inn later. 'It's quiet,' he said.

I think he knows that today is our pocket money day!

Tomorrow is the last day of the year. There's talk of celebration. I do not want to celebrate. What is there to celebrate? All I want to do is get out of here!

31 December 1929

I can't stop thinking about Maisie today. I wonder if she enjoyed Christmas, I wonder what day she'll be back.

Today is the last day of 1929. I look back at the year and weep.

Mother, Mother, Mother!

This afternoon there's a barn dance and party in the Main Hall. Mr Randall told us that the day before New Year is always a big day on the calendar.

'Staff and people from the village have their own big party here tonight,' he said.

He's expecting Mr and Mrs Juett from the Nag's Head Inn to be there. I think he likes Mrs Juett. He's always talking about her.

1 January 1930

This morning Nobby had somehow managed to climb up to the top of the Water Tower. One of the attendants or workmen must have left the bottom gate unlocked. Nobby was shouting 'Happy New Year' to everyone and was swearing at us while we all stared back up at him. He then started throwing pieces of masonry down at us. Mr Randall, Mr Elliott and two other attendants raced up to get him. After about an hour he was brought down kicking and screaming. They took him off to one of the refractory wards to calm him down. Lionel thinks that he might not be back in our ward after that. Good! I have always despaired of Nobby. Harry Horlock pulled up in his fire engine just after all the fuss was over.

'Imbeciles,' he shouted, 'imbeciles!'

Today I saw Mr Mycroft; he was standing outside the porch of his cottage and giving out confectionary that he'd brought back from Cornwall. He also gave me some homemade clotted cream that his sister had made. I had never tasted Cornish clotted cream before, it was delicious.

This evening, a church choir from Guildford is coming to sing for us. Mr Randall said that they are normally very good and are quite famous in these parts. They come over every New Year and sometimes at Easter.

'Albert will fetch them in his omnibus,' he said.

I wonder what 1930 will bring. I need to get out of here. I MUST get out of here but how?

4 January 1930

I'm writing with my new fountain pen.

It's been snowing. It's very cold. I thought I had lost my tin and everything else but it had fallen down further in the tree hollow and was hard to reach. It was covered in leaves and snow. I might have to move it soon.

Today is Saturday. I don't think Maisie is back yet. I haven't seen her. I long for Maisie. It seems such a long time now since her father or whoever it was, came to collect her.

This morning, I helped in the laundry again. It was nice and warm in there. Mrs Skilton and I were singing the song Mrs Evenden had given me to learn. She told me that her brother was always singing it when he first got back from the Great War.

'At least he got home in one piece,' she said.

> *'Pack up your troubles in your old kit-bag*
> *and smile, smile, smile,*
> *while you've a Lucifer to light your fag,*
> *Smile, boys, that's the style.*
> *What's the use of worrying?*
> *It never was worthwhile, so*

pack up your troubles in your old kit-bag,
and smile, smile, smile.'

I'm helping in the laundry again on Monday and on Tuesday I'll be feeding the pigs and helping clean out their pens.

5 January 1930

I had a long talk with Bertie this morning. He was telling me about his time in isolation. He was very tearful and is still shocked that he was blamed for putting the female patient in the family way. He's very angry and hurt. He told me that he was given some strong medicines and felt very weak. He found it very difficult getting out of bed and had to be treated for bedsores. He told me that Dr Carlisle entered the room one night and bent over him. He started nibbling at his ears and forced his hand inside Bertie's long johns. The next thing Bertie knew, he was being buggered.

'It lasted about two hours that night. There were other nights when the same thing happened, but they didn't last as long.'

Bertie had to explain to me what being buggered meant. I didn't know. He also told me that on one of the days, Nurse Applejack came in and lectured him about the error of his ways and continuously struck him across the backside with her copper-stick.

'She just wouldn't stop.'

I asked Bertie if he had reported this to anyone. He said he did but no-one has listened. He told me that he feels shameful and is still in lots of pain. He just needed to tell someone and said that he trusts me on my mother's life not to speak of it. He's going to write a letter to his father but all post is examined by Miss Rance before it's allowed to be sent.

'Maybe she'll do something,' Bertie said.

What Bertie has told me is very unsettling and has made me angry. Very angry!

We had church this morning. Parson Jaggs is away and a vicar from the Wesleyan church came to take the service. I think I've lost my faith. How can there actually be a God?

7 January 1930

Yesterday I helped in the laundry. Mrs Skilton said that she thinks my singing is good and that my voice is very clear now. I know all the verses of *'Pack up Your Troubles...'* off by heart now as well as just the chorus. I wonder what Mrs Evenden will say. Mrs Evenden is coming to see me again next Wednesday I think.

This morning I helped feed and swill the pigs. Gertrude the pot-bellied pig was being seen by Mr Hampton, the farm vet.

'We may have to put her down,' he said.

Donald the farmhand said that she is quite old now and has been at the farm for as long as he can remember. Jack cut his hand on some barbed wire, there was lots of blood. Mr Hampton put a bandage on and Donald poked lots of fun.

'Mr Hampton might have to put you down.' He laughed.

Bertie told me that he saw Maisie come back this morning. I haven't seen her yet, how I long to see her.

8 January 1930

Raymond set fire to his bed again last night. When the porters took his mattress away, it was still smouldering. The attendants restrained him with straps and took him to the side room. He was very quiet but kept trying to kick them as he was taken away. The fire klaxon never went off.

'We could have all died,' Lionel said rather angrily.

Getting out of the airing courts is becoming easier again. I saw Maisie earlier. She looked gaunt and sad and didn't want to talk. I tried to ask her about how her Christmas was but she just flinched and walked away as if I wasn't there. It felt like I was almost invisible. I worry!

It's just started to rain.

10 January 1930

I've just found a new tree. It has a big hollow about ten feet up inside the trunk where it's safe to hide my tin. It's an old chestnut tree; sweet chestnut I think. My things should be safe up here. At least I can't be seen from the Chief Clerk and Attendant's house anymore.

I saw Maisie again this morning. This time she waved and smiled but she looked so pale and deep in thought. I wish I knew what troubles her so much. We didn't have a chance to talk.

Nobby Hatch has been moved to one of the refractory wards just to keep him out of trouble,' Mr Randall said. 'He needs to be kept secure for his own good.'

A new man has come into our ward called Carlos Brignall. He's half Spanish and he used to be a soldier in foreign fields. I haven't heard him talk yet. He's about fifty years old, has black hair with a wide middle parting and a droopy moustache. He just sits on his bed pulling and clicking his yellow fingers. He constantly stares at us and it's unnerving but he reminds me a bit of Reginald. Raymond just stares back at him.

14 January 1930

Yesterday we had to all come out of the ward and weren't allowed back until after teatime. A porter told us that the wards had to be fumigated and all the curtains and linen changed. We had to file one by one to the ablutions. An attendant hosed us down with cold water and then Nurse Applejack and another nurse dried us and painted us all over with a smelly white lotion. Thankfully I was allowed to do my private parts myself.

'There had been a scabies outbreak on the male wards,' Mr Randall said. 'They're like tiny fleas that get under your skin.'

I wondered what the big red blotches on my tummy were and why I had been itching all over since Christmas. Everyone is blaming Raymond because he never likes washing and is always scratching his head.

'He must have spread it,' Lionel said.

Tomorrow is Wednesday and Mrs Evenden will be here. I hope she will like me singing *'Pack up your troubles in your old kit-bag and smile, smile, smile'*... like Mrs Skilton did.

I haven't seen Maisie for a few days. I hope she is alright. I worry.

15 January 1930

It's Wednesday. I waited and waited with Edward but Mrs Evenden didn't come. Miss Rance said that she should have been here at 11 o'clock but she has not had word.

'These things happen sometimes, she said.

I went with Jack to feed the pigs. Gertrude had gone. Donald told us that the vet had to put her down with a bolt as there was a danger that she could infect the Middle Whites. We were all very sad.

Harry Horlock was across the road. He has a newer fire engine which he has acquired from Inkerman Barracks. It has a bigger wheel at the back with a longer hose. He kept tooting the horn and ringing the bell. He was frightening the pigs.

It's just started to snow again. There are lots of starlings chirping around up in the trees today.

17 January 1930

I had to go and see Miss Rance this morning. Edward was there. Miss Rance explained why Mrs Evenden didn't come to see us for our elocution on Wednesday.

'Mrs Evenden had come off her bicycle on the ice and has broken her hip,' she said.

She told us that she didn't think she would be back because of her age.

'It's a long bicycle ride over to here from Camberley and I don't think that Mrs Evenden will be able to ride here again,' she warned.

This is bad news. Miss Rance told us that she will now look for someone else to help us with our speech.

'It may take some time. Speech therapy nurses are always very hard to find.'

Edward's speech is much worse than mine but I don't think he realises how bad this news really is.

On Monday I'm helping in the laundry again. I wonder what Mrs Skilton will say when I tell her what's happened!

18 January 1930

At last I've had a chance to talk to Maisie while she was on her way to the Recreation Hall. She seems very frail but at least her spirits are high. She told me about her Christmas. Her father has told her that he hopes to take her home for good in a few months so that she can help on her uncle's farm. He has lots of sheep and a couple of horses. Maisie's pony is also being looked after on the farm. I sensed that Maisie has a big problem with her uncle though and I wonder if he could be the cause of all her troubles.

I told Maisie about Mrs Evenden's accident and what Miss Rance had said about it being hard to find another elocution nurse to help with my speech. Maisie told me again that she thinks I'm speaking much better now and that she finds me much easier to understand than she did a few months ago.

This afternoon there's another football match out on the field. It's very cold and icy out there. Lionel, Raymond and I helped Mr Randall and the grounds men clear away all the horse shit from the pitch this morning. The match is only going to be an hour long and is being played between the porters and attendants. We're going to watch and Carlos is coming too. He's very odd and always looks like he's going to run off and do something stupid at any moment. Perhaps that's why the attendants are always paying him so much attention!

21 January 1930

Yesterday it was my turn to help in the laundry again. Mrs Skilton was having trouble with the water supply and Mr Mycroft and a man called Mr Armstrong took nearly all morning to sort it out. Mrs Skilton made me two cups of tea and I told her about was has happened to Mrs Evenden. Edward and I have no-one to help us anymore. Mrs Skilton suggested that she could talk to Miss Rance to see if she can bring me any good news, but said that it's not normally her business to get involved. She gave me a hug and called me a poor old soul. I hadn't had a hug like that since before poor Nanny died.

It's very sunny today and all the ice is beginning to melt away. There are still a lot of starlings up in my tree. They're very noisy. There's also a little brown squirrel that comes to eat nuts from my hand. I've called him 'Quickie' because he runs away fast afterwards; looks back, then comes back for more. He likes eating breadcrumbs too.

23 January 1930

Carlos kept everyone awake last night. He was rattling his bed and the night nurse had to slap him a couple of times. This morning there were nuts and bolts from the bedstead all over the floor. Lionel told me that he thought Carlos had been playing with himself.

'We all do it for satisfaction sometimes. Lots of men used to be brought here because they masturbated too much but not so many now,' he said.

I've never thought about playing with my dinky!

Lionel then told me about a man called Jeremy Johnson who was here a couple of years ago. He used to do it every night and in the mornings when it got light his bed would be in the middle of the floor.

'We called him Jerking Jeremy. He died from arthritis in the end.'

It's very quiet today and the noisy starlings have all gone. Quickie the squirrel has been down from the tree again but I had nothing to give him, he nibbled my finger and then ran off and found some nuts under another tree.

Miss Rance has asked to see me later. I wonder what she wants.

24 January 1930

Mrs Evenden is dead. Miss Rance told me and Edward yesterday. She had died from her injuries after coming off her bicycle on the ice in Camberley. She was on her way to see us. Miss Rance said that she wouldn't normally tell patients about this sort of thing but said that she was aware of the close relationship we both had with her. I despair. Mrs Evenden was starting to prove why I shouldn't be here and helped with my speech. I've already been told that it will take a long time, if at all to find anyone else. Mrs Skilton from the laundry is going to talk to Miss Rance but I don't think that will really help.

Every time there's someone nice around who can help something happens to them. I need to get out of here, I am not a lunatic!

I saw Maisie earlier. We couldn't talk but she waved and smiled. I waved back. I always have a warm feeling when I see her. I wonder if she feels the same for me!

25 January 1930

Last night I had a strange dream. I dreamt that I was in a barn. It was raised up from the ground and I had to walk up some steps to get inside. Inside there was a big feast going on with a pig, a peacock and roast chickens on a long table. Around the table were all the dead people. Some I knew, some I didn't. Colonel Peter, Reginald Smyth, Linda Spooner and Mrs Evenden and others who have passed on since I've been here. Everything moved slowly. Somehow it was a comforting dream, I don't know why but everyone looked at peace. At the end, my Uncle Charlie came in and then I awoke.

Today is Saturday. I have brought some biscuits for Quickie. I thought that squirrels were meant to hibernate this time of year? There's a deer in the grounds. I hope Mr Drake doesn't see it. When he shoots them he gives the venison to the important people. I've never eaten venison before. Mr Mycroft said that everyone turns a blind eye.

'He's only supposed to kill rabbits and pheasants and that should only be twice a year,' he told me.

26 January 1930

I hate Sundays. Nothing ever happens on a Sunday, except church. I hate church. We don't even get taken to the village this time of year. Mr Randall told us that it's because it's too cold. There's nothing else to do. The laundry and all the workshops are shut on Sundays. There's only really dinner to look forward to. Missy Hope in the scullery told us that we all have roast chicken today. 'There'll be parsnips, carrots and runner beans too.'

She made me a cup of hot milk then told me to be on my way.

Lionel told me that Nobby Hatch has been causing trouble again. He's still in the refractory and might be sent back to Broadmoor.

'He tried to strangle an attendant one night last week,' he said.

I wonder who tells Lionel all this stuff but then it does explain why all the klaxons were going off. Lionel is nearly always right. I asked Mr Randall about it and he told me that Nobby is still here but has a 'review' next Wednesday.

27 January 1930

Today I mourn. This morning Aunt Betty came with Cousin Clifford. They informed me that Uncle Charlie has died of pneumonia. He died on Friday night.

'Your mother is in a terrible state,' Aunt Betty said.

When Miss Rance came for me and took me to the reception I knew something was wrong. I now think back to the dream I had the other night. I think it was a sign. I told Miss Rance and she told me not to be so evil. Uncle Charlie was the person who watched over me all my life until I was sent here. I will miss him dearly. I am not evil!

Aunt Betty told me that the landlords have already taken the house back in Raynes Park and all the possessions are being sent for auction on Friday. 'The rent hadn't been paid for weeks,' she said.

The possessions must include all of my things that I had to leave behind. It's difficult to be angry when I mourn so much. There will be a funeral tomorrow but Aunt Betty and Miss Rance said that I would not be allowed to go.

'Your mother will be too upset to see you on top of everything else,' Aunt Betty said.

29 January 1930

Miss Rance came to see me again today. She told me that I am no longer required to help in the laundry.

'You are a man and you should only be doing male jobs!'

She told me that I can carry on helping with the pigs but said that I will now be employed at least three days a week in one of the workshops.

'You spend too much time up in those woods; God knows what you do up there!' She said.

I do fear that this could be because Mrs Skilton has spoken to Miss Rance about my speech. I hope Mrs Skilton is not in any kind of trouble. I worry.

THERE IS NO GOD! – Why do people keep talking about God?

Yesterday Uncle Charlie was buried. I wonder how the funeral went. I wonder how Mother is. I want to see her but how can I pray for her now that I have lost my faith?

30 January 1930

Today is just another day. I was talking to Bertie earlier. He hasn't been very well over the last few weeks and has been getting treatment. He told me that it's a new thing but it's made him very drowsy. He can't remember what it's called but it has something to do with malaria. He said that he has had an X-ray.

'It doesn't hurt and they take pictures of the inside of your body,' he said.

Mr Randall told us that some people have died from the malaria treatment recently.

'I think that it's supposed to treat syphilis and things. Though many do get better and then are allowed to go home.'

Last night all the lights came on. Carlos was choking. The night nurse and two attendants had sat him up and they were slapping him hard on his back. He had gone to bed with his false teeth still in, they

53

had broke and he swallowed some. He was rushed off somewhere, for an operation I think.

After dinner I saw Maisie with one of the horses. She was in the bottom field. She was too far away to talk to. The sun came out just as she started to stroke its mane. It was a very beautiful moment.

31 January 1930

Soon I will find out which workshop I will be working in. I don't know if I'll have a choice. I want to work more on the farm. I love the smell of the animals. There are more cattle now. It's always sad to see some of them go off for slaughter though and that seems to happen quite often now.

I want to speak to Mrs Skilton from the laundry. I want to know if she's spoken to Miss Rance about my speech and if that's the reason why I'm not allowed to work in there anymore. Miss Rance also told me to stop pestering Missy Hope in the scullery. I do NOT pester!

Tomorrow is Saturday. After dinner, Mr Randall is going to take some of us for a walk along the canal to Pirbright Lock and back.

'We'll stop for a drink in the Nag's Head Inn on the way. I want to say "Hello" to Mrs Juett and Jack and some of my other friends,' he said.

Now, I spare my thoughts for Uncle Charlie.

1 February 1930

Today we went on our walk. We only had time to go to Sheets Heath Bridge and back because Mr Randall wanted to spend a longer time in the beer house. He was over an hour talking to Mrs Juett. I don't think he even spent any money on ale because he was helping Bertie and Lionel spend their pocket money. I didn't have any money but Lionel bought me some cider. Jack was there and was pulling barrels up from the back cellar. He thinks that quite soon I'll be helping out at the farm every day. No-one has told me yet but I would like that. I hope he's right!

Along the canal there was a barge laden with timber but it was stuck in the mud because the water was too low, Mr Randall said that it won't be too long before the whole canal is all in ruin.

'They say it's been heading that way since the railway came about 90 years ago, soon nothing will be able to get through!' he said.

2 February 1930

This morning in church, I closed my ears. Parson Jaggs was shouting away and I mimed when we had to say 'Amen'. I didn't sing along to the hymns. I think Nurse Applejack was watching me. I wonder if she'll say anything.

Jack was right. I will be working on the farm and helping with the pigs and other animals and will start tomorrow. Jack let on that Mrs Skilton had told him when he saw her with her new gentleman friend on Saturday night. He thinks that she had 'fixed it' with Miss Rance on Friday. She must have been over to her office to see her about my speech. She wanted to help but knew I liked working with the animals so must have said something. I will miss helping in the laundry. I don't think that men are allowed to work in the laundry anymore. It's a woman's job now I think. Lionel says it is!

3 February 1930

Nurse Applejack kept staring at me at breakfast this morning. I wonder if it's because I didn't sing in church yesterday. Do I have to go to church every Sunday? Lots of the other patients don't!

I had to report to Donald the farmhand at 9 o'clock this morning. Donald is always very jovial and tells silly jokes. He told me that I'll have to meet the Farm Bailiff and his wife tomorrow for afternoon tea. He said that the Bailiff is a very kind man, unless you cross him. He lives in a house near the North Lodge entrance called Almond Villa. It's a very smart house with a nice lawn and two greenhouses right on the edge of the grounds. We always walk past it when we go to the shops. I think that it's the same house which had the Fuchsia Show last year.

4 February 1930

Yesterday an American soldier came just after breakfast. He had an invitation to instruct everyone at the asylum who could do work to help us with our fitness. He had a long red neck and big white teeth, his khaki uniform reeked of mothballs. He was wearing big brown boots, almost knee-length - they were very shiny. There were fifteen of us, we were all under twenty-five years of age and he made us run around the cricket field five times. He kept shouting... *'Hip, hip, hip,'* as we ran around - I puffed a lot. I'd never had that kind of exercise before. Mr Randall said that his friend Silas had arranged it as some American soldiers are staying as guests at Inkerman Barracks and he has made friends with them up at the Anchor Hotel.

Later I went to help with the cattle and was shown how to fill the milking pails. The cows have big udders that have four dinky things that have to be pulled to get the milk out. After dinner I watched some new stag boar pigs arrive. Donald said that they desperately need them to mate with the sows.

5 February 1930

Last night was a bad night. Parson Jaggs came to me when he was doing his bedside rounds. He told me that Nurse Applejack had made him aware that I was not paying attention to him in church on Sunday. He asked me if I had a problem with God. I said that I did because I don't think that there is a God. He said that if there wasn't a God I wouldn't be here.

'God is looking down on you all the time,' he said.

He made me get out of bed and kneel on the floor. He said that I should repent and cleanse myself of the devil. After he left Nurse Applejack took me to the side room and beat me with her copper-stick. I have bruises on my back and arm. There was no-one there to stop her and I didn't really have time to shout. Lionel saw but he couldn't do anything. He whispered that I should tell Miss Rance but that might get me into even more trouble.

I may have to pretend that I believe in God just to survive this place. It isn't fair. THERE IS NO ~~FUCKING~~ GOD!

7 February 1930

I spoke to Maisie today. She told me that she doesn't like my whiskers.

'You don't need to grow a beard to prove to me that you're a man,' she said and then laughed.

I smiled and laughed back. Lionel is going to show me how to use a razor later but said that an attendant will have to be there when he does.

Maisie asked me how I got the bruises on my arm and I told her that I have them on my back as well. I told her what Nurse Applejack had done on Wednesday after my conversation with Parson Jaggs. I told Maisie that I don't believe in God. She told me that she doesn't either.

'How can there be a God?' she said rather curtly. 'If there was we wouldn't be rattling around in this awful place.'

That's exactly what I think! I love Maisie but she's got her own problems. One day I hope she'll tell me all about them. It might help me to understand exactly why she's here.

I have brought some biscuit bits for Quickie but I haven't seen him yet.

8 February 1930

Today I met The Tall Man. I've seen him before but we've never spoken. He stays in another ward and he is not allowed to leave the airing court. He's been here for about twelve years and has never been let out of the grounds. Lionel told me that he was sent here in 1918 at the end of the Great War just because he was tall; he's nearly seven foot high.

'No-one knows his real name, he's always just called The Tall Man but there must be something else wrong with him. It can't be just his abnormal height that brought him here,' he said.

The Tall Man has a very deep and booming voice and looks nearly as high as the water tower.

'He knows everything about everybody and claims to be a sorcerer. You should never look him in the eye or speak to him. He often predicts when people are going to die and he's normally right!' Lionel added.

Lionel also knows a lot about everyone, especially the older patients.

This morning we went to Embledon's with Mr Randall to get some buns. I saw Mrs Skilton. She asked me if I was happy now that I've been given more work on the farm. I said 'Yes!' She told me that she was sorry that I couldn't work in the laundry anymore. She let me know that the jobs are now being given to the female patients as they are not strong enough to do some of the work that the men can do. I asked her about the speech teaching. She confided that Miss Rance has told her off for getting too emotionally involved with me. She grabbed my arm and said that she was worried about me because of what had happened to Mrs Evenden. She then gave me a hug and said sorry. I think it's me who should be saying sorry to Mrs Skilton. I made sure that I thanked her and said goodbye properly before we left the shop.

10 February 1930

BANG! BANG! BANG! There was some shooting going on in the grounds just as it was getting light this morning. It was Mr Drake and one of his friends from Bisley. They were out to kill the foxes after they had got into the coop and killed dozens of hens during the night. No-one was allowed out until lunchtime, when all the shooting had stopped. Mr Randall later told us that they had shot three foxes and that they had taken their brushes to the scullery for cleaning.

Yesterday was church. Nurse Applejack kept staring at me during the whole service and Parson Jaggs looked over a few times. I tried to hide behind the person in front of me so that they couldn't see me, but Parson Jaggs kept moving and waving his arms about. Nurse Applejack scowled at me as I left the chapel. I'm not good with this. I don't want to keep feeling like a hypocrite because I have to go to church and pray to something which isn't there!

11 February 1930

Carlos is dead. He wouldn't wake up this morning. No-one knows why he has died. The attendants and porters came and took him away just before breakfast. No-one wanted to eat. It's sad. Nearly every week someone dies and it's not nice when I keep seeing bodies being taken from the ward with blankets pulled over their faces.

Bertie has been acting very strange since his last treatment. He's not the same person anymore and he thinks that his new best friend is the ghost of a soldier killed in the war.

15 February 1930

Yesterday Mr Randall and Mr Elliott took four of us for a walk along the canal towards Woking. Mr Drake came. He was carrying an old canvas army kit bag. We stopped at a place called St John's and Mr Drake gave us some stale bread to feed the ducks. Mr Drake had a long piece of string with a noose on the end and started trying to catch the ducks. He caught two by strangling them and pulled them in. Mr Randall said that we mustn't tell anyone what we saw.

'The ducks are for a special dinner. Shush! We're not supposed to do this,' he whispered.

We sat on a lock gate with Mr Elliott while Mr Randall and Mr Drake went off to a beer house called the Rowbarge Inn. Mr Elliott told us that it was built at the same time as the canal so that the navvies had somewhere to sleep and drink.

'Further along the canal there was an old camp where some of them lived in tents and shacks,' he said.

On the way back we passed a matron and three female patients. From a distance I thought that one of the ladies was Maisie but it was another girl. I was very disappointed.

Carlos was buried at Brookwood Cemetery on Thursday.

On Thursday night there was a full moon and there was a lot of commotion and howling noises coming from the refractory. Then all the klaxons went off. It was worse than usual. Mr Randall told us today that it was all caused by Nobby Hatch.

'They say that it took six attendants to restrain him. I think they'll definitely be taking him back to Broadmoor now, he's been given too many last chances now,' he said.

16 February 1930

It was church again this morning. Nurse Applejack wasn't in the chapel; she has leave of absence for two days. I think Parson Jaggs may have forgotten about me now.

There's something banging against the trunk of my tree. It must be a woodpecker but I can't see it because of the bright sunshine when I look up into the branches. A woodman came up here yesterday and painted some red crosses on some of the elms. He told me that they're diseased and need to be cut down. I think my tree is safe but I don't want anybody to find my tin.

There's a new person in our ward who is a dwarf. He has dark skin. Lionel said that Mr Randall had told him he's a Hindu and is the son of a servant who lives in the village. Lionel thinks that he's been sent here because he reads too many books and won't do anything else.

Quickie has just come down from the tree and taken some pieces of biscuit out of my hand.

Next Saturday there's a concert in the Main Hall. It's a coach builders' band from Guildford. Mr Randall told us that he has a good friend in the band who is the older brother of Silas Greenwood.

'Look out for the man with the French Horn, that'll be him, his name is Toby,' he said.

18 February 1930

It was very hot at the farm this morning. Donald told me that it was very warm for this time of year and that I could get a sun tan. Very funny! I like Donald though, he has a way of making me laugh and forget about all of the bad things.

Lionel keeps using the word 'fastidious' to describe The Dwarf. I looked at it in the dictionary Maisie gave me and it says that it means: 'very attentive to detail and concerned about accuracy.'

That's right because The Dwarf as I call him is very tidy and wants to fold his own bedding down every morning. He's very peculiar and doesn't like the nurses looking under his pillow or anyone touching his books. He's already asking where the library is but I don't think that he'll be allowed to go. Mr Randall said that he's trying to find him something to do in one of the workshops.

'He needs to be weaned off the books,' he said.

After dinner The Dwarf told me that his name is Emile. Emile Bashir. He added that his mother is actually French and works in service up at Mrs Woolston's house at Hilltop Place. She's the lady who had peacock for her Christmas dinner and comes here to help us with the arts and crafts sometimes. His father is from India and is a servant at Hilltop Place where they both live in a tied cottage. The Dwarf told me that everyone he knows calls him 'Basher'. He wants everyone here to call him that and asked me if I liked reading books and if I had any. I told him that the only book I had was a Gideon's bible and I mentioned to him why I don't read it anymore. I told him that I don't believe in God. He said that he has his own god but no-one in England understand his religion and that they always laugh at him when he mentions it. Emile is very talkative but he's very weird and creepy. I'm glad he sleeps further down the dormitory away from me.

19 February 1930

Today has been very quiet. We went out by the North Lodge gate and watched some sheep being herded towards the village past the Farm Bailiff's house. Some men were working in our own slaughterhouse at the farm. They want to get it operational again. The water supply had somehow stopped; it hadn't been working properly for months. I think that's why some of our pigs have been going to Grimditch's in the village for slaughter.

'No-one apart from the Chief Clerk really wants to slaughter the animals here anymore. It's the stench and having to watch them all dying,' Donald said.

20 February 1930

Last night there was another fire. All the klaxons went off and everyone rushed to the windows. Some electrics had blown out in the laundry and piles of bed linen had caught alight in one of the drying rooms. There was howling coming from the female wards. Harry Horlock had to get help. He was unable to put the fire out and couldn't raise some of his own firemen. Some men from who live in the village came with their own pails to help the porters and attendants but it wasn't enough. A fire engine from Woking came and then everything calmed down at about 4 o'clock. I can still smell the smoke now.

This morning I saw Mrs Skilton being taken to the Medical Superintendent's office. She was very tearful. Mr Randall thinks that she may be dismissed as she hadn't turned everything off properly before she went home yesterday. I hope Mrs Skilton is alright and that she keeps her job. I worry.

22 February 1930

Mr Randall told me that Mrs Skilton still has a job but she's been severely reprimanded and demoted to a laundry orderly.

'She will not be in charge in there anymore. It's probably cost her about half a crown a week in wages too,' he said.

This morning I saw The Dwarf looking up at The Tall Man in the airing court. The Tall Man was looking down at him, they didn't talk. It was a very odd sight, a very funny thing. Lionel and Bertie were laughing but Mr Randall told them both to stop.

24 February 1930

I've been wondering about how to get myself out of here. I shouldn't be here anymore. My speech has got better and I can grow whiskers. Two things which Mother always said made me out to be mental. Now Uncle Charlie is gone I don't know what to do. Mrs Evenden gave me much hope and Mrs Skilton too. I think I will write a letter to Aunt Betty to see what she can do. I need Mother to know that I need to get out of here. I don't want to become like some of the others. I am NOT a lunatic. Many have been here too long and they have no-one outside anymore to come and get them.

I must speak to Maisie too. She knows me inside out. She always listens to me and agrees that it's wrong that I was ever sent here. Why is Maisie here though? She always seems very normal, although just sometimes very sad.

I think I will write the letter to Aunt Betty then show it to Maisie before I send it. Last time I spoke to Maisie she said that I should get my own envelope and stamp and post it in secret next time I go to the village.

'Miss Rance or anyone else won't be able to alter or stop it then,' she said.

The coach builders' band from Guildford, were very good at the concert on Saturday night. Albert the busman came. He told us that some of the men in the band helped build his omnibus. He told us that he will be getting a new one soon.

26 February 1930

Today at 10 o'clock I was taken to the reception. Mr Elliott took me and told me to sit down in the waiting area.

'You have a visitor coming,' he said but didn't say who.

At just before 11 o'clock a lady attendant brought a man into the room. He was wearing a sharp blue suit but looked a bit ruffled. He said that his name was Mr O'Leary. George O'Leary. He was about fifty years old with brown hair going grey and rotting teeth. He asked me how I was and if I was comfortable. He told me that he hadn't seen me since I was two years old and that he had recently met with Cousin Clifford who had told him where I was. He felt that it was his duty to come and see me and sought after my welfare. He said that he had become very concerned. I asked him if he knew Mother, indeed he does. He told me that in 1907 he and Mother had a big falling out over one of her so-called gentleman caller friends. I know what that is now so I shuddered, partly with shock and then with rage. I asked him how he knew her and he said that they had known each other since childhood. He had moved from London and taken a butcher's job in Frimley Green just before the Great War.

'Then everything became blurred, very blurred.'

He told me that he was sorry to learn that Uncle Charlie was dead and that Nanny had died too. He said that Nanny hated him because she thought that he was just another one of Mother's gentleman callers.

'In fact we were very close, your mother and me, right up to that day in 1907.'

Just before he left, he jangled some change and gave me five shillings in two half crown coins.

'Spend it wisely and enjoy,' he said.

I never thought to ask him who he was. Yes, his name was George and he knew so much. I didn't ask him if he was my father but he never told me that he was either. I don't know who my father is, I wonder. I now wonder if it's him!

27 February 1930

I had a long conversation with Lionel today. It was raining and we sat in the shelter in one of the airing courts. He normally just says one word or one sentence and then goes quiet. Today he was telling me everything about his life. He told me that he actually likes it in here.

'It's safe and it takes me away from all the worry and pressure I used to have,' he said.

He told me that he thought his wife was carrying on with other men and told her father about it. The problem was that her father is a policeman of high rank. He told Lionel that he was delusional and disrespectful and was not the right man to have his daughter as a wife, despite the fact they had two young offspring at the time. Lionel told me that he thought his wife was also obsessed with lesbianism.

'She always liked kissing other women. I feel free and I don't have to put up with that shameful indignity any more now.'

I've never heard Lionel talk so much and I laughed when he spoke about lesbians but I was glad when the bell went for dinner time. It felt like my ears were aching. I mean, really aching. I didn't expect to hear so much.

I keep thinking back to yesterday and the visit of George O'Leary. I should have asked him outright if he was my father. I didn't have time to think. I didn't know that he was coming to see me. I ache with wonder but do now have a sense of optimism which I haven't had before.

1 March 1930

'Hip, hip, hip'...

Yesterday was the last day of February. February is the shortest month but it felt like the longest. Today is the 1st of March. There's a slight smell of spring and the birds were chirping much louder this morning.

This morning, after breakfast the American soldier came to see us again, this time with two others.

'It will be our last time as our detachment is taking a ship from Southampton back to New York next week,' he said.

I meant to ask him what a detachment was. We ran around the cricket field ten times. There were more of us this time including two very ugly twins from another ward. Mr Randall persuaded The Dwarf to join us, he did but he insisted on bringing a book that he was reading. The American soldier kept shouting out... *'Hip, hip, hip – hip, hip, hip'* as we run around. His two friends ran with us. The Dwarf ran faster than all of us and was still reading his book which he had raised high in his left hand as he run. It was very odd, very funny.

If I am mad – then its days like this that have made me mad!

2 March 1930

Yesterday and today there's a display of arts and crafts in the Recreation Hall that have been painted and made by patients. Some are for sale. Mrs Woolston is helping with everything. A lot of people have come from all over the county and people from the newspapers have even come. Mr Elliott said that it's an annual event. We were allowed to have a look at the display after church today and I saw some splendid drawings and paintings. Someone has drawn a portrait of The Tall Man sitting down, it has considerable likeness. I then saw two beautiful paintings, one was of a unicorn and a flying horse, the other was of two shire horses in a poppy field. When I looked closer I noticed that they had both been signed by Maisie Albright, that's my Maisie. I didn't know that she's such a clever artist! Now I must talk to her and tell her that I've seen her paintings. I must tell her that I like them very much.

3 March 1930

Today Mr Randall told us that Maurice has been taken back home by his family. Maurice had been in one of the senile wards since the incident with Raymond in December. I think he was happy until then. He should have stayed in our ward. It's Raymond who should have gone. Nurse Applejack always picks on the wrong people.

Donald the farmhand told me that some of the sows should be having their piglets soon.

'That could be over the next few days. We need to make sure that Mr Hampton, the vet is here this time as there was a lot of trouble with them last year, some were born dead and others born blind,' he said.

Cyril the Farm Bailiff came over and said that it's all different stock now. 'I don't think we'll have any problems this time, they're noisy buggers when they're first born.'

Donald told me that Cyril has a tough load on at the moment because the last Farm Bailiff was dismissed for striking out at patients in his charge and the farm's reputation needs to be repaired.

5 March 1930

Albert came in his new omnibus today. He was very proud.

'It's a Dennis E version,' he said with a big beam on his face.

It's painted cream with a dark blue stripe. He told us that it was built in Guildford at the same coachworks where the concert band came from a few weeks ago.

'It's just called a bus!' he said rather smugly.

Toby, the brother of Mr Randall's friend Silas was with him. He was the man who played the French horn in the band. Albert said that he doesn't want anyone being sick in his bus when he starts to do the outings.

'You lot always cost me a fortune in disinfectant.'

Mr Randall told me not to worry.

'He's only joking; he gets paid enough to clear it up.'

I think I knew that!

I need to write a letter to Aunt Betty but what do I say? Where do I start?

7 March 1930

I saw Maisie near the Recreation Hall this morning before I went to help at the farm. For once no-one was watching, except for Mr Elliott who never seems to mind. We had time to talk. I told Maisie that I had seen her paintings and said how much I liked them.

'There are many more,' she said.

She told me that sometimes her uncle comes and collects them and sells them to art galleries all along the south coast from Brighton to Weymouth.

'He makes a lot of money selling my paintings.'

I told her that I hoped that the money would be ready for her when she leaves here but she avoided what I had said and started talking about me instead. She said that my speech sounds nearly perfect now.

'You only have a slight stammer and you shouldn't be here,' she remarked.

I had already told her about Mrs Evenden and what had happened to Mrs Skilton. They were the two people who were helping me and could have got me out. I told her that I didn't want to leave her behind. She smiled. She told me that she didn't think that Mrs

Skilton caused the fire in the laundry, someone else did, but Mrs Skilton took the blame.

I always feel warm when I speak to Maisie. She makes me feel like I have a heart.

8 March 1930

Nurse Applejack is being promoted to a Sister.

'She starts in her new position next week,' Mr Elliott said.

He thinks that Parson Jaggs must have influenced the Visiting Committee when they came on Monday last, because she is a God-fearing woman and they are always talking together, especially after church and when Parson Jaggs does the bedside rounds.

'The hospital can't keep the younger nurses very long and most fall in the family way to soldiers based at Pirbright, Deepcut or Inkerman Barracks. Nurse Applejack is black and is definitely not young or pretty, she was always going to get promoted sooner or later,' he said.

Lionel thinks that her new duties might mean that she leaves us alone now.

'She'll be the first ever Negro Sister at the asylum,' he reckoned.

There's a football match on the field this afternoon between the doctors and the attendants. Mr Elliott says that he's the goalie today. I will watch.

9 March 1930

The doctors won the football match 12-1. Mr Randall didn't play because he has a sore foot. He told us that the attendants lost because they all went to the beer house just after dinner and got too tipsy. Mr Elliott isn't talking.

It's a church day today. There were people from the village in the chapel this morning. Some important men from the council were there too. Nurse Applejack was trying to be nice to everyone. There's another service this afternoon but that's for patients from some of the other wards.

10 March 1930

I have written a letter to Aunt Betty and I bought my own stamp and posted it in a letterbox in the village in secret like Maisie suggested. Donald the farmhand and one of the new attendants went with me. I've tried to remember what I wrote and have written it all down again...

Dear Aunt Betty,

I hope this letter finds you and Mother well.

I am sorry about what happened to your friend Mrs Evenden, she was very helpful to me and Edward but now everything has stopped.

I am told that my speaking is much better now and I eagerly request that you arrange my release from here. I understand that I cannot go back to Raynes Park but ask if there's room in your new house for me.

I am NOT a lunatic and I think that Mother was wrong to send me here.

A gentleman came to see me on 26 February last and he said that he knew Mother and Nanny. He said that his name was George O'Leary and remembered me from when I was small. I beg and ask respectfully if this man is my father? He never told me so, and I did not ask him. I don't know if I will see him again. He said that Cousin Clifford had told him that I was here. He seemed to be a very kind man and said that he had a certain interest in my welfare.

Please tell Mother that I love her so and long to see her. I forgive her. Please tell her that a very special friend has given me some heart.

Your humble and loving nephew

Tommy xxx

I wanted to tell Aunt Betty about Maisie and her paintings. I know that she takes an interest in art and may like to see them. I will tell her about Maisie another time. I wonder how soon Aunt Betty will reply.

12 March 1930

I saw Mr Mycroft today. It's the first time that I've seen and spoken to him for a few weeks. He has a new puppy called Rex. It's a black mongrel bitch with tight curly hair and it licked my hand a lot. Mr Mycroft said that he had noticed that I'm talking much better now and asked why I was still here. I told him about what happened with Mrs Evenden and how everything has stopped since she died. I told him that I feel trapped and that I had written to Aunt Betty on Monday to ask if she could help get me out. Mr Mycroft told me that the letter would probably not have been posted if I was making that kind of request. 'They look at all patients' letters before they're sent.'

I told him that I had sent it in secret from the Post Office in Knaphill. He called me 'intelligent'. I've never been called that before!

We spoke about Maisie's paintings and how I loved the ones that I saw at the arts and crafts display. Mr Mycroft told me that he had read about Maisie's paintings in a newspaper once and that her uncle is always coming to collect her new ones.

'He must make a lot of money selling them,' he said.

I must tell Maisie what Mr Mycroft said.

16 March 1930

There's a female patient who walks around the grounds with a small pram. She pretends to have a baby. I think she must be new because I have only noticed her over the past week or two. One of the female attendants is always walking just behind her. She's very strange. She looks too old to have a baby. I mentioned her to Mr Mycroft when I was walking to the chapel and he said that she's quite notorious outside.

'She's been reported in the *Surrey Advertiser* before. She had been stealing babies from their mothers while they shopped in a town called Staines and another called Weybridge. She was arrested but was sent here because the doctors found that she is ill,' he said.

He told me that she suffers from something called phantom pregnancies.

'She thinks she's going to have a baby but no-one has put her in the family way so she can't.'

He added that her name is Angela Reeves and that she's also a liar and a thief.

'Patients in her ward are already complaining about their belongings being taken,' he said.

I think that some starlings are nesting in my tree. There's a lot of noise and commotion and I've seen one bird taking twigs up there today.

I haven't heard back from Aunt Betty yet but we don't get any post on Sundays.

17 March 1930

Today Mr Hampton, the vet came to the farm with a pig farrowing man to inspect all the pregnant sows. Donald thinks that it's because things went very wrong last year.

'They are not taking any chances this time,' he said.

Mr Hampton told us that he needed to make sure that there would be no still births.

'Last year some of the sows were killed by the state of their own dead embryos within, it was a clear disaster.'

His friend told me quite a lot about how pigs get pregnant, their litter sizes and how older pigs usually have larger litters than the younger pigs do.

'Sometimes we have to abort the piglets or pull dead foetuses out of the sows, it's not nice but we eventually get used to it. If you're really interested in pig farrowing I'll get you a book on it,' he said.

Mr Hampton told me that when I leave the asylum, pig farming is perhaps something I should do. Donald agreed. I liked that!

When we finished on the farm Mrs Luscombe, the Farm Bailiff's wife invited us all over to her garden for tea. It's been a sunny afternoon and she said that we should all celebrate the start of spring.

Harry Horlock's wife was also there chatting with some other ladies from the village.

19 March 1930

Yesterday Nurse Applejack came for me and took me to the reception for my review. It was Mr Stevenson again. He asked me how I was. I told him that I am much better now and that I'm looking forward to leaving the asylum. He asked me why I thought that I might be leaving. I told him that at least three people have told me that my speech has improved greatly and that I should not even be here. He told me that I was delusional.

'Yes, your speech has improved, but it's only slight,' he said.

He told me that I was wrong to get my hopes up and said that there's a lot else which needs to be looked into before he can consider letting me go. He told me that he had received a report from Nurse Applejack which Miss Rance had given to her. He said that that it also contained a revision of my case notes from the nurse which suggests that I have a bigger problem.

'Nurse Applejack has been very thorough with you. What she is saying about you, young man, gives me grave concern about your general welfare. Miss Rance has stated here that you think you can predict when a person is going to die and that you see dead people. In my mind that is delusional and certainly not good for other patients if they hear it. You will require further treatment before I see you again.'

I despair. I don't know where I am now. Miss Rance must have told Nurse Applejack about the dream I had just before Uncle Charlie died. She has misunderstood me. I am not evil. I am not delusional.

Last night I couldn't sleep. There was a moth flying round and round a gaslight that had been left on in the ward. I watched it until I could see the sunrise come through the window. The light went out and the moth dropped to the floor. Then the ancillary nurse came in and swept the moth away and then took my linen.

'Have you wet the bed?' she asked.

I hadn't, it was just sweat from my body. I don't care if she didn't believe me. Many of the other patients wet their beds every night but I'm not one of them.

I wanted to see Maisie or even Mrs Skilton today but it will be dark soon. I need to talk. I need to let them know what Mr Stevenson said yesterday. I need someone to listen. I need someone to help me. I need to release this burden of despair. If there is a God, please help me. Help me!

20 March 1930

Today I spoke to Donald and told him about what Mr Stevenson said. He noticed that I was trembling a lot and said that I shouldn't help on the farm today. He told me not to weep.

'Real men don't cry and you aren't going to get away with that while I'm around,' he said.

He took me over to Rose Cottage just across from the farm where he lives with his mother. She works as an assistant in the Bursar's office. She was there and gave me a cup of tea. A man came in, one of the senior cowmen I think. Donald told him why I was there. The man took out a flask.

'Have a nip of this, it's Irish whiskey and it'll be better for you than any medicine, and certainly better than tea,' he said.

Donald's mother let me stay there until it was time to go back to the dining room for dinner. She's very kind and explained that Donald is always talking about me.

'He tells me that you will make a great pig farmer one day,' she said.

This morning has helped, but I still need to talk to Maisie. I still need to get a reply from Aunt Betty. I still need to get out of here.

21 March 1930

Last night was another night without sleep. All the klaxons went off at about 2 o'clock and all the lights came on. The attendants and porters were running up and down the corridor and there were some men outside with hand torches. Nurse Eley and another nurse told us all to lie down and go back to sleep. Later, I could hear dogs barking and all the lights came back on again. I looked out of the window and I could see lots of policemen running around. A lorry came and then some soldiers got out. The klaxons eventually stopped just before it got light with the sunrise. It all went very quiet and then the dawn chorus started. The birds are very tuneful this time of year.

After breakfast, in the airing court there was much excitement. A man from another ward told me that Nobby Hatch had escaped from a back ward in the refractory block during the night and had stabbed the night attendant there in the eye with a pencil. The Surrey Constabulary was called and the Staff Sergeant thinks that Nobby had run into a garden in Queens Road and was hiding in a shed. I noticed that Mr Randall and Mr Elliott weren't around this morning. It's very unusual for both of them to be away at the same time. There was a new attendant watching us but I don't know his name yet. Lionel had been talking to him earlier and was told that all the senior attendants were helping the police search for Nobby. According to what Lionel was told Missy Hope had been attacked in the village last night by a man matching Nobby's description. She disturbed him after he got into the house where she lives and was knocked to the floor. Nobby ran off with some food from the pantry. I hope they catch him soon.

It was a great morning on the farm even though I was very tired today. Donald is expecting the first piglets of the spring to be born next week.

'There shouldn't be any problems this year now that they have all been checked,' he said. I hope he's right!

23 March 1930

Nobby Hatch is still missing. In the chapel Parson Jaggs asked everyone to pray for him.

'He must repent his sins and find it in his heart to come back,' he yelled.

He didn't mention Missy Hope at all. Mr Mycroft told me that she's still very poorly and will not be back on duty for a number of days.

'That's if at all!' he said.

Mr Mycroft remembers Missy Hope when she was a patient here and thinks that the incident with Nobby will cause her much more mental strain. He is worried that she may be readmitted and it's not her fault. I hope someone helps her. He told me that he's sure that the family she is living with will support her.

'She'll be fine I think,' he added.

This afternoon I've been at the lake feeding some mallard ducks. In one corner of the lake there are hundreds and hundreds of frogs laying their spawn. Their noise is very loud when they all croak at once. I've never seen more than one frog at a time before so I found this exciting. I'm going to go back each week, I want to see the spawn turn into tadpoles and watch them grow into frogs. In my dictionary I have found the word metamorphosis. It's an interesting sight. I'm beginning to like nature now. I'm beginning to like it quite a lot!

24 March 1930

There's a problem with the sewerage works today. There's a horrible pong. Mr Mycroft and Mr Armstrong are waiting for some equipment to arrive so that they can mend a pipe. The sewage has overflowed and gone into the water supply and there's raw shit seeping into the canal.

'The canal men are very angry. Last time this happened it killed hundreds of fish,' Mr Mycroft said.

It was Mr Mycroft who told me once that there had been a typhoid epidemic. I wonder if that will happen again.

Today on the farm I've been helping to milk some cows. I'm getting used to it now but I still prefer working with the pigs. Eight new cows came today. Mr Luscombe, the Farm Bailiff told us that they were Blue Albion's.

'We've just brought them up from Bisley; they're quite rare these days,' he said.

Donald's mother, Mrs Pengelley came across to the farm this afternoon and asked how I was. I liked that.

25 March 1930

Nobby Hatch has been caught. He was arrested in a village called Ripley after he tried to attack a woman behind her shop. Mr Randall told us that her screams disturbed some neighbours and they jumped on him until the police arrived. He told us that the night attendant who Nobby stabbed in the eye is very poorly.

'He might die and the Medical Superintendent is very concerned. The Constabulary are holding him for two counts of attempted murder, on the attendant and Missy Hope and one count of alleged rape on the lady in Ripley,' he said.

I asked Mr Randall if he thought Nobby would be coming back.

'No, no, no, he'll either be sent back to Broadmoor or if the attendant dies, he could hang,' he replied.

Mr Elliott thinks that because he was allowed to escape, the asylum will be held accountable so he may avoid the noose if it comes to that.

I'm glad they've caught him though.

27 March 1930

Gladys Compton R.I.P. One year ago today dear Nanny died. I miss you Nanny. That's all I want to say today.

28 March 1930

Today has been a very quiet day. Everything seems to be standing still. There has been weeks of commotion and much has been happening. I sit and think about it all now.

I still await a reply from Aunt Betty but now I fear that Miss Rance will have sent a letter to Mother about me for Aunt Betty to read out. I dread that it will contain all the lies that Nurse Applejack has said about my condition and that Mother and Aunt Betty will believe them. I worry.

Bertie has told me that he's going home to Sutton Green on Sunday next. I will miss him but I fear for him as he's just a shadow of who he was. He's a very quiet man now since his last treatment but I suppose that's how his father will wish to see him.

29 March 1930

It's Saturday and Mr Randall is taking us to a beer house this afternoon in a special farewell for Bertie.

I saw Mr Mycroft this morning and I told him about the kindness shown to me by Donald's mother at Rose Cottage.

'Oh that'll be Mrs Pengelly, she's a good sort. She comes from down my way, Downderry in Cornwall. It's a quaint and whimsical place. You'd like it there, plenty of sheep and pigs as well,' he said smiling.

He told me that her full name is Thirza Jayne Pengelley and that her husband Michael was killed on the very last day of the Great War.

'So sad, so bloody sad but she has a new man now who looks after her well, have you met him yet?'

'I think so. A man came in and offered me some Irish whiskey from his flask,' I replied.

'Oh that'll be him, that's old Jimmy Flynn, he's a fine specimen of a man but he can get very moody if he doesn't have it all his own way. The Medical Superintendent has told him to make Thirza an honest woman again so that they can both live together legally in the cottage. Parson Jaggs will be marrying them in the chapel soon. They don't usually have weddings in there,' he said.

I'm going to see if I can find Maisie now. Saturday is normally her day for doing crafts at the Recreation Hall.

30 March 1930

At last I saw Maisie yesterday but she was very upset. Angela Reeves, the woman with the pram has been moved into her ward. She's been stealing Maisie's things and has been very spiteful. Maisie told me that she has stolen and broken all her pencils and paint brushes and ripped some of her best clothes to shreds.

'She is very unsettling to me.'

77

It felt unfair to burden Maisie with all my sorrows, so I didn't. She was hoping to get some new pencils and brushes from the crafts teacher at the Recreation Hall, I hope she did.

We went to the Nag's Head Inn after dinner yesterday. Jack was outside helping his father with the lawn.

In the field behind I could see some of the cows I helped milk on Monday last. This must be where they're brought to graze. I'll ask Donald if they really are the same ones.

Bertie, Lionel and I drank lots of cider. Mr Randall stood at the bar hatch talking to Mrs Juett and only spoke to us when he wanted a drink. I like him a lot even though Bertie said that he doesn't.

'I've never trusted him,' he said.

Lionel laughed and then I remembered that someone told me once that that Mr Randall was a bit of a rogue.

Bertie was collected by his father after church today. I shall miss him!

31 March 1930

I asked Donald about the cows and he told me that he and Mr Flynn were just about to go to the field to herd them up for milking.

'Yes, they are the ones in that field,' he said.

Mr Luscombe got permission for me to go with them. There were a total of twenty-two cows. I counted them as we walked up the Broadway. A lady came out of one the houses with a shovel and picked up some shit. Donald told me that she always does that; she uses the muck for her garden.

'It makes bloody good manure.'

Donald told me that he had expected there to be piglets this morning but they haven't been born yet.

'They'll be there tomorrow; they normally pop out just before dawn, so I'll have to get up very early again,' he said.

I offered to help but Mr Flynn told me that patients are not allowed to work before breakfast. I didn't know that.

1 April 1930

Everyone was late getting up this morning. The breakfast bell didn't go off. Nurse Applejack woke us up by screaming and banging her copper-stick on the bottom of our bedsteads. The night nurse had already gone home. The Dwarf was jumping up and down on his bed and pointing and laughing but I didn't know why. Later Mr Randall told me that one of the porters had hidden the bell for a joke.

'It's April Fool's Day today,' he said.

At the farm Donald was scratching his head. There are still no piglets. 'They're very late popping out this spring now,' he said.

The vet came and told him not to worry. I think Donald is a bit put out because he's been getting up very early and nothing has happened yet, he's very tired.

'I'm very frustrated,' he told me.

Mr Hampton told him that he was just being impatient and told him to go home and rest.

2 April 1930

Hurrah! The piglets have arrived. I knew just before I got to the farm because of all the noise.

'We've got thirty-nine of the little buggers.' Mr Flynn said excitedly.

Before he went off to see to the cows he asked me to help Donald get the newborn cleaned and washed down. I had to get more water for the sows.

'They get very thirsty after giving birth.' Donald said.

I'm still waiting for a letter from Aunt Betty. It seems a long time since I wrote. I don't understand why she hasn't replied to me yet. I worry.

4 April 1930

Nurse Applejack came for me yesterday. A new doctor had come to interview me. He said that he was a psychiatry specialist and that his name was Dr Barnes. He told me that he had received a report from the Medical Superintendent who had concerns about me becoming delusional. I am NOT delusional! Dr Barnes asked me if I thought I was delusional. I answered 'No!' He then asked me why I thought I wasn't delusional, it was hard to explain. He kept asking awkward questions and I didn't understand all the things that he was saying. He asked me what I thought about the institution and what I liked and what I hated. I told him that I liked helping with the animals and that I hated going to the chapel. He asked me if I felt that my speech had improved since I've been here, I told him that I thought it had. I know it has because of Mrs Evenden and Mrs Skilton. I told him that Mrs Evenden had died and that I was still waiting for a new person to help me with my speaking. He told me that Mrs Evenden had obviously helped me because he could fully understand everything that I was saying. I liked it when he said that! He asked me if I could see dead people. I answered 'No!' but I told him about the dream I had just before Uncle Charlie died. I told him that I thought Nurse Applejack and Miss Rance had twisted everything around to make me look stupid. I told him that I am not stupid and that I am NOT a lunatic. He told me that he could help me.

'There's a lady called Mrs Jenkins who specialises in cases like yours. 'She's very good but because she's good there's a long waiting list of patients from all over Surrey and beyond waiting to see her. I will see what I can do for you but it may take some time,' he said.

All the time I was with him, Nurse Applejack was listening. I forgot that she was there, she was sat behind me. On the way back to the ward she slapped me around the back of the head and called me a 'liar'. I am NOT a liar. I was only telling the truth!

I missed helping at the farm yesterday and I couldn't go today. Today was my weights and measures day. I have some new working shirts and trousers now.

There's still no letter from Aunt Betty.

5 April 1930

Today is Saturday. At last a letter came from Aunt Betty. It's quite short, I write it here:

Dear Thomas,

Thank you for your letter dated 10th March last.

Your Mother sends you her love. She says that she is trying to summon some strength and will to come and visit you one day. Cousin Clifford will drive her over when she is ready.

I have received a letter about you from Miss Rance. She says that the Medical Superintendent is arranging for a specialist doctor to visit you as he has concerns about your welfare and that you are showing signs of being delusional. Your mother is worried.

The man called George O'Leary is not your father, your mother wants to be honest with you but she doesn't know who your father is herself and feels ashamed.

There's no room for you here. Cousin Clifford and Gloria are expecting a baby.

Yours truly

Aunt Betty

This is as I feared. I've waited so long for Aunt Betty to reply. This is not at all good news but at least I should see Mother soon.

6 April 1930

I didn't really have the heart to go to the chapel but I thought I might draw undue attention to myself if I tried to get away with it so rather reluctantly, I went. I always think of Reginald when I'm in the chapel. It takes me away from what Parson Jaggs keeps saying about God. I still have Reginald's tin soldier. I keep it by my bed. No one has tried to steal it yet but last night I noticed that The Dwarf kept looking at it. I think I will bring it here and put it in my tin. It should fit, I think.

I'm looking forward to going back and helping on the farm tomorrow, I can't wait to see how all our piglets are.

7 April 1930

Nobby Hatch has been temporarily sent back to Broadmoor for some special assessments. Mr Randall and some of the other attendants went out to the beer house last night to celebrate. Mr Randall told me that Nobby probably won't have a trial if he's been found to be of unsound mind. The bad news is that he could still come back!

'I bloody well hope they throw away the keys on him this time,' he said.

At the farm only one of the piglets has died. Eight more were born on Saturday. There are forty-six piglets all together now and they're all snuggled up to the sows. It's a wonderful sight!

8 April 1930

Today The Tall Man spoke to me in the airing court. I've always been told to avoid him and not to catch his eye. He thinks that he's a sorcerer and a magician. I asked him if he could predict death and if could see dead people. He said he could. I asked him if he knew when I would die but he laughed and said that he just saw an old man. There was a howling wind around us when he spoke.

'The winds have come a bit late this year,' he roared.

He then pointed up at the sky. There was a single raven circling above us. 'That is your spirit,' he said.

When I looked up again the raven was gone.

Jack came and helped us with the pigs on the farm today. He doesn't come as much now. He said that it's because things are getting very busy at the beer house and that his father is becoming very frail.

'Something to do with an old war wound,' he told us.

Quickie has just run up the tree. I think I can hear baby squirrels.

9 April 1930

I keep thinking back to yesterday and The Tall Man. I'm
surprised that I actually spoke to him and asked such questions but
he seemed very kind even though he is quite strange. He thinks that
he can predict when someone is going to die and says that he can see
dead people. These are the two things that Miss Rance and Nurse
Applejack have been saying about me. I cannot predict death. I don't
see dead people, yes, I dream about dead people but I don't see them.
There's a difference. I'm not mad. I am NOT delusional!

There's a trip to a place called Virginia Waters on Saturday. Mr
Randall told me that there's a big lake and waterfall there. Albert
will be taking some of us in his new bus with Mr Elliott.

10 April 1930

This morning an ambulance came and then some police.
Everyone had to go back inside. It was just after breakfast. I saw
Nurse Applejack outside. She looked like she had been crying. Mrs
Eley and another nurse had their arms around her. All the policemen
raced over to the reception. Later Miss Rance came out. She had
been crying too. All the attendants were in a big group on the lawn
and were talking to the police sergeant. Later, just before dinner Mr
Randall came into the ward and said that we could go out. Lionel
stopped me from asking him what had happened.

The rest of today has been very quiet and I've been wondering.
When I was at the farm no-one seemed to know what had happened
either. Mr Hampton was there and said that he had seen all the police
arrive.

'A few more of them buggers than normal,' he said.

Eight more piglets had been born this morning. Donald thinks that
they would be the last ones this year now. I worked out that we now
have fifty-four piglets but Mr Hampton said that one has been born
blind and will have to be put down. Donald told me that the
slaughterhouse is now ready and it can work again.

'The Medical Superintendent is advertising for a new slaughter
man.'

I told Donald that I don't want to see the pigs being slaughtered. They're beautiful animals.

'Don't be soft, you'll soon get used to it,' he said.

I don't think I will!

11 April 1930

It's Friday. Whispers are going around that Dr Carlisle is dead. People are saying that he was found hanging by a porter in the reception's storeroom just before dawn yesterday. Most patients are very happy and there's much commotion. I thought back to what Dr Carlisle had done to me and I remember what Bertie said was done to him when he was here. Lionel thinks that Dr Carlisle may have hung himself because important people were catching up with him. Lots of people had been complaining.

'I'm one of them,' he said.

Lionel told me that he thinks that Dr Carlisle might have thought that he was going to be dismissed or arrested by the constabulary.

'I heard that he had been seen by a policeman just last week.'

Mr Randall came over and told us to stop gossiping but wouldn't tell us anymore.

'I'm bound by my own silence,' he said.

Now I wonder!

12 April 1930

We've just got back from Virginia Waters. It's a very nice place and we had a picnic by a waterfall. There were lots of people walking their dogs and I saw a man and a lady kissing for a very long time under a tree. The Dwarf came with us and stayed in the bus all the time with his book. Albert and Mr Elliott tried to get him out but The Dwarf was very stubborn. He didn't even want to eat. Mr Randall didn't come on the trip.

'That's because he likes spending his Saturday afternoons in the beer house staring at Mrs Juett's big boobies,' Mr Elliot quipped.

Mr Elliott told me that Royston Melledew is coming back tomorrow. He left and went home just after I came here last summer.

Mr Elliott said that things haven't gone right for him so he's coming back for awhile.

I asked Mr Elliott if he knew what had happened to Dr Carlisle. He told me that he was due to appear before the Visiting Committee on Monday.

'I think they had found him out. There had been some very serious complaints about him buggering and fiddling with patients and now they are all being treated as a matter of urgency. Even the newspapers have somehow got hold of the story,' he said.

Mr Elliot asked me if I had a cause of complaint against Dr Carlisle. I told him that I did but didn't want to talk about it anymore now that he is dead. Mr Elliot said that I should write a letter saying what had happened to me.

'That's what all the other patients have done,' he added.

I worry that if I did that Nurse Applejack and Miss Rance will make things even more difficult for me. Mr Elliott said that he understood then told me not to repeat what he had been saying.

'I've told you too much already.' he whispered.

13 April 1930

On the way back from the chapel Nurse Applejack came over to me. She said that she didn't want me talking to anyone about Dr Carlisle. She told me that I must never mention his name.

'The poor man is dead now, so we must all let him rest in peace,' she said.

Indeed, I wonder why she said that to me!

Lionel told me that his wife had visited him just after he got back to the ward from the chapel.

'I think that she's taken all my savings, about £400.'

He thinks that she's using it to keep another man and to buy expensive perfumes and lotions for herself. I feel concern for Lionel. He's started cutting himself again.

Royston came back today. All his hair has fallen out and he's very melancholy. He's very quiet and hasn't spoken to anyone yet.

14 April 1930

Nurse Applejack was missing this morning. Another nurse from one of the female wards was carrying out her duties. She told us that Nurse Applejack had to go before the Visiting Committee to tell them what she knew about Dr Carlisle. She told me not to ask any more questions.

'That's how rumours start,' she said.

She's coloured just like Nurse Applejack but seems very nice. I think her name is Primrose Starkey or something. She's asked us to just call her Nurse Primrose. I wish that she could be in charge of us all the time. She told me that she hopes to become a Ward Sister one day, just like Nurse Applejack. I had forgotten that Nurse Applejack had been promoted. No-one calls her Sister anyway, perhaps that's why!

17 April 1930

There's been lots of rain since Tuesday. Today the sun is shining. Mr Drake has just walked past. He showed me a brace of pheasants that he'd just bagged. He looked very proud of himself.

After dinner I went down to the Sparvell fields behind the beer house to help herd the cows up the road again. Mr Luscombe and Mr Flynn are concerned that they're not producing enough milk and think that they may need to buy some milk in from Hilltop Place or from the farm at Stafford Lake.

'The Chief Clerk won't be very happy if we have to do that,' Mr Luscombe said.

Nurse Applejack was back today. She must have had some leave of absence to take.

18 April 1930

On Saturday while we were on the bus trip to Virginia Waters I thought about running away. I lost courage and thought - where would I go? I realised that I don't have anywhere to run to. Albert would have only found me and brought me back and Mr Elliott would have got into lots of trouble for losing me. Last time I tried to escape all my treats were stopped for awhile and Mr Randall watched me all the time for nearly three weeks. It was hard to come up here and write and I couldn't see Maisie.

Royston spoke to me today. He's suffering from general paralysis and he's had to come back for some treatment.

'They have a new way of treating what I have and they can cure me here but I don't like talking about it.'

I think he'll be having the same kind of treatment that Bertie had.

I asked Royston how he lost all his hair and he said that he had drunk some poison by mistake.

'It had been put in an enamel mug in our scullery and I thought it was milk, when I woke up the following morning all my hair was on the pillow and some of my teeth had fallen out. It was the last thing I needed on top of everything else,' he said.

Royston thinks that he will only be here until the summer and then he hopes to go home again. I wish I was lucky like that, if that is lucky!

It's Good Friday. Mr Flynn came up from the fields in his new green tractor this morning.

'We're going to use it to plough the fields down there when the time is right,' he said.

He wanted to show it off I think. He told us that it was a John Deere Series 8 and that he got it cheap from a place called Harrisons near Aldershot. He showed me the serial number... No 823.

Mr Mycroft came by the farm with his puppy and told me that he had something important indoors that he wanted me to see.

'You'll find it very interesting!' he whispered.

He wouldn't tell me what it was and he kept smiling to himself as he walked away. He told me to knock on his door the next time that I was to pass by his cottage.

19 April 1930

I couldn't wait to see what Mr Mycroft wanted to show me so Mr Randall let me go round to see him straight after breakfast. Rex, his puppy came out of his front door and kept licking me.

'Here you are, take a look at this,' Mr Mycroft said.

He seemed very excited. It was a newspaper supplement from last week's *Times of London*.

'Look, look further down the Arts page,' he said and pointed to an article about Maisie's paintings.

I copy it here...

Maisie Albright was born on the 17th day of December 1904 and is an established artist who lives as a recluse at Tilford in the Surrey countryside. She studied art at the Gallery in Winchester and was a member of the Winchester Art School. She has painted a number of contemporary landscape visuals of the Surrey and Hampshire countryside and much of its wildlife. Her late grandfather was a member of the Victorian Artists' Society. Miss Albright's method of work is most sound, always as a preliminary step making charcoal and pencil studies of her subjects and frequently smaller studies in the colours of the intended picture. She paints freely and with a firm touch. Her paintings are in much demand at art galleries throughout the South of England and sales are aggressive.

Mr Mycroft thinks that she is very famous.

'She's a good artist.'

I asked him why it says that Maisie lives in Tilford when she lives here. He thinks that it's because most families do not want everyone to know that their kin are tucked away in an asylum.

'It's a shameful thing to tell people,' he said.

I asked him what aggressive sales meant and he told me that a lot of guineas are being paid for Maisie's art.

'She should be a very rich lady when she leaves here,' he replied.

He cut the article out for me. I must give it to Maisie but I can't help thinking that something might be wrong.

22 April 1930

Nurse Applejack took me to see the Medical Superintendent this morning. On the way there she kept saying...

'Remember what I told you, remember what I said.'

When we arrived she sat beside the Medical Superintendent and just stared at me with her big white bulging eyes. I felt very unsettled. Miss Rance came into the office and sat beside me.

'If you need to hold my hand, please do,' she said.

I noticed a waver in her voice. She's normally very stern. It was very strange. I haven't seen her like that before. The Medical Superintendent is called Mr Deane, he normally only talks to important people or very difficult patients when he has to write to their families with reports or requests. He told me that he had received a report from Attendant Elliott which was dated Monday 14th April. It said that I had mentioned an incident involving the late Dr Carlisle. He wanted to ask me questions about it. Nurse Applejack was still staring at me and she made me feel very hot.

'What did Dr Carlisle do to alarm you?' he asked.

I couldn't answer.

'Don't sit there in silence, you need to tell me everything, I am your friend, you can tell me anything.'

I didn't want to talk but then he asked me if Dr Carlisle had tried to touch my lap. I said 'Yes!'

'Did he remove your trousers?'

'Err, yes!'

'Did he penetrate you?'

I didn't know what that meant. I felt Miss Rance squeeze my hand. Nurse Applejack was still sat there just staring and glaring at me.

'Do you know what penetration is?' he asked.

'No!' I replied.

He asked me if Dr Carlisle had pushed his penis into my bottom. I said 'Yes!' Miss Rance squeezed my hand again.

'How many times did this happen to you?'

'Err, about seven,' I replied.

'Can you remember the dates?' I said that I couldn't.

'It's something that I had found hard to write down and I wanted to forget.'

'One more question!'

'Was anyone else there when these incidents supposedly took place?'

I couldn't answer. Nurse Applejack was unsettling me and was still looking at me with a frown. Afterwards she took me back to the ward and said 'Tommy, Tommy, it's alright now, now we can be friends.'

I feel very ashamed. One day someone should know the truth, the real truth. That is why I have written it all down here.

It's getting late now and it will be dark soon. I haven't seen Maisie today. I so wanted to find her and give her the newspaper cutting Mr Mycroft let me have.

28 April 1930

For nearly a week I've had a fever. Nurse Applejack had given me some new medicines. I've been very drowsy and it's been hard to get out of bed. For four days I've been in the sick bay at the infirmary. I still feel very weak but Mrs Eley has been bringing me cups of milk or Ovaltine at night to help me build up my strength. Lionel thinks that I should be very careful about the pills Nurse Applejack is giving me.

'You were alright until she started giving you those,' he said.

I think he's right!

29 April 1930

Mrs Eley screamed during the night and woke us all up. She was led away by two porters. It was very eerie. Lionel said that he thought he saw a small ghostly child with black eyes standing in the shadows by one of the windows in the dormitory.

'Mrs Eley must have seen it too.'

He told me that it's the ghost of a little girl and it came at about the same time last year.

'The night nurse who was on duty that night never came back. I'm used to it now but I don't talk to anyone else about it. They think I'm off my rocker already,' he said.

I saw Maisie today but she was too far away to talk to. She was walking towards the bottom field near the canal with the Matron and two others. I think she was going down to see the horses. I still have the newspaper cutting that I need to give her.

30 April 1930

At last I have been able to talk to Maisie. We were undisturbed for about half an hour and I had time to give her the newspaper cutting. She's having more trouble with Angela Reeves, who is still stealing and breaking her things. Maisie told me that didn't know her paintings were being sold to the art galleries for lots of money like the newspaper says. She's very upset and told me that she thinks her uncle is betraying her.

'Father may be too,' she said.

I asked her what she meant and she told me that her uncle is the man behind nearly all her problems.

'He bullies my father and is a tyrant. He's a very cruel and callous man,' she said with a catch in her voice.

I had time to tell Maisie about my letter from Aunt Betty. She put her hand softly against my face and told me not to worry.

'One day, everything will work out for you, just be patient my sweet love,' she whispered.

Maisie said the word 'love'. She has given me back my hope. I think that I'm in love with Maisie. I've never been in love before!

1 May 1930

Today some children from the Knaphill School came and danced around the Maypole. Later all the nurses and lady attendants danced around. The Asylum Band was playing the music and Mr Elliott was pressing the keys and buttons on his accordion. It's the first time that I've seen him in the band. There was a big tent and there were lots of cakes, sandwiches and beer. People from the village came and some of our crafts were on sale. Mrs Woolston was there again. She's always helping out with things.

3 May 1930

Missy Hope is back at work in the scullery. She was helping Sarah take the skins off some rabbits.

'The attendants are having rabbit stew for tea tonight.'

She told me that there's not enough rabbit to feed the all patients as well. 'That's why you never get any,' she laughed.

Missy's hair has been cut short since Nobby Hatch attacked her.

'He pulled most of it out when he tried to rape me,' she said.

I didn't expect her to talk about it but she felt comfortable telling me what had happened.

'Nobby is a monster, I'm glad that he's been sent back to Broadmoor but Tybern would have been better.'

Tybern Gallows is where they used to hang murderers and rapists in public right up to the last century I think.

Miss Rance came into the scullery and asked me what I was doing there. I didn't answer and she told me to be on my way.

Tomorrow is Sunday. I don't want to go to the chapel. I need to think of a plan.

4 May 1930

Lionel has taught me how not to swallow the pills that Nurse Applejack's been giving me. He showed me how to move them under my tongue. I then have to push my tongue against my lower teeth. When I open my mouth it looks like the pills have gone. I tried it just before church today but I need to practice more. I don't want Nurse Applejack to find out that I am cheating. I went to the chapel and sat there smiling throughout the service. Nurse Applejack just stood there frowning at me. I think she was confused. I laugh!

5 May 1930

There are two new men in the ward. One appears to be very strange. I think he wants to be a girl. He's brought a lady's hand mirror with him and keeps twirling his long black hair into curls. He hasn't had it cut yet. Last night just before the lights went out he was using some crayons as cosmetics, blue for his eye lids and red for his lips. The Dwarf was smiling and waving at him all the time from the other end of the dormitory. The other man is called Stanley Bevan. Part of his forehead is missing. Lionel told me that he has been here before. He thinks that something must have happened to him since he left because he didn't have a hole in his head the last time he was here.

I helped with the cattle again today. I went down to the field behind the beer house and herded them up to the farm with Donald and Mr Flynn. They're still not giving up enough milk and Mr Flynn thinks he may be in trouble. The Chief Clerk now has to buy in milk supplies from Hilltop Place, just as Mr Flynn feared. Donald said that he shouldn't worry too much. He told me that it often happens.

'That's exactly why I am worried!' Mr Flynn uttered.

6 May 1930

Mr Mycroft asked me if I had given Maisie the newspaper cutting yet. I told him that I had and that she didn't know that her paintings were being sold in art galleries like it says. She didn't know that she was sort of famous.

'I suspected just as much,' he said.

Mr Mycroft told me that he would mention the newspaper article to the Medical Superintendent.

'I don't know what he'll say, he already thinks that I'm an interfering old so and so.'

I told Mr Mycroft that I always have a warm feeling in my heart whenever I think about her.

'That's love, that's love alright,' Mr Mycroft said with a smile.

He told me that love is a dangerous thing and that he's glad that he's too old for that sort of rubbish now. He asked me if Maisie knew how I felt about her. I told him that I didn't know and that I was thinking about writing her letter to tell her. Mr Mycroft said that it would be an honourable thing to do but told me to be aware that she might not love me back.

'You also need to be aware that relationships between patients are very much discouraged here. 'It's hard enough for the asylum staff, let alone patients to have relationships with each other even though some do,' he said.

I do hope Maisie will love me back!

7 May 1930

Head, cheek, spare rib, blade, hand, loin, belly, leg, hock, trotter are all the parts of a pig. Mr Flynn wants me to learn all of this so that I will make a good pig farmer. He said that a pig provides lots of different kinds of meat; gammon, ham, bacon, pork. He wants me to learn where all these things are and wants me to mark them on a pig with a small paint brush before one goes to slaughter on Friday.

'Hey, don't worry, Donald will help you with that, he's used it,' he said.

I'm not really looking forward to seeing a pig being slaughtered but Mr Flynn thinks that would be a good initiation for me if I want to be a real pig famer. In the dictionary that Maisie gave me it says that 'initiation' means 'an occasion when someone is first introduced to an activity or skill. Now I wonder if I'm doing the right thing!

8 May 1930

Today I have written a letter for Maisie. It's been hard to write and I've had to look up at the big blue sky to get all of the words. I don't know whether I will have enough courage to give it to her yet, but one day, I hope I do. I love Maisie with all my heart and I hope that Maisie really does love me too.

Dear Maisie,

How I long to be with you. How I long for us to be free from this place. Sometimes I am lost without you, but when I think of you I feel that at last, I am whole and my heart sings.

Every time I write down your name, I think of you smiling. You are such a beautiful thing. When I see you in the field, beneath the sunset with the horses I see an image of real beauty and I feel love, true love. I think I know what love is now; it's like a welcome pain. I don't ever want this wonderful feeling to go away.

I want to walk away with you into our own special sunset somewhere hand in hand, away from everything that stops us from being together.

Forgive me Maisie for these words and I hope that they do not offend but I wish that you could forever be my love. I do hope that you can find it in your heart to love me back. I sincerely hope you will.

Yours always

Tommy xxx

9 May 1930

This morning I had my test with Mr Flynn. He asked me questions about how a pig should be cut and what all the joints are called. He seemed happy with my answers. Mr Luscombe had come to watch and listen and he asked me what different kinds of meat came from a pig. I told him: Gammon, ham, pork, bacon. He told me that nothing goes to waste.

'Even its heart, its brain, its liver are all sold,' he said.

The brain is made into brawn; it's something that all the soldiers had to have in the Great War,' he laughed.

Donald then asked me to draw lines on the pig to show where it should be cut after it had been killed. It was hard so Donald took over. When the pig was taken into the slaughter room it began to squeal. Suddenly it stopped and then there was lots of blood on the floor which spilled over my boots. The Slaughter Man is new but didn't say anything. Donald helped him lift the pig on to a table. They cut it open. I couldn't watch anymore. Now I ask myself again, do I really want to be a pig farmer; do I really want to do all this?

Tomorrow is Saturday and there's a concert in the Main Hall. A group of melody men are coming from London to play for the staff and patients.

10 May 1930

Saturday is always a good day to find Maisie. I saw her walking towards the reception. I wanted to give her my letter but I changed my mind at the last minute. I lost courage. She told me that her Uncle Sylvester is coming today to visit and collect three of her paintings and arrange some more pocket money. She had a roll of paintings under her arm but as they were wrapped I couldn't see them. She told me that her uncle will arrange for them to be framed. She's going to ask him what he does with them afterwards. She told me that she's also going to show him Mr Mycroft's newspaper cutting from *The Times*. I worry.

Mr Randall is taking some of us to a beer house this afternoon. I wonder if that will be the Nag's Head Inn! Stanley will be coming with us. The other new man who wants to be a lady is not ready to go out on walks yet and might be moved to an isolation room or on to another ward.

'He's very mixed up, not everyone is allowed out of the grounds. You might have noticed that those who aren't allowed out wear different coloured shirts and jackets from you chaps so that we can watch them easier, some get out anyway which always keeps us busy,' Mr Randall said.

Tonight after dinner it's the concert with some melody men from Jamaica and their instruments.

11 May 1930

Yesterday afternoon Stanley Bevan, the new man came with me, Lionel, Mr Randall and two others to the Nag's Head Inn. We all sat outside on a bench while Mr Randall watched us from inside. Lionel asked Stanley what had happened to his head. He told us that he tried to shoot himself with a rifle and that it went off too quickly.

'I was in the shed in the garden but I couldn't reach the barrel back far enough and I pulled the trigger by accident before I was ready,' he said.

He told us that when he left the asylum last time his wife had promised to care for him but she kept treating him like an idiot.

'I had fought for King and Country and was fed up by being treated like a bloody fool by that woman,' he said.

He told us that the gun had been in his shed since he came back from the trenches in 1918.

'I should have killed her with the thing. That bloody woman will be the death of me.'

Lionel laughed and said...'it sounds like she nearly was!'

Stanley told us that he's finished with women now, especially now that half his head is missing and all his good looks have gone. Lionel laughed again and said 'Good looks? I don't remember you having any good looks!'

The most memorable thing about yesterday was that Mr Randall paid for all the booze. He normally uses <u>our</u> pocket money for that!

12 May 1930

There was another fire on the ward last night. It was Raymond again. This time his bed and a pair of drapes caught light. A sideboard and the gramophone player got damaged. There's a new night nurse who is a man. It was his first night and Raymond kept swearing at him and calling him names. He kept telling him that being a nurse is a woman's job. He also picked on Anton Shelton, who he calls the 'Girly Man'. Anton wouldn't leave the ward when the klaxons went off because his hair was a mess. One of the night porters was trying not to laugh. Harry Horlock was angry because his sleep had been disturbed again but it was the first time that he had had the opportunity to use his new fire engine so he looked quite happy. At least he didn't call us all a bunch of imbeciles this time. I think that's because the Medical Superintendent had come over to see what was going on and he would have heard him.

13 May 1930

Today after we finished at the farm Donald and Mr Flynn invited me over to Rose Cottage for some cold drinks. Mrs Woolston was there and she was showing Mrs Pengelley how to make a Knaphill Pie. Mr Flynn said that it's his favourite.

'Best in the winter though, it warms the old cockles,' he said.

Mrs Woolston said that it's nice anytime of the year and told me not to listen.

'It's a bacon and leek pie but it has a secret ingredient which gives it its own flavour, that's why it's called a Knaphill Pie, it's a village recipe that I inherited from my old grandmother,' she said.

Unfortunately it was still cooking when I left so I never tasted it but I saw some cheese and garlic on the side. They must have been the secret ingredients!

14 May 1930

This morning on the way to the farm I saw Mr Mycroft and asked him what the real difference was between Brookwood and Knaphill. I have always been a bit confused. Mrs Woolston began telling me yesterday when she was talking about the pie but was disturbed by something falling on the floor. Mr Mycroft told me that the asylum is really a village within a village.

'It's really in Knaphill but it's always been known as Brookwood Lunatic Asylum or the Brookwood Mental Hospital as we should be calling it now. It's all to do with the railway station down at Brookwood. People can find us easier apparently,' he said.

'It's all a bit sad, mad and bad around here,' he added.

I asked him what he meant and he said 'Sad because of the cemetery, mad because of the asylum and bad because of the old prisons.'

He told me that there used to be two prisons where Inkerman Barracks is now. I remember Maisie telling me once that Mr Mycroft knows everything. I think she's right!

I asked Mr Mycroft if he had told the Medical Superintendent about Maisie's paintings yet and he said that he was just waiting for the right moment. 'You have to catch that man in the right mood,' he said.

16 May 1930

Parson Jaggs came into the ward yesterday to do his bedside rounds. He always waits until everyone is in their beds before he comes in so it's difficult to avoid him. I went to the ablutions but he was waiting for me when I got back. I hoped that he wouldn't recognise me but he asked me if I had rediscovered God yet. I stayed silent for as long as I could but then he asked again. I told him that I find it hard to believe in God when there's so much death and pain about. He asked me about pain.

'What pain?' he asked.

I told him that I had suffered an emotional pain ever since I had been here. Being brought here, not seeing Mother, seeing my friends die, losing Uncle Charlie and finally losing hope!

'This is all my pain!' I told him.

He went on about God again and told me that I should embrace him. I cannot embrace God. I cannot embrace something that does not exist. He told me that I should pray to Jesus.

'He is God's servant,' he snapped.

Parson Jaggs told me that I must pray for my soul. I told him that I do. He then went off to speak to Royston. Jesus if he existed was no more than a conjuror. He's just a silly statue in the chapel. I have decided that religion or faith and all its hypocrisy can have no place in my heart anymore.

17 May 1930

Nurse Applejack came over to me this morning and told me to 'Repent!' Parson Jaggs must have told her about the conversation we had on Thursday evening. She kept banging her copper-stick on the bottom of my bed like she always does. Gradually there was a circle of people standing around her, Lionel, Royston, Anton, Stanley and even Raymond. She stopped shouting at me and then told everyone to go down for breakfast. She leant over me and then whispered...

'Thomas Compton, you must repent, you must deliver your soul to God, that's the only way that you will ever free your conscience!'

I didn't answer; I couldn't say anything because I was shaking with so much rage.

This afternoon Mr Randall and Mr Elliott took me and Lionel to the beer house. Later, Mr Drake came in. They were talking about going on a long walk out of Knaphill tomorrow and asked us if we would like to go.

'We may have to bring a couple of the others,' Mr Elliott said.

I saw Jack and he told me that he's not allowed to come to help with the pigs anymore.

'There's too much to do here and my father is very ill now,' he said.

Mrs Juett was standing behind him. Later I saw her and Mr Randall talking under a tree outside.

'They just needed to get away from all the smoke,' Mr Elliott said.

It's always very smokey from all the tobacco in the Nag's Head Inn but as it was raining quite hard today we all had to sit inside.

18 May 1930

It's Sunday. Sunday is always awkward for me. Going to the chapel is becoming very hard and it enrages me even more now. The church was very full this morning because the Visiting Committee was here. During the service I tried to hide at the back behind one of the pillars. Each time Parson Jaggs looked over I pretended that I was interested in what he was saying. Most of the time I was there I just closed my eyes and thought about Maisie. I think that Parson Jaggs thought that I was actually praying. I was but NOT to God!

After church I went to help Donald feed and swill the pigs because one of the other farmhands is very sick and Donald needed an extra pair of hands. Patients don't usually work on Saturdays or Sundays but Mr Luscombe got permission for me to help. Our piglets are already starting to grow quite big now. Mr Flynn and Mr Luscombe had just come back from herding the cattle back down to the Sparvell fields. Donald told me that both men are very happy because the Blue Albion cows have started producing more milk.

'That will bring the farm back up to its full quota and we can now supply enough churns to the kitchens each week if the cows keep doing their bit. That means the Chief Clerk will also be happy!' he said.

He also told me that Mr Luscombe and Mr Flynn were both celebrating in Rose Cottage past midnight last night.

'They must have drunk a gallon of Irish Whiskey between them,' he laughed.

I've just had roast beef, peas and potatoes for dinner and I'm going on a walk with some of the others this afternoon. Mr Drake is taking us to see a hidden badger sett in Bisley near the church.

'It's huge!' he said with his arms wide apart.

Mr Randall thinks that all the badgers have gone from there now but it's big enough for people to get in and have a look around inside. Mr Elliott is coming and is bringing his lantern. Mr Drake says that he hopes to shoot a couple of rabbits in the fields behind the old mansion house while we're out so he's bringing his gun.

'Just shout if you see a policeman,' he said.

Lionel, Stanley and The Dwarf are coming with us. I don't like The Dwarf. I find him very irritating. He makes me flinch. I wish that he wasn't coming with us; he'll probably spoil the walk for the rest of us like he always does.

19 May 1930

Yesterday was very disappointing. When we got to the badger sett it had gone. There was just a very big hole in the ground. Mr Randall thinks that the farmer must have dug it out.

'I know he thinks that the badgers come out at night and bother his cattle,' he said.

He told us that the farmer is related to the Woolston family but that he used to be a gypsy.

'His ancestors used to camp here and then claimed the land about 200 years ago for the whole tribe,' he said.

Mr Drake told us that a number of pottery pieces and even some Roman coins had been found in the field at the start of the century.

'They're all kept in a museum over Guildford now,' he said.

The badger sett could have only been destroyed recently as the soil and clay smelt fresh. I could also see some chalk. There were some black and white cows in the corner of the field and they just stared at us all the time that we were there. We then went on to have a closer look at the church. It's quite small and there were some graves and a bell was ringing. Everything took a lot of time because The Dwarf wanted to stop and read his book whenever he found something to sit on. He didn't really seem interested in anything else at all!

20 May 1930

For the last few days I have had a very itchy bottom and there are little white bits in my shit. I told Lionel. He told me that quite a while ago he'd had them too. He told me that I need to tell the nurse. He said that it might be tapeworm.

'It's very common in here and it lives in your bowels,' he said.

I told Lionel that I didn't really want anyone looking up my bottom or even touching it and that I didn't want Nurse Applejack anywhere near me. He told me that when he had tapeworm he was given some lotion which he had to put on himself in the ablutions while an attendant watched. I asked him if it would go away on its own but Lionel didn't know. It's very uncomfortable. I wonder what has caused it!

There are eight more new cows at the farm. They look like Blue Albions but could be a different breed. I'm not sure. Donald doesn't know and Mr Flynn is the best person to ask but we didn't see him today. Donald told me that Mr Flynn had gone back to the market with Mr Luscombe. There's a cattle market in Guildford,' he said.

I think I remember someone telling me that before.

21 May 1930

Cousin Clifford came to visit me today. Mr Randall came up to the farm and I was excused from helping for the rest of day. Clifford said that he was passing on his way to Woking and that he thought that he would drop by and say 'Hello!' He told me that he knew Aunt Betty had written to me and mentioned the baby. Clifford and Gloria expect it to be born in September. He told me that he was sorry that there was no room for me at the house in Watchetts Road. He and Gloria are staying there because Aunt Betty is giving them the house when she dies.

'I do hope that's some years away yet,' he said rather sympathetically.

I told Clifford that I feel very angry and frustrated that I'm stuck in here. He agreed that there has never been much wrong with me and that Mother should not have sent me here. I told him that Nurse Applejack and Miss Rance have been making things very difficult for me by telling the Medical Superintendent that I've been seeing and talking to dead people. I told Clifford that it was all about a dream I had and that a doctor called Dr Barnes had been to see me and told me that he would get some help but nothing has happened yet. Clifford said that he would go and speak to Miss Rance before he left. I asked him about Mother and told him what Aunt Betty had said in her letter about Mother being well enough to come and see me soon.

'She's back on her feet again now but she doesn't walk too well. She feels very guilty about everything,' he said.

He asked me if the man called George O'Leary had been back to see me again, I told him 'No!' I asked him if he thought Mr O'Leary might be my father but he went silent and just smiled rather nervously.

'Who knows, who knows, even your Mother doesn't know, she's very confused and very ashamed. I don't think she even remembers. Apparently there were so many gentleman callers around in those days.'

Before he left Clifford said that he will try and bring Mother over to visit me one Sunday over the next few weeks.

'Anyway, my lovely Gloria would love to see you again,' he added.

I still find it very hard to believe that my mother was a prostitute but I think that she's actually admitting it now. It sounds like she's telling everyone that she feels ashamed.

23 May 1930

I saw Nurse Eley today. She has a new position in one of the female wards. She told me that she doesn't have to work on the ward at night anymore. She told me that the female patients are far more trouble, especially Angela Reeves. I worked out from what she had said that she must be working in Maisie's ward and I told her that Maisie was having trouble with Angela.

'You're not supposed to know things like that!' she said.

She asked me if the ghost had come back in my ward and I told her what Lionel had said about it only appearing once a year.

'That's still once a year too many.'

I told her that there's a male nurse in our ward at nights now.

'That's no comfort for me,' she said.

She then gave me a caramel toffee before she toddled off towards the laundry. I like caramel toffees.

24 May 1930

Mr Flynn told me that he's very relieved that the cows have started to produce more milk.

The eight new cows are also Blue Albions but have had their horns tapered back which is why they look a little different. They're also branded.

'These ones came from the market in Guildford so they should be fine. If not, they'll all be off for slaughter. Our slaughterhouse can only deal with pigs and sheep although that might change soon,' he said pulling a face.

Miss Rance wants to see me at 10 o'clock on Monday. I wonder what she wants, I wonder if it's anything to do with what Cousin Clifford might have said!

25 May 1930

After chapel Lionel told me that it's his wife's birthday today. He did tell me her name once but I can't remember. I think it begins with the letter J. It could be Jeanie or Janet but I'm not sure. It's also his sister's birthday today. I told Lionel that I didn't know he had a sister. I also mentioned that I'd heard Nurse Applejack tell one of the other nurses that it's her birthday today as well. He laughed and rolled his eyes...

'My sister is more evil than my wife and Nurse Applejack put together, all the old witches must have been born on this day.'

I thought about it a bit and then I realised that Nanny was also born on the 25th May. I told him that Nanny wasn't a witch, just a bit strict and funny in her own way. Lionel laughed again.

'Well maybe bitches, not witches then,' he said.

We both laughed for about a minute but I felt like I was betraying my Nanny, I didn't mean it. I've always loved her and I miss her.

26 May 1930

Today I went to see Miss Rance. It was about a conversation she had with Cousin Clifford when he visited last Wednesday. She told me that she thought Clifford is a very honourable man and that I should be glad that he is championing me. I asked her what she meant. She told me that he's very concerned about my welfare and has been speaking to her on Mother's behalf. Miss Rance told me that she showed him my case notes. I thought that they were personal and I told her so. She then told me that Clifford has declared himself as appropriate kin, an appropriate relative who is now entitled to ask questions about my treatment.

'He was very concerned when I told him that you were delusional,' she said.

I told her that I am NOT delusional.

'It's all a big mistake, a fraud.'

She snapped at me and told me not to become too emotional about it. I told her that I was brought here because of my speech, I had an impediment and it has gone now. She told me that I still had an impediment and that is why Dr Barnes has been to see me and is arranging for a specialist person for me.

'The Medical Superintendent is doing everything he can for you,' she said.

I told her that everyone else has been telling me how much my talking has improved and how I find that people always seem to understand what I'm saying now.

'I can only comment on what I see. You still have a speech defect and you are delusional,' she argued.

I felt myself nearly crying with despair. Cousin Clifford has tried to help but she's told him a pack of lies. I'm now frightened that he's gone away believing everything that she has said. I worry!

It's a fine evening. I'm glad that I've been able to sit here undisturbed. It's just the birds chirping in the trees and me. There's a deer getting rid of its winter coat on a bush just behind me, it hasn't seen me yet otherwise it would have run off. There are some rabbits scurrying around in the grass. I hope Mr Drake doesn't come with his gun. There's a beautiful orange sunset which has been split by a long thin indigo cloud. How I wish Maisie was here to share this moment. In the dictionary there's a word: 'tranquil' - I think that this must be what tranquil means, or is it tranquillity?

28 May 1930

Mrs Pengelley called me over today and invited me in to Rose Cottage. She was looking very proud.

'Try some of this, try some of this,' she said.

There was a big pie on the kitchen table.

'I've made my first Knaphill Pie all on my own.'

Donald was with me and he tried some first.

'It's been made with the meat from one of our pigs,' he said.

Suddenly my appetite was lost. The bacon must have come from the pig that I saw being slaughtered the other day. I was too embarrassed to say no, so I just tried some. There was a lot of leek and the potato tasted of cheese and garlic so I tried to eat that instead of the bacon. The green stuff on top was rosemary I think. When I did eat the bacon, it tasted very nice and I felt guilty.

I saw Maisie this afternoon just before tea. She was walking with a nurse so we couldn't talk. We smiled and waved at each other. The nurse smiled too. I think that Maisie was talking about me; my ears were going all funny!

29 May 1930

I had a chance to speak with Maisie this morning. She was on her way to see the horses down in the bottom field. I asked her if she had shown the newspaper cutting to her uncle.

'Oh, he looked very confused and angry and asked me where I had got it from. He told me that he was keeping it all as a big surprise and that all the money was being put into saving bonds for me to spend when I leave here. I didn't believe him, he was obviously lying but I chose not to say anymore,' she said.

I fear for Maisie because I think something has happened to her which she hasn't felt comfortable telling me about yet and I think that her uncle maybe cheating on her by selling her paintings. Maisie told me herself that she thinks she's being exploited!

Maisie asked me if I was going to The Ball on Saturday. I didn't know about it.

'It's a Ladies Ball where the women have to ask the men to dance. I will come and find you, so be smart!' she said.

Mr Randall told me that Silas Greenwood who works at The Anchor Hotel is coming to work at the asylum from next week. He's got himself a position of attendant in the senile block.

'Silas was always arguing with the landlady woman up there. There was no real man supporting her and he didn't know whether to hit her or fuck her so he left before he hit her,' he said.

The way he said that made me laugh.

Mr Flynn ran over a chicken in his tractor this morning. There was blood and feathers everywhere. Another chicken was injured and Donald pulled its neck to put it out of its misery. It was all very messy. I heard Mr Luscombe tell Mr Flynn to watch where he was going and to be more careful in future. Mr Flynn wasn't very happy!

31 May 1930

This morning some of us went for a run around the cricket field. It's not as much fun without the American soldiers. Mr Elliott doesn't bark loud enough and there's no *'Hip, hip, hip'*. The Dwarf didn't come, he runs the fastest! A man from another ward won our race and his attendant gave him a knob of sugar.

'He thinks he's a horse,' Mr Elliott said.

Tonight it's The Ball. I have a nice clean shirt and have polished my boots. They're the boots I was wearing when I came. Uncle Charlie bought them for me. I'm looking forward to dancing with Maisie but I don't know how to dance. I worry!

1 June 1930

Last night at The Ball I had one dance with Maisie. I kept tripping over my boot laces but it did make her laugh.

'I'll have to teach you how to dance!' she joked.

For most of the evening we sat in the corner and looked and smiled at each other. I wanted to hold her hand but I was aware that Nurse Applejack was watching us nearly all of the time. Nurse Applejack looked very strange in her own clothes. She was dressed all in yellow and orange and had a floppy green hat on her head. Maisie felt uneasy because Angela Reeves kept staring at her. She said that Angela was probably still angry because she wasn't allowed to bring her pram.

'That's not my fault!' she said.

Angela was taken away by an attendant before all the dancing had finished. After that, Maisie felt that she could relax and enjoy the rest of the evening. I enjoyed her good company, despite Nurse Applejack.

At the chapel there was another vicar taking the service and Nurse Applejack wasn't there. I didn't know where Parson Jaggs was but the new vicar said that he would join us later for High Tea.

It's been very hot today and a lot of us were just sitting around with our shirts off. The Tall Man was walking around the airing court still wearing his winter overcoat just like Colonel Peter used to. He must have been very hot and smelly.

Mr Drake has put down some snares and traps in the woods. There's one near my tree. There are white arrows painted on the trees near where they are. Mr Drake told me to watch where I tread.

'I don't fancy a patient for dinner,' he laughed.

I think Mr Drake is very funny. He talks to me as if I'm a normal person although sometimes I think he jokes with me. Actually, I am a normal person. I am NOT a lunatic!

2 June 1930

Mr Randall told me that Parson Jaggs is having an operation and will not be back at the chapel for at least four weeks. The vicar who took his place is from one of the churches in Knaphill. He's new and didn't seem very religious. He just wanted to talk about other things all the time and at High Tea last night he told us all about what he did in the war. He shot two German soldiers.

'I saw the whites of their eyes, I had to kill them, and YES, it was either them or me,' he said.

Miss Rance has given me a note. Dr Barnes is coming here on Wednesday and wishes to see me at 10 o'clock.

4 June 1930

Nurse Applejack took me to the Chief Clerk and Attendant's office. There was a lady sitting there.

'I'm here on behalf of Dr Barnes, my name is Mrs Jenkins and you must be young Thomas Compton,' she said.

I sat down and Nurse Applejack left the room. It was just me and Mrs Jenkins. She offered me a cup of tea. I said 'No thank you.'

'Perhaps you would like some coffee then?' she asked.

I said 'Yes please.'

I think I had only drank coffee once before and that was about six years ago at Nanny's house.

'I am here to assess you, your case notes are very interesting but I want find out all about you myself. I understand that you prefer to be called Tommy, is that correct?'

'Yes,' I replied.'

'It says here that your Mother has moved to Camberley and is living with your Aunt, is that correct?'

'Again, yes,' I replied.

'Your birthday is on the 9th August and you are now twenty-four years of age.'

'Yes, yes, yes, why are you asking me so many questions?'

I felt uncomfortable and very agitated. Every time I have to go to the office I'm asked about the same old things. Do these people expect me to give a different answer every time? Mrs Jenkins told me to calm down. I think that she noticed that I was trembling. A maid came in and poured me another cup of coffee and gave me a biscuit. The coffee tasted very nice.

'Right, let's see what we can do to get you out of here,' Mrs Jenkins said.

I felt my ears prick up, I felt alert. I was very interested to find out what she was going to ask me next.

'You have been here since Monday 22nd July last year and were brought here because of a speech defect and a bit of late maturity. I understand you well and I see a fine mature young man sat before me,' she said.

I smiled but told her that I wasn't aware that 'late maturity' was one of the reasons why Mother had sent me here.

'You were simply late coming through adolescence,' she said. 'It happens to lots of young men and all for different reasons.'

She asked me if I thought that I was delusional and I told her about the dream I had just before Uncle Charlie died. I told her that I thought Miss Rance and Nurse Applejack misunderstood me on purpose to make me look bad.

'I am NOT delusional!' I said quite angrily.

Mrs Jenkins thinks that it was my comment about them, rather than what I thought I had seen, which is what had probably got me in to trouble.

'People don't like being criticised or being made to look like fools, especially by patients when there are other people around, it's no excuse but I think I understand what's been going on here now.'

She then asked me about church and God. I told her that I no longer believe in God. I hate going to the chapel and that if there was a God then all these bad things would never happen. She told me that I don't have to go to the chapel every Sunday.

'It's a matter of choice, your choice, and no-one can force you to go, it's all written down in the hospital rules.'

I told her that Nurse Applejack has always forced me to go to church and that Parson Jaggs has been very forthright in making me attend also.

'No, no they're wrong, they're not allowed to do that. I will get you dispensation from going to the chapel.'

I asked her what dispensation was and she told me that it means that I won't have to go to the church any more. I smiled and felt happy. Mrs Jenkins then asked me about my friends. I told her that Lionel who is in the bed next to mine in the dormitory is a good friend. I told her about Colonel Peter and Reginald who have both died. She remembered Reginald.

'The way he passed was so sad, so sad.'

I told her about Donald and all the others at the farm and how friendly and helpful they are. She then asked me if I had any lady friends. I went quiet.

'Come on, you can tell me if you have, there's nothing wrong with having a friend of the opposite sex so long as you are both responsible. You are at an age where a boy/girl relationship should be very healthy for you as long as you behave yourselves within the rules,' she said quite stealthily.

I finally told her about Maisie and how beautiful she is, how she loves horses and is very good at art. Mrs Jenkins said that it seems like Maisie has been very important to me.

'Yes, she is very important to me.'

This all took about an hour and at the end Mrs Jenkins got up out of her chair and looked out of the window.

'Look I can't promise anything, but you have a good case for going home, the problem is that you don't have any home to go to, I will make some enquiries to see what can be done. I shall come and see you again in three months time.'

I thought that three months is a long time, the summer will nearly be over by then and I will still be here. But now at last, I have some hope!

6 June 1930

Last night all the lights came on. Raymond was missing from his bed and the nurse was arguing with one of the attendants. Two porters came into the dormitory with another attendant. They looked under all the beds and searched the ablutions. Suddenly all the klaxons went off, there's a big new electric one now which is very loud. We all looked out of the window and could see people running towards the Recreation Hall. This morning Mr Randall told us that Raymond had been caught on the roof and that he was threatening to jump off. He'd been chased by another attendant who had caught him in the mortuary interfering with an unclaimed corpse. Mr Randall told us that there are only two dead bodies in there at the moment and they have no kin, they are waiting for the council to finish the paperwork before they can be buried. Raymond has been put in to isolation and is waiting to be seen by the Medical Superintendent later.

'He'll probably be moved over to a room in one of the refractory wards now,' Mr Randall said.

At the farm two of the pigs have been found with a disease and are going blind. Donald has separated them from the others and is waiting for Mr Hampton to come.

'They'll probably have to be put down; we can't slaughter them for meat,' he said.

He told me that last year when they had all the problems, all the dead pigs were taken down to the Sparvell field at night and burned before first light.

'It was sad and the smell was something that I've never forgotten.' Donald said as he put his fingers to his nose.

He was very upset because he really cares for the pigs and was hoping that this year there would be no health problems with them.

7 June 1930

This morning I played football in the field and scored a goal. The backs of my legs ache now and I have a pain all down my right side. Maisie and some of the other female patients watched us and were cheering. We were playing against a team of attendants and porters. They kept kicking us and pushing us over. I don't think that's in the rules! They beat us by three goals to two and then we all went to dinner.

I saw Mr Randall just now. He looked very drunk. He must have been in the Nag's Head Inn all afternoon. I know he likes it there!

Tomorrow I do NOT have to go to the chapel. I hope Mrs Jenkins has told everyone including Nurse Applejack about the dispensation!

8 June 1930

Just as I feared, Nurse Applejack came for me and told me to get dressed ready to go to church. I told her about what Mrs Jenkins had said and that I do not have to go to the chapel anymore.

'What?' she shouted.

'Who is she to tell you what you can do and what you cannot do? I'm in charge of you, no-one else,' she screamed.

I started shouting back at her; I was trembling and can't remember exactly what I said. She swung her copper-stick at me but missed. I ran to the door and Mr Randall was standing there. He asked what all the fuss was about and I told him that I had been given dispensation from going to the chapel by Mrs Jenkins. He told Nurse Applejack that it was true. Miss Rance had told him about it. Nurse Applejack wasn't very happy and then rushed off mumbling things under her breath.

Mr Randall said that I could go for a walk with him and Mr Elliott although some other patients including The Dwarf were going with them too. The Dwarf doesn't go to the chapel because he's a Hindu. He says his prayers on a mat in the side room instead. We walked along the canal to a place called Deepcut locks and back. There was a fishing match going on and I saw some very huge carp and other fish being caught. It's been very hot today. I sweat.

9 June 1930

The two diseased pigs were taken away from their holding pen last night. Mr Hampton has been to check the others and has given them the all clear. One of the piglets has been found with a deformed trotter but it's alright apart from that. Mrs Pengelley came over and gave us all a cold orange drink with some ice. It's been very hot again today but Mr Luscombe says that he thinks there will be a storm tonight.

'The air is very close and it's hard to breathe, we need a bloody good storm to clear it,' he said.

Donald said that there's full moon due on Wednesday night.

'That'll keep you all howling,' he laughed.

I laughed too but I don't howl. I just lay there and listen to all the others. 'A woman called Isabella Browne is the one who howls the loudest, she's notorious for it,' Mr Luscombe said.

'I know. I've heard her before!' I replied.

11 June 1930

Today a letter came from Aunt Betty, it was quite short but it contained some good news. Well, I hope that it is good news!

Dear Thomas,

I hope this letter finds you well.

Your cousin Clifford tells me that he visited you at the asylum on 21st May last. I hope you are pleased that he has volunteered to be your 'appropriate relative.' He has promised your Mother and me that he will visit you once a month if he can.

He has also persuaded your Mother to come and see you soon and he will drive her over one Sunday when the weather is not quite so hot.

Your mother is very frail these days so please may I respectfully ask that you treat her with calm when you see her.

Yours truly

Aunt Betty

I long to see Mother again and it will be difficult to remain calm. There are so many questions that I need to ask. I hope that if Mother does come and that she'll tell me everything without me needing to ask. I don't want to press her but I need to get out of here. She was wrong to send me here and I haven't forgiven her yet. How can I?

12 June 1930

Last night there was a full moon and a storm all at the same time. It was very noisy on the ward and I could hear lots of howls and screams coming from the female blocks The Dwarf was hiding under his sheets and Anton was pressing his nose up against the window trying to lick the raindrops but the rain was on the outside. There was lots of lightning and thunder, it must have lasted for about an hour but then came back. Royston was very sick and was taken away by the porters. Stanley was throwing books and things at The Dwarf. All the lights came on and I noticed that the new night nurse was crying. I haven't seen a man cry before. Eventually the Medical Superintendent came into the ward and took him away. Later Nurse Starkey came over from one of the female wards and stayed until Nurse Applejack arrived. There was a horrible stench this morning, vile almost. Lionel reckoned that The Dwarf had done a shit in his bed.

On Saturday Albert is bringing his bus and we are going to Bognor Regis. It's at the seaside. Six of us from our ward are allowed to go this time and eight from another. Mr Elliott and Silas are also coming I think.

13 June 1930

Today has been a beautiful day. Not because of the weather but because of Maisie. She came and sat with me under the tree for a little while. No-one else was in sight. It was only for about ten minutes but I think it was the best ten minutes of my life. We didn't say much but we held hands and stared into each other's eyes. The moment was tender. We kissed. I had never kissed a girl before. Her lips were warm and sweet and I felt a tingle in my heart. Then she ran off and then turned and waved and smiled, her long red locks shimmering in the low evening sunlight. I felt suspended in time. I felt overcome by her beauty and for the first time in my life I felt love, true love!

16 June 1930

Yesterday Albert came with his bus and we were all ready to go to Bognor Regis at 8.30. There was Lionel, Anton, Royston and me and two other men from our ward, who I don't really know. There were eight others from another ward including the two ugly twins. Lionel told me that they were brought here as 'Idiot Children' twenty years ago. They have very large protruding foreheads, walk in the same steps and talk at exactly the same time and always say the same thing. They are very odd. I remember them running around the cricket field with us when the American soldier came. When we set off the sky was very grey and Mr Elliott wasn't very happy. There had been very hot and sunny weather for the last two weeks. On the way we stopped for drinks at a little village called Northchapel. We had to wait for an extra half an hour for one of the others to come out of the beer house toilet. Mr Elliott was getting very impatient and angry and kept looking at his pocket watch. When we got to the beach everyone took their socks and boots off, rolled their trouser legs up and then went into the sea for a paddle. The sun had come out and the sky was blue again. I saw Mr Elliott look up and at last he was smiling. Anton stood in the sea and spent the whole time looking at his face in his silver hand mirror. He was wearing real ladies' cosmetics on his face and everyone was staring at him. When we got out of the sea Albert took as all to a tea house, which was in a road called Lennox Street. We all had scones and cakes and a cold drink. We then went for a walk along the promenade until we got to the pier. Mr Elliott and Silas bought us all some chips. When we got back to the bus Anton was missing. Mr Elliott and Silas went off to hunt for him. They found him in a ladies toilet after a very posh lady screamed and ran out shouting 'Freak, Freak!' Silas said that the incident had spoiled the day. I think everyone fell asleep on the way back and it wasn't until I saw the lights on the clock face of the tower that I realised we had got back to the asylum. When we got off the bus Albert asked if we had enjoyed the day. I said 'Yes' and remembered to say 'Thank you.' I had never been to the seaside before!

17 June 1930

There was a strange hush in the ward this morning. Mr Randall came in and told us that Raymond had been found dead in the refractory ward last night. The constabulary had been because Raymond was manic and suicidal but it appears that he has died from his illness. Lionel thinks it was the general paralysis. 'Raymond was very unclean and so could have been bitten to death by fleas,' Lionel said.

Nurse Applejack heard Lionel talking and screamed at him and told him to show respect and pray for Raymond.

Jack was back helping at the farm today. His father is getting better now and is able to work normally at the beer house again. He told me that his father and mother keep arguing lately and that he needed to get away.

'This is the best place to come to get away from them. I hate it when they argue,' he said.

Mr Luscombe and Mr Flynn have gone off to the market at Guildford today to look at some sheep. The Chief Clerk came up to the farm and was a bit concerned that they had gone to buy some more livestock without permission and had been talking to Donald and Mrs Pengelley. One of the other farmhands rushed over to Guildford on his bicycle to warn them. We still don't know if he got there in time!

Tonight there's a party in the Main Hall. The asylum band is playing and the Bisley Ladies Choir will be there. Mr Randall told us that each year there's a big event to celebrate the opening of the asylum.

'It opened on this day in 1867,' he said.

117

It has rained very hard for the last couple of days and there hasn't been much sun. In fact I haven't seen any sun since we were at the seaside on Sunday.

This morning at the farm it was very eventful. We had just finished feeding and swilling the pigs when Mrs Woolston came by on her way home. She had been helping at the Recreation Hall with the female patients' arts and crafts lessons again like she does every Thursday. As she waved at us her bicycle skidded and there was a terrible bang. She lay on the road for quite a few moments before she began to wake up. There was a lot of blood on the ground. Mrs Flynn and Donald rushed to help and I followed behind. Mr Horlock charged out of the North Lodge.

'I think she needs an ambulance now, urgently!' he shouted.

Mrs Horlock came out and then rushed back in to call for help on their telephone. Donald noticed that Mrs Woolston's bicycle had skidded on a cowpat in the exit road. After the ambulance had taken her away Mr Horlock picked up the bicycle and her shopping bag fell from the handle bars and lots of arts and crafts materials spilled out all over the road.

'I think she's been stealing from the stores, she's a thief!' Mr Horlock shouted.

His wife came out again and said that there must be a logical explanation.

'She's a very rich woman and she doesn't need to steal things!'

Mr Horlock shouted back at her. 'I've never trusted her; there's always been someone fishy about that toffee-nosed woman!'

Mrs Horlock seemed to disappear very quickly after he said that. Mr Luscombe had overheard the conversation and said that he would report everything to the Medical Superintendent when he sees him tomorrow.

'Things are not looking very good for Mrs Woolston now are they?' he said.

At tea tonight Lionel told me that everyone thinks that The Tall Man is to blame for Raymond dying so suddenly. He'd heard that he had approached Raymond in the airing court a couple of weeks ago and told him that he was going to die.

'He warned him that he would die a horrible death and that is his demons would come for him in his sleep, that's why poor Raymond was acting the way he was,' Lionel said.

Mr Randall came in and told us that the Medical Superintendent had not been able to contact Raymond's family yet and asked us with a big 'please' NOT to talk about him anymore.

'Let's just respect the dead, he's gone!'

I think Mr Randall was a bit upset!

21 June 1930

Everyone has been talking about Anton today. Lionel thinks that he should be in an isolation room or in one of the mixed wards. I didn't even know there were any mixed wards.

'I don't think they know what to with him, it's probably the first time they've had anyone like him in here.' Lionel said. 'If they're trying to stop him from behaving like a woman then why are they letting his relatives give him cosmetics when they visit him?' he added.

I noticed that The Dwarf had developed a peculiar interest in Anton and that he has been sitting on the end of his bed reading him stories most evenings for about an hour before the lights go out. Stanley thinks that The Dwarf is a bit confused. Lionel reminded us that he does have a name.

'He's called Emile Bashir!' he snapped.

I'm not sure why Lionel mentioned it but he's right, no-one actually calls The Dwarf 'Dwarf' to his to face.

'It's about respect, the same thing that Mr Randall was talking to us about on Thursday,' Lionel said.

I think he's right. Perhaps I should respect The Dwarf even though he does unsettle me.

23 June 1930

There are quite a lot of squirrels about today including some grey ones. I haven't seen Quickie for a long time so I'm wondering if he's still alive or has just moved off to somewhere else. Mr Drake doesn't like the grey squirrels and shoots them when he can. I remember him telling us once that they're taking over from the native brown squirrel or reds as he calls them.

'The greys are much stronger and were brought over from America towards the end of the last century, they're annoying little buggers,' he said.

Anton had another assessment today. I wonder what they're going to do with him!

24 June 1930

This morning Mr Randall came to into the ward just after breakfast whilst I was still getting ready to go and help at the farm. He told me and Lionel that he had been talking to the Head Mortuary Attendant who had told him that Raymond had died from a sudden cardiac episode.

'I think Mr Randall means a heart attack,' Lionel said.

After Mr Randall had left Lionel said that The Tall Man must have caused it by saying those things to Raymond.

'It must have all been too much for him,' he added.

I remember my conversation with The Tall Man. He never said that I would die but he did say that he could see me as an old man. I don't really want to talk to The Tall Man anymore. I must avoid him if I can but it's very difficult if we are in the airing court at the same time and he looks at me.

Anton has told us that he's staying in our ward. He had his assessment yesterday and a special nurse is being brought from another asylum to help look after him. He told us quite openly that he wants to turn himself into a woman and live a woman's life but he's not allowed to go to the female block or to a mixed ward in case his condition upsets the female patients. I think that his condition is upsetting the male patients, it's certainly quite amusing! He told us that the Medical Superintendent thinks that he's suffering from something called a transvestic disorder. He seemed to be quite happy about this and said that he thinks that people are at last beginning to understand him now.

'I am a woman; I'm just stuck in this awful man's body with a penis, I've always felt like this,' he said.

Stanley laughed but Lionel told him to stop. I noticed that The Dwarf was listening to everything that Anton was saying quite attentively. It was all very odd and quite unsettling!

25 June 1930

Last night after dark it was still very warm and I went with Lionel and Stanley and Mr Randall out in the grounds and we sat on a pile of freshly cut logs at the edge of woods. We looked up at the stars and Stanley began telling us their names and what all the constellations are. He told us that he used to have an expensive telescope when he was younger so that he could look at them more closely but his wife sold it at auction the last time he was here. Mr Randall gave Stanley something to smoke. It smelt very different to their normal tobacco. Stanley's pipe fizzed and he started to say strange things. Lionel told me to ignore it and not to get involved. We could see bats flying around in the moonlight. Mr Randall told us that they always come down from the clock tower at this time of the year.

'They swoop down very fast and are always very interesting to watch. Just watch them!' he said.

Afterwards we went back to the ward and Nurse Applejack was still there. The night nurse hadn't come in for her shift and she was very angry. At about 11 o'clock Nurse Primrose came. The lights didn't go off until after midnight so everyone was happy!

29 June 1930

Today, Mother came. Mr Randall came to fetch me from the airing court just after 11 o'clock. We walked over to the reception and Cousin Clifford was stood by his car outside. Miss Rance came out and there was a woman just behind her leaning on a walking cane. It was Mother.

I felt myself freeze and then tremble. I felt happy and angry, I suppose a bit confused. Mother had changed so much. Her hair was cut short and was turning grey and she was stooped, almost hunched and I noticed that she had got very thin. Her knuckles were turning white as she held tight on to her cane. There was nicotine stains all over her fingers. Mother used to take pride in her fingernails but now they were chewed off and all gone. Miss Rance asked Mr Randall to find somewhere quiet outside for us to go and sit so we could talk alone. Cousin Clifford said that he would drive himself to Woking and then come back and collect Mother at 1 o'clock so that I could then go and have my dinner as usual. We went to the corner of the bottom field and sat on a bench. There are a lot of poppies growing down there and there was a slight breeze. I wanted to hug Mother but she seemed like she didn't really want to talk although she did try to smile. We sat there for about five minutes just looking up at the clouds. Maisie walked by with a nurse and someone else from her ward.

She shouted out... 'Hello Tommy, how are you today, is that your mum?'

I waved at her and said... 'Yes, this is my mother!'

Mother also waved and told me that she thought Maisie was a very pretty girl.

'I know!' I said.

I told Mother that Maisie is my special friend. Mother smiled and then we began to talk.

'Thomas, Tommy, I am so sorry.'

I could see that Mother was trembling so I reached out my hand. She pulled it towards her and then pressed it against her chest.

'Thomas, I am so ashamed.'

I wasn't going to ask her why she sent me here, I would have preferred it if Mother could tell me without me asking but I couldn't hold on to my patience. I felt anxious and eager, I just wanted to know. Mother then commented on how I was talking.

'You speak much more clearly now, I can understand everything you say, it looks like they have done wonders for you here,' she said with a slight smile.

I told her about Mrs Evenden and what had happened to her. Mother already knew because Mrs Evenden and Aunt Betty were friends. I told

Mother that I was still waiting for a new speech nurse and that a lady called Mrs Jenkins had been to see me and said that she would try and get me out of here. Mother went silent. Miss Rance came over with a maid and gave Mother a cup of tea. I had a glass of water. We sat there quietly for awhile and then Mother started talking about my childhood and how she needed to entertain the gentleman callers to 'make ends meet'.

'Your Uncle Charlie was the only person who was there for me; if it wasn't for him things could have been a lot worse.'

She told me that his poor health was one of the reasons why she thought that it was best for me to come here.

'You were late growing up, I never thought that you would grow up and it was entirely my fault.'

Mother squeezed my hand very tight and I thought that she was going to give me a kiss but she seemed to flinch at the very last minute. I turned away and then I felt her hand on my shoulder.

'I'm sorry Tommy,' she said again.

I asked her about the man called George O'Leary who had come to see me and if he was my father.

'No, no, no I don't know who your father is, it could be anyone,' she said. 'Why do you think I am so ashamed?'

I held Mother's hand but felt very awkward. We then sat in silence again and then the sun came out from behind some clouds. Mother started talking about the birds and how beautiful they sounded.

'It seems very nice here.'

I then told her about all the things that have been going on. I told her about Dr Carlisle and what he had done to me. I told her about Nurse Applejack and Parson Jaggs.

'There are some very evil people and there are patients like me who should not be here, like Maisie,' I said.

I asked Mother if I could go with her today but I already knew the answer. There's nowhere for me to stay, I asked Mother if that was the only reason I was still here. She told me that Aunt Betty had read her a report from the Medical Superintendent telling her that I was now delusional.

'That's why you're still here,' she murmured.

I raged and felt angry. I told Mother that it was a story made up by Miss Rance and Nurse Applejack. It was about the dream I had.

'I don't really see dead people, it was just a dream.'

Mother looked confused and shrugged her head and then asked me about Mrs Jenkins. I told her that she seemed to understand me and that she had already got me off from going to the chapel every Sunday.

'You must go to church, we must pray for ourselves,' Mother said.

I couldn't believe it, I had never known Mother to pray, never mind go in to a church before. I called Mother a hypocrite. She stood up but looked very weary on her walking cane so I helped her sit back down. She appeared to be quite faint but then said that she was feeling better and tried to smile.

'I was just having one of my little turns,' she said.

I asked her about what had happened to her in London when she was found hurt in a drinking house doorway.

'It was that man Rufus; he didn't want me going off with other men and when he found out where I was going he followed me. He attacked me from behind but another man saw what went on and recognised him and reported him to the constabulary. They did nothing; I think he's still walking free,' she said.

I remember Rufus; he was one of Mother's gentleman callers from a couple of years ago. He's not a very nice person and always shouted at Mother and scowled at Uncle Charlie and me. Mother told me how much she missed Uncle Charlie and then started to cry. We hugged. It was the closest I had ever felt to Mother and then I found myself beginning to sob. Mr Randall came over and told Mother that Cousin Clifford had returned from Woking and was waiting to take her back to Camberley. We hugged again.

'You must hate me Tommy, I'm sorry for what I have done, all of it,' she said quite sincerely.

She waddled off on her cane with Clifford then turned and waved; Clifford put his thumb up and smiled. I don't know why he did that, perhaps he knows something? I saw them drive off and then turn right as they left the grounds through the exit gate. I never thought to ask when I would see Mother again.

I sat on the bench for about an hour. I didn't want to go for dinner. Mr Randall came over and put his hand on my shoulder and asked me if I was alright. He could see that I was shaken.

'Hang on a minute.'

He went off and then came back about ten minutes later.

'Silas is going to cover for me for the rest of the day; I'm taking you to the Nag's Head Inn for a stiff drink.'

When we got to the beer house it was very full and Mr Flynn was there with Donald and another one of the farmhands. Mr Randall brought over a big glass of Scotch whisky.

'Get that down you.'

Mr Flynn laughed. 'You don't want to be drinking that scotch piss,' he said... 'Try this.'

It was Irish whiskey and Mr Flynn let me have a sip. I finished the scotch and then Donald went over to Mrs Juett who was at the counter and bought us some cider. I was beginning to feel better, Mr Randall looked very happy and Mr Flynn brought over a whole bottle of the Irish stuff. Everyone started singing and then an old man began playing a piano. It was a very jolly afternoon. I think we were all a bit tipsy.

It has been a long hard day. I don't know what else to write. Mother, I love you but yes, there are still so many questions to be asked. Why didn't she get me out of here?

30 June 1930

It was very hard helping at the farm today. I couldn't concentrate because I kept thinking back to yesterday and my conversation with Mother. People were talking to me and I was just nodding back. I don't think that I was really listening. Mr Luscombe said something about a test, I remember agreeing to take it but now I don't really know what test he meant or what the test is for. It must be something to do with pigs, I hope so, and I think I know all about them now.

Just after tea, I had a chance to talk to Maisie. She asked me about yesterday and Mother. I told her about how I felt, how emotional it was and how Mother had left everything still the same.

'Nothing has changed at all,' I said.

I told Maisie that Mother thinks I'm delusional now because of the Medical Superintendent's report. Maisie told me that I must not lose my spirit.

'I'm here for you!' she whispered.

Those words meant so much to me. I love Maisie with all my heart!

1 July 1930

It's July. I've been here for nearly a year now. Some days have gone quick and others slow. I think back to the good days. There are a few. Those are all the days I've seen and talked with Maisie.

Mr Luscombe came over to see me this morning and gave me a drawing of a pig. It had lots of shapes drawn on.

'Right, tell me what all these cuts are.'

At first I didn't know what he meant and I felt stupid.

Donald said... 'You know, bacon, pork, gammon and all that, what part of the pig to they all come from?'

Mr Luscombe told me to write down in each shape what the all the joints were. When I gave it back to him, he laughed and then walked away.

'I'll see you later.'

When he came back he remarked... 'Well, there's just one bit you've got wrong, and it's the big piece, it's the loin and you've put 'back', never mind, we'll make a pig farmer out of you yet,' he chuckled.

Just afterwards I saw Mrs Woolston ride by on her bicycle; she waved and was looking well. Last time I saw her she was taken away in an ambulance after falling off. Donald told me that she's alright now but it was funny that she fell off because she skidded on a cowpat. I asked him what had happened about her stealing the materials from the arts and crafts stores. Donald didn't really know but said that he had heard his mother talking to Mrs Horlock about it. 'Mrs Woolston is too important around here. She'll get away with anything,' he said.

I remember hearing once that her husband was something to do with the council. 'Perhaps that's why?' I thought.

3 July 1930

Maisie has been having more problems with Angela Reeves, the pram woman. Someone had taken her pram and she's blamed Maisie. Maisie has scratches on her face where Angela has attacked her. Someone had taken the pram and hidden it in some bushes. Maisie told me that if it hadn't have been for the attendant she could have been hurt much worse. Angela is an evil looking thing; she has a small head with rodent-like features and wears spectacles that are always perched on the end of her nose. She has shoulder length light brown hair that is awry and her mood always looks to be malicious.

'I think that she should be put in Broadmoor to rot,' Maisie bemoaned.

I spoke to Mr Randall about it and then he started talking about Nobby Hatch.

'We're getting him back from Broadmoor, although he'll probably be locked away in the refractory ward where he belongs until he sorts himself out. It was only temporary anyway,' he said.

The night attendant he attacked has made a recovery and has returned to work on light duties although he wears an eye patch.

'He's been reprimanded for inciting Nobby, so not everything was really Nobby's fault,' he added.

This really isn't the news that I wanted to hear.

5 July 1930

Today was another outing day. We went in Albert's bus to see some old ruins. There was an old lady walking around and she was telling us a story about some monks who came from France, an order of Cistercians. I don't even know where it was we went, it wasn't too far away and no-one really said, or if they did, I didn't hear them. I remember Mr Elliott saying how bored he was and that the only good thing about the trip was the sandwiches! The Dwarf and Anton came on the trip; I think they are becoming good friends but Mr Elliott said that he thinks their friendship is unhealthy and that he would report it to the Medical Superintendent. I'm not sure what he means by that but the more I think about it, the more I can guess.

Lionel hasn't been himself today and didn't want to come on the trip. When I asked him why, he didn't really want to say. I struggled to get him to talk.

'It's because today is my wedding anniversary. I've nearly forgotten all the years and it's not my fault, it's not my fault,' he said.

Lionel had already told me about his wife and what she had done to him but I think her father is to blame for much of his weak demeanour. Demeanour is a word I found in my dictionary and describes a person's way of looking and behaviour.

6 July 1930

I've now read the dictionary Maisie gave me all the way through; I've looked at all the words and have tried to remember them all. Last year I didn't even know some of these words but now when I hear people speak them, if I don't understand, I can look them up. Donald says that I use too many long words and that he wants to have a look at my dictionary. I will not part with it. It's so precious because Maisie gave it to me. I don't want Donald to think that I'm being selfish so I might buy him a dictionary with some of my pocket money when I can.

7 July 1930

Mr Mycroft called me over again this morning and showed me a snippet from last week's *London Illustrated News*. There was a short article about Maisie and her paintings that says...

'Maisie Albright of Tilford is a reclusive artist of some repute, whose fine and subtle paintings are fetching sums equivalent to the price of a typical London townhouse. Her uncle who acts as her agent is the revered and shrewd patrician Sylvester Albright, noted for successfully procuring and selling on the artwork of many previously unknown painters in London and across the south.'

I don't think that Maisie will be very happy with this news. Mr Mycroft said that he will definitely mention the newspaper articles to the Medical Superintendent now.

'I hadn't done so yet, but there's something very fishy going on there,' he said quite inquisitively.

10 July 1930

When I saw Maisie this morning I told her about the article Mr Mycroft showed me. She told me that she was called to go and see the Medical Superintendent yesterday. Someone had told him about the article but she didn't know who. I thought it best not to say but now I think she'll guess that is was Mr Mycroft because of what I've said. The Medical Superintendent has taken three of her paintings and is keeping them safe. He asked Maisie not to paint anymore until the whole affair had been sorted out. Maisie told me that one of the attendant's from her ward must be present the next time her uncle visits. Maisie is very worried and feels that she could now be in much trouble with him because of this.

Stanley came to help on the farm today and Mr Flynn showed him how to milk the cows. He had to stop after about an hour, I think he was tired. Mr Randall came to collect him and I could see him fighting back tears as he was led away.

11 July 1930

Patients don't usually have visitors on Fridays but today Cousin Clifford come back and got permission to see me for twenty minutes from Miss Rance. Mr Randall called me back from the farm whilst I was attending to one of the pigs. We sat in the waiting room at the reception and Clifford asked me how things went with Mother on Sunday. I told him that it was very emotional and that I didn't rage at Mother too much. I told him that I was disappointed that she believed what the Medical Superintendent is saying about me being delusional, which just isn't true. I was also disappointed that Mother left without saying that she would make arrangements to get me out of here or when she would come and see me again. Clifford told me that on the Friday before Mrs Jenkins and another woman visited Mother at Aunt Betty's house to discuss my case. Mother was very upset because Mrs Jenkins asked her a lot of questions about why I was sent here last year. She asked Mother about her own circumstances and criticised her because she couldn't read and write and that had almost certainly contributed to matters.

'It wasn't just your speech defect that was the problem; it was your mother's poor education and the fact that she accepted gentleman callers to help put food on the table,' Clifford said.

I told Clifford that Mother asked me questions about Mrs Jenkins but never said that they had met. I did notice that Mother seemed very agitated when we talked about her, especially when I told Mother that Mrs Jenkins was going to do something to get me out. He smiled and said that he too had spoken to Mrs Jenkins that day because he is now registered as my appropriate relative. He asked me if I knew Hope Harrison.

'Yes, that's Missy Hope who works in the scullery with Sarah,' I replied.

He told me that Mrs Jenkins helped her at one time, and when she was allowed to be discharged as recovered, she found Missy accommodation with a family in Knaphill.

'Mrs Jenkins is thinking of doing the same with you, so you can be employed here to work on the farm and live nearby,' he said.

I was amazed by this news and wondered why no-one had been to see me to mention it yet. Clifford told me that it's all now about what's in the report from the Medical Superintendent.

'That's probably the real fly in the ointment and what's causing the biggest problem at the moment, although your speech still needs a little work,' he said a bit sarcastically.

Miss Rance then came over and told Clifford that he had already spent over 20 minutes with me and asked him to leave and come back another time. I'm now left to wonder about everything he's been talking about.

12 July 1930

Mr Randall was telling me today about how he loves going to the beer house. 'Drink is what saves me from my demons and is what keeps me sane and separates me from you lot,' he said.

He kept using the word irony but never really explained why. I thought that perhaps I'd missed something that he'd said. Lionel told me that Mr Randall once confided to him that reality is a delusion created by an alcohol deficiency. I think now that's what Mr Randall meant by irony. The word delusion keeps coming up in conversations lately. Another irony is that Mr Randall is taking us to the beer house this afternoon. I quite like going to the Nag's Head Inn. I get the chance to talk to Jack and I like it when one of the old men starts playing the piano and we all join in a big sing song.

I saw Maisie this morning. She has had word that her uncle is visiting her tomorrow. She looked very worried and told me that she fears what he might say. I tried to comfort her but Nurse Applejack was standing close to us and I didn't want her to hear our conversation.

15 July 1930

It's Tuesday. I haven't seen Maisie since Saturday. Her uncle was coming to see her on Sunday and I've been wondering what he said about her paintings and the newspaper articles and if she's alright. I fear for her and can't get her out of my mind. I think about her about her all the time.

I've also been thinking about what Cousin Clifford said on Friday last. I'm not sure what to do. I've been wondering about asking to go and see Miss Rance but I don't want a negative response. She's one of the people who have been making things very difficult for me. Miss Rance is so two faced she may as well have two heads!

Royston was sent to the infirmary today. He looked very pale and poorly. His skin had a yellow tinge and his eyes were almost gone. He looked like he had already passed to the other side although he was still breathing.

BOOK TWO

21 July 1930

I have had a bad few days. Last Wednesday Nurse Applejack mentioned Mother's visit and asked me how I felt about having a whore for a mother. I remember screaming at her and lashing out. She chased me along the dormitory and out into the seating area of the ward. A porter jumped on me and held me down until an attendant came. I remember seeing Nurse Applejack with a needle and then for awhile everything is blurred. When I woke up I felt very weak. I was strapped to the bed in the side room. My body was very tight and my jaw felt locked. I tried to speak but the words wouldn't come out. I remember Nurse Primrose giving me a bed bath and rubbing in some lotion. Parson Jaggs came into the room one day, placed his hand on my forehead and said a prayer. I thought I was going to die.

Yesterday when I woke up I found myself back in the ward with all the others. Lionel asked me if I was alright. I felt my arms and legs beginning to work again. I think the medicines they had given me were beginning to wear off. Lionel said that he thinks that all my rage happened because I've been thinking too much about things lately.

'It's because you've had a lot going on,' he said.

He told me that I must also stop worrying about other people and start looking hard at myself. Stanley said that just before I woke up I was talking about dead people.

'You were having conversations with them,' he told me.

Lionel said that the night nurse and Nurse Applejack were standing by my bed and heard everything that I was saying. Nurse Applejack was writing things down. Now I worry.

Today Mr Randall had been very kind to me and has tried to make me laugh with some funny jokes. We sat on the logs chewing toffees most of the afternoon. He told me that he understood why everything had happened but advised that now I must try and stay calm and not rage at people anymore. Donald came over and said that they are all hoping to see me back at the farm tomorrow.

'We'll go easy with you,' he said quite sympathetically.

22 July 1930

I've been here exactly one year today. I remember the train from Raynes Park to Brookwood and then a taxi. I remember the silence. I didn't really know what was happening then. I remember Uncle Charlie walking away in tears. He looked very ill that day. I remember the pale green room in the reception. I remember asking 'Why?' It's then that I realised what Mother had done. I remember hating her. I remember calling her names. I remember wanting her dead!

Today I've also been thinking about Maisie. I haven't seen her since before they put me into isolation. I still don't know what happened when her Uncle Sylvester came to visit. I'm very worried about her. I saw Mr Mycroft when I was walking over to the farm this morning. I asked but he said that he hadn't heard anything. I told him that Maisie will probably have guessed who told the Medical Superintendent about what her uncle was doing with her paintings. He told me that I shouldn't worry.

'I would have taken great pleasure in confronting the bastard myself as old as I am.'

He told me that Maisie is a sweet young lass, who is another person who shouldn't be in here. I asked him... 'Why?'

'You need to ask her that yourself, even I'm not sure about that,' he said.

Today at the farm Mrs Pengelley came over and gave me a hug. She's a very nice lady but she always wreaks so much of tobacco and I didn't like being that close to her for too long. It's another problem I had with Mother and why I could never embrace her. People don't understand me when I tell them that I hate the smell of tobacco which is probably why I have no desire to smoke the stuff. Nanny always used to give me glasses of sherry or milk stout when I was little. I suppose that's why I like alcohol and especially cider so much.

23 July 1930

Today has just been a normal day but it was hard helping at the farm. My body still feels weak from the medicines I was given when I was in isolation. Nurse Applejack keeps asking me if I'm alright. I don't know why, she normally just screams and shouts and shows no feelings. I have said sorry for nearly hitting her but she should never have called my mother what she did. What she said was wrong and I'm wondering if she has realised that now. Perhaps somebody has said something to her, there were plenty of other patients who had heard what she had said and had seen what went on.

I still haven't seen Maisie yet. There's a pain in my heart and I feel very anxious. I want to know how she is. I want to hold her hand again. I want to look into her beautiful green eyes. I just need to know that everything is fine with her.

25 July 1930

At last I've seen Maisie and we had a long talk. She's been in the infirmary with very bad stomach pains but she's alright now. She told me that she saw Royston being taken in.

'He didn't look very well at all,' she said.

She then started to tell me about her uncle and what happened when he visited. She began to cry and I let her dry her tears on my shoulder because neither of us had a handkerchief. She said at first that her uncle was very abrupt with her and told her that people should mind their own business and not interfere with his affairs. She said that he showed her some bank documents and that some money was being put in trust for her but she could only see a couple of hundred pounds. He said that more would be added to her funds soon. He has increased funds to her pocket money account here but that is only about a guinea a month.

'It's not a lot considering how much he's been selling my paintings for,' she confided.

Maisie told me that it helped having an attendant with her; she thinks that her uncle could have been quite nasty if they were left alone. He told her that he would make arrangements for her to go back home as soon as he could but her father is her appropriate relative so it's not really his decision. I remember Maisie saying once that her uncle bullies her father so he may get his way. Again, I worry. I asked Maisie if her uncle had something to do with her being here.

'He's everything to do with it; he's ruined my life, my father's life and sent my mother to an early grave,' she whispered.

Maisie said that she will tell me everything one day. I know that it must be hard for her to speak about everything. Just before she left she told me to close my eyes and then she opened the palm of my left hand and then closed it again. She told me not look until after she had gone. When I opened it, it was a tiny lock of her lovely red hair.

26 July 1930

Lionel has been telling me about what happened to Anton while I was in isolation. He was visited on Sunday last by a woman who left some ladies clothes for him. He came back in to the ward wearing a long black wig and a pink frock. Emile, The Dwarf, kept jumping up and down on his bed and got very excited. Just before the lights went out the Medical Superintendent and two porters and a female attendant came. Anton collected all his things and has now been given a room near the reception.

'There's a special nurse looking after him over there now,' Lionel said.

I also missed a trip to Southsea while I was away. Lionel told me that on the way back, Albert's bus broke down at a place called Petersfield and everyone had to get off. Mr Elliott took everyone into a beer house called the Red Lion and there was complete mayhem.

'People in there hadn't seen people like us before and The Dwarf upset the bar-wench when he jumped up on the serving hatch. She screamed very loud and we were all asked to leave. Albert couldn't get the bus working but managed to telephone a friend of his who came over from Aldershot in a big green bus to collect us. We'd all been sitting on a wall by the road and it was nearly 3 o'clock in the morning when we all got back to the asylum. The Medical Superintendent is very angry about what's happened and is going to see Albert to make sure that it doesn't happen again. I don't think there'll be any more outings for a while now,' he said.

Tomorrow is Sunday and in the afternoon we're going for a picnic down at Stafford Lake near Bisley. There's a nice big house down there which is holding a fête.

It's usually a pleasant afternoon when we go down there so long as everyone including the attendants try and behave themselves,' Mr Randall said.

I laugh!

27 July 1930

Today we went to Stafford Lake. It was very grand. There was an army band and lots of dancing and many refreshments. Mr Randall found a lady selling cider and we all had some. Stanley sat by himself most of the time and the lady who was selling the cider later went over to sit and talk with him. It was actually his sister who lives in Bisley, I didn't realise that he came from a family that lived so close to the asylum. Mr Drake came with us and he took us down to a place called Larkin's Yard. There were a lot of cattle and some horses there. The lake has a road going over it so it looks more like two ponds. There was some giant goldfish in the pond. Mr Drake told us that they were from Japan and were called Koi Carp.

They're an exotic species but they have trouble with the herons here so there's wire all around to stop them wading into the water and catching the fish,' he said.

On the way back we got as far as the police house and Mr Randall waved us all goodbye.

'I'm going down to the Nag's Head Inn for a few,' he chortled.

He was staggering around a bit and looked like he'd already had too many ciders at the fête!

When we got back to the grounds some of the female patients had just come back from a walk. They'd been for a picnic along the canal at Pirbright. Maisie was with them and waved and smiled at me and I waved back.

28 July 1930

I'm not sure that I should say this but there are many nights when I lay awake and just think of Maisie. I'm able to shut out the groans and snoring of all the others and I just lay there watching the reflected light from the night nurse's table lamp flickering on the ceiling. Some nights my dinky goes hard and I put my hand on it and stroke it slowly. I don't want to be caught playing with it so I stop. I have an incredible longing for Maisie. I'm sure that if we were not both lost in here we could share our love properly somewhere outside. I'm still not sure if Maisie really loves me, I hope she does. If we weren't here though, we would never have met so that's at least one small blessing about this place. If there's a God I wonder if he would look down on us and give us direction? Somehow I don't think so. I think that we need to be strong by ourselves until we can walk free into a normal life together, hand in hand away from here. I would really love that but my silly dreams have already caused me so many problems!

29 July 1930

Today was my hardest day at work on the farm. Just before dinner the lorry which brings all the hay up from the Sparvell field lost its load and it went all over the road. Some of the bales had broken and the breeze was blowing the hay into the Broadway. Mr Flynn couldn't get in with the cows and had to take them along Queens Road and back around to the farm through the East Gate in Lower Guildford Road. All the farmhands rushed to help with some attendants and patients from another ward. We had a break for dinner and then went back. A policeman came and he arranged for some other officers to come and help clear the Broadway. All the people had come out of their houses and were leaning over their front gates watching the commotion. Harry Horlock appeared and started moaning about all the mess and called us all idiots. He had a big row with Mr Luscombe, it was all quite fun. Mr Luscombe called him a 'lazy good for nothing oaf' and said that he would report him to the Medical Superintendent for being rude and unnecessary. Mr Horlock did nothing to help although Mrs Horlock gave the lorry driver, who was upset, a few cups of tea. We finished clearing up about 5 o'clock. My back aches and I have blisters on my hands now from all the lifting.

30 July 1930

Mr Randall was talking to us about Nobby Hatch again today. It was because Lionel had asked him why he was allowed to come back from Broadmoor if he had really attacked those women when he escaped. Mr Randall told us that he did attack Missy Hope but it wasn't really too serious, he just pushed her over when he went into her house whilst he was hiding from the constabulary. Lionel asked him about the lady in Ripley who Nobby is said to have raped. Mr Randall told us that a lady screamed 'rape' but then later admitted that he hadn't actually touched her.

'The constabulary got it wrong and because of that he's allowed to come back here but has to be locked in the refractory ward at least until it's time for his next assessment.'

I asked him if Nobby would ever come back to our ward.

'I don't know, I can't answer that,' he said quite blankly.

Lionel said that he thinks Nobby's leading a charmed life.

'They should throw away the key,' he said.

I agree.

2 August 1930

Today will forever be one of my most memorable whilst I've been here. This afternoon I went for a walk around the woods. It was very fine and the sun was shining brightly through the trees. I sat down by some bushes where I lifted up an old manhole cover that had been left on the ground. Underneath there was a lizard and lots of eggs. I put the cover back down gently. There were lots of squirrels running about and the birds were singing quite tunefully. Apart from that, it was very peaceful. No noise from the other patients and no shouting from the cricket field. I walked on a bit further and then I heard someone giggling. It was a woman's voice. I stooped down but couldn't see anything. I walked on even further and then I could hear voices more clearly. Suddenly I saw something hanging in a rhododendron bush; it was a pair of ladies bloomers. This time I crouched down and I was able to see. There was a man on top of a lady, the lady stopped giggling and then started making a groaning noise. I could see a man's bottom going up and down, up and down. I felt myself freeze. The lady started screaming louder and shouting... 'Yes, yes,' and then the man started groaning. The leaves on the bush kept getting in my way but I didn't want to move them in case they heard me and caught me watching. I was curious but I think they were trying to make a baby. It all went on for quite a long time, about half an hour I think. Then the groaning stopped and there was silence. Suddenly they both sat up. It was Mr Randall and Mrs Juett, Jack's mother from the beer house. I felt shocked and I froze again. They started kissing and I could see Mrs Juett's bosoms. I've never seen bare bosoms before! Mr Randall seemed to grab the nape of her neck and then they lay down again, Mrs Juett started groaning even louder and I heard her say...

'I love you Algernon, I love you!'

That's Mr Randall's Christian name. By this time I thought that it may be best if I got away but I didn't want them to see me. If Mrs Juett reached for her bloomers she might because they were hanging on the bush I was hiding behind so I decided to crawl away as quickly and as quietly as I could. They were both making lots of noise so I hoped they wouldn't hear me; it was my best chance to get away without being noticed. When I got back to my tree I could still hear them, they were making some very funny noises for at least another hour.

Mr Drake came over and asked me why I hadn't been out for a walk today and I told him that there were no attendants available to take us. He said that Mr Randall had a day's leave and that Mr Elliott was working in a different ward.

'They seem very short of attendants and staff all round just lately,' he said.

When he stopped talking, he walked off in the direction where I had seen Mr Randall and Mrs Juett. I wondered what he would do if he saw them. What Mr Drake said to me might explain why no-one had come looking for me today, I'd been away from my ward for quite a long time, even Nurse Applejack hasn't been about.

When I got back I told Lionel what I'd seen and he said that it would be best if I kept it all to myself.

'You could get into a lot of trouble if you talk about things like that; you know how they twist things around in here,' he said with a funny grin.

Lionel is always a good person to give advice. This is my big secret now, but should I tell Jack?

3 August 1930

Nurse Applejack appeared in the ward this morning and asked me if I would like to join her in going to the chapel. For once, she was quite polite and there was no abruptness in her voice.

I said 'No thank you' and then went off for breakfast.

Breakfast was awkward because I knew that the bacon had come from one of the pigs at the farm.

Today I have been looking out for Maisie; I haven't seen her for a few days. I hope she's alright. Mr Mycroft let me take his puppy Rex for a walk around the grounds and Stanley came. We both talked about the fête at Stafford Lake last week. He says that he's hoping to go back home soon. His sister is making arrangements to look after him and she will give him accommodation, which is what they were talking about when I saw them sat together last week.

'I'll be able to come and visit you then,' he said.

I wish I had a sister who would do that for me. I wonder when I will see Cousin Clifford again.

Silas came into the ward this afternoon and told us that Royston is very, very ill in the infirmary.

'It's not looking good for the poor man, not good at all,' he said.

4 August 1930

Mrs Pengelley has invited me to her wedding to Mr Flynn on Saturday. She's getting married in the chapel and they have got permission from Miss Rance for me to go. Mrs Pengelley said that I can wear one of Donald's best Sunday suits and a pair of his shoes. He's about the same size as me so she thinks that everything will fit quite snugly. Mr Cohen is here on Saturday morning and will cut my hair.

'I'm hoping that you will look quite dapper. Please make sure you have a shave!' she said.

Saturday is also my birthday. I'll be twenty-five years old, that's a quarter of a century!

I keep thinking back to last Saturday and what I saw Mr Randall and Mrs Juett doing together. I wonder if Maisie and I will be able to do that one day. I wonder if Maisie would like us to. I think that's what they call fucking or making love and I think it's now about time I found out for myself what it feels like. It must feel nice because of all the pleasurable noises I heard. Lionel told me that I mustn't tell Jack.

'That would cause a lot of trouble, especially for Mr Randall. Mr Juett is good friends with the shooting men from Bisley, you must not say a word, promise me that you won't say anything to anyone about what you saw,' he pleaded.

Lionel is a good friend. He always stops me from saying or doing silly things.

6 August 1930

Cousin Clifford came to see me this morning.

'It's just a fleeting visit to see how you are,' he said.

I told him what happened with Nurse Applejack on Wednesday 16th July last. Clifford told me that he knew and that he'd received a message from Miss Rance. He had come over on the Friday to visit but I was sedated and asleep when he came so he wasn't allowed to see me. He told me that Miss Rance had mentioned that I had suffered from a maniacal attack. I told him about what Nurse Applejack had said about Mother being a whore.

'Well she was, but she isn't anymore and the nurse was wrong to say that.'

I told Clifford that Nurse Applejack is actually Sister Applejack; I just call her nurse because of habit. Clifford said again that she was definitely wrong to say what she did about Mother.

'It's a poor example to the other nurses; I will mention it to Miss Rance,' he said.

I asked him not to. She will only make things worse for me and I don't want any more trouble. Clifford was adamant though.

'Don't be a fool, let me deal with it,' he said quite sternly.

I fear now that there could be more repercussions if Clifford says something. I'm becoming quite paranoid about everything and I worry.

9 August 1930

Today is my birthday and I had the best present I could have had. I saw Maisie twice. She gave me a small card that she had made. On the cover it was a picture of a young man sitting under a tree.

'That's you!' she said.

Inside she had written: '*I find I'm needing every word you say.*'

I don't know why she's written that, but it's so beautiful and I feel glad.

I told Maisie that I was going to Mrs Pengelley and Mr Flynn's wedding at the chapel today and that I would be wearing one of Donald's best suits. Later, when I came out of Mrs Pengelley's house all dressed up; Maisie was standing across the road with one of the female attendants and a couple of other patients. They all waved and shouted across and remarked on how smart I looked. Donald patted me on the shoulder. I felt very proud.

The wedding in the chapel was a grand affair. It was the first time that anyone had been married in there. I tried to shut my ears when Parson Jaggs started talking about God. I just stared at the windows and thought about Maisie. When we came out the bell was ringing and everyone was throwing grains of rice. Missy Hope was there and she caught a bouquet of pink roses, Donald joked that she would be next.

'Next?' I asked.

'Yes, the next woman to marry, its tradition,' he said. I laughed.

We all went off to the Recreation Hall and there was a big feast with plenty of turkey and cakes and beer. Albert came in his bus and took Mr and Mrs Pengelley to the station. Donald told me that they are on their way to Cornwall for their honeymoon and are staying in a cottage which is owned by one of Mr Mycroft's family. I wish them well; they have both been very good to me and I will have to learn to call Mrs Pengelley Mrs Flynn from now on!

11 August 1930

Last night I had another sleepless night. I laid there awake watching the moonlight through a gap in the curtains until it passed. Then I felt all my demons come at once, it was like they were queuing up in a long line with Mother at the front. The Tall Man was there bending over me for some reason and I could see the ghosts of Reginald, Colonel Peter, Dr Carlisle and Linda Spooner beckoning me. Suddenly Royston came into the picture and now I worry. Royston is very ill and I pray that he hasn't died. Does this mean that I really do see dead people even when I'm awake? I don't think that I should tell anyone what I've seen, they will only say that I'm hallucinating or delusional again but I think that it was my imagination playing tricks with me. I know that it was all just in my thoughts but everything seemed so real, so real.

On the way back from the farm I saw Mr Randall, he's been on a week's leave and was acting a bit strange and wasn't his normal self. I felt a bit embarrassed and I didn't know how to react after what I'd seen the other Saturday. I thought that it was best not to say anything and just said 'Yes' when he asked me if I was alright. I wonder now if he knew that I was watching him and Mrs Juett. I worry.

12 August 1930

Just as I feared, Nurse Applejack told us that Royston died in his sleep last night. She told us that he had been in a lot of pain but went very peacefully at the end. Lionel reckons that the poison Royston took may have been mercury.

'That makes your hair and teeth fall out, they use it in barometers,' he said.

I'm now wondering about the thoughts I had on Sunday night. I think it's just co-incidence but I remember back to when Uncle Charlie passed away and the dream I had then. I hope I'm not becoming a soothsayer like The Tall Man!

It was difficult helping at the farm today with everything going on in my head. Donald kept asking me if I was alright, I was tempted to tell him everything that was going on but in the end, I felt is best just to smile and carry on with my work. It was very busy with Mr Flynn being away on his honeymoon and I had to help milk the cows when they came up from the field. Mrs Horlock came over to help for awhile; I'd never seen her working at the farm before.

Now I think about Royston, more death in this forsaken place and another poor soul that has sadly passed.

13 August 1930

Miss Rance called me to the Clerk and Attendant's office today.

'Sit down Thomas.'

She asked me how I felt about myself. I wasn't sure why she was asking, no-one else was with her so it all seemed quite odd. She then told me that she had a long conversation with Cousin Clifford on the day he came to visit but wasn't allowed to see me. She told me that I must now do what I can to help myself.

'Don't lash out at Sister Applejack anymore, don't pretend to talk to dead people anymore, and don't keep disappearing up into the woods all the time,' she said.

I told her that the time I spend in the woods is very valuable to me.

'It helps me cope with being here.'

I asked her about the conversation she had with Clifford and she told me that he's going to have a meeting with Mrs Jenkins before she comes to see me in September.

'We may be able to decide your fate then,' she chuckled.

I asked her what she meant and she told me that if things go well I could be away from here by Christmas. Now I hope and wonder. I remember what Clifford had told me about staying here to work on the farm but living somewhere outside. Missy Hope does that and I think that she is very happy. I will have to go to the scullery and ask her about it all, maybe I should go and see her tomorrow and ask.

Donald spent all morning trying to get the tractor to work. It wouldn't wind up; no-one else could get it going either. Mr Flynn has a knack and always gets it going straight away when he's there so I think they're missing him.

'Never mind, he's back on Saturday, it can wait until then,' Donald said.

I asked if I could have a go, they all stood back and laughed. The handle was very stiff, I felt it jerk and then it turned very suddenly and the tractor sparked into life. I had got it working and I felt very strong and proud. Mrs Horlock was there and she said... 'Oh look, we have a proper King Arthur in our midst.'

I wasn't sure what she meant. Later Donald told me about the sword in the stone and all about the Knights of the Round Table. I laughed.

14 August 1930

Today I've been very depressed and melancholy. All the good things seem to have got lost in my heart and all the bad things are taking over again. The demons are coming back and I keep hearing voices in my head. It's only the thought of Maisie that keeps me strong, but even she can't help me, circumstance won't allow it. I'm going to sit by the lake and ponder. I need to clear all this negativity out of my mind. I know that it's only me who can really do that, only me who can help me. I think Miss Rance is right, I need to look at myself very differently now, I need to be me, I cannot pretend anymore, but how can I not pretend when everything is so real?

15 August 1930

Royston's funeral is on Monday. He's being buried down at Brookwood. Lionel asked Mr Randall if we could go but he said 'No!'

Mr Randall told us that he should never have taken us down to the cemetery last year to visit Colonel Peter's grave.

'I nearly got severely reprimanded for doing that,' he said.

On the way to the farm I saw Mr Mycroft and I told him about what had happened to Royston. He already knew something about it as he had been talking to one of the mortuary attendants.

'His body was in a terrible state when they took him in,' he said.

Mr Mycroft seemed to know that it was mercury poisoning that killed Royston. He also told me that all funerals for patients are carried out at first light at the cemetery so as not to draw attention.

'There will only be Parson Jaggs and someone from the Chief Clerk and Attendant's office down there and of course the undertakers and a grave digger,' he said.

When I spoke to Mr Randall this afternoon I was glad that he didn't say anything about the other Saturday when I saw him and Mrs Juett in the woods. Perhaps he didn't see me after all. I hope he didn't! Maybe I'm just being paranoid. Paranoia is not something that I want to add to all my other problems.

16 August 1930

Nurse Primrose was on duty doing the night shift last night. I couldn't sleep again so she got me a drink and we went and sat in the seating area outside the dormitory for a while. Everything was very quiet for a change so our conversation had to be in whispers. She asked me what I thought was keeping me awake so I told her nearly everything. Nurse Primrose is a very kind lady who is the very opposite to Nurse Applejack. I don't think that she likes Nurse Applejack very much and I sensed that she didn't really what to talk about her. I told Nurse Primrose that I found it hard coping with all the death that was about. Too many friends have died. Nurse Primrose said that she thinks that about four people a month die in the asylum.

'Sometimes it can be a lot more. Particularly if there's some sort of epidemic about, such as tuberculosis,' she said.

I told her about Maisie and how much she has helped me and stopped me from going really mad. Nurse Primrose laughed and said that she remembers Maisie well from when she has worked in the female ward. I asked Primrose why Maisie was here and she said... 'Oh Tommy, Tommy, I can't tell you that, you will have to ask the poor sweet girl yourself!'

I thought about it a bit more and then realised that I was wrong to ask. But why is Maisie here? Primrose thinks that it must be very difficult loving someone in such circumstances.

'I understand everything,' she said.

She then told me about the time when she was doing her primary nurse training and how she fell in love with a white man who was doing his doctor's examinations at the same place in London.

'He was very handsome and had lived in Africa before so he was used to having black people around him. His mother didn't like me and her family had been a keeper of slaves in the old days and her son was the only man left in the family after the Great War. She was very protective of him and was fearful that one day we might have a half-caste child. She always said to her son that she didn't want black blood in her family so that was the end of that. I loved him so dearly though.' She said with a hint of a tear.

I felt very sorry for Primrose and I thought about the story of Romeo and Juliet. It must have been a bit like that. It was nearly 4 o'clock when I got back into the dormitory, just in time to see Emile, The Dwarf be sick.

This afternoon Mr Randall and Mr Drake took me and Lionel to the village. We got some buns from Emlenton's and then sat outside the Crown beer house. Mr Randall said that he fancied a change of scenery and thought that a walk into the village would make a nice change. They're starting to build a new Wesleyan church near the corner of the Broadway. Mr Drake told us that they had to pull the old one down, before it fell down. In a funny way, it was a very enjoyable afternoon. I think I needed that!

17 August 1930

Today we had a surprise trip in Albert's bus to Stonehenge. It's an ancient monument with lots of big stones near a place called Salisbury. Mrs Woolston came with us and told us about its history and about the druids who worshipped the sun. We had a picnic by a river and I could see hundreds of big fish. Mr Elliott told us that they were trout.

'You won't find them in the canal, they only like rivers.'

I noticed that some of the trout were white in colour and had pink eyes. 'They're albinos!' he said.

When we got back to the ward someone called Edward was being moved into the space where Royston was. I recognised him as the man who was having speech lessons with poor Linda Spooner and me until Mrs Evenden died. I tried to talk to him but his speech must have got worse, he couldn't say anything or answer any of my questions. He kept just gripping his fists; it was in frustration I think.

18 August 1930

When I finished at the farm this afternoon I was walking back and I saw Maisie talking to Mr Mycroft. She was holding his puppy in her arms and making a great fuss of him. When she saw me, Maisie gave the puppy back and rushed over to me and gave me a hug. Mr Mycroft had been talking to her about her uncle and her paintings. I asked if there had been another report in the newspapers. Maisie said 'No!' Mr Mycroft told me that the Medical Superintendent and the Chief Clerk had been talking to a detective from the constabulary. He wasn't allowed to interview her because she's a patient but the Chief Clerk had been talking to him on Maisie's behalf.

'I think Uncle Sylvester is in big trouble now,' she said.

She also told me that she doesn't want to stay in Tilford at Christmas this year and has refused to see him if he visits here again.

'I loathe that man, I loathe him terribly and he bullies my father,' she said quite angrily.

Just then one of the female attendants came over and asked Maisie to walk with her back to the ward. Mr Mycroft scratched his head and then told me that he thinks it's actually her uncle who is keeping her here.

'I think he's been lying about her condition and is stopping her father from getting her out,' he said.

Later I wondered about Maisie. Every time we speak, her uncle is the main topic of conversation. I agree with Mr Mycroft, perhaps her uncle is the real reason why she's here. It must be more than just something to do with him selling her paintings. Something much more sinister I think.

19 August 1930

I went to the scullery today and had an interesting conversation with Missy Hope. Sarah was there and she gave me some left over rabbit stew from the attendants' dinner. It was very nice; there was lots of garlic and parsley and other stuff in it.

'It's Missy Hope's own recipe,' Sarah said.

I remember Missy giving me some rabbit stew before, she looked very proud. When Sarah went back to the kitchen, I asked Missy about what happened when she stopped being a patient and came back to work in the scullery. She said that it was Mrs Pengelley who really helped. She told me that she didn't think that there was much was wrong with her and told Fiona who used to work in the Chief Clerk and Attendant's office. I asked Missy why she was put in here and she said that her father thought that she was an imbecile.

'My sisters were very good at receiving their education; they're very bright and I didn't like it. I just wanted an ordinary life with a husband and children. My father objected and he hit out at my mother when she tried to intervene. The next thing I knew, I was here.'

I asked her about Mrs Jenkins and she told me that she didn't do very much. It was Mrs Pengelley and Fiona who did everything.

'They spoke to my father when he visited one day and he admitted that sending me here was a bit harsh. He had a big reputation and had already told everyone that all his daughters were going to have long careers in medicine. I didn't want that and I think that he was frightened that he was going to lose face. I saw Mrs Jenkins just once, she made a lot of promises but that was all. Yes, she's a nice lady but I think she is the sort of person who takes credit for other people's actions, so, perhaps, she's not that nice after all,' she said.

149

I found out that the family who Missy Hope stays with are good friends of Mr Flynn. After all this, I'm not sure about anything anymore. I must speak about this again with Cousin Clifford the next time he comes. I think I need some kind of reassurance that things will happen for me in the same way they as they did for Missy. I worry.

20 August 1930

I was able to talk to Maisie again today. I was on my way to the farm and she was walking by with one of the Percherons. She told me that there has been a lot of trouble in her ward and that she doesn't know what to do. Angela Reeves and one of the female night attendants have struck up a very odd relationship and have been meddling and interfering with other patients, even torturing them. Maisie is fearful that she could be the next. She told me that ever since Angela had her pram taken away she has changed. The attendant took pity on her and now they are sort of friends. During last night at about 2 o'clock, they forced another patient called Katherine into the side room and tried to pull her fingernails out. They had put something into her mouth to stop her screaming and then also took it in turns to hold her down while the other one interfered with her private parts.

'Her genitals, I think,' Maisie whispered.

I asked Maisie how she knew all this and she told me that she could hear it all going on, Katherine confided everything else to her when they walked to the dining room for breakfast this morning.

'It's all quite disturbing, the night nurse was asleep, she's always asleep, so wouldn't have heard anything.'

Maisie wants to report the incident but she doesn't know how, she thinks that she's caused enough problems for the Medical Superintendent and the Chief Clerk already lately because of what her uncle has been doing with her paintings.

22 August 1930

It's been very wet and windy over the last couple of days and some trees have been blown down in the woods. It's very muddy and now and it feels like the summer is nearly over. The woodmen have been here burning logs, it's a nice smell but the fires are spitting a lot because the wood is still wet from all the rain. I always remember Uncle Charlie telling me once never to try and burn wet wood... 'You will only get smoke.' He was right. I can't see any flames, just a big plume of smoke drifting over the canal.

After dinner I played conkers with Stanley and Lionel. Mr Drake joined in. He smashed ours to bits. I think he cheated. Lionel told me that Mr Drake had pickled his conkers to make them harder.

'How do you think he kept winning?' he laughed.

Colonel Peter died a year ago today. This evening I think of him.

23 August 1930

This morning some of us went for a walk along the canal as far as Pirbright with Mr Elliott and Mr Drake. There's been a problem with the lock gates and a lot of the water has drained away. I saw a barge stuck in the mud and it was nearly over on its side. There were ropes holding it to a tree so it didn't list any further. There were lots of men in the mud trying to save the fish. Many fish were already dead. There were also hundreds of clams in the mud; I'd never seen a clam before. Mr Drake told me that it will take weeks to get the water level back up, if they ever do.

'It's just as well we don't use the canal for our own water supply anymore,' he said.

Later I told Mr Mycroft what I'd seen. He told me that the canal had always been the main source for water at the asylum but it was contaminated and that's what caused the typhoid that was here twenty or so years ago.

'Our reservoirs keep running try and that's why we have a water tower, but even that's not always sufficient,' he said.

After tea I saw Maisie. She's still worried about what's going on in her ward and is finding it very difficult to sleep. She's thinking of telling the day nurse about what's happening each night but is frightened that she won't be believed. Maisie has also thought about mentioning it to Miss Rance but doubts that she will help. She already thinks that Maisie's a troublemaker who makes things up just to get attention.

24 August 1930

Sunday is now a day when I sit down and think about religion. Am I right about God? Am I right about Jesus? I know I believe in spirits but I cannot believe that there is a higher being. I don't think there can be anyone up in the sky looking over us. I think that we all just control ourselves, it's just that other people take over and control us when they shouldn't sometimes. I think that's what might have happened to Maisie and me. Someone has stolen our souls and put us here when there's nothing wrong with us and we should be free. We should be out in the world living a life far away from here and walking hand in hand towards a brighter destiny.

Uncle Charlie told me once that life itself is all about destiny. We are born and then we die.

'It's just a matter of when,' I remember him telling me.

25 August 1930

On the farm two of the pigs have suddenly died. They always seem to die two at a time. Mr Hampton has been over and inspected all the others but is coming back again tomorrow; he's not sure what's wrong. Mr Flynn is back from Cornwall and is very worried; he's been talking about it all to Mr Luscombe. Donald told me that he thinks that there's some sort of disease about again.

'It's a problem that we normally have when we get new stock from the market but these are our own and were born here, so it's all very unusual,' he said.

Mrs Pengelley, or Mrs Flynn as she's called now has gone back to work with the Bursar. Mr Flynn took us all back to Rose Cottage and we drank Irish whiskey until it was time for me to go back to the ward. I'm now worried what I might find when I go back to the farm in the morning. Everyone is very sad and upset.

26 August 1930

Mr Hampton was at the farm this morning and has found out what it was that killed the pigs. Someone had put some rat poison down too close to the pen and somehow it got mixed in with the feed. One of the new farmhands is getting the blame and he has already said 'sorry'. Donald reckons that Mr Luscombe is going to dismiss him from service this afternoon.

'Luckily all the other pigs are fine and in good health,' he said.

There's a plague of rats coming up from the sewer and Lionel has been helping out by catching them. He told me that he uses a big log, a stick, a length of string and bits of rotting food to catch them.

'That usually does the trick, there's a knack to it and they pay me a penny for each one I take to Mr Drake, he then clobbers them over the head again to make sure they're dead,' he said.

27 August 1930

It's all a bit strange but I was trying to help Edward with his talking this morning. Lionel and Stanley were trying to help too. I reminded him about what Mrs Evenden taught us... '*How now brown cow.*' Now he's been saying it to himself all day. Edward sounds very posh when he manages to speak and I get the impression that his family have made him an outcast because of his impediment.

The woodmen have been about cutting trees and burning the logs again today. This time they've waited until the wood is dry and there's a lot of flames shooting up into the sky. One of the men has been walking around painting big red crosses on more of the trees. He told me that they're trying to make a clearing so that some of the younger trees can grow. A man from the nursery has been and taken away some rhododendron bushes, the ones that flower red or yellow, it's only the ones with purple flowers that are left now.

Mr Luscombe has let the farmhand off with a reprimand over the dead pigs. His name is Stephen and he's very relieved. He's gone off to the Crown beer house with Donald to celebrate his good fortune. Mr Luscombe is a very kind man and I think that he knew that it was all just a big mistake.

28 August 1930

I saw Maisie this morning, she looked very down and agitated and was being led to the Medical Superintendent's office by a nurse and two attendants. She looked like she was being restrained and her hands were tied behind her back. She looked over but her face was expressionless, we did not have a chance to talk. I need to find out what's going on. I need to make sure that she's alright.

All day I've been thinking about her, it was hard to concentrate at the farm and I didn't want to trouble anyone else with what is going on in my head, although I think that Donald guessed that something really big was playing on my mind.

There's a beautiful, magnificent sunset tonight. The sun is red and whole and there's an incredible orange glow all over the bottom field. I wish Maisie would come running to me so that I could hold her in my arms; I wish that she was here so that we could share this moment and watch the sun go down together.

30 August 1930

At last I had a chance to talk to Maisie. She's very frightened. She told me that she was attacked by Angela but was restrained by the nurse and two attendants when she tried to hit back.

'She was poking fun at me and being rude about my hair and then scratched my face with her long fingernails,' she said.

Maisie told me that when she explained what had happened to the Medical Superintendent he called her an attention seeker and told her to stop making up stories. It reminded me of the time Bertie had a fight with Nobby Hatch. He was the one bullying Bertie and he got away with it because everyone believed Nobby instead!

Maisie said that she wants to be moved to another ward. I told her that I thought it would be wrong to move, there's always a chance that it might cause even more problems for her and that she would have to get to know everyone all over again. The women in some of the other wards are even more fearsome than Angela Reeves so I don't think that Maisie should move. I think that she just needs Angela to be taken out and then everything will go back to normal.

31 August 1930

Yesterday Mr Randall took me and Stanley to the Nag's Head Inn. After seeing Mr Randall with Mrs Juett I felt very awkward. It's been very hard not to say anything, especially to Jack but I thank Lionel for his advice, it probably stopped me from causing a lot of trouble. Jack was outside helping his father paint the porch but I noticed that when Mr Randall said 'Hello' to him, he just looked the other way as if he wasn't there. Mr Randall wasn't himself and kept looking over at Mrs Juett. She had a big smile on her face and kept waving at us. One of the old men then started playing the piano and everyone started singing the war songs. The third song was *'Pack up your troubles in your old kit bag...'* I knew all the words and sang along too. Mrs Juett clapped.

'Well done Tommy,' she shouted.

I didn't know that she knew my name but I felt very proud.

When we got back for tea, Parson Jaggs was there. I've never seen him on a Saturday before and he was dressed in normal clothes. He came and sat beside me in the dining room and said 'Oi Look! I'm human too you know!'

I smiled and laughed because I didn't expect him to say that. Lionel told me that he does that every now and again; he thinks it's a good way of getting all the non-believers to go back to the chapel.

1 September 1930

Today I went down to the Sparvell field to help bring up the cattle for milking. In one corner of the field there was a big hole with smoke coming out. I went over to see what it was and it was the two dead pigs. It wasn't very nice and the sight of their half-burned carcasses upset me. Donald said that I shouldn't have looked.

'There's been heavy dew over night and it's put the fire out. The other farmhands couldn't have noticed what's happened yet,' he said.

On the way back up we had trouble getting the cows through the Broadway. A new house is being built and a builder's lorry was blocking the road. The builders didn't want to move and there was a big row. Mr Luscombe and Mr Horlock came down and there was nearly a fight. Donald told me later that when they took the herd back they had to go the long way round down Limecroft Road and one of the cows ran off. They got it back after it ran down towards Bisley and went into someone's garden.

2 September 1930

I saw a woodman walking away from my tree with some branches under his arm. There wasn't a red cross on the trunk so I wasn't expecting it to be cut. I asked him if he was going to chop the whole tree down, luckily he said 'No!' But then I panicked and worried about my tin and what if he had found all my stuff. Fortunately, I'd hidden it well enough for him not to find it. He's chopped all the low branches off so probably didn't reach up high enough, but now the tree is harder to climb. The woodmen have cut more trees down than I thought. There's a big clearing now and it's easier to be seen from the Clerk and Attendant's house. I might have to move all my things and find another tree, again.

Earlier, I watched Lionel catch a rat. He killed it stone dead with one jerk of the string, the log went down on its head and flattened it. The rat's blood was everywhere and Lionel spilled some all down his trousers when he picked it up. He put the rat in a hessian bag but the blood just seeped out all over him. He's caught four rats so far this week and said that he will pay for the cider if Mr Randall takes us out on Saturday.

3 September 1930

This morning I asked Lionel why he has never been to the chapel. He told me that it's because his father was a Jew. I asked him what he meant; he said that his father worked for the gentry somewhere in East London making suits and drapes

'Yes, my father was Jewish but I'm not a proper Jew,' he said.

I was confused but then he told me that his mother was an English rose and that she was born into the Church of England.

'Everyone was very upset with my father when he married her but she was a very pretty woman and they were so much in love, no-one was ever going to stop them from tying the knot,' he added.

For some reason we then started comparing the size of our noses.

'I have my mother's nose if I had my father's nose then my nose would be twice the size of yours,' he said with one of his big grins.

I laughed. Lionel can be very funny when he's in such a frame of mind.

5 September 1930

The thought of Maisie kept me awake again last night or at least half awake. I think that I just kept drifting in and out of sleep, half thinking and half dreaming. I saw her walking into the sunset and then coming back with the dawn as the sun came up again. She was running across a field, spinning and dancing and blowing kisses towards the spot where I was standing. There was nothing else, there was no background, just Maisie twirling and twirling and then falling on the ground, and the sun, it seemed to follow her until suddenly there was darkness. Everything went cold; I could even feel the chill. Some long dark shadows appeared on the ground and then I could hear the sound of crows, I looked up into the sky and I could see them circling and then The Tall Man came. His voice was booming but I couldn't understand what he was shouting about. Everything went still again and then turned white. I could see Maisie waving at me from the distance but she was fading. A long row of nurses walked across the field and then a row of nuns. I could see Parson Jaggs, he was standing on something and reading a verse from his bible, and then there were cheers. Everything seemed to go blurred and then I opened my eyes. Everyone was getting ready for breakfast. I felt relief.

Parts of the dream, if it was a dream were very comforting but then it all seemed to turn inside out. I worry now and I wonder what I've been thinking of in my sleep. I wonder what's been stirring inside my head to bring such thoughts. I hope that I'm not really going mad.

6 September 1930

Saturdays are always a bit different but today has been another day of thinking for me. I'm looking at all the good things and I want to be positive but sometimes the darkness comes back and I worry. I know that I should say something to someone but I think that if I do it will just make everything worse. I may tell Nurse Primrose the next time that I see her and when it's safe to talk. She's good at listening but I don't know whether I can trust her, trust is very hard to find. I trust Maisie but sometimes I don't even trust myself! I need to share this burden, I need to talk to someone and I need someone to tell me that I have not gone mad!

It's a church day tomorrow and I've been thinking about going back to the chapel to pray. I'm now wondering whether I was wrong to judge my faith and question God because of what happened to Reginald. Was I wrong to walk away and not believe? I need answers and I hope that God, if he's there, might help me. At least this time it will be my choice if I do go back and maybe that will help. Perhaps I need to look at doing it but I'm still not really sure.

7 September 1930

This morning I got up and went to the ablutions. There's a big mirror there and I had a long look and thought that I could see something behind my reflection staring back at me. I had a shave and used some posh soap that was Royston's. Then I went down and had breakfast. It was boiled eggs, bread and wheat cereal. Some of the others then went to the chapel with Nurse Applejack. I stayed behind for about ten minutes and then followed. When I got there the door was still open but I chose not to go inside. I could hear Parson Jaggs shouting his sermon like he normally does. Then everything went silent. Then the organ started and everyone joined in a hymn. I had never heard it before but it was very uplifting. I felt like I had fallen from grace so I stood up from the mound of grass that I'd been sitting on and walked around the outside of the chapel until the music stopped. I looked up at the sky and thought that if there is a God, he's out here with me looking down from the clouds. As I was thinking that, the sun came out and shone for just a brief moment. It felt like someone actually was trying to say 'Hello.'

Afterwards I walked down through the woods to the fence and got onto the canal towpath. All the water in the canal is nearly gone and the barge I saw the other day was still stuck in the mud. It was only some ropes that had stopped it from going right over on its side. Mr Drake came along and told me that there had been a problem with a lock gate down at St John's which was why the water was low, and then he told me to get back in the grounds.

'I haven't seen you,' he said.

I've realised that I keep questioning everything lately. Today I've been thinking about love and what it really is. There must be different kinds of love. I know that I love Maisie and I think that she loves me. There's always an ache which I feel in my heart when I don't see her or when I think that something's wrong. It's a different kind of ache which sort of hurts but doesn't, it doesn't feel like pain. Sometimes my head starts playing tricks and then I wonder if what I'm feeling in my heart really is love. I think that I need to talk to Maisie about love. I need to know if she feels the same, I need her to tell me what she thinks love is. I need her to tell me if she loves me!

No-one has really been interested in me today and apart from Mr Drake, there's been no-one about. If I had walked out of the asylum today I don't think that anyone would have noticed.

8 September 1930

Emile, The Dwarf has been acting very strange again lately. This morning when I woke up he was sat on my bed reading poems.

Nurse Primrose pulled him off then he started jabbering something in Urdu or whatever the blessed language is called, he also speaks. He then ran down the dormitory and hid under his bed.

Lionel isn't very well. He woke up with a fever and his face looks all yellow. The doctor has given him some extra medicines and he might have to go to the infirmary if he doesn't improve.

On the way to the farm Mr Mycroft called me over. He said that there had been some trouble in the female ward last night where Maisie is. He told me not to worry, Maisie wasn't involved but one of the other patients was attacked, he thinks it was caused by Angela again but wasn't sure.

'There's been a lot of bother, one of the women had been howling all night and the Medical Superintendent has been over there since the crack of dawn, he won't be very happy about being called out so early.'

I asked Mr Mycroft how he knew that it wasn't Maisie and he told me that he'd already seen her this morning, she was with one of the horses and was taking it down to the bottom field.

'She's fine, don't worry yourself young man,' he said.

9 September 1930

Today I received a letter from Aunt Betty. I wasn't expecting a letter but for once I have received some good news - well sort of.

Dear Thomas,

I hope this letter finds you well. Your mother sends you her love and good wishes.

I hear that you are talking much better now.

I am pleased to be able to tell you that your cousin Clifford and Gloria are now the joyous parents of a little baby girl, she was born on 2nd September last in Frimley. They have named her Amanda Louise and she is in fine health.

This may mean that Clifford will not to be able to visit you as much now that he has fatherly duties to undertake.

Yours truly

Aunt Betty

Clifford is my appropriate relative and if he can't come and visit as much then it could be a long time before I see Mother again as well. I thought that he was going to help get me out of here but now I'm not sure.

Lionel is much better today but is very drowsy. He thinks that he may have caught the fever because of the rats. The doctor has told him to stop catching them for awhile. Stanley thinks that the rats might cause a plague!

11 September 1930

I was able to speak to Maisie today. I asked her what had happened in her ward on Sunday night. She said that there was a fight between the night attendant and Isabella. Angela had caused it, she had been sat there just staring and pulling faces at Isabella all evening. Isabella seemed to snap and went for Angela but the attendant came from nowhere and pushed Isabella on to the floor. She dragged her all along the dormitory floor by her hair and then started kicking her.

'Isabella has lots of bruises.'

She told me that the night nurse didn't do anything but then decided to call for the Medical Superintendent at about 5 o'clock. When he came, Angela told him that it was her who attacked Isabella, not the attendant and then started crying.

'The night attendant got away with it all; everyone was too frightened to say anything.'

I wanted to ask Maisie what she thought about the word 'love' but I didn't think that it was a good time to ask. I told her that Cousin Clifford had just had a new baby. Maisie laughed.

'I think that you'll find that it's his wife who's had the baby,' she said.

It made me feel silly, so I just laughed as well.

12 September 1930

I have seen a magpie today. Uncle Charlie used to warn me about them, especially if I ever saw one on its own. He always told me to salute and ask... 'How's your wife today?' It would stop bad luck. He called it 'superstition'. I always thought that it was funny saluting a bird to stop bad luck but Uncle Charlie was adamant about it. I remember him telling me that a single magpie is an omen of bad fortune and it will always send you to a bad place.

'You must always salute it to let it know that you're showing it true respect,' he said.

I don't know if he was right but I saluted the magpie anyway and then it flew off. Now I wonder about superstition and bad luck. I'm already in a bad place but I don't ever remember seeing a magpie in Raynes Park, so why was I sent here? Uncle Charlie once told me that he always looked for two magpies. 'It's a sign of joy!' he used to say.

I remember that I used to hate treading on the cracks in the pavement between the slabs. Mother used to shout... 'The bears will get you, they will eat you alive!'

It's sort of funny how I always think of Mother mostly with affection now.

13 September 1930

Mr Randall took me and Stanley to the Nag's Head Inn. Lionel didn't come because he is still too poorly. We sat in the corner by the piano, there was no-one playing it today. We didn't see Mrs Juett, I think she was upstairs. Mr Randall went outside and we saw him arguing with two men. I thought they were going to hit him but then he came and got us.

'Come on you chappies, we're out of here!' he said.

We didn't even have time to finish our cider. He walked us down to another beer house in Bisley.

'Come on, I'll buy you a few but don't let me get drunk,' he said.

Mr Randall is nearly always drunk on Saturdays. I think something must have happened between him and Mrs Juett which was why he was arguing with the two men; he seemed very agitated and wanted to get away very quickly. Perhaps they know that he's been seeing her behind Mr Juett's back?

Tonight there's an End of Summer Ball in the Main Hall. An orchestra is coming down on the train from London. Mr Randall reckons that it should be another grand affair.

14 September 1930

Today was another church day. I thought about going to the chapel again but I decided against it. I went for a walk around the woods instead and thought about God. I thought that if there is a God he would be here with me. I felt strange and hollow, empty. It felt more like Maisie was with me, probably because I would have liked that. I kept looking up at the sky but there was no break in the clouds this time, no sunshine, no sign that someone was looking down. I kept thinking about all the dead people, all the sick people, all the odd people. I found myself praying for them. I felt myself praying for me. Perhaps I think of religion differently to everyone else. Perhaps I have my own religion, my own God, most probably though I have nothing at all except these thoughts!

17 September 1930

It's been very windy and it's rained for the last few days and everywhere is flooded. The pig pens are very muddy and all their swill has been washed into the road. Mr Horlock has been out with his pumps and hoses trying to stop it all from running into the gutters outside the North Lodge gate. It's a terrible mess. The cows haven't been up for milking since Monday and things are getting a bit desperate now. Some trees are down in the Broadway so they're going to have to bring the herd in another way. Mr Flynn is very anxious, he doesn't like bringing them up by a different route.

'The cows get very confused and it causes more problems than it's worth,' he told us.

Donald broke his arm doing something with the tractor yesterday and hasn't been with us. Mr Flynn said that he will be helpless for at

163

least three weeks. Mr Luscombe is looking for a new farmhand to fill in and asked me if I knew any patients that might be suitable. I didn't know. I'm the only one in my ward who works although Lionel catches the rats but he's not strong enough to lift things or work with big animals.

'Don't worry, I'll ask the Medical Superintendent if he can nominate someone,' he said.

Miss Rance has told me that Mrs Jenkins might be coming to see me tomorrow.

18 September 1930

Today has not been easy. Mrs Jenkins came. Nurse Applejack was sat down beside her in the Medical Superintendent's office.

'Now then, Thomas, I have your case notes here and they make every uncomfortable reading since the last time I came to see you,' she said.

'When I was last here there were signs of improvement, yes, it states here that you were delusional and that you were talking to dead people, I was happy with your explanation at the time for all that but what of this, what of this? She asked.

I had no idea at what she was referring to and looked at Nurse Applejack but she then looked away towards the window.

'The Medical Superintendent has recorded some very stern recommendations about your welfare here and I'm not sure that I can help, some of this is beyond my field of medicine,' she said.

Mrs Jenkins then stayed silent for about a minute as if she was waiting for me to talk. I looked over at Nurse Applejack. She turned to Mrs Jenkins and pointed to something on the desk. There were more papers and I could see my name written in the top left hand corner. Mrs Jenkins then began reading but remained silent. The silence was quite disturbing and I began to worry. It felt like my heart was racing. I didn't know what has happening. Suddenly, Mrs Jenkins looked up.

'Thomas, Thomas, what have you being doing, you silly man?' she asked.

I felt tense and aghast but couldn't answer.

'Mania, melancholy, delusion, it's all written down here. It says in Sister Applejack's report that you attacked her and that you had to be restrained on 16th July last, is that correct?'

'Yes,' I replied

'You have had occasions of depression and some melancholic episodes, is that correct?'

'Yes.'

'You have been talking to dead people again, is that correct? She asked.

I said 'No, no, that is NOT correct.'

I remember waking up one morning from a dream and Lionel told me that just before I awoke that I'd been talking in my sleep. Nurse Applejack, I mean Sister Applejack came over and started writing down all the things that I had been saying. I told Mrs Jenkins about what Lionel had told me. Mrs Jenkins then asked Nurse Applejack to go outside the room with her. An attendant who I had never seen before came into the room and sat down opposite me. He just frowned and tutted which made me feel very uneasy, he didn't speak. He just stared at me as if I was some poor caged animal. Perhaps I am? After about 20 minutes Mrs Jenkins came back into the room.

'Sister Applejack has gone back to the ward to resume her normal duties,' she said.

Mrs Jenkins then mentioned Cousin Clifford and asked me if he and Gloria had been blessed with their new baby yet.

I said... 'Yes, it's a baby girl she was born a few days ago and is called Amanda Louise.'

Mrs Jenkins then asked me why I had attempted to attack Nurse Applejack. I told her that it was because she had insulted my mother.

'She called my mother a whore and was very disrespectful.'

Mrs Jenkins shook her head and said... 'That was very stupid Thomas, I know it can't be very easy for you knowing that your mother is a prostitute, but you can't lash out at people just because they say what they think, Sister Applejack has told me that she was only giving you her honest opinion of your situation and that you unduly lashed out at her because of it.'

I couldn't believe what I was hearing and I felt myself sinking down into the chair.

'Right, that's it. I will see you again in January. Make sure that things improve by then otherwise I cannot help you,' she said.

Suddenly she was gone!

I felt motionless, angry and sad. I was hoping for some good news but Nurse Applejack has made things very bad for me. She's exaggerated lots of things about my situation and told lots of lies. I need to tell someone about her and how she abuses us. She is my biggest demon. Now I doubt if I'll ever get out of here.

19 September 1930

This morning when I awoke I felt very hollow. There was a kind of numbness in my mind. I had breakfast, went to the farm, did my work and then went back to the ward. Mr Elliott was there and for some reason he could see that I was down and melancholy. He told me that he was taking Edward up to Embleton's in the village for some tea and cakes and asked if I would like to go as well. I remembered the lardy cake and the iced buns that they sell but I didn't have any money.

Mr Elliott said... 'Don't worry son, I'm paying, if I don't Silas will, we're meeting him up there.'

When we got to Embleton's we sat inside at a table by the window. Mr Elliott asked for some scones and a big pot of tea, there was no lardy cake so I was a bit disappointed but it was very interesting sitting by the window; it was like watching a whole world go by. There were all different kinds of automobiles driving up and down outside. A lady came over and started talking about a new bus service.

'Look, there it is!' she said.

'There's now a bus which goes to Chertsey Ridges all the way from Camberley and back, it stops outside here once every two hours,' Mr Elliott told us.

Just then a man in a posh blue Bugatti motor car pulled up outside, when he took his hat and goggles off I could see that it was Silas or Mr Greenwood as we have to call him now. He walked in and shouted...

'Hello, one and all. Do you like my new toy?'

I had only ever seen Silas on a bicycle before so this was all very different.

While Silas and Mr Elliott were outside looking at the car I started talking to Edward. His speech seems much clearer now.

'I've said a lot of *how now brown cows.*' he kept saying.

I laughed because I remembered a time when I had to say that a lot as well when Mrs Evenden was still alive. I found out that Edward is the same age as me; his birthday is a week before mine on 2nd August. He looks quite a bit older but I felt it best not to tell him. Edward told me that he is a mad keen football supporter and that missing his favourite team playing on Saturdays is what hurts him most about being at the asylum. I told him that we play football here; he laughed.

'It's not the same thing as standing in a crowd of 20,000 people at Fulham on a terrace with the person behind you piddling down your back because there's nowhere to go to the toilet,' he said.

I laughed but was quite surprised at how well he spoke. I don't think that Edward has any demons anymore but I felt I had to warn him about Nurse Applejack.

'If you don't have any demons, she'll invent some for you!' I said.

When Silas and Mr Elliott came back into the shop, another man appeared. I recognised him as one of the men that Mr Randall had been arguing with at the Nag's Head Inn on Saturday. They were all laughing and I heard them talking about Mr Randall and Mrs Juett and everything they had been doing.

I heard the man say 'That Randall bloke needs to watch his back; Old Man Juett will have his guts for garters and as old as he is doesn't take any prisoners.'

The lady who was serving in the shop joined in the conversation and I heard Silas tell her that Mr Randall had been knocking Mrs Juett off for months. 'He keeps her fresh!' he said.

I think I knew what they were talking about and remembered what I had seen in the woods a few weeks ago. I just sat there and smiled to myself but now I think Mr Randall could be in lots of trouble!

20 September 1930

For some reason I felt very perky today and I've tried to be positive. I've looked for Maisie all over but haven't been able to find her. I want to know that she's alright after what Mr Mycroft had told me about what's been going on in her ward again. It really is only the thought of Maisie that keeps me going now!

This afternoon I went out in the grounds with Stanley and Edward collecting chestnuts for Missy Hope. Chestnuts are very prickly things. Most of the chestnut trees are near the fence at the Broadway. I saw Mr Flynn and a couple of farmhands bringing the cows up for milking. Everything is back to normal with them now after the recent flood but yesterday Mr Hampton was checking the pigs for disease again, there were some worries that their food might have become contaminated because of all the rain.

When I got back to the scullery Donald was there, his left arm was all up in a sling. He was kissing Missy Hope. They both looked very amused when they saw me standing in the doorway. Donald told me that he and Missy are very nervous. They've asked to see the Medical Superintendent at 4 o'clock. 'We have to declare that we're having a relationship, it's in the rules, if we don't, then we could be dismissed,' he said.

I remembered Missy catching a bouquet of roses at the wedding and there being lots of laughter. I wonder if Donald and Missy being together now is anything to do with that. They then started kissing again and didn't seem to care that I was watching!

I haven't seen Mr Randall today. I wonder if he went to the Nag's Head Inn.

21 September 1930

It's Sunday, a church day and God. I will not go. After what happened to me on Thursday I cannot and will not go to the chapel. Today must be the start of something different, a new outlook. I need to reinvent myself and perhaps become a different person. I need to not to be 'Me' anymore. The mirror is not a friendly place, not a good place to start, so I thank my own heart for the love of nature. At least there is a sense of freedom and freewill up here between the trees. I have convinced myself that there can be no God, or if there is, his name is Lucifer!

I wandered out on to the canal towpath again. It's something I seem to do most Sundays now that I don't have to go to the chapel. The water levels are back up following all the recent rain and a canal man told me that the lock gates have been fixed down at St John's. The barge that was stuck in the mud is still there and has taken on water.

'The ropes didn't have enough give when the water came back into the pound,' he said.

He then asked me if I was a worker or a patient at the asylum. I told him that I worked with the pigs at the farm. I didn't want him to know that I was a patient in case it upset him and he became violent. He was a very big man. When I saw Mr Drake in the distance I said goodbye and came back into the grounds. Mr Drake was good about it when he caught me outside last time but I didn't want to out run my luck.

Luck is seeing Maisie in the bottom field with one of the horses. I ran down and we chatted for what seemed like the whole afternoon. She told me that she is very tired because of what's been happening in her ward, she said that she cannot sleep at night because she lays awake feeling scared.

'Nothing has happened to me yet but they keep picking on Isabella because she used to be a nymphomaniac who couldn't leave men alone, which is the reason why she's in here.'

Maisie had to tell me what a nymphomaniac was. She told me that Isabella is not allowed to be near men and that Angela and the night attendant have both been constantly abusing her because of that. Another lady called Katherine who was attacked a few weeks ago has since been moved to a special care ward in the infirmary.

'She's very poorly and her memory has gone.'

I asked Maisie what the night attendant's name was.

'Miss Maunders,' she replied.

I think that I'll remember that name, especially if anything ever happens to Maisie now!

22 September 1930

Today I had a medical check. No lice, no scabies, right weight for my height, no organ failure, no syphilis, no dementia. The doctor looked at my dinky.

'Do you masturbate?' he asked.

'Yes, sometimes but not all the time,' I replied.

He told me that nearly all men masturbate if they can't be with a woman.

'Do you think of a woman when you masturbate?' he asked.

I said 'Yes!'

'What woman?'

I didn't answer that but then he laughed and said... 'Don't worry. I was just playing with you.' No he bloody well wasn't!

I think there's a name for people like him and I felt very uncomfortable. He reminded me a bit of Dr Carlisle but he's much younger and spoke with a high pitched tone. Emile, The Dwarf, went in after me and seemed to be in there a very long time! When I got back to the ward I told Lionel about the doctor.

'Oh him, Dr Brownbill-Smith, they say he likes men but he's quite harmless, just very odd, but you have to watch him though,' he warned.

I'm beginning to think that some of the doctors, nurses and attendants should be patients here themselves. Some of them are definitely not right in the head!

23 September 1930

Nobby Hatch is dead! He was found under his bed with his wrists cut just before dawn. Mr Elliott came into the dining room at breakfast and told us.

'He had used a broken bottle to sever his veins and there was blood everywhere.'

Nobby had been very unsettling to me but I had forgotten about him after he was sent to the refractory wards. No-one deserves to die but he has chosen to do it himself. Perhaps his demons came to get to get him. I've been sat here wondering what his final moments must have been like, what must have been going through his head? How he found the courage to kill himself? It must take courage to do something like that, but if the mind is playing tricks, maybe Nobby thought very differently and just killed himself anyway.

24 September 1930

Everything seems to happening all at once this week. I was on my way to the farm this morning and Mr Mycroft was walking towards me with his dog.

'Have you heard?' he asked.

'Heard what?'

He told me that Mr Randall was in the infirmary. Two men had set upon him on late on Sunday night and that he has been badly beaten. One of the men has been arrested by the constabulary and is under lock and key at Woking Police station.

'Apparently Mr Randall's been carrying on with the landlord's wife from the Nag's Head Inn,' he said.

I tried not to agree or let it be known that I knew what was going on. It was hard. I guessed that Mr Randall might be in trouble and now this news has proved it. I hope he will be alright.

26 September 1930

When I was in the bottom field with Maisie last Sunday I should have asked her about what she thinks 'love' might be and how it feels. We were too busy talking about everything that's been going on in her ward and I forgot to mention it. Maybe it wasn't the right time anyway. Perhaps love is something that should be spoken about at a special time, when the moment is right and when there are no other things to talk about. I still have the letter I wrote for Maisie. Maybe I should have been brave enough to give it to her and then she would know what I think about love and how it feels for me. I feel Maisie inside me with each heartbeat. I wish that she was here in this very moment and beside me now.

28 September 1930

Cousin Clifford and Gloria came to visit me today. Gloria had their new babe in arms in a thick grey blanket. It wasn't a very long visit because I made Gloria cry. The baby was asleep when Gloria pulled the blanket away from her. Its face was all scrunched up and I told Gloria that it reminded me of one of the gargoyles on the roof at the Chief Clerk and Attendant's house. Clifford didn't look very happy either and they left quite quickly. I tried to apologise because I didn't really mean to say what I said. It just came out. Now I don't know when I will see Clifford again and if he is still going to help me. I worry.

7 October 1930

I've been in the infirmary for a few days. All the bones and joints on my right side became stiff and very painful. I couldn't move my shoulder, pick things up or walk properly. The doctor there gave me some new medicines and I've been given a special diet of fish, milk, vegetables and fruit. The doctor said that I have the bones of an old man and that I'm too young to suffer from such a disease. He never told me what it was but Lionel thinks that it could be some kind of arthritis. I hope not. Uncle Charlie had arthritis and had to use a walking cane most of his life.

Mr Elliott came into the ward to say 'Hello' and asked me if I remembered the airship that had passed over on a test flight last year. I remember it well, it was all very exciting and quite a few aeroplanes came over just behind it. Everyone thought that the airship was going to hit the water tower. Mr Elliott then showed me his newspaper.

'Look it's crashed on its proper maiden flight in France in the early hours of Sunday morning. There were bodies everywhere, over 40 dead, it's a real tragedy,' he said.

I have lost so many days and I wonder how Maisie is... And, I wonder how things are at the farm?

9 October 1930

Therapy is a word that I keep hearing lately. Last night I couldn't sleep. It was very peaceful and Nurse Primrose noticed that I was quite restless. She brought me over a cup of my favourite Ovaltine and checked my temperature. Everyone else was asleep. We listened to the rain pouring down outside and I could see raindrops glowing on the window pane caused by the lights outside. It all felt very therapeutic. Nurse Primrose kept using that word so I had to ask her what it really meant. It was a long night and she stayed with me until I must have fallen asleep. This morning when I awoke there was an eerie stillness about the ward and everything was unusually calm. I hadn't seen or felt that before. Mr Randall came in. His face is still black and blue with bruises from his beating. Today is his first day back on duty and he told us that he was glad to be back although he had been reprimanded by the Medical Superintendent for fighting. 'But I never threw one bloody punch!' he said.

The farm was also very quiet today. Donald will back next Monday, his arm is nearly better but he won't be able to lift anything heavy for a while. Now I must look for Maisie. It's been a long time since I've seen her. I don't think she even knows where I've been or why. I must tell her and see how she is. I hope that nothing else bad has happened in her ward. I haven't been told anything so hopefully all is well.

10 October 1930

This morning there was a big thunderstorm, I think it must have gone on for about three hours. No one could go out because it rained so hard. Just after it stopped we were only allowed to go as far as the airing court. The Tall Man was there and he was going wild. He was holding his arms up and his voice was booming.

'I am your Antichrist! I am your Antichrist!' he kept shouting.

Emile, The Dwarf, was running around excitedly, round and round and through The Tall Man's legs about a dozen times. I tried very hard not to catch The Tall Man's eye, it's always very uncomfortable when he latches on and sees you looking and I never know what he's going to say. This time though, he was arguing with God or something else which wasn't there. The two attendants, who normally look after him, were sat on a bench just chuckling away as they smoked their pipes. It was all very odd and they didn't seem too bothered by all his antics.

Later, the sun came out and I was allowed to go to the farm and help with my normal duties. My bones still ache a bit and my joints all down my right side still feel very sore, so it was very hard pushing the pigs around in their pens while I was mucking them out. I feel very weary now.

11 October 1930

It's Saturday, it's very hot and it feels like the summer has come back. I sat on the porch with Mr Mycroft this morning,

'It's the start of an Indian Summer,' he said.

I asked him what that was and he told me all about the North American Indians, the Sioux and the Cheyenne. He told me stories about the Wild West in America with all the cowboys and cavalry, it was all very interesting and he said that he would find me some books that he has in a cupboard somewhere.

This afternoon Mr Randall came to take us out. Lionel is still not strong enough to leave the ward and Stanley was expecting a visit from his sister, so it was just me and Edward. Mr Randall told us that he was going to take us for a long walk by the canal, it was a nice day and I somehow guessed that we wouldn't be going to the Nag's Head Inn to see Jack. Instead we ended up at an old barn near a bridge where there was a bar inside and lots of old men drinking. Mr Randall knew a lot of them, so he left us outside with a big jug of cider while he went inside to talk and drink.

I spoke to Edward about his speech, it really does seem much better now and he said the same about me. He too, is upset that he was sent to the asylum but thinks that it's more to do with the way he looks than how he speaks. Edward has a hair lip, a cleft chin and his eyes are quite close together.

'My father said that I could never be trusted and my sister always called me ugly,' he said.

174

Edward then started talking about football. His favourite team is called Fulham. They play in London and are playing a team called Walsall today. He said that he will find out the score on Monday.

'I hope they win, I love it when they win,' he said.

Edward told me that he used to go to the football with his older brother Brian, but he had drowned after falling off a boat in the River Thames about two years ago. Edward told me that since then everything had become very difficult for him.

'My brother was also my best friend,' he said with a slight tremble.

When Mr Randall came out of the beer house, he had Mrs Juett with him and she was clinging to his arm.

'Hello Thomas, what do you think of my hero?' she said.

She meant Mr Randall. I was shocked to see her. Mr Randall then told me that they were going to find a house and live together.

'She's had enough of her old man at the Nag's Head Inn and needs to start a new life and I'm her man now,' he said.

I asked about Jack and Mrs Juett told me that he is going with Mr Juett to run another beer house over Bracknell way.

'I'll be well shot of the old man and his evil ways,' she said.

Just then Mr Randall and Mrs Juett kissed. I felt very awkward!

12 October 1930

It's another Sunday. At last I've seen Maisie. She told me that things have been quite quiet in her ward lately. Miss Maunders has been away on Annual Leave and Angela won't talk to anyone else so she has just been sat on her bed.

'She just sits there with her legs crossed. She stares at us over her spectacles and keeps giving me dirty looks but at least she's quiet and hasn't been attacking people recently,' she said.

I then plucked up the courage to talk about love. I asked her what she thought love was. She said that love is lots of things.

'You can be in love with someone, you can love someone but not be in love with them, you can love people and you can love things like animals and places,' she said.

'Are you in love?' she asked.

I replied 'Yes, I think I am, actually I know I am!'

'What do you love?

By now I felt my heart racing and I was beginning to tremble.

'What's wrong with your speech - it's all gone funny again?' she laughed.

I told Maisie that I was nervous.

'It's not what I love. It's more about who I love.'

Maisie grabbed my hand and asked... 'Who do you love Tommy?'

Now I knew this was it, probably the most important thing I that was ever going to say to anybody in my life.

'It's YOU, Maisie, it's you I love!'

Maisie squeezed my hand very tight.

'Thank you Tommy, Thank you.'

For a few seconds it went very quiet and we just sat there staring into each other's eyes, I was lost in the beauty of the moment. Maisie has such beautiful green eyes and then she said it.

'Tommy, I love you too, I really am in love with you. I have been since the very first day that I saw you!'

I felt goose bumps pop up all over my body and my heart raced along even more. I kept hearing the word 'Hallelujah' in my head. Everything was wonderful, everything was great and I felt much relief that Maisie had told me that she loved me too. This was it - the greatest moment ever in my life!

Maisie grabbed my hand back again. She said that we need to talk.

'I need to tell you everything about me and why I'm here and what has happened to me, it's only fair that you should know, we must find a time and place so that we can talk again properly.'

We were about to talk about a plan when Nurse Applejack walked over, she was on her way back from the chapel.

'Come on Thomas, what have I told you before about cavorting with female patients,' she said.

Maisie just smiled and then ran off, she turned and waved and then smiled again.

I will never forget what has happened to me today.

13 October 1930

Last night was quite amusing. Stanley and Lionel were both playing with themselves and Nurse Primrose turned the lights on and caught them both. Everyone else was woken up and there was a lot of kerfuffle. Stanley and Lionel looked very embarrassed. Lionel told me that Nurse Primrose is usually very good at stopping people from masturbating.

'She normally just puts her hands under the covers and I finish straight away,' he said.

I didn't believe him and then he laughed.

'Only joking; only joking,' he said.

Now I know Lionel is getting better and is almost back to his old self.

Donald was back on the farm today. He told me that he and two of his friends had found an old tunnel up at the Hermitage near St John's. They were crawling through it when it all collapsed. Donald said that they thought that it led to the cemetery at Brookwood but weren't sure.

'It was a bit of an adventure but please don't tell Missy that I nearly killed myself,' he pleaded.

14 October 1930

Today I received a letter from Aunt Betty. She has asked me to write and apologise to Cousin Clifford for being rude about the baby.

Dear Thomas,

I hope this letter finds you well.

Your cousin Clifford has told me what you said to Gloria about young Amanda Louise. Your comment was not only thoughtless but also very wicked. You must be very ashamed.

Your mother is also not very amused and she has asked me to scold you for what you have said.

I would urge you to write a clear letter of apology to Gloria and tell her that you think the baby is bonny and is a daughter of whom she should be very proud.

I have also enquired; there are no gargoyles on the roof of the Chief Clerk and Attendant's house.

Yours truly

Aunty Betty.

Yes I do feel very ashamed and now I must decide what to say to Gloria when I write. I still need Cousin Clifford to be my friend. I need him to get me out of this place.

15 October 1930

Lionel told me that I'd been talking in my sleep again just before I woke up this morning. Luckily it was before Nurse Applejack came on duty. Nurse Primrose was helping the porters with some linen so didn't hear me either. Lionel said that I was talking about love and saying Maisie's name a lot.

'At least you weren't talking about dead people this time!' He laughed.

I told him about the conversation that I had with Maisie on Sunday and I asked him what he thought love was.

'Love is shit, it's blind and perilous,' he snapped.

I should have known better than to ask. Love I think is what's behind most of Lionel's problems. At least he's getting better now and he was allowed to come and watch me working at the farm today. He's been told by the doctor that he's not going to be able to catch rats anymore. He was seen yesterday and the doctor confirmed that his illness was caused by a disease called leptospirosis that he must have caught from a rat. It's what must have made his skin turn a bit yellow I think.

At the farm I helped Donald and Mr Flynn paint the tractor. It's still quite new but they wanted to paint it before the winter to help keep the rust off. Mr Flynn is hoping that the lumbermen will come and build a special shed for it soon.

16 October 1930

Today I had to go and see the Medical Superintendent. He informed me that he had received a report from Mrs Jenkins concerning her visit on the 18th September last. He asked me if I thought that I might have any psychological problems and if there may be other things bothering me. I told him that I had always been confused about why I was sent here, why I am still here and why everything is seemingly always going against me. He asked me about my general health. He knew about my time in the infirmary.

'It looks like you haven't been eating properly. I see you have a special diet now and the staff in the dining room have been instructed to ensure that you abide by it,' he said.

He then asked me about Mother and what her residential situation was like. I told him that she now lives at Aunt Betty's house at Watchetts Road in Camberley with Cousin Clifford and his wife Gloria and their new baby. 'There's just no room for me there,' I said.

'I see here that Clifford is named as your appropriate relative and that he has been in conversation with Miss Rance of late, is that correct? He asked.

I said that it was and then told him about the letter I had received from Aunt Betty the other day and he laughed when I told him what I had said about Amanda Louise.

'Some people are just too over sensitive but don't worry, when they get their faculties together they will forgive you in good time,' he advised.

He then told me that he's arranging for Mrs Jenkins to come back and see me again but it won't be until the end of January at the earliest because of her other appointments.

'I want you to dust yourself down and take a long hard look at yourself young Thomas. You have to help yourself; it's not just about other people helping you. I need to see an improvement, no mania, no melancholy and certainly no more delusions,' he said.

He then asked me if there was anything that I would like to say. I reminded him that Mother had me sent here because I had a speech problem.

'Mother couldn't read and write so it was always a problem.'

He looked and nodded.

'Yes, there are pauses between your sentences and some of your words when you talk, however, I do believe your speech and general elocution is actually much better now.'

He then asked me if I enjoyed working on the farm and if I knew Donald.

'Of course I do.' I replied. 'He's been very helpful and is a good friend to me.'

He then told me that he had the pleasure of speaking to Donald and Missy Hope Harrison on 20th September last.

'I have given them both my blessing to become engaged to be wed,' he said.

I was very happy with this news but wondered why Donald hadn't told me yet.

When I got to the farm Donald was there and he asked where I'd been. I told him what the Medical Superintendent had said. He laughed.

'I knew that he wanted to see you about all the other things and when we saw him the other day I mentioned you. I told him that you are a good patient, a strong worker and now a fine friend. The Medical Superintendent didn't give us a final decision until yesterday so I didn't want to say anything until we had got that.'

Donald was very happy and we hugged and we did a little dance in the mud. Now though, I must think about all the other things that the Medical Superintendent has mentioned.

17 October 1930

This morning I saw Maisie talking with Mrs Woolston near the farm. Maisie was giving her a painting. I stopped working with the pigs and Maisie came over. She told me that since all the trouble had started with her Uncle Sylvester and with all what's been happening in a ward, she has only managed to paint one picture.

'I finished it in the Recreation Hall a few Saturday's ago. Mrs Woolston said that she liked it so I gave it to her, it's called *Angels Descending* and she's going to have it put on the wall in the hallway at Hilltop Place.'

Maisie seemed very proud that Mrs Woolston wanted the painting so I decided not to tell her what Mrs Woolston was really like after she got away with stealing all those things from the stores in the summer. Maisie told me that her Uncle Sylvester is coming to see her on Sunday.

'I'm not sure what he'll say when I have no paintings to give him but I do have some very good reasons for not painting anything,' she said.

I could see that she was very worried about what might happen and she appeared to shake when she mentioned her uncle's name. Just then, Mr Luscombe called out and I had to get back to work. Maisie blew me a kiss and ran off. I've been thinking about Maisie all day. I suppose that I must think about her every day and I'm glad.

18 October 1930

Saturdays without going to the Nag's Head Inn are now rather boring. I miss the old men singing around the piano. Mr Randall has told us that he can't take us there anymore.

Mr Elliott took us for a walk instead through Bisley. It rained most of the afternoon and we had to shelter from a thunderstorm under a tree on Bisley Green. Mr Elliott wanted to take us into a beer house across the road called the Hen and Chickens but the old man who was serving the beer wouldn't let us in because he knew that we were from the asylum. Mr Elliott thinks it that it has something to do with what's happened between Mr Randall and Mrs Juett at the Nag's Head Inn.

'Word travels fast around here but never mind, it will all blow over soon but I can't see Algernon going back in the Nag's Head Inn for a very long time,' he said.

I smiled when he said 'Algernon'. I had nearly forgotten that Algernon is Mr Randall's Christian name and I remembered the time in Guildford when Silas first told us. That day was quite funny!

Emile, The Dwarf, came with us and didn't even bring a book. He was very quiet but when we got back to the ward he told us that he hopes to be discharged before Christmas. His family are planning to move to go and live and work in a large chateau at a place called Lille in France.

Now it's just started to rain again. There's been too much rain this year!

19 October 1930

Maybe I am delusional. Today I have invented my own God and he came and sat beside me underneath the tree. He is bald, has pointed ears and wears an attendant's uniform. He is kind and he listens to me. I can talk to him and he can give me all the answers.

I worry about myself, the power of imagination and what happens in my dreams. This sort of thing never happened to me until I came here. I remember Lionel telling me once that the spirit of the asylum can get under the skin and it affects us all in different ways. The Tall Man is a fine example of that and Colonel Peter was very similar. The same must happen in the female wards, which could be why Maisie is always scared.

Is there an end to this? If there is, I can't see it. I definitely cannot see it, but yes, I do need a god, I need someone to pray to, I need something to be there!

20 October 1930

I went with Donald across the way to help Mr Horlock with his gate this morning. He was putting new hinges on and wanted us to help lift the gate while he screwed them in. The gate was very heavy. Mr Luscombe came over and told us off because we should have been working with the pigs. Mr Horlock and Mr Luscombe then had an almighty argument and now Mr Luscombe is going to report him to the Medical Superintendent for 'stealing' his workers. It was all quite amusing really and it made me laugh. Donald told me to make sure that Mr Luscombe didn't see me laughing.

'He would take a very dim view of that!' he said.

I wonder how Maisie got on with her Uncle Sylvester yesterday. I hope that he wasn't mean or cruel to her about why she has no paintings for him. I hope that he understands why Maisie hasn't been able to paint lately. I suppose, at least he can't make off with all her money, if that's what he's been doing.

21 October 1930

On the way back from the farm, I saw Maisie with one of the Percheron horses. We were able to talk for a little while and she told me about her Uncle Sylvester's visit yesterday. She was quite upset.

'Actually, he was rather nice to me. I think it was because he had spoken to Miss Rance before he saw me and she had told him about some of the things that have been going on, although she doesn't know everything.'

Maisie told me that he's going to make a provision for her to spend more time at home during Christmas so that she can do some paintings there but she doesn't want that and feels very uncomfortable about the idea. She's adamant that she's not going to stay with him even though her father lives in the same house. I remember her telling me once that her father is a very weak man and that he is often bullied by her uncle. She told me that when she mentioned to her uncle that she had given her only new painting to Mrs Woolston, he was furious.

'He never even gave me anything for my pocket money allowance this time.'

Maisie was very tearful and I wanted to hold her hand but Nurse Applejack and some attendants were nearby and then the horse became restless. We smiled at each other and then parted. A feeling of love came back into my heart again. I have so many questions for Maisie but we haven't had a chance to sit down properly and talk again like we did the other Sunday.

22 October 1930

This morning when I woke up Lionel was screaming at me.

'You were shouting in your sleep and saying things about God and how you've met him and that he's your only friend. Nurse Applejack had just come on duty and she wrote everything down that you'd been saying. She was laughing and said, "Ha-ha Thomas, I've got you now!" You should be worried,' he warned.

Now I worry that she's going to write a report but at least I have the proof that Nurse Applejack wants to get me. Lionel heard her.

'I think she's the devil!' Lionel quipped.

Later, Emile, The Dwarf, started jumping about. He has been given a note and is being discharged from the asylum on Friday.

'I'm cured, I'm cured!' he kept shouting.

I will be glad to see the back of him but felt jealous that it wasn't me who was given a note, not me who was going to be discharged on Friday. I then thought lucky Emile, that there had been no real difference in him between the day he first came and now. All he's done is read books and irritate people. In a strange way, I think I will miss him though.

23 October 1930

The evenings are getting dark much earlier now and it's very depressing. The dark grey sky makes the whole place look much more sinister. Yesterday, I was standing in the bottom field about an hour before the sun went down. There was a big black cloud in the sky, it kept swirling and moving. It looked like it was folding itself inside out and was shifting very fast above the Bagshot Road. Mr Drake came over and I pointed at the cloud. He laughed.

'That's not a cloud, that's a flock of starlings. They often get together in their thousands at this time of year. It's called a murmuration,' he said.

I had never heard that word before and it's not even in the dictionary that Maisie gave me. I saw Mr Drake again this morning and I told him that I couldn't find the word when I tried to look it up. He told me that he has a big book all about birds and their habits in his house and that he would let me have it if I promised to look after it.

On the way back from the farm I saw Mr Mycroft. He gave me a book of Wild West stories to keep.

'I bought it for my grandson but he never grew old enough to read it. Look after it, it's yours now,' he said.

I could see a tear in Mr Mycroft's eye and I felt very sad but I didn't want to ask about his grandson and I think that he had already said more than he wanted to say. I just said 'thank you' and came away.

Today has been all about reading and books.

24 October 1930

Albert came today with six new patients, four men and two women.

'They've been transferred from another asylum in London because it's overcrowded,' he said.

There are two spare beds in our ward so I'm wondering which two of the new male patients we'll get. They all looked so pale and thin and under nourished. Albert told me that he's coming back tomorrow to take us on an outing to a farm on the other side of Godalming.

'You'll see lots of other kinds of animals there, not just pigs and cows,' he said.

I asked Mr Randall about the outing but he didn't know.

'You won't see me around much on Saturdays anymore, I think Mr Elliott and one of the others will be going out with you lot tomorrow.'

Emile left today. He was very excitable and I met his father. He was a very smart man and wore a very bright suit. He had a gold tooth. Emile's left some of his books behind and there's one about Hinduism, which is all in a different language. It's all written in little shapes and squiggles. Nurse Applejack has taken it to the library.

25 October 1930

Stanley, Edward and some men from another ward all came on
the trip to Godalming today. Mr Drake and Silas came as well and
were drinking Scotch whisky at the back of the bus. When we got to
the farm there was some very tall sheep, I hadn't seen sheep like that
before.

'They're not sheep, they're South American Alpacas,' Mr Drake
laughed.

There were three of them, some donkeys and lots of goats. In
another field there was a herd of deer. They were very tame and we
were allowed to feed them by hand. When we finished at the farm we
went and found a beer house and sat outside with our sandwiches. It
was quite bright and sunny and it felt quite warm. Mr Elliott brought
us out some cider. Edward had never drunk cider before and didn't
like it very much. Later, Mr Elliot came out again, it was getting dark
and I think they had all forgotten about us. I think Albert was drunk
as well and on the journey back to the asylum the bus kept swaying
from side to side. Everyone was singing and one of the men from one
of the other wards knew all the words to everything.

'I used to work in a beer house, so I know all the songs,' he said.

He was very jovial and kept telling jokes. There didn't seem to be
anything wrong with him at all so I wondered why he's in here as a
patient. I must ask. I think his name is Marcus.

26 October 1930

Today is a church day and this morning Nurse Applejack asked
me why I wasn't going to the chapel. She knows now that I have
dispensation and do not have to attend. I can't be forced.

'But you do believe in God now, I heard you talking to him the
other morning,' she said.

I told her that I do NOT believe in God because I have my own
God now. I think that was a bad mistake, I shouldn't have told her.

'So Thomas, you are delusional, so delusional that you have to
make up God now. GOD is already here and he's here for everyone
you SINNER!' She shouted.

She then said that she would be having words with Parson Jaggs.

'You need exorcising Thomas.'

Now I worry about the consequences because I know that she writes everything down and reports it all back to the Medical Superintendent.

I walked around the grounds all day looking for Maisie but there was no sign of her. I so want to talk to her about everything. She said that she would tell me why she's here but we still haven't had a good chance to sit down and talk about it yet. I fear that when we do it will take a while. She knows everything about me; I just need to know about her, it will help me understand her more. I want us to be together forever. I want it to happen but so many things are in our way. I wonder if she thinks the same.

3 November 1930

It's been raining very hard for quite a few days and everywhere has flooded again. It's been very muddy on the farm and we have had to make sure that we've been very careful with the pig feed this time.

Lionel is much better now and he is allowed to go out catching rats again. I went with him yesterday and we caught six, they were all quite big. Lionel has been looking for Mr Drake to pay him but I think that the money gets paid straight into Lionel's pocket money allowance. I'm sure Lionel must know that but he does seem a bit confused about a lot of things since he's been ill.

The man who came on the bus trip to Godalming has moved into our ward. Nurse Primrose says that it's more suitable for him and he shouldn't be with us too long. His name is Marcus Ventura. He told me that he was sent here because he was melancholy and suicidal but he feels alright now.

'I've learnt to look on the bright side,' he said.

He didn't say what caused his situation and I didn't like to ask although Lionel said that there's probably a woman behind it.

'There nearly always is,' he said with a grin.

I told Lionel that I didn't think that what he had said was completely true. Reginald was like that because of the Great War and he never recovered from it.

'I don't think that it was actually a woman who caused him to die by his own hand,' I said.

Lionel looked surprised after I had challenged him but agreed that I was right. I've come to realise today that I'm now able to speak up and that people listen to me. I wonder if Mother will.

I've also remembered that I still have to write a letter to Gloria and apologise for what I said about her baby. It's been a long time since Aunt Betty wrote and I haven't done anything about it yet.

4 November 1930

Dear Gloria and Cousin Clifford,

I hope this letter finds you both in good health and that everything is well with little Amanda Louise.

I am very, very sorry for what I said about the baby when you came to visit me on 28th September last. I'm also sorry that I have taken so long to write this letter of apology for which I have no excuse.

I had to spend some time in the infirmary at the beginning of October because I had pains all down my right side but I think that I'm alright now and I've been back helping on the farm again.

I look forward to your next visit and hope it will be soon.

Yours truly

Tommy

I hope Clifford and Gloria will forgive me. I wasn't used to seeing a baby up close and so young and I didn't know what to say. I need Clifford to come back, he was doing something to get me out of here and I hope that what I said about their baby hasn't ruined it all.

5 November 1930

At breakfast I spent a long time talking to Marcus. He told me that he will be forty years old soon. He has a beer house which used to belong to his father in London where he lives with his wife and three daughters. His wife is called Phoebe and she's running it with her brother while he's away. He told me that he saw his best friend Konrad shot on one of the last days of the war.

'He died in my arms,' he said quite sadly.

That's not why I'm here though, I had syphilis and it nearly got worse, it changes into something called general paralysis which can make you mad, a lot of soldiers caught it but there's a sort of cure for it now and after some malaria treatment it starts to go away.

'I'm nearly free of it now and luckily my wife was not infected by it. A lot of us caught if off some frisky Belgian girl called Liza before the big battle. We all thought we were going to die anyway so we didn't really think about the consequences and she was enjoying herself. All we saw was the bodies of dead British soldiers being wheeled back on carts as we marched towards the Front, so we thought, this is it, certain death, but in the end we won and some of us were lucky enough to make it home.'

Marcus was very interesting to listen to and he told me that he had lots more stories to tell. After we had finished talking Marcus went over to Edward and started telling the story all over again. I seem to remember Mr Mycroft telling me about soldiers coming back from the Great War with things wrong with them. I think that it was really syphilis that brought Lionel here.

Tonight there's going to be a big bonfire in the bottom field. I hope no-one catches alight this time.

6 November 1930

This morning before I went to the farm I had to go to the Medical Superintendent's office. No-one wanted to see me this time but I was helping Mr Randall and one of the porters carry over some boxes of paperwork from the ward. When we got to the waiting room there was a lady in a dark blue dress with long black curly hair sitting by the window.

'Hello Tommy!' she said.

I didn't recognise her and her voice sounded very deep. Mr Randall grabbed my arm and pulled me away before I had a chance to answer. On the way back to the ward he told me that it was Anton. I remembered Anton. They took him away from our ward because he wanted to be a woman. Mr Randall told me that he's being kept in isolation for his own sake. He must have been waiting to see the Medical Superintendent for an assessment or a check up.

'You do see some right old sights around here sometimes,' he said.

I told Mr Randall that I had seen men dress up as women before but that was only usually in fancy dress. Mr Randall told me that the whole thing is giving the Medical Superintendent and the Visiting Committee a major headache.

'They just don't know what to do with him,' he said quite wryly.

7 November 1930

I thought that I was hearing voices in my head again this morning and for a moment I was very worried. I listened harder and then I realised that it was the lumbermen shouting at each other on the other side of the farm. Their voices seemed to carry on the wind. I'm glad it was nothing more sinister but certain things have been making me very paranoid lately and I don't want to start suffering from any new problems. My bones and joints all down my right side have been aching again today, Mr Mycroft said that it could be to do with all the wet weather.

'My joints have been giving me problems for donkey's years,' he said.

He asked me what I've been eating and I told him that the doctor had given me a special diet since I was let out of the infirmary.

'Mind you haven't got rickets and make sure that you take plenty of milk and cod liver oil,' he added.

I had to tell him that I hated cod liver oil. Nanny used give me spoonfuls of it when I was a small boy and I've loathed it ever since. I think I would rather have aching bones and joints.

'Well don't come back complaining to me when you can't walk anymore,' he chuckled.

He made me feel a bit guilty; he always seems to care about me and the other patients and how we get on. He appears to takes an interest in what we're doing and likes sharing his stories with everyone. Lionel calls him 'Old Mr Nosey.'

This year we are entering some pigs into the Christmas Village Show. There are some new pot-bellied pigs coming on Monday which Mr Luscombe bought at the market last week. Donald thinks that they could be put in the arena with the Middle Whites.

'They're a popular breed because of their size and shape. The Middle Whites though are an English breed and people at the shows always like that, so who knows?' he said.

I can't really tell the difference yet. Donald is the real expert on pigs these days and when I told him so he laughed. I remember that there used to be a pot-bellied pig here before called Gertrude. She did look different from all the others and was a pet but got ill and had to be put down.

8 November 1930

From Monday I have a new routine because all the medical staff, attendants and porters have been given different duty hours and their handover times have been changed. Miss Rance gave me the note and told me to memorise it.

'All patients must now work to this new schedule. There's one for weekdays and one for Saturdays and Sundays. 'Yours is an artisan's schedule,' she said.

Artisan means that I work on the farm I think.

Monday, Tuesday, Wednesday, Thursday, Friday

6:00am	Morning Bell
6:15am	Ablutions
6:45am	Prepare for Breakfast
7:00am	Breakfast in Dining Room
7:30am	Airing Court/Social (or Medical Checks)
8:30am	Farm
10:45am	Elevenses at Farm
12:30pm	Prepare for Dinner
1:00pm	Dinner in Dining Room
1:30pm	Airing Court/Social (or Medical Checks)
2:00pm	Farm
3:00pm	Free Time
5:00pm	Ablutions
5:15pm	Prepare for Tea
5:30pm	Tea in Dining Room
6:00pm	Airing Court/Social (April to September)
7:30pm	Ablutions
8.30pm	Night Cap/Hot Drink on ward
9:00pm	Bed Time/Evening Bell
9:45pm	Lights Out

Saturday

6:00am	Morning Bell
6:15am	Ablutions
6:45am	Prepare for Breakfast
7:00am	Breakfast in Dining Room
7:30am	Airing Court/Social
9:00am	Recreation including elevenses
12:30pm	Prepare for Dinner
1:00pm	Dinner in Dining Room
1:30pm	Airing Court/Social
2:00pm	Recreation/Free Time or Trip
5:15pm	Prepare for Tea
5:30pm	Tea in Dining Room

6:00pm	Airing Court/Social (April to September)
7:30pm	Ablutions
9.30pm	Night Cap/Hot Drink on ward
10:00pm	Bed Time/Evening Bell
10:30pm	Lights Out

Sunday

7:00am	Morning Bell
7:15am	Ablutions
7:45am	Prepare for Breakfast
8:00am	Breakfast in Dining Room
8:30am	Airing Court/Social
9.30am	Chapel or Free Time
12:30pm	Prepare for Dinner
1:00pm	Dinner in Dining Room
1:30pm	Airing Court/Social
2:00pm	Recreation/Free Time or Trip
5:15pm	Prepare for Tea
5:30pm	High Tea in Dining Room (Parson Jaggs)
6:30pm	Airing Court/Social (April to September)
7:30pm	Ablutions
8.30pm	Night Cap/Hot Drink on ward
9:00pm	Bed Time/Evening Bell
9:45pm	Lights Out

I don't think it's too different from what I've been doing already but I would love to have more free time especially during the winter months. It doesn't say what we have to do at 6.30pm from March to October. I think that it has something to do with the darker evenings. I will have to ask.

Miss Rance told me that she has given the scullery maid a new diet chart for me.

'There's a lot of fish and beans on there for you!' she said with a smile.

9 November 1930

Yesterday afternoon Mr Elliott took some of us for a walk around
the village. It was quite cold and all we really wanted to do was get
back and warm up. Lionel, Stanley, Marcus and one of the other new
men came. Mr Elliott took us into a field and showed us a badger sett
and some fox holes. We saw some dead rabbits that had been shot.
Mr Drake came over with one of the shooting men from Bisley.

'This time next week we'll be shooting rabbits and pheasants in
the asylum's grounds,' he said.

When he eventually walked off Mr Elliott told us that it will all be
very awkward as it was the same man who had that fight with Mr
Randall and put him in the infirmary.

'I doubt if we'll see Mr Randall about at all next Saturday,' he
quipped.

When we got back to the asylum I saw Maisie. She was smiling
and waving and I ran over to her and we hugged.

'Hey, leave the little lass alone!' Mr Elliott shouted.

I ran back and he laughed.

'I know all about your love life, you can't keep anything from
me!'

I laughed too. Some of the other attendants are not so lenient and
I was very glad that Nurse Applejack wasn't around.

I meant to ask Maisie when we might be able to find some time to
talk but the darker evenings are making it much more difficult now
and I couldn't find her this morning. I think that a Sunday morning
would be the best time for us. It's also one of my favourite times of
the week now that I don't have to go to the chapel anymore.

10 November 1930

Today is the first day of the new schedule and already it's been
messed up. I was called over to see Miss Rance. Dr Barnes was
there.

'Hello young Thomas. I'm just on a flying visit and thought that I
would check up on your welfare whilst I was here. I see from these
reports that you've had a couple of relapses and that you've been

194

poorly and have been in the infirmary since the last time I saw you,' he said.

I asked him what he meant by relapses and he mentioned the mania and melancholy.

'What's all this about your delusions Thomas, you're supposed to be getting better not worse and these reports from Sister Applejack do not make comfortable reading,' he said.

He then asked me what my relationship was like with the medical nurses and I told him that I felt it very easy talking to Nurse Primrose but not with Nurse Applejack. He didn't know who Nurse Primrose was and then I remembered that her surname was Starkey.

Miss Rance butted in... 'Thomas, you must only address the staff by their surnames and remember that it is Sister Applejack, she is not to be called 'Nurse' anymore!'

Miss Rance can be very harsh sometimes and I also know that she is very friendly with Nurse Applejack and that's why things have been very difficult for me. Dr Barnes then asked me about Mrs Jenkins' visit on 18th September last.

'I see here that she terminated your interview early because she had concerns about your welfare and general progress. She wasn't expecting to see any relapses and that's why she's trying to give you more time. You have really got to help yourself Thomas,' he said with a frown.

I was trying not to get angry and felt I very let low. I wondered if I had been letting myself down. Then I thought about the farm and how well things have gone there and I told Dr Barnes that working there was really helping me. He then asked Miss Rance to obtain a report about me from Mr Luscombe and ensure that it's available to Mrs Jenkins on her next visit. Miss Rance then asked Dr Barnes when Mrs Jenkins will next be available.

'February or March, she is a very busy woman,' he said.

Now it really does feel like I'll be here forever. Every time there are signs that I might get out of here, something gets in the way.

13 November 1930

Today I received a letter from Aunt Betty about my apology to Gloria and Clifford about what I said about the baby. I don't think that she's very satisfied with what I said and she seems very angry that I took so long to reply.

Dear Thomas

I do trust that this letter finds you well.

Your cousin Clifford and Gloria have showed me the letter written by you on 4th November last.

Whilst they have accepted your apology I find that the lateness of your letter is both patronising and insolent. Your tone is disrespectful and the way that you have tried to say sorry appears to be very hollow and without true feeling and this angers me. The only saving grace is that you remembered to mention the baby's name.

Clifford has asked me to inform you that he will try to come to the asylum and visit you soon, so can I trust that you will show him your utmost respect?

Yours truly

Aunt Betty

P.S. Your mother sends you her best wishes although she is quite detained by a cold.

I know my letter to Gloria was late but I did write it with true feeling and I am sorry for what I said about the baby. I don't know what else to do. Perhaps when Cousin Clifford next comes to visit I can explain.

14 November 1930

This morning while I was working on the farm some boys from the village rode into the grounds on their bicycles. They started poking fun at me and kept shouting... 'Loony, Loony.' Donald and Mr Flynn raced over from Rose Cottage and Mr Horlock came out of the North Lodge.

'Be off with you,' he shouted.

They rode off and then he came over to talk to us. He recognised one of the boys and said that he will tell his father.

'He'll put a belt to the lad when I tell him,' he said.

Mr Horlock then asked if we could go over and help him carry some wood into his shed. Mr Flynn laughed.

'Are you asking for another argument with Mr Luscombe again?'

Mr Horlock started walking back to his cottage and then turned and shook his fist and shouted back at us... 'That's the last time I'm coming out of my house to help you horrible lot of imbeciles.'

He keeps using that word. Donald told me to ignore him.

'You know how rude and ridiculous that man is and he's really no better than those young boys from the village he's just chased off!'

Next Monday Marcus is coming to work on the farm. He's hoping to be discharged before Christmas and the Medical Superintendent is giving him a chance to work out in the fresh air before he goes back to live in a smokey beer house. He told me that he's looking forward to seeing his wife and children again.

'Phoebe has been very patient and loyal with me,' he said.

When I got back to the ward I told Lionel that Marcus was going to be working with me on the farm and that he hopes to be out of the asylum before Christmas. Lionel told me that knows why Marcus is here.

'Well lucky him, a wife that stands by him who is patient and loyal, I wish mine was. There's no bloody such thing as a loyal wife!' he snarled.

Lionel's voice was quite loud which was unusual apart from when he screamed at me the other morning. I think that now he's just jealous about Marcus.

16 November 1930

I saw Maisie this morning and at last we had time to talk. The weather was grey and still and the rain had stopped just after breakfast. We sat on some logs to the side of the woods and out of view of the buildings while most people had gone to the chapel. Maisie has received a letter from her father warning her of her Uncle Sylvester's possible intentions. The letter is very long and drawn out and Maisie thinks that her uncle has been fighting with him again. She told me that she doesn't want to go home for Christmas and is trying to make an arrangement with her cousin. She's written to her for help but has had no reply. Maisie is very upset and is not really sure what is happening at home. I think all the uncertainty is what concerns her most.

I remembered what Maisie had said about her uncle before and decided to ask her again if it's because of him that she was at the asylum.

'Yes,' she replied.

I wasn't sure if Maisie was actually going to tell me anymore than that but then she started.

'My father was away on business and my mother had just died. Uncle Sylvester came to live at the house to help my father make ends meet. At the time I was courting a boy called William but Uncle Sylvester chased him off and told him never to see me again. My father didn't come home as expected and he ended up going on a voyage through the Mediterranean Sea. He was gone for over a year. It was early in 1927 and my uncle discovered that I could do oils and watercolours. He told me that he could sell the paintings for lots of money. He'd seen the reports about my work at Winchester that he found in my mother's things and then found a way of selling the paintings to lots of art galleries. All the time my father was away he kept me locked inside the house, he only let me out to see my pony or hang out the washing but he always came as well. I felt suffocated,' she said.

Maisie told me that one night in the spring just after she had gone to bed her uncle walked into her bedroom in the attic and forced himself on her.

'He ripped my nightdress and entered me. No-one could hear my screams. Afterward he went downstairs and poured himself a big whisky from the canter and just cried. I sat at the top of the stairs and

I could hear him sobbing. I felt very sore and there was blood coming out. I had scratches all over my chest and on my legs.'

I started to weep as Maisie carried on telling me what had happened. We were holding our hands together very tight. She could see that my eyes were watering and she began to weep as well. There was a pause and we placed our foreheads against each other's then helped each other wipe away the tears.

It was then that Maisie said that she had more to tell me.

'Things then got much worse. In the summer my doctor told me that I was pregnant and that I could expect a baby before Christmas. I told Uncle Sylvester and he was furious. He accused me of seeing William again. I hadn't and I told him that the baby was his. He started beating me and he locked me in a room for days on end. In the end December came and my tummy was very large. He knew a lady who called herself a midwife and she visited me a couple of times. Both times she looked concerned, very concerned. On the evening before my birthday she came around again and told me that it was time for the birth. Uncle Sylvester just sat downstairs out of the way all the time. The nurse held my hand and then told me to start pushing. Nothing was happening and then she put her hand in. She got me to sit up and told me to push again. The pain was too much and I felt myself doubling over. Just then the baby came out but it fell from between my legs dead on to the floor with the chord still dangling. I screamed for hours. An ambulance came and I was taken to the infirmary at Winchester. I was in there for five weeks.'

Maisie then had to stop talking and I had to take in everything that she had said. The whole story was very disturbing and I told her that she didn't have to tell me anymore.

She said... 'No Tommy, I must tell you the rest.'

Her father came back from his voyage just after the New Year and her uncle had told him that she had become pregnant while he was away and that William was the father. Her father asked where the baby was and her uncle told him that it had died at birth. It was a boy.

'Father then went to see William's family and looked very confused when he came back. William had killed himself in London some months previously. It didn't add up and my father became very suspicious. He came to my room and I told him precisely everything that Uncle Sylvester had done to me. When Father confronted him Uncle Sylvester said that he would shoot him and that he would tell everyone that his daughter, meaning me, was a whore. There was a big fight and father hit his head. He has been very frightened of Uncle Sylvester ever since, without him, he could lose the house. Father eventually went to the police and I was becoming very hysterical, the policeman didn't believe what Father had told him and I later found out that the midwife had disposed of the baby's body secretly. There was no record of its birth or death. It later turned out that the midwife wasn't real and that she was just an evil woman who Uncle Sylvester had paid to help cover everything up. She could not be traced. As a result I was taken away for being delusional. I had a medical check but the doctor said that he could only see signs of a miscarriage. The next thing I know I was sent here.'

This was all very difficult to understand and Maisie asked me if I was alright. I told her that I was a bit confused but what she had told me has helped me understand why she's here. We then sat in silence and then Maisie said that she would understand if I didn't want to see her anymore. We clasped hands again and I told her that I loved her. She looked into my eyes and we just sat there staring at each other in silence.

'Thank you for listening to me. This has been a very heavy burden for me,' she said.

Just before we parted Maisie told me that she thinks Angela has guessed why she's in the asylum and that she has heard her whispering to Attendant Maunders about things. She's worried in case something bad might happen now.

17 November 1930

Mr Randall walked with me to the farm this morning.

'I need a quiet word with you Tommy.'

I was curious and I thought that it was very unusual. He told me that Mr Deane, the Medical Superintendent, had asked him to speak to me.

'Were you in the woods with the young Albright girl yesterday morning?' he asked.

I paused and then felt my heart sink. I decided to be truthful. 'Yes.' I replied.

He told me that I need to be very careful about what I was doing. He told me that while I was with Maisie Mr Deane and his wife walked by with their dog.

'They stopped and watched you both for awhile. They could see that you were both in deep conversation, so didn't intervene. Did you see them?' He asked.

I said 'No!'

'You must be more careful in future. Remember that you're not supposed to associate yourself with female patients and there can never be any physical contact. Did you kiss each other?' he asked.

'Actually, no we didn't,' I replied.

I told him that Maisie was telling me the whole reason why she was sent to the asylum.

'It's such a sad story and it made me cry,' I said.

He told me that he knew little bits about Maisie and remembers her being brought here as a very hysterical young woman.

'She's very calm now by comparison,' he said.

Just as we reached the farm gate he grabbed by shoulder and turned me round. He winked and told me to be more careful in future.

'Be alert and always look around you, you never know whose watching. Mr Deane asked me to have a word with you. This is that word so please don't let me down otherwise I will not be able to let you go beyond the airing courts anymore.'

I suddenly warmed to Mr Randall and felt that he was on my side. It means a lot. I don't think he's the scoundrel that some people say he is, despite what's happened between him and Mrs Juett.

19 November 1930

There was lots of commotion in the ward this morning. Marcus was being jovial, he's happy because he's leaving the asylum soon.

He was making fun of Nurse Applejack and she was getting very angry.

'She was very flustered,' Lionel said gleefully.

Suddenly there was a big scream and I turned and saw Marcus fall to the floor and hit his head on a table on the way down. I wasn't sure what had happened but Nurse Applejack was standing over at him and screaming at him very loudly. I didn't understand what she was saying. She seems to talk very gibberish when she loses her temper. Lionel told me that Marcus had sneaked up behind her and pinched her bottom. She quickly turned around and hit him on the side of his head with her copper-stick. Two porters came and took him away to be patched up.

'Let that be a lesson to you all!' she shouted.

Both Lionel and I agreed that Nurse Applejack should get into trouble for what she had done.

20 November 1930

Some peacocks arrived at the farm this morning. Last year we had to fatten them up for Christmas and I remember Mrs Woolston taking one home to Hilltop Place. Mr Flynn came out and said that they were having one for their Christmas dinner this year. He actually marked the one he wanted. The peacocks are very loud and jump around a lot but can't really fly too well. Tomorrow we have some turkeys coming and lots more chickens. The lumbermen have been building some new sheds, pens and coops to make room for them. Mr Flynn's wife came over to talk to us. I still want to call her Mrs Pengelley but she's called Mrs Flynn now. She said that she had arranged for me to have dinner with them all today so I did not have to go to the Dining Hall. We had rabbit stew with lots of garlic. Mr Flynn brought out some of his favourite Irish whiskey.

'You had better wash it down with some water before you leave and go back to work,' he said.

Donald and Missy Hope were there as well and we listened to lots of old stories about the asylum and the farm. Most of them were about all the arguments that had been going on between Mr Horlock and Mr Luscombe. Everyone was laughing and we were still talking about it all when we went back over to the farm.

Today was very bright and sunny. It was the first time that I've seen the sun come out for quite a few days.

21 November 1930

Because of what happened with Nurse Applejack, Marcus has left the asylum already. A porter came and got his things this morning. No-one had a chance to say goodbye. Lionel told me that he thinks that it was to stop anything else nasty happening between them. He was going to be leaving soon anyway and now we all think that someone must have contacted his family to arrange for him to be collected. Stanley told us that he saw him being driven away.

Later Lionel told me that he is going to write a letter and send it direct to the Visiting Committee. He thinks that if he can get someone to post it in the village without the Medical Superintendent or Miss Rance seeing it, something might actually get done about Nurse Applejack.

'She's brutal, a liar, an abuser and is also very clever because she gets away with everything but not this time.'

I told him that if he writes a letter I would get a stamp for him.

This afternoon Miss Rance came to the ward and gave me a note. Some extra money had been put into my pocket money allowance.

'It's from a man you know called George O'Leary. He came by yesterday and has left five pounds for you, it's a lot of money so spend it wisely and not all at once,' she advised.

I had almost forgotten about him. He was a friend of Mother's. When I asked Mother, she couldn't tell me if he was my father, she didn't seem sure. I wonder if I will ever see him again. I now have more questions and I need answers, honest answers. Perhaps I should see if someone has an address for him, I would like to write to him and thank him for the money. I also wonder why he's being so kind. Does he know something that Mother, Aunt Betty or Cousin Clifford have not been telling me?

22 November 1930

At first light this morning I could hear gunshots. It was the men from Bisley out in the grounds doing their annual shoot with Mr Drake. Nurse Applejack told us that no-one would be allowed out into the airing courts or around the grounds until after the men have finished their shoot at mid-day. After breakfast I had to go to the Bursar's office to be measured for a special overall for next week's Christmas Village Show. Mrs Flynn was there and she had a long tape measure. She looked at my working trousers and gave me a pair of new ones. She then went out to the stores and came back with my overall. It's a sort of long brown coat which reaches down to my knees.

'It's called a parading overall, you must make sure that you give it back afterwards, oh, and good luck with your pig at the show.'

She told me that Mr Flynn and Donald had been talking last night and that they are going to let me parade one of the new pot-bellied pigs around.

'The show is on the cricket field and there will be lots of people from the village there,' she said.

This afternoon Mr Elliott took me and Edward to Embleton's and we met with Silas who had driven up to the High Street in his new car. Embleton's had some of my favourite lardy cake today, so I was very happy.

Tonight there's a concert in the Main Hall by a silver band from Sandhurst. I wasn't sure what that meant but Lionel told me that they're called that because all of their instruments are made of silver. I had heard of a brass band before, perhaps I should have guessed!

23 November 1930

This morning I walked around looking for Maisie. I remembered what Mr Randall said to me last week so I kept looking over my shoulder. The morning went by and it had started to rain just before dinner time but I still didn't find her. Mr Drake saw me just now and told me that they got twelve pheasants and 22 rabbits during their shoot yesterday.

'We even got a March hare. We don't often see them in the grounds, particularly at this time of year.'

He told me that he was going with Mr Randall and Silas to the canal to catch some ducks this afternoon.

'The canal men don't care about us anymore and they seem to let us do whatever we want, they sometimes join us for a beer and are now good friends. Most of them speak a bit different and we don't always understand them. It's their accents. They're nearly all from up north or come from Ireland,' he said.

I still haven't seen Maisie.

24 November 1930

All the klaxons went off just after breakfast and we could see a tall plume of black smoke in the sky. It looked like it was coming from the bottom field. The attendants rushed us all back in to the wards and Mr Horlock stopped outside with his fire engine. Mr Randall and Silas ran down and jumped on the back and they all rushed off. I was looking out of the window and I saw the hose fall off. They had to stop and wheel it back in again. Mr Horlock was very angry. We could then hear other sirens in the distance. It was more fire engines I think. The smoke was still in the sky at dinner time. When Mr Randall came back this afternoon he told us that there had been a fire at the screening tank and all the oil had gone up in flames.

'We had fire engines over from Camberley, Guildford and Woking trying to put it out.'

He wasn't sure what had caused it, but there had been a tanker delivering new crude oil about twenty minutes before so they are blaming the driver.

'Perhaps he was smoking near the tank?'

There are now fears that the asylum could run out of fuel and he told me that the Visiting Committee has already called for an emergency meeting with the Medical Superintendent. The constabulary have all gone off to try and find the man they think caused it.

'He'll be in for the high jump,' Mr Randall said.

26 November 1930

On the way back from the farm this morning I saw Maisie. At first she looked at me a bit strangely. We both quickly looked around to see if it was safe to talk and make sure that no-one important was watching. She told me that Miss Maunders had kept her in the ward all day on Sunday and wouldn't let her out. 'It's because the Medical Superintendent and his wife saw us talking together in the woods last Sunday,' she said.

I told her that Mr Randall had spoken to me about it but it seems that Miss Maunders has treated Maisie more harshly.

'She's been very mean and saying nasty things to me and she called me a whore.'

I felt anger and went to touch Maisie but she flinched and pulled away. She suddenly burst into tears and ran off. Now I worry!

27 November 1930

When I was getting up this morning I remembered that today is Mother's birthday. I sat on the end of the bed for a little while and thought about her. I can't even remember how old she is. Lots of childhood memories flashed by in my head and I remembered a time when she got chased down the road by a donkey. It tried to buck her up the bottom. That day was very funny. I think Lionel must have wondered what I was smiling about. Just then Nurse Applejack came into the ward so I couldn't sit there thinking about it all anymore.

After dinner we had a dress rehearsal on the cricket field for Saturday's show. It seemed really strange walking around a field with a pig on a leather strap. Mr Flynn told me that on Saturday there will be ropes up and I must keep the pig inside the arena. Mrs Flynn came out to watch and clapped as I walked past.

'I'm the crowd today but on Saturday there will be hundreds of people here,' she shouted.

Donald told me that it's a lot like the summer show but that there's more Christmas things including a Father Christmas for the children.

'There'll be plenty of things to do. We just need the weather to be fine,' he said optimistically.

28 November 1930

Just after dinner I saw Maisie. She was on her way to the bottom field with one of the horses. We were too far away from each other to talk but she smiled, waved and blew me a kiss. I feel much happier now.

Tomorrow, it's the show!

30 November 1930

Yesterday was a good and bad day. It was the Christmas Village Show. The rain held off until near the end and I think that everyone was happy. The pigs' parade was at 2 o'clock. There were lots of people watching and I could see Maisie with some of the other female patients. She was cheering and clapping and spinning around. All her friends were clapping me too. It was a grand affair and I could smell all the chestnuts roasting that some of us had collected for Missy Hope a few weeks ago. When I was nearly at the finish line, there was a big bang which made me jump and I accidently let go of the pig. The bang had frightened it and she ran off into the crowd. Mr Drake and Mr Luscombe had to get her back into the arena. Mrs Flynn ran over to make sure that I was alright. Maisie came over as well. She said that a small boy had burst his balloon on a holly branch that his mother was carrying. It all made me feel quite squidgy and it ruined my day. Mrs Flynn said that I had looked very confident and I agreed that I had felt quite proud but now I feel down and melancholy. The moment the pig ran off embarrassed me. Later, Mr Randall came over and told me not to worry.

'Shit happens to the best of us sometimes,' he said.

Today I've been looking for Maisie and I fear that Miss Maunders has stopped her from leaving the ward again. It will soon be Christmas and I need to ask Maisie if she's been able to avoid going to stay with her uncle. I know her father will be there too but I think that she's still very worried about what might happen. After everything that she's told me I do hope that her cousin has replied and will allow Maisie to stay.

2 December 1930

Just before light this morning something jumped on my bed and then jumped off again. I sat up very quickly and could see the outline of something running across the floor. Nurse Primrose turned her lantern up and I could see that it was a big tabby cat. It had somehow got into the ward and had brought a mouse in. Just before breakfast Mr Randall came in and he saw it.

'What are you doing in here old boy?' he asked.

He recognised it as the cat from the Nag's Head Inn.

'They must have left him behind when they moved out, there's been new people there for about a week and I suppose that he doesn't want to be there with them, that doesn't explain what he's doing right over here though.'

Mr Randall took the cat and told us that he would get one of the porters to take him back.

'He belongs over there, he'll just have to get used to the new folk,' he said.

On the way to the farm, I saw Maisie. She was very happy. She has received a letter from her cousin and she will be staying with her in a little village called Wrecclesham at Christmas instead of going to her father's house in Tilford Green.

'It's only for a few days but at least I won't have to see Uncle Sylvester now although I would have liked to have spent some time with my father,' she said.

I told her that I hoped to see her a few more times before Christmas. I also remembered that it's her birthday on 17th December. I must try to buy her a gift but what?

3 December 1930

It was very busy at the farm today. More poultry arrived and I noticed there was some mallard ducks running around with the chickens. Donald told me that their wings have been clipped and that

Mr Drake and Mr Elliott had brought them back from the canal on the day of the shoot. He also told me that Mrs Woolston won't be having a peacock for her Christmas dinner this year. Her husband's already been round and ordered a large turkey instead.

'I think that she's far too embarrassed to ask for much this time because she got caught stealing those things from the Recreation Hall in the summer,' he said.

I remembered that last year it was very busy in the scullery and Sarah and Missy Hope struggled to kill all the chickens.

'Don't worry. You and my good self are helping them to wring their necks this year,' Donald added.

I don't think I'm looking forward to that!

4 December 1930

Everyone seems very excited that Christmas is just three weeks away. Edward is the only one in our ward who is going home to spend it with his family although Stanley told me that he's going out on Christmas Day to have dinner at his sister's house in Bisley but he will be back in time for tea.

On Saturday Albert is taking us on a shopping trip to Woking in his bus. That will be my chance to buy Maisie something for her birthday. Nurse Primrose suggested that I could buy Maisie some perfume from a big shop called Robinson's.

'If you don't buy anything for Maisie, you can always buy something for me,' she said. I think she was joking.

Nurse Primrose told me that Nurse Applejack is going away for Christmas for about four days and that Nurse Montague will be coming back on our ward to cover her day time duties. I think I remember her being our night nurse for a little while some months ago.

'It should be very nice for all of us this Christmas, so long as everyone behaves themselves and no-one dies,' she said.

I hope no-one dies either!

5 December 1930

Lionel was very ill during the night and was sick quite a few times. He was taken away by the porters but brought back again just after breakfast. The doctor has told him that he may have an allergic reaction to rats and has been told to stop catching them once and for all. Lionel is very upset. He's quite weak which is why he can't do much work but I know that he enjoyed catching the rodents and was very capable. I could see a tear in his eye when I spoke to him earlier.

At the farm we spent the whole morning hosing down the pigs. The water supply kept going off and it caused lots of problems. Mr Flynn started to lose his temper. I'd never seen him do that before! Donald told me to keep my distance.

'When he flies, he flies!' he said.

I was expecting him to take off but he didn't have any wings. I told Donald what I was thinking and he told me to shut up.

'You're getting too bloody cocky lately,' he said and then laughed.

He then told me that Mr and Mrs Flynn had their first big argument while they were in bed last night.

'It went on for hours and I never got any bloody sleep,' he said.

6 December 1930

There was a thin layer of snow on the ground this morning and I was worried that Albert was not going to be able to come in his bus and take us shopping in Woking. When the sun came out the snow thawed away quite quickly. Albert picked us up at 11 o'clock and everyone from our ward except Lionel came. The town was very busy and everyone was pushing and shoving. Mr Elliott told me that when you get into town at this time of year, people can be quite rude and nasty.

'Their Christmas spirit disappears and they become quite selfish,' he said.

I took the five pounds that Mr George O' Leary had left for me and looked for a gift for Maisie. I thought about what Nurse

Primrose had said about buying perfume or scent but I found a little china ornament. It was of a horse with an angel standing beside it. It reminded me of Maisie straight away. I had 1/6d left after that and bought myself some buns and sweets from a bakery near the railway station. When Albert came to take us back we had to wait in the bus while Mr Elliott went looking for Edward. He had got lost for a while and was found crying underneath the railway arch. He had lost all his money and looked very upset and afraid. Stanley put his arm around him to try and cheer him up. He hadn't bought any presents. Mr Elliott said that he would make an arrangement to take Edward into Woking again on Monday.

'I'll get Mr Greenwood to take us in his car,' he said.

I think Edward liked that because he began to smile.

Tonight there's a carol concert in the chapel. Children from the Knaphill School are coming to sing for us. The Bisley Ladies Choir will be there too. Mr Elliott told me that Mrs Skilton is coming with all the ladies from the laundry and some other friends. I haven't seen her for a long time so I'm looking forward to seeing her again. I like Mrs Skilton.

7 December 1930

This morning was very awkward. There was no service in the chapel because of the carol concert last night. The church service is being held this afternoon instead and is being taken by a vicar from Knaphill because Parson Jaggs has gone to London. When I came out for my walk, Nurse Applejack followed me and called me back.

'I thought I'd join you for a brisk walk in the winter air,' she said.

My legs went like jelly and I didn't want to walk anywhere at all. I wondered what she was going to say. She asked me about Christmas and what I thought about it. I stayed silent for as long as I could and then said that I thought it was all about 'goodwill to all men.'

Nurse Applejack glared at me and said 'Isn't that something that Jesus has taught us?'

I felt trapped but agreed that it was.

'So you do believe!' she said.

She made me feel very uncomfortable and it felt like she was trying to get me to say something that was wrong. She put her hand on my shoulder and asked me to make a promise.

'What promise?' I asked.

'Promise me that you will reconsider God and what you think about Jesus, learn to believe in God the Father, the Son and the Holy Ghost, I know you do really!' she replied.

She smiled and then turned and walked back to the ward. It was rare to see her smile but I think that it was just a false smile to make me feel at ease with what she was saying. I didn't feel at ease at all.

I had hoped to see Maisie today and now I think that Miss Maunders hasn't let her out again because it's Sunday.

After dinner Mr Elliott and Silas took us to the Nag's Head Inn. Edward and Stanley came. It was all different and very quiet. There was an old lady pulling the beers who wasn't very friendly and the piano had gone. It was very cold and Mr Elliott bought us some hot mulled cider. It reminded me a bit of cinnamon.

10 December 1930

Today I found out the address for Mr George O'Leary. It's a butcher's shop in Frimley Green. I want to thank him got the five pounds he left me and I'm still curious as to why. I remember what Mother had said about him when she came to visit me but I still wonder why he's interested in me and why he came to visit in February last. I wasn't sure what to write. Should it be a long letter? Should I ask lots of questions? In the end I decided to write a short letter:

Dear Mr O'Leary,

I do hope you are keeping well. I am writing to thank you for the five pounds that you left for me on 21st November 1930 last. I'm not sure why you left it but I appreciate it very much because I had no other money in my pocket money allowance.

I have only spent £1.00 and that was on Saturday when we went on the bus to Woking for our Christmas shopping trip.

Since you came to visit me I have seen Mother, it was just once. When she left, I felt very confused about everything. My cousin Clifford told me that he knows you but hasn't really told me much more than that.

I do hope you can visit me again one day so that I can thank you sir for the five pounds in person.

Yours truly

Tommy

If he does come to visit me, I must find the courage to ask him if he is indeed my father, or at least ask him if he knows who my father is. He seemed quite a fine gentleman and I think he might tell me the truth. I do hope so. I need to know the truth!

12 December 1930

Nurse Primrose told me that some of the other staff members have gone sick. There's a nasty epidemic of influenza. Some of the porters are helping with the attendant's duties and the Medical Superintendent is asking for help. He's hoping to bring in some nurses from other hospitals and asylums.

'He is very concerned and so am I. I don't want to catch the blessed thing and it can kill sometimes,' she said.

I asked her if Nurse Applejack had caught it but just then Nurse Applejack appeared.

'No Tommy, I haven't!' she shouted.

Nurse Primrose smiled and whispered...'Bad timing, Tommy, bad timing.'

Now I feel like I'm in trouble again.

It was very sunny today and on the way back from the farm I went for a walk down to the bottom field. Maisie was there with her favourite horse, it's a Percheron called Sorrell. She told me that she is looking forward to Christmas now that she will be staying with her cousin. Her cousin's husband is coming to collect her at dinner time on the day before Christmas Day and she'll be back on the 29th

December. She asked me what I would be doing and I said that I would come out into the grounds and just think of her. She grabbed my hand and pulled me close.

'Thank you Tommy, I will be thinking of you too,' she whispered.

We both looked around behind us, there was no-one about and so we kissed. It was a long and warm kiss and I pulled her closer. I could feel her heart beating against my chest. We stopped and looked around again. I ran my fingers through her long red hair and we just stared into each other's eyes. Her green eyes are so beautiful. We kissed again, this time for even longer. Maisie gently pushed me back.

'Go, Tommy, go, we must not chance our luck, I love you Tommy!' she said.

I told her that I loved her too and then slowly walked away. I kept turning back and looking over my shoulder. Just before I lost sight, I watched Maisie in the distance with Sorrell; she was stroking its mane. She saw me watching and she waved. I blew her a kiss and then walked until I could see her no more. Its days like this that make me realise that I am in love. Days like this which make me realise how important Maisie is to me. Days like this that make me realise that we should both be free of this place.

14 December 1930

Yesterday we had a treat none of us were expecting. Albert came in his bus just after dinner. Mr Randall and Mr Elliott told us all to dress up warm and told us that Albert was taking us to the circus. I'd never been to a circus before so I suddenly felt very excited. Albert had already made one trip because he had taken some female patients over and they were waiting for us so I guessed that the circus couldn't be too far away. As we got on the bus Albert told us that we were going to Pirbright. The circus was on the green by a pond. When we arrived there was also a fair and we split into little groups of four, there were sixteen of us altogether. I was with Lionel, Stanley and Edward who are all my friends so I was very happy. Mr Randall was watching over us and another group while Mr Elliott helped as well with the other eight. I could see the female patients but Maisie wasn't with them. I felt disappointed but then I noticed that none of them were from her ward. Perhaps they may come on another day. Mr Randall said that the circus is here all week until next Sunday. Outside the Big Top I could see some elephants, they were very big and a man was making them stand up on their hind legs. It was all very exciting because I had never seen elephants before. There were some clowns and midgets. One of them reminded me of Emile, The Dwarf, because his skin was brown and he ran around in circles just like Emile used to do. When the circus performance started we were sat in the second row. We saw horses being charged around, then gymnasts, then fire-eaters and then the elephants came in. There was an intermission, a lady with lots of tattoos on her arms came round selling ice-cream and Mr Randall bought us all one each with his own money. It was very odd eating ice-cream in the middle of winter but no-one seemed to mind. When the circus started again the clowns came out, they were shouting and falling over. One of them was juggling balls and another ran over to us and pulled faces. There was a lot of music and then some tigers came out from nowhere. The man in the middle was guiding them around the ring with a stick and then made them all get up on a big wooden stand. They growled and it felt very dangerous but the man was just laughing and shouting at them all the time.

Lionel said... 'I think he knows what he's doing.' I wasn't that sure!

When we came out of the Big Top we went into a thing called a marquee. There was a painted lady in a big glass box and she was covered in snakes. Lots of other things were going on but people were in the way so I couldn't see everything. We got back to asylum too late for tea so Mr Randall and Mr Elliott had to arrange for some sandwiches and hot drinks. We were all shivering from the cold but very excited about where we had just been.

I have looked around for Maisie all day today. There's been no sign of her so I think that she's been stopped from coming out again. I want to make a plan so that I can make sure that I see her on Wednesday and give her the ornament which I wrapped up this morning.

215

15 December 1930

It's been very busy again on the farm today and I've had to help with the chickens. Some foxes tried to get in last night but an attendant from the mortuary came up and chased them off. He then ran over to alert Mr Flynn. Mr Flynn is very tired as he's been out checking all the fences all morning to make sure the foxes can't get in.

'It would not be very good if we lost all the chickens just before Christmas,' he said.

Later I went back to feed and swill the pigs. One of them tried to bite me as I stroked his head and then he just rolled over, he looked like he was laughing at me.

Donald came over and I said... 'Look at him, look at him!'

He asked me how I knew it was a boy. I was just about to tell him when I noticed him smiling. He was joking with me again.

'Of course I know how to tell the difference,' I said.

This evening Parson Jaggs is coming to say Christmas prayers in the ward. He's bringing some carol singers. I don't remember him doing that last year.

16 December 1930

Donald and I spent most of the morning looking up at the sky. It was very grey and we were trying to decide whether it would snow or not. Donald thinks that it's too warm. Mr Flynn came over and asked us what we were looking at. 'We're talking about snow,' Donald said.

Mr Flynn has always told us that he's an expert when it comes to the weather.

'No, it won't snow yet, it's too warm, in a day or two it might, maybe just in time for Christmas, just to make every where look nice for the season. It just needs the temperature to drop a little bit more,' he said.

On the way back to the ward I looked out for Maisie but I didn't see her. I have been carrying her present around and have been trying to keep it safe, it's made of china and is quite fragile, I don't want to break it. I hope I can see her tomorrow otherwise it will be too late and it won't be the same if I give it to her belatedly.

17 December 1930

Last night I couldn't sleep. There was a lot of noise in the ward and Lionel was being sick again. I sat up and just looked at a beam from the lamplight outside that was shining through a gap in the curtains. Nurse Primrose came over and brought me a cup of Ovaltine. She asked me if I enjoyed the circus on Saturday. I said I did. She told me that she's going there with some of the other nurses and some friends on Friday. When she went back to her desk I laid back down on my side and thought of Maisie. I always see her in the field with one of the horses when I think or dream of her.

At about 2 o'clock I began to hear screams and shouts coming from outside. I think the noise was coming from the female block. I peered out of the window and it looked like all their lights had come on. Suddenly the klaxon went off and all our lights came on. Now everyone was awake. After about 20 minutes everything died down again but no-one wanted to go back to sleep. The porters came in and tried to help Nurse Primrose get some of the men down the other end of the dormitory to calm down. No-one really knew what was happening. No-one was saying anything.

I haven't seen Maisie yet. There's still time but it will be dark soon. I've decided to hide her ornament inside the tree with my tin until I see her again.

Happy Birthday Maisie!

20 December 1930

It's now Saturday. There's been thick snow on the ground since Wednesday when it first fell. I've been able to go out and help at the farm with the pigs and chickens for a little while each day but that is all, they have to be fed and cleaned out no matter what the weather is like. Today was the first day since the snow came that Mr Flynn was able to bring the cows up for milking. It took four other farmhands to help him because the snow is still quite deep in places.

The grounds are very white and everything is very peaceful. I haven't seen Maisie but no-one has really been able to go out over the last few days and it's been very cold. Mr Randall is trying to get us some gloves and tomorrow he's going to help us make a sledge.

'We'll have lots of fun tomorrow,' he said.

21 December 1930

Last night Nurse Primrose took me to the side room.

'I need to tell you something very important but you must promise me that you won't tell anyone about what I'm about to say,' she said.

I wondered what she was going to tell me and then she grabbed my hand. I felt my heart sink and I began to feel very cold. She told he that there had been an incident in the female ward on Wednesday night. Maisie was taken to the infirmary. She's been placed into an induced coma and is very poorly.

'The incident involved a patient called Angela Reeves who has now been placed in isolation in the refractory. It also involved the attendant Miss Maunders, she's been suspended from duty and will probably be dismissed or transferred, I know nothing more than that, so please don't ask me what has happened,' she added.

My mouth felt dry. I wanted to speak but I couldn't get the words out. I eventually managed to ask Nurse Primrose what an induced coma was.

'Your Maisie's been put to sleep to aid her recovery. Remember to keep this to yourself. The Medical Superintendent will have my guts for garters if he ever finds out that I've told you this.'

Now I worry about Maisie. I know that she's been scared of those two for a long time and I remember her telling me about what they had done to the nymphomaniac lady, Isabella.

When the time came for me to go with the others to make the sledge I couldn't. I told them that I felt a bit ill. In a way I do. My stomach hurts and my heart is really aching. I can only think of Maisie and I'm trying to piece together in my mind what could have really happened.

22 December 1930

Today I haven't been able to think properly. My mind is full of all the wrong pictures. I don't like what I see. I told Donald what has happened to Maisie. In fact, I don't know what's happened, all I know is that she's in the infirmary. I'm trying to find out more but I don't know who to ask. Donald suggested that I should talk to Nurse Primrose again tonight.

'All the nurses talk to each other and she should be able to get some news for you.' he suggested.

I couldn't concentrate very well today but Donald helped. He tried to reassure me that Maisie would be alright and told me that if he can find out anything more then he would let me know.

23 December 1930

Last night I spoke to Nurse Primrose. She told me that Maisie is still in an induced coma and that the doctors hope to bring her out of it tomorrow.

'She was very hysterical when she was taken in and had a bad injury to her stomach,' she said.

Nurse Primrose told me that she had heard that Maisie's father and uncle came to visit yesterday but were sent away without seeing her because she was still asleep.

'The Medical Superintendent would have given them a full report.'

I asked her if she knew exactly why and how the incident happened but she told me that all she has heard is rumours, although Katherine one of the other patients witnessed everything.

'I'm not sure how reliable her account is, so I can't be sure about anything yet,' she said.

24 December 1930

Tomorrow is Christmas day. This morning I have been helping Sarah and Missy Hope kill some more chickens ready for the Christmas dinner. Donald joined in while Mr Luscombe and Mr

Flynn did the turkeys. There was blood and guts and feathers everywhere and the floor was very slippery. Donald told me not to look in the chickens eyes when I'm about to wring their necks.

'You won't get so much of a bad conscious about what you're doing to them,' he said.

I hate killing animals but I don't want people to think that I'm a coward. I love working on the farm and when I get out of here that's what I want to do for a job so I have to look brave. One of the other farmhands walked into the scullery with a sack of sprouts and it split and the sprouts went all over the floor. Mr Flynn went mad and whacked him around the back of the head.

'There's enough mess in here already without you adding to it you stupid boy,' he shouted.

Donald and I just looked at each other, grinned and then carried on with what we were doing.

Nurse Applejack has gone on leave for Christmas today and Nurse Montague will be our day nurse until Sunday. Tonight I must ask Nurse Primrose if she has anymore news about Maisie.

25 December 1930

It's Thursday 25th December, Christmas Day. This morning nearly everybody went to the chapel. I walked over that way because Nurse Applejack wasn't around to bully me. Whilst everyone was inside I walked around outside and listened to them all singing carols. I could hear Parson Jaggs shouting and I could hear the choir boys from the village singing *Once in Royal David's City* and it reminded me of last year. I remember it as one of the songs that Mrs Evenden had given Edward, Linda and me to learn as part of our speech therapy. Both Linda and Mrs Evenden are dead now. The thought of them being dead made me go cold and then I thought about all the others who had died since last Christmas. In my own way I said a little prayer for all of them and I could feel them out there walking with me. I felt goose pimples all over but rather strangely it was all very quite comforting.

At dinner time some people from the village came with lots of gifts; I remember getting a fountain pen last year. This year when I opened my present it was a hairbrush. Mr Randall laughed and asked if he could borrow it.

'It's some weeks before Mr Cohen is due to come and cut our hair again,' he said.

After dinner Nurse Montague came over to me.

'Let's go outside,' she whispered.

She told me that she knew Maisie very well and had been her day nurse in her ward for the last few months. She told me that she knew there had been lots of problems with Angela Reeves.

'Most of it happened at night time when I wasn't there but nearly always, Attendant Maunders was involved as well.'

After she finished speaking, Nurse Montague took my hand and said that she had a little treat for me.

'A special Christmas treat but you must not tell anyone, not a soul,' she said.

She led me through the grounds until we got to the infirmary. There's a male ward and a female ward in there. There were a lot of visitors and most of the patients were sitting up and talking and drinking tea. Miss Montague took me to a side room in the female ward. Maisie was laying there but she was fast asleep. Miss Montague told me that I had two minutes to wish her a very Happy Christmas. It was difficult because I knew that she wasn't having a very nice Christmas and she was a still asleep. Nurse Montague walked away for a moment and I held Maisie's hand.

I whispered 'Merry Christmas, I love you Maisie, please get better soon.' Maisie gave my hand a slight squeeze and I could see a faint smile around her lips. I'm sure that she heard me.

On the way back to the ward Nurse Montague told me that Maisie had been given lots of medicines to keep her drowsy for her own good.

'She should be back to normal in a week or two but she's been through a lot of trauma, it will all take time.'

I asked her if I could speak to Katherine, Maisie's friend to find out what had really happened.

'No, you have been told too much already, I shouldn't have even taken you to the infirmary but its Christmas, it's just that Nurse Primrose and myself think that your relationship with Maisie is very sweet. It should be forbidden, but we always turn a blind eye when there's true love about,' she said.

I liked that.

26 December 1930

Today has been very cold but Donald persuaded me to play football for the farmhands against Mr Drake's team of ground-keepers and woodmen. I was the only patient in the team! We only played thirty minutes each way instead of the normal forty-five. Mr Flynn is very good at football and scored two goals. Donald scored one as well but we let in seven and lost 7-3. Lots of other patients and staff were watching. Afterwards there was another match between the doctors and the attendants which the doctors won 9-0. Donald thinks that the attendants were all too drunk to play properly which is why they lost. I think he's right.

Nurse Primrose said that she would try and give me some more news about Maisie when she comes on duty this evening. It was very nice of Nurse Montague to take me to see her yesterday. I hope that she doesn't get into any trouble. I hope that Maisie gets better soon. It's such a shame that she missed staying with her cousin for Christmas, I know that she was looking forward to being with her.

28 December 1930

Today I had a surprise visit from Cousin Clifford and Gloria. It was too cold for them to bring the baby so they left her at home with Aunt Betty. Clifford gave me a big hug and at last I was able to say 'sorry' to Gloria properly for what I had said to her about Amanda Louise.

'It's all water under the bridge and I was far too over-sensitive with my reaction. Having just had a baby leaves you quite raw,' she said.

Clifford told me that Mother is well and wanted to come over to see me but she has a very bad headache.

'She had too many glasses of sherry over Christmas and her head still isn't right.'

I had forgotten that Mother liked drinking sherry so much. It was always her favourite Christmas tipple.

I asked Clifford if he knew if anything was happening about getting me out of here. He told me that Miss Rance had informed him that Mrs Jenkins was coming back to see me in February.

'The good news is that there's a proper job waiting for you here on the farm if everything else goes well. The Medical Superintendent and Mr Luscombe have been talking. It all depends on how things go with your treatment and I've been told that they need to be sure that you don't have any more relapses regarding your mania or so-called delusions. The big problem they'll have is finding somewhere for you to live but I do know that they've been talking to a lady called Mrs Skilton. Do you know of her?' he asked.

I told him that I knew her from when I helped in the laundry.

'She helped me a lot with my speech and we sang lots of songs together when we were working. It was only when they decided that they only wanted female patients to help in the laundry it stopped,' I said.

Clifford told me that he was going to speak to Miss Rance again before he left today and that he would try and let me know if there was any more news.

After they left I felt that at last I have some hope. If Mrs Skilton does agree to accommodate me then she is being very kind. I'm now wondering what will happen to me next.

30 December 1930

The last couple of days have been full of hope but now a dark shroud has come over me and I feel quite melancholy. I think that it's all to do with the realisation of different things. Maisie is still very poorly and I'm still thinking about the conversation I had with Cousin Clifford. Everything seems very hard and I don't know what to do. I have some good friends, Donald, Lionel, Stanley and Edward but apart from Donald they all have their own problems. Maisie is the only person I can talk with properly but I can't because she's still asleep in the infirmary. I don't want to feel like this. I don't like it when my head is down and I know that Nurse Applejack will make more of it and tell more lies to Miss Rance and the Medical Superintendent about me if she sees me like this. I'm trying to leave God out of my thoughts because I need a real person to talk to, someone who actually exists. Someone to guide me, help me - but who can I trust?

31 December 1930

Tomorrow it's going to be 1931. Last night Nurse Primrose told me that Maisie is sitting up in bed and taking her food properly now. That is the news I hoped for and I feel a little better now. I still have the ornament I bought Maisie for her birthday but two weeks have already passed by and now Christmas has been and gone as well.

On the way back from the farm I saw Mr Mycroft. He'd been down to Cornwall for Christmas. I saw him reaching for something in his inside pocket. When he pulled it out, I could see that it was a newspaper cutting.

'Read that young Tommy,' he said.

It was about one of Maisie's paintings and it had been sold at a very high price to a gentleman from a town called Polperro in Cornwall. When I read down a bit further it said that the painting was entitled *Angels descending.* I remembered that the painting Maisie had given to Mrs Woolston was called that and so I told Mr Mycroft.

'Are you sure?' he asked.

I told him that Maisie had been advised to stop painting for awhile because of what was happening with her uncle. She had only painted one picture called *Angels descending.* I told him that I saw Maisie with it on the day just before she gave it to Mrs Woolston. Again, Mr Mycroft asked me if I was sure.

'Yes, yes,' I replied.

I felt quite excited and annoyed at the same time.

'Maisie's uncle must have got in contact with Mrs Woolston somehow to get the painting from her,' I said with a sigh.

'Well if he has, he's sold it on for a very big profit. You could almost buy a house with that money.'

Mr Mycroft took the cutting back and said that he would show it to the Medical Superintendent.

'There's some real mischief going on around here and the Medical Superintendent needs to be told, especially if Mrs Woolston is involved.'

I now wonder how Maisie's uncle knew how to get hold of the painting. Someone must have told him where Mrs Woolston lives. He must have gone there and offered her a price.

Tonight there's going to be a ball and dance in the Main Hall. I don't really want to go. It doesn't seem appropriate for me to celebrate a new year when I already know that it's going to be a bad year. Lionel told me to keep my chin up but it's difficult, very difficult.

2 January 1931

Yesterday morning I helped at the farm and then had the rest of the day free. It was raining very hard so I stayed in the ward. Mr Mycroft had given me a book about the Wild West and the native Indians. I really enjoyed the story of the Battle of Little Bighorn and the fight between General Custer's 7th Cavalry and the Cheyenne. Lionel told me that he had read the book when he was a child and asked to borrow it when I had finished.

Last night Nurse Primrose told me that Maisie should be well enough to go back to her ward on Sunday.

'I've heard that she's sitting up and talking but is still very frail.'

I asked her about Angela Reeves and the attendant Miss Maunders. She told me that Miss Maunders had been reported to the constabulary for her misconduct and has been dismissed. Angela is being assessed in the refractory ward.

'As she's done this sort of thing before and caused harm to other patients, I doubt very much if she'll go back to Maisie's ward,' she said.

'Good.' I thought!

4 January 1931

This morning I was walking around the edge of the woods. Someone called out my name. It was a female voice.

'Tommy, Thomas. Tommy.'

I could hear my name being called quite clearly. Eventually a female patient appeared in front of me. I sort of recognised her, but didn't. She had short black hair, big blue eyes and was very thin.

'Hello Tommy, I'm Katherine. Maisie is my friend.'

I then recognised her from a time when I was helping at the farm. She was walking past with Maisie and a nurse, it was quite a long time ago and I think that her hair must have been much longer then. She asked me if I knew what had happened to Maisie on the night before her birthday. I told her that Nurse Primrose had confided little bits but she wasn't allowed to say too much because she was worried that she might get into trouble for telling me things. 'She took me to see Maisie in the infirmary for about five minutes on Christmas Day; she shouldn't have even done that. It was very quiet and not very many staff members were about so I don't think anyone really noticed me,' I said.

Katherine then told me that she had been attacked by Angela Reeves and Miss Maunders herself some months ago.

'They tortured me, tried to pull my fingernails out and they cut off all my hair. I was very poorly and had to go to another part of the asylum to convalesce for a while. On another night they attacked another girl called Isabella too. The poor girl has suffered very badly and will probably never recover from it.'

Katherine then told me that they started picking on her again on the night Maisie was attacked. Maisie tried to intervene but then was attacked herself. 'They pushed her into the side room and started pulling her hair. Miss Maunders held Maisie down very tight and kept her hand over her mouth to stop her from screaming. Angela then ripped Maisie's night dress right open and then started interfering with her private parts. "Where's the baby? Where's the baby?" Angela kept shouting. She then forced her hand right up inside Maisie; she was almost punching her inside. "Where's the baby? Where's the baby?" Angela was being exceedingly vicious and had a very mad look in her eyes. Maisie was trying to scream but no noise was coming out because of the pressure Miss Maunders was putting on her. It all went on for about half an hour.'

I asked her how it finally stopped.

'Miss Montague who is normally very quiet and acts like a little door mouse heard the commotion and called two male night attendants over. She couldn't call for help anywhere else because Miss Maunders was the night attendant on duty. When they pulled the two of them off, Maisie was hysterical, there was blood all down her night dress and on the floor.'

Katherine told me that a doctor came and sedated Maisie and then he and a porter rushed her over to the infirmary.

'The doctors then put her into a coma mainly to stop her from harming herself.'

I asked Katherine why she thought Angela was shouting 'Where's the baby?'

'I know that Miss Maunders had access to Maisie's case notes and had read that she had been raped by a person unknown and had lost a baby during childbirth. Angela is obsessed with new born babies and pregnancy and has always wanted her own but for some reason she can't have them.'

I remember that when I first saw Angela she was pushing an empty pram around the airing courts. Someone told me once that she had tried to steal some babies from their prams near London and that was why she was sent here.

Katherine put her hand on my shoulder and asked me if I was alright.

'I felt I had to tell you this, you need to know exactly what Maisie's been through. I know you love her,' she said quite calmly.

I thought that it was best not to tell Katherine that it was Maisie's uncle who had raped her. I asked her to pass my love back to Maisie and thanked her for telling me everything. The news was very upsetting but it's best that I know what's really happened.

5 January 1931

Mr Elliott came into the ward this morning just after we got back from breakfast and told us that he is leaving his post of attendant at the end of next week.

'I'm going back to sea,' he said.

I remembered someone telling me once that he used to work on the ships. This time he's got a steward's job. Mr Randall joked that he'd have to look a lot smarter when he joins his ship than he does now.

'A shave might help,' he said. We all laughed.

Mr Elliott is bald but he has a long black beard, he's very friendly and I think that we shall all miss him very much. Another attendant was with them who was wearing an eye patch.

'That's Attendant Arthur Dyke, he's the one Nobby Hatch stabbed in the eye, they've let him come back now but he's not allowed to work in the refractory or isolation wards,' Lionel whispered.

He said that Mr Randall was telling him all about it on the way down to breakfast earlier.

'Apparently Dyke is a lazy old so and so who is also known for liking a tipple, he's quite good at upsetting people which is probably what he did to Nobby and that may be why the Medical Superintendent doesn't want him working on his own anymore.'

Nurse Montague will be back working in Maisie's ward from tomorrow and has promised that she will give her the ornament that I bought for her birthday. It seems so long ago since I last saw her now.

8 January 1931

There was some commotion coming from the ablutions block at one of the other wards this morning. We saw two porters and a doctor taking The Tall Man out on a trolley. They were rushing him off to the infirmary. Mr Randall and Mr Elliott ran over to help. Later I found out that The Tall Man had slipped into a bath of scalding water. The attendant who was looking after him had been distracted by another patient. The Medical Superintendent called all the attendants over for a special meeting and the porters had to watch over us in the ward with the doctors and nurses until they all came back. Mr Randall later told us that they had all been told to do their jobs properly or they would be dismissed. The Tall Man is in a very serious condition and they don't expect him to make it through the

228

night. They think that he might have also tried to grab an electric light bulb when he slipped.

'All the lights went out and it was hard for anyone to see what had really happened. Only The Tall Man would have been able to reach the bulb because of the high ceilings. It's possible that he received an electric shock or was electrocuted as well,' Mr Randall said.

I asked him who was supposed to be looking after The Tall Man.

'Mr Dyke, he's an idiot,' he confided.

Mr Elliott then joined in the conversation and said that he thinks Mr Dyke is leading a charmed life.

'Maybe he won't be my replacement after all,' he said.

This afternoon I've been watching a deer walking around the woods. It keeps reaching up into the branches in the same tree looking for food. I'm not sure what kind of food deer eat but there must have been something there that it was interested in. It was there for about half an hour before I accidentally startled it which made it run off. I didn't know that deer could run so fast. Just after that Mr Drake came by with one of the woodman. He told me that they were marking some more trees for 'the chop.'

'Some of them are petrified and the asylum can do with some more logs to get us through the winter.'

I asked him what he meant by 'petrified.' He told me that it's just a nickname they have for diseased or dying trees. A real petrified wood is all fossilised.

'I don't think that there's anything like that in this country, it's just that some of our trees are a bit peculiar!'

He told me that they were looking at all the trees which had twisted trunks and odd branches.

'They need to be cut down or cut back, they're ugly bastards,' he joked.

It reminded of the time when I was up here and it was getting dark and some of the trees frightened me because I thought they had started growing faces and were whispering at me. It was just the fading light and the wind that had disturbed my imagination. Maisie says I have a vivid imagination!

9 January 1931

The Tall Man is still alive but he has had to have his legs amputated. Mr Randall told me that having his legs cut off is the only chance for him to survive. The doctors are trying very hard to save him but are they not holding out much hope.

Nurse Montague came and saw me this morning just before I went to help at the farm. She told me that Maisie went back to her own ward yesterday. She's very drowsy and still needs her body massaged.

'She's been laid on her back for three weeks and her muscles need to start working again. I must warn you though; she hasn't spoken to anyone at all yet, she's still very traumatised by what happened to her.'

I asked Nurse Montague if Maisie liked the ornament.

'Yes of course she did, she smiled when I gave it to her and then smiled even more when she realised that is was you who had bought it for her,' she said.

I felt glad and relieved. Now I just want Maisie to get better so that I can see her again.

12 January 1931

There's been snow all over the weekend and it's been very cold. Mr Drake told me that the temperature had gone down below freezing. I asked him how he knew and he told me that there's a new barometer outside on the wall of the female block where the clock tower is. He took me over to see it. Mr Mycroft was walking by and started telling us what the difference is between Centigrade and Fahrenheit.

'We always use Fahrenheit.'

Next to the barometer was a long strand of seaweed.

'Oh, I put that there so that we can tell when it's going to rain, I always bring a bit back with me from Cornwall when I go,' he said.

Mr Drake told me that when the seaweed goes limp it means that it's going to rain or snow. When it goes hard it means that it's going to be dry and the sun might come out. I asked Mr Drake what happens when it's frozen like it is now.

'It's all gone hard so is the sun going to come out?' I asked.

He laughed and then gave me a pretend clip around my ear.

'Don't try and be clever with me Sonny Jim,' he said.

We all laughed. It was the first time I had ever heard Mr Mycroft laugh before. Maybe it's because he didn't have his pipe, it's the first time I've ever seen him without it. Mr Drake told me after he'd gone that smoking was giving the old boy a bit of a bad cough and that he had been having some trouble breathing.

'When he was down in Cornwall his family told him to stop.'

Later I helped Mr Drake clear away the snow from the path outside our ward.

15 January 1931

This morning I awoke and felt all melancholy again and then I thought about what has happened with other people and it reminded me of a conversation I once had with Mrs Skilton in the laundry.

'Life is all about perspectives. You take a long hard look at yourself and then look at other people. Only then will you realise that things are not as bad for you as they may seem,' she had said.

At the time I didn't know what 'perspective' meant but the dictionary that Maisie had given me has helped me with lots of things. So has the advice I took from Mrs Skilton. It has saved me from slipping further into the abyss. Lionel sometimes calls the asylum 'The Abyss', he must think that we're already there!

Mr Randall told us that The Tall Man had a heart attack last night but the doctors managed to save him.

'He is still very ill and it's all very touch and go,' he said.

We then started to ask each other what The Tall Man's real name is but no-one seemed to know including Mr Randall. He said he would try to find out.

'I've never known him to be called anything else,' he admitted.

Lionel joked... 'Well now he's got no legs we can't really call him The Tall Man anymore can we?'

Mr Randall told us all off for laughing and Lionel apologised.

'Sorry. I couldn't help it,' he said rather churlishly.

16 January 1931

Mrs Skilton stopped by the farm gate this morning and leant her bicycle on the fence.

'Tommy, Tommy, come over here and let us both talk for one minute,' she said.

She told me that she had received a letter from the asylum's Visiting Committee. Her name had been put forward by the Medical Superintendent suggesting her as a person who could accommodate a patient who is ready to leave the asylum to live in the community. She asked me about Mother and asked me if Clifford Compton was my brother.

'No, he's my cousin, he and his wife Gloria and their baby live in the same house as my mother and Aunt Betty. There's no room for me there,' I replied.

Mrs Skilton said that she has been asked to meet with Clifford, Miss Rance and a lady called Mrs Jenkins at the end of February.

'The meeting will really depend on you having a successful assessment Tommy.'

I told her that I knew Mrs Jenkins was coming to see me again in February but no-one had given me a date yet. She then asked me how I've been. I told her that there have been days when I have felt melancholy, down and depressed.

'It's because I feel that I shouldn't be here, can't see a way out and there's always a lot of pain and death about, it's depressing.'

She then asked me about Maisie. I was surprised that she knew, I couldn't remember speaking to her about Maisie before. I then told her what had happened and that Maisie was attacked and had been in the infirmary. I still haven't seen her since before her birthday in December. Mrs Skilton said that she would come by and talk to me again.

'I can't promise anything, I do have a room but there are two other patients who also need accommodating but I would like it to be you if I do decide to take someone in.'

I thanked her and she smiled. She put her hand on my shoulder.

'Be good, be strong,' she whispered.

As she was riding off Mr Luscombe came over.

'Young Thomas, do you still want to be a farmhand?' he asked.

'Yes of course!' I replied.

He then reminded me that I have another test on Monday.

'If you're interested in working on a farm after you leave here then this will be an important examination for you. Who knows? You could be working for me quite soon,' he said with a big grin.

He then gave me a little red book. It was all about farm animals, their weights and diets, diseases and how they should be cut at slaughter.

'Learn that over the weekend, just the piggy bits,' he said.

I had been given a test before but this looks much more complicated. Now I hope that I can remember it all. I worry.

18 January 1931

I've been reading the little red book Mr Luscombe gave me. There's lots of things I need to remember but I'm glad that it's just the pigs that I'm being tested on. Donald told me that if I passed the test it would be the first time a patient has been successful. He also told me that he didn't think I would find it hard.

'Trust me,' he advised.

I do trust Donald and I don't want to let him down. He's become a good and faithful friend. The parts about looking after pigs I already know but it's the bits about detecting diseases that I think I really need to learn. The diseases a pig can get are tuberculosis, anthrax, erysipelas, swine fever or plague, cysticerci, trichinae, sacrcosporidia, dropsy and urticaria. I know Mr Luscombe will ask me about those. He's always talking with Mr Flynn and Mr Hampton about diseases. I just hope I can pronounce them right when he asks. I might even have to write them all down on a separate piece of paper. If a pig is diseased is has to be slaughtered separately and its carcass burned. After slaughter a fully grown pig's head normally weighs 5lbs. I have to remember all the cuts like, leg, loin, spring, hand, spare rib. A pig's heart weighs 1lb. I wonder how much a human heart weighs; it must be about the same. There are lots more things to remember. I have read the book through about three times but I still worry that I might forget something.

There's been more snow lying on the ground since last Sunday but it's beginning to thaw now. Today is quite warm after a lot of cold days. I still haven't seen Maisie yet. Nurse Primrose is back on duty tonight. I must ask if there's any more news.

20 January 1931

I passed my pig test yesterday. Mr Luscombe told me that he's going to send a report to the Medical Superintendent and then shook my hand.

'Congratulations young Thomas, this is a good step in the right direction for you, well done!'

I felt very pleased with myself.

Yesterday afternoon I saw Maisie, she was being taken for a walk around the grounds by one of the nurses and an attendant. She looked very thin and pale and her hair looked shorter, I noticed that it was now very straight and all her beautiful curls and ringlets had gone. She didn't look up so she never saw me. Nurse Applejack was nearby so I didn't want to call out. It was a very frustrating moment, I just wanted to run over and give her a big hug but at least I've seen her now. I hope she gets better very soon.

22 January 1931

Mr Mycroft told me this morning that there's been a big problem at the mortuary.

'There's been a mix up with two bodies and they've already buried the wrong one.'

He told me that the family of Nancy Springer had come down from London for her funeral. They visited the mortuary first and asked to view her body. When the attendant unscrewed the coffin lid they discovered the wrong person inside. The body belonged to Amy Tench, a lady who had died of old age.

'Nancy was only twenty-four years old and it's turned out that she's already been buried at Brookwood Cemetery a couple of days ago by mistake. They'll now have to dig her up and bury her again. The family is very upset and heads will roll over this.'

Mr Randall came over and joined in the conversation.

'Yes, heads will roll. This has happened at least once before and within two days the Medical Superintendent and the Head Mortuary Attendant were gone,' he said. 'The Visiting Committee will take a very dim view of this.'

When I got to the farm I mentioned what I had just heard had happened to Donald and Mr Flynn. Mr Flynn told us that nothing surprises him by what happens in the mortuary anymore.

'These things seem to occur all the time. More people die at the asylum during the winter months and it gets very crowded in there. If the family hadn't asked to see the body, on-one would have known.' Donald laughed.

The rest of the day was spent talking about dead bodies.

23 January 1931

Today Mr Flynn let me have a go at driving the tractor. Donald was up on the seat beside me and had to grab the steering wheel a couple of times to stop me from crashing into the fence. Mr Horlock rushed out of his lodge and started shaking his fist at us.

'You pair of irresponsible idiots, imbeciles!' he shouted.

Donald told him to 'Fuck Off!'

He didn't like that and we saw him run over to the Farm Bailiff's house. Mr Luscombe came out and there was a big argument. Donald told me to jump off the tractor and make myself scarce. He then drove off towards the cricket field. Mr Flynn who had been busy milking the cows came out and asked me what had been going on. I told him that Donald had been rude to Mr Horlock.

'He wasn't happy that you had let me drive the tractor. He shouted at us and Donald swore back at him,' I said.

Mr Flynn then went over to speak to Mr Luscombe. Mr Horlock came back out again and then there was another argument. One of the other farmhands took me to one side.

'Let's go over to Rose Cottage and get out of the way. We'll wait for Donald to get back in there,' he said.

Mrs Flynn came in and asked us what was going on. I told her that there was a big argument going on outside. It was then that she told us that she had just seen the new Medical Superintendent arrive.

'Mr Deane has been dismissed and no-one seems to know why,' she said.

I wondered if it had something to do with what had happened at the mortuary the other day. Mrs Flynn didn't know anything about that. Just then Mr Flynn came back in with Donald. He told us that he was going to meet the new Medical Superintendent at his house with Mr Luscombe later this afternoon.

'He's called Dr G.Aitken but we don't know what the 'G' stands for yet,' he said rather nervously.

24 January 1931

Today Albert came and took us to Guildford in his bus. It was our first real outing of the year. Mr Elliott was with us and today will be the last day we will be with him before he goes back to sea.

'I stayed for a few extra days to work my proper notice,' he said.

We stopped outside a beer house. It was very cold. We weren't allowed to go inside but Mr Elliott bought us all some drinks and we stayed on the bus. There was Lionel, Edward, Stanley and three men from another ward who I hadn't seen before. The drink helped wash down our sandwiches and cakes. Albert then drove us to down to the river. We watched some men and boys fishing. There was a man in a canoe, he was talking to us about boats and said that we should all go back in the spring.

'The River Wey will be full of boats around Easter time, there's a pageant every year and you'll really enjoy it here then,' he told us.

Mr Elliott then asked Albert if he could remember it and perhaps take us back to Guildford to see it when it's on. Albert told us that he would see what he could do, although that's not really his decision to make.

'That'll be Mr Randall's prerogative.'

Tomorrow is Sunday. I'm hoping that I can find Maisie and see how she is and have a proper talk. I miss her. It's now been nearly five weeks since she was attacked.

25 January 1931

Whilst everyone was at the chapel I walked around the grounds hoping to see Maisie. It was very cold and the wind was harsh against my face. The trees were bending rather peculiarly and I suddenly realised that I was sat under my tree in a storm. There was no rain but some clouds came over very fast and they got blacker and blacker. I decided to put everything away and run back to the ward. When I came back later after dinner it was calm but some trees were down and Mr Drake and the woodmen were out looking at all the damage. I looked again for Maisie but couldn't find her although I did see her friend Katherine. She told me that Maisie is starting to get better but is still feeling very weak because of the amount of time she had to spend in the infirmary.

'She's having nightmares and has been screaming every night in her sleep. It's all very hard for her to take in and understand what's happened.'

I thanked her for telling me and asked her to tell Maisie that I'm thinking about her and that I can't wait to see her again. Katherine told me that it might take a while.

'She's going to take a long time to heal,' she warned.

I'm now wondering when I actually will see Maisie again.

26 January 1931

When we were getting up this morning Mr Randall came into the ward and told us that The Tall Man had died in his sleep last night.

'He passed away because of his horrendous injuries and the amputations. However, I think that he must be in a much better place now. His life would have been very uncomfortable and the pain considerable had he survived.'

Lionel knelt down by a chair and said a little prayer.

'I wonder if he will meet his Anti-Christ now,' he said.

Just then Nurse Applejack came in and asked Mr Randall what was going on. It was then that we found out that The Tall Man's real name was Elijah Williams.

'He used to be an army chaplain in the war but lost himself unto God and became very confused after suffering shell shock,' Mr Randall said.

After he left Nurse Applejack started banging her copper-stick on the bedsteads and told us to hurry up.

'You're all late for breakfast, get down there now!' she shouted.

I noticed that Edward was not looking very well and that he wasn't paying attention to anything Nurse Applejack was saying. Suddenly she pulled him up from his bed and pushed him through the door and then hit him on the back of the neck. He fell to the floor and I tried to help him up but then she hit me too. Fortunately it didn't hurt too much but Edward cried all through breakfast time and wouldn't eat his food. Lionel whispered to us that he was worried that Nurse Applejack is already starting to go back to her bad old ways now that there's a new Medical Superintendent here.

'I think the old one had her card marked. She probably thinks that she can start getting away with things again now.'

Both Stanley and Edward agreed. I then asked Edward why he was looking ill but he didn't know.

'It's just a pain in my chest,' he muttered unconvincingly.

Lionel suggested that he should ask Nurse Applejack if he could see a doctor. Edward said that he would wait until Nurse Primrose comes on duty tonight. I told Edward that it could be too late by then - at least that made him smile. Lionel noticed a red swelling on the back of Edward's neck from where Nurse Applejack had struck him.

'You should report that too, it might help get rid of her,' he laughed.

28 January 1931

It was very wet and windy last night. The wind was making all the doors and shutters bang and everyone in the ward was very restless. Nurse Primrose had to get the night attendant and two porters in to help calm some of the others down.

I noticed that Edward was acting very strangely today. He's not been quite right since Nurse Applejack pushed him over and hit him round the back of his head. I don't think he's spoken to Nurse

238

Primrose about seeing a doctor yet. I should have reminded him and I'm not sure if she's on duty tonight.

Just now Mr Drake came by with a dead roe deer over his shoulder. He told me that he had caught two gypsy lads coursing at the edge of the grounds.

'They had shot it but didn't kill it. I had to shoot it again myself to put it out of its misery.'

Mr Drake then asked me why I sit up here under the tree reading or writing in all weathers. I think he could see that I was hiding something under my shirt. It was my notebook and the only person who knows about it is Maisie. I didn't want him to see it or know what I really do so I told him that I just come up here to think and get away from everybody else where its quiet and I can be on my own.

'I sometimes scribble things down but it's nothing important,' I said.

He laughed and then told that he can't read or write very well.

'I never went to school because I lived so far out in the countryside when I was a lad. My old grandfather taught me what little I do know but I've always got by and managed somehow – somehow!' he said with a snort.

He then picked up the dead deer and walked off down towards the scullery. I think that he and some of the others will be eating venison tonight.

30 January 1931

Today is Friday. Mr Randall told us that it's the Tall Man's funeral today. 'There's a special service being held for him in Aldershot and he's being buried in an army cemetery over there.'

After he left Lionel started talking about amputated limbs and how the infirmary got rid of them. He told us that he thinks there's a special man who comes to collect them and takes them somewhere to be incinerated. Stanley told us that there's a crematorium at St John's.

'I think they burn them all down there,' he said.

Lionel laughed but couldn't come up with anything better. I told him that we get all the limbs and human organs from the mortuary at the farm to feed to the pigs.

'My friend Donald told me that once,' I said.

Everyone went quiet but I couldn't keep a straight face and then we all started laughing. They knew that I was only joking then. Stanley said that we were being callous and very cruel.

'We shouldn't make fun of the dead. Let's say a quick prayer for The Tall Man to redeem ourselves,' he demanded rather passionately.

Just then Nurse Applejack walked in through the door.

'Lordy, Lordy I never thought I would see the day!' she screamed.

We were all still knelt on the floor with our hands together. We just looked at each other and grinned. She then walked off down the ward and I could hear her muttering something under her breath. Just before she got to the end she did a little jig and a jump and shouted 'Lordy, Lordy' again.

Lionel told me to be careful.

'She might expect to see you in the chapel on Sunday now.'

'Ha Ha, there's no chance of that, I have much better things to do with my time on a Sunday,' I said.

I then began to think of Maisie and became all melancholy. It made me remember where I am.

31 January 1931

Last night it was very wet and windy again. I couldn't sleep. Edward was awake as well and we watched the rain lashing down outside and against the windows. Nurse Primrose brought us both a mug of Ovaltine and took us to the side room so that we could talk without waking up any of the others. Edward told us that he was finally seen by the doctor yesterday. The doctor told him that he has an irregular heart beat and that is was causing some of the funny feelings he has been getting in his chest. I asked Edward if he also told the doctor about the bruise on his neck. Edward said that he did but didn't want to tell him how it happened.

'What did happen?' Nurse Primrose asked.

Edward didn't say anything. Then I told her.

'Nurse Applejack pushed Edward to the floor and then hit him around the back of his head with her copper-stick. It has caused a lot of bruising.'

Edward then told us that the doctor has arranged for him to have an X-Ray next Tuesday. Nurse Primrose took a look at his neck and said that she would try and get Edward to have the X- Ray much sooner.

'I'll arrange it for later today if I can, even though it's Saturday,' she promised.

I then asked Nurse Primrose if there was anything that could be done to stop Nurse Applejack from saying and doing such nasty things.

'I'm the wrong person to ask, you will need to speak to Miss Rance or Parson Jaggs about that sort of thing,' she suggested.

Later, just after breakfast Silas came into the ward and told us that he has taken Mr Elliott's place on the attendants' roster.

'I'll be seeing a lot more of you all now,' he said with a laugh.

He also told us that he has gone back to work at The Anchor Hotel in the evenings.

'There's new people running it now and I need to earn more money to pay for the upkeep on my Bugatti,' he said with a smile.

He told us that Mr Dyke, the attendant who was going to replace Mr Elliott, has been dismissed after what had happened to The Tall Man.

'The Visiting Committee found him to be wholly responsible for Elijah Williams' death,' he confided.

I'm glad that Silas is Mr Elliott's replacement but he told us that we will all have to call him Mr Greenwood now.

1 February 1931

After breakfast I went for a walk over to the farm with Mr Randall to see the pigs. Mr Mycroft was there chatting to Mr Flynn. They were talking about the new Medical Superintendent and are worried about some of the changes that he's planning to make. Mr

Mycroft has been asked to move out of his cottage because he's not in full employment anymore since he retired.

'They need my cottage for a new full-time gasman,' he said.

Mr Flynn told me that there's a boarding house for elderly men in the Broadway near the Village Hall.

'I'm going to try and get old Mycroft a room in there although he won't be able to take his dog,' he whispered.

Mr Mycroft looked very upset and I saw him wipe away a tear. He said that he felt he had some good friends around him and that he was grateful they were here to help. Mr Flynn told us that the new Medical Superintendent wants to bring in some of his own staff from other asylums to help him change a lot of Brookwood's outdated practices and culture.

'There's a big meeting with him and the Visiting Committee in the Main Hall on Monday where we should find everything out.' Mr Flynn reckoned.

Mr Randall told us that he didn't think that it was just the mix up between the bodies in the mortuary that had caused Mr Deane to be replaced as the Medical Superintendent

'That was just an excuse I think. This must have all been pre-arranged before.'

I then asked Mr Randall if I could leave them all and go off for a walk on my own.

'You don't normally ask these days,' he said. I laughed and ran off.

When I got to the bottom field I noticed that the gate had been left open by the pump house so I went through and had a walk by the canal. I noticed some barges berthed along the bank. It was good to see them back now that the water levels are up again. There were some tow-ponies grazing along the bank and a lady was hanging out some washing in the trees.

'Hello boy, are you from the nuthouse?' she asked.

I laughed and told her that I was from the hospital on the other side of the fence.

'That's not a hospital, that's a loony bin but you look quite normal to me,' she said.

She waved me closer and asked me if I would like a drink of tea.

'Don't be afraid, I don't bite,' she laughed.

There was another woman on the barge and a young boy who was about nine.

'We come from up Camden Town way.'

I didn't know where that was but the two women's husbands have come down to Knaphill hoping to find work at the asylum.

'We've heard that they pay good money over there,' she said.

I told her that I thought that was an unexpected comment because whenever I've heard the staff at the asylum talk about money all of them say that they don't earn enough.

'Ah but when you only earn a pittance or don't have any wage at all then any job that puts food on the table will be worth its weight in gold. If our men get the work then we'll all be staying put here on the canal. We'll be looking for some proper bricks and mortar then as well,' she confided.

When I got back into the grounds I told Mr Randall about my conversation with the barge lady. That was a mistake. He told me off for sneaking out of the grounds on my own.

'Well at least you came back. If their men are looking for jobs they had best see Mr Drake tomorrow. He's looking for a couple of new woodmen. I'll walk down there later and tell them.'

2 February 1931

I haven't been able to speak to Maisie since the middle of December and its February now. I now worry that she may be forgetting about me. I looked around for her everywhere until it was nearly dark yesterday but I didn't see her. I really need to speak to her soon. I need some peace of mind and a lot of reassurance that she's alright. Tonight I'll ask Nurse Primrose if she can find anything out. I think Nurse Montague is working back in her ward so perhaps she might be able to get some news for me.

3 February 1931

This morning I helped Mr Randall carry some boxes over to the office for Miss Rance. When we arrived there was a big black car outside about to drive off. As it moved and got closer I noticed Maisie sitting in the back with another lady. It must have been her cousin. Both of them were dressed in black. I recognised the man driving the car as Maisie's uncle as I had seen him before. Maisie saw me and waved and I waved back. She looked very drawn and sad. I watched the car go down the driveway until it turned left at the end and went out of sight. When we got into the office Mr Randall asked Miss Rance about the car and what had happened.

'Poor Miss Albright's father died on Wednesday last after a short illness. It's his funeral in Tilford today. The poor girl will be back with us on Sunday after spending the rest of the week with her family,' she said.

I felt Mr Randall put his hand on my shoulder. I think he knew how I must have been feeling.

'Come on, let's get you back to the ward and arrange a hot drink,' he whispered.

I noticed Miss Rance frown and give me a funny look over her spectacles when he said that. She must have heard! On the way back Mr Randall told me that I shouldn't have got involved with Maisie.

'These emotional things don't help with your treatment and can often make things worse. That's probably why Miss Rance frowned at us. As you've been politely told before, relationships between patients are not encouraged,' he said with half a grin.

I wanted to say something to him about how I really feel about Maisie but I felt it best to stay silent. I wonder now what must be going through her mind. She must be wondering what really did happen to her father. I now wonder if her uncle had anything to do with his death. Maisie has told me some very dark stories about him.

6 February 1931

This morning Mr Luscombe came over and asked me some questions about the pigs.

'Thomas, if I asked you want I meant by the gilts are going to farrow would you understand what I was on about?'

I waited a bit and then said... 'I think so.'

Donald was there and put up his thumb at me.

'Tell Mr Luscombe, of course you know,' he shouted.

I hesitated for a bit and then told Mr Luscombe that gilts are female pigs that haven't had piglets before.

'When the gilt looks like it's going to farrow then it will be having its babies for the first time.'

He laughed and said... 'That's about right but now tell me how many times a year a pig can have piglets?'

I told him that our pigs could have two litters a year.

'By the time the gilt has its second litter it's called a sow.'

'Well done Thomas. I'm off to see the new Medical Superintendent this afternoon and I want to give him an update on your progress.'

Mr Luscombe nearly caught me out because I wasn't expecting to be asked any questions today. Donald said that he had faith in me and that he knew I would know all the answers. Now I wait to find out what the new Medical Superintendent will say about my progress. People are saying different things about him and I already know that he's upset Mr Mycroft and that Mr Randall doesn't like him. I keep overhearing that some of the staff are becoming very worried about how all the possible changes could affect their jobs.

8 February 1931

Yesterday was very wet and windy and no-one could go anywhere or do anything so we had to stay in the ward. Lionel showed me and Edward how to play a game called Ludo. Stanley joined in later and kept winning all the games. Lionel accused him of cheating but Stanley said that it's impossible to cheat. Edward wasn't really concentrating. He was thinking about football and kept talking about Fulham. They were playing a big local derby game against Queens Park Rangers yesterday and he's very frustrated because he has to wait until Monday to find out the score from the newspapers.

Today is bright and sunny although the ground is still very wet from all the rain. I went for a walk near the chapel and could hear everyone singing inside. I think the sound of people singing hymns is very uplifting but I still have a lot of unanswered questions about God which is why I won't go inside there anymore.

On the way back to the ward I saw Katherine. She told me that Maisie was brought back earlier.

'Don't worry, she's in good spirits, she stayed at her cousin's cottage in Wrecclesham. Her father died from a liver complaint. They say that he'd been drinking over a bottle of Scotch whisky a day, so his death was no real surprise to the family.'

I was pleased about that and glad to hear that she didn't have to stay with her uncle. I must stop thinking the worst all the time. I probably won't see Maisie today but at least I know that she's sort of alright now.

9 February 1931

I had just got to the farm this morning when Donald said that I should go over to Rose Cottage immediately. When I got in there Mr Luscombe and Mr Flynn were sitting at the big table in the kitchen. Mr Luscombe told me to sit down and asked Donald to leave the room and get his mother.

'I have some good news and some bad news. I know that you won't like the bad news so I've arranged for Mrs Flynn to come in and sit with you,' he said.

Mr Luscombe's voice was trembling which made me feel very uneasy and I was beginning to feel very sick with worry.

'As you know, I was called over to see the new Medical Superintendent Dr Aitken on Friday afternoon. I told him about your progress on the farm and he was very pleased indeed with you Thomas. He has asked me to congratulate you on what you have achieved and to tell you... well done!'

I tried to smile and said 'Thank you.'

Just then Mrs Flynn came in and took my left hand and held it very tight. Mr Flynn offered me a glass of his Irish whiskey.

'I think you might need a drop of this,' he urged.

Mr Luscombe stood up and looked out of the window. It was only for about a minute but it seemed like an eternity. The silence was almost unbearable.

'Now for the not so good news; because your time with us on the farm has been so exemplary, Dr Aitken feels that other patients

246

should also benefit from the experience of working with us here and from Monday 2nd March he's going to rotate all the patient's jobs around. Each month patients who are able to be employed will rotate and do different jobs.'

This was not the news I was expecting to hear. I've already decided that I want to be a pig farmer and I've been studying everything to make sure that I knew what I needed to. Mrs Flynn then produced a handkerchief, I didn't realise that I had started crying.

'Is there anything we can do for the poor lad?' she asked.

Mr Luscombe said that he had a suggestion.

'The way the rota will work means that you will be with us for just one month twice a year. You could volunteer and come and help us out on Saturday mornings, there's still plenty of work to be done and the farmhands could do with your help. Obviously if there's a bus outing like there is on some Saturday's then you won't be able to do it. What do you think?' he asked.

I said 'yes' straight away.

I feel that Mr Flynn and everyone else at the farm are my friends now so I knew that this was an opportunity to keep on seeing them. Donald came back into the room. He must have known about everything and gave me a hug.

'I'm so, so sorry Tommy,' he said.

Mr Luscombe told me that I could spend the rest of the day with the Flynns. It was actually Mr Flynn's day off and he didn't want us all going back over to the farm smelling of whiskey.

'What would that old fart Harry Horlock say, if he noticed you'd all been drinking?' he joked.

I now feel like I'm being punished for my good progress but know that it's not really anyone's fault.

10 February 1931

When I got back into the ward yesterday evening I noticed that Edward was missing. Lionel told me that I had a missed everything.

'Edward saw the football result he'd been waiting for since Saturday and then went absolutely berserk. He jumped up on his bed and tore down a drape, threw a flower vase at the window which smashed a pane of glass and then kicked Nurse Applejack up the bottom. He was restrained by Silas and two porters and then taken off to the side room and then to isolation.'

I picked up the newspaper and saw the football score. Fulham had lost the match two nil against Queens Park Rangers. Lionel told me that Edward was fine until he saw the result. He's usually very quiet and doesn't really say too much so I'm surprised that this has happened. I then thought that perhaps that's one of the reasons why he's here though. We don't always know the reason!

13 February 1931

People say that Friday 13th is an unlucky day. Today I have been lucky. Today I have been able to speak to Maisie for the first time since before her birthday in December. She thanked me for the ornament and told me how much it means to her. She still looks very pale but her curls are back and she's making ringlets in her hair with her fingers again. Her voice was very soft and I noticed that she was pausing a lot between sentences which I hadn't noticed before. I told her that I was sorry to hear about the death of her father.

'Don't be, he's in a much better place now and away from Uncle Sylvester, he's safe with my mother now and that's the only place he really wanted to be.'

Maisie asked me how I was and I told her what was happening with my job at the farm.

'You must be very disappointed.'

I told her that I was.

I asked her about the painting that she gave to Mrs Woolston. She told me that her uncle had asked for it.

'To keep him quiet I told him where it was and he offered Mrs Woolston a tidy sum. He bought it and then sold it for a big profit at an auction in London. He's apparently put some money in a special bank account somewhere for me. We then started talking about the night she was attacked by Angela Reeves and Miss Maunders. I told her that Katherine had told me all about it all.

'Whatever Katherine told you, it was ten times worse.'

'I will never ever be able to conceive a child again after what they have done to me.'

Maisie is very worried that Angela may be let back into her ward because of her good behaviour in the refractory. Miss Maunders was dismissed but re-instated following an appeal.

'She's now been transferred over to Broadmoor which is why no-one has seen her since I was so viciously attacked,' Maisie said.

We were just getting deeper into conversation when we noticed two female attendants walking towards us. We cut the conversation short and parted very quickly. We didn't want to draw attention to ourselves. I feel much better now that I have spoken to Maisie but feel that all is not right with her. The death of her father probably hasn't helped but I do think that something else is still troubling her.

15 February 1931

I was sitting under the tree reading my dictionary when Maisie appeared out of nowhere.

'SUPRISE, TOMMY!' she shouted at the top of her voice.

She then sat down beside me and we started to kiss. I kept looking over her shoulder to make sure that no-one was about. She grabbed my hand and pushed it inside the top of her dress and down onto her bosom. I felt her tongue go deeper into my mouth. I then pushed my tongue in her mouth. I could at last taste the sweetness of love. I felt her heart pounding against my chest.

'I love you Tommy, I want to marry you Tommy, Let's get out of here Tommy,' she whispered.

I slowly pushed her away so that I could look into her eyes. I was lost for a moment. Her green eyes are so beautiful and I felt transfixed, almost spellbound. We kissed briefly again and then began to talk.

'What really is troubling you?' I asked.

She told me that she expects to be released from the asylum by the end of March.

'It all depends on a final assessment by the new Medical Superintendent. Don't worry. I will be going to live with my cousin Suzanne in Wrecclesham permanently then,' she confided.

Whilst I was pleased to hear her news I felt very sad. I think Maisie noticed and she pulled me closer towards her.

'How are things going with your Cousin Clifford, is he still going to help get you out of here?' she asked.

I told her that things had been very quiet about that lately and that I was still waiting for something to happen.

'There's a possibility that I could go and live in a house outside in the village and then come back here and work as a farmhand, but since the new Medical Superintendent has arrived, I can't be sure about anything.' I said.

Maisie told me that her cousin lives near a pig farm.

'Come and live with us, then everything will be perfect.'

After that Maisie got up and said that she'd better go before she was missed. I can't stop thinking about what she said. I feel sort of happy and sad all at the same time.

16 February 1931

Nurse Applejack came into the ward singing something in African at the top of her voice this morning. She was wearing a new uniform. It was a very dark blue and she had a new hat which was a different shape from her old one.

'None of you have any excuses not to call me Sister now,' she said rather proudly.

I heard Lionel snigger and then he pointed out that she wasn't carrying her copper-stick. I've never seen her without it before. On the way to breakfast Mr Randall told us that the new Medical Superintendent is already putting his mark on the place. There are a lot of things that Mr Deane didn't do that he should have done and Dr Aitken is already starting to put everything right as quick as he can. He told me that Nurse Applejack has had her copper-stick taken away.

'We can only assume that someone must have told Dr Aitken what she's been doing with it.'

I asked Mr Randall why the new Medical Superintendent was called doctor and not mister like Mr Deane was but he didn't know.

'Contrary to what you may think, I don't know everything. Mr Mycroft is the expert at that,' he replied.

He then told me that Mr Mycroft is moving out of his cottage today.

'He's got some lodgings down the Broadway. You'll probably see him when you're walking up and down with the cows.'

I realised then that Mr Randall didn't know that I wasn't allowed to help on the farm all the time and I told him about the new patient's work roster.

'Well I didn't see that one coming,' he said.

'Me neither!'

After dinner Edward was brought back into the ward. His head was bowed and he was very quiet. No-one spoke to him either but he did smile at me as I walked out of the room. I think that he must be very embarrassed about what had happened.

17 February 1931

Today Donald was talking to me about the other jobs I would be doing when the new roster starts.

'Will you go back and work with Mrs Skilton in the laundry?' he asked.

I told him that only female patients are allowed to help in there now. On my list there are jobs gardening in the grounds, helping in the stores, working with the waterman, helping with electricity and gas and helping Miss Rance and the porters in the reception.

Donald laughed... 'You've got a fair old mix of work there and do you know who might be coming to work here on the farm in March?' He asked.

I took the roster from my pocket and told him that it was marked down for man from another ward but it didn't show his name. Donald grabbed it for a moment and said that it looked very complicated.

'You could pretend that you don't understand it and just turn up here on Monday 2nd March anyway,' he suggested.

We both laughed and I told him that I didn't want people to think that I was an idiot.

'Oh, the irony,' he shouted.

I then realised what I had said and felt a bit angry.

'Don't worry Tommy, I know you're not an idiot and you must not let other people think that you are. I'm sorry for making that silly suggestion,' he added.

Mr Flynn has decided to take all the pot-bellied pigs to market today.

'Mr Luscombe and the new Medical Superintendent have agreed to just keep the Middle Whites. Our farm needs to produce and it's not all about parading the fancy pigs around an arena when there's a show,' he said.

It was sad to see them being taken away on the lorry and I did feel a bit of a tear in my eye. They were my favourites.

20 February 1931

This morning I saw all the attendants and porters rushing off down towards the bottom field. Mr Luscombe, Mr Flynn and the farmhands were already there. Donald's mother came out and invited me over to Rose Cottage for a cup of tea. She told me that an aeroplane had flown over and one of its wheels had fallen off and made a big hole in the ground. The aeroplane then got lower in the sky and had come down with a big bang on the other side of the canal in the Lye.

'There was a lot of smoke and I think they've all gone looking for it, I hope the pilot's alright,' she said.

She told me that she had never known such drama.

'I've never seen Jimmy and the others run so fast,' she laughed.

Jimmy must be Mr Flynn's Christian name, although I do think that I've been told that once before!

I later discovered that the pilot was found alive. He was sitting by the aeroplane wreckage with just a few scratches and smoking a cigarette when Mr Luscombe and the others got to him. Mr Flynn told me that an army truck came to pick him up and that there are lots of soldiers and policemen guarding the crash site now.

'The aeroplane is a Sopwith Pup, I think. It just seemed to fall apart in the sky. We saw it go over as we were gathering at the farm gates this morning. We knew it was in trouble just by the strange sound it was making. I think they're waiting to take the wreckage to Farnborough later but we've still got one of its wheels,' he said with a massive smile.

21 February 1931

At half past eleven this morning I saw Albert drive his bus up to the reception. The bus was full of young coloured ladies. Not one of them had white skin. Silas told me that Albert had been to collect them all from Southampton.

'A ship load of African students arrived last week and the new Medical Superintendent has agreed to take fifteen and have them trained here as nurses. Since he's been here he's already had to dismiss seven young nurses because they'd all been 'knocked up' by squaddies from Pirbright. There'll be less of a chance of that happening to these girls as they're more studious and the squaddies won't want to be ridiculed by their mates for going with a blacky,' he said.

Lionel laughed and said... 'That's all we need, a busload of trainee Applejacks.'

Silas pretended to ignore him but I did see a little smile on his face, I reminded Lionel that Nurse Primrose has black skin and is very nice.

'In fact she's the very opposite to Nurse Applejack,' I said.

After dinner Silas took Stanley, Lionel and me to Embleton's in the village. Mr Randall was there and everyone was talking about Mrs Juett. Mr Randall was telling them that she's gone back to her husband and son Jack and is now helping them to run the beer house in Bracknell.

'Never mind, I'll be out looking for a new woman tonight, another one with big boobies I hope,' he said.

Silas laughed and told him to be careful.

'Don't go and pinch another man's wife this time, it might save you from getting a beating,' he said. We all laughed.

Mr Randall stood up, took his cap off and bowed.

'Thank you, thank you.'

Lionel whispered that he thought that Mr Randall was behaving like a puppet master.

'He's very upset by it all, I can tell. He's making light of everything so that he doesn't lose face,' he whispered.

I asked Lionel how he could know.

'That's exactly what I used to do, that's how I know,' he replied.

I'd forgotten that Lionel once told me that he used to be a bit of a womaniser himself when he was younger.

26 February 1931

There's been snow on the ground for the last few days and no-one has been able to get out and do very much. This is my last week helping at the farm for a while and I feel very sad. Next week I will be helping in the stores. Donald's mother works in the Bursar's office and she knows the man who's in charge of the stores very well.

'He hardly ever leaves the place. He would sleep in there if he could. He's always miserable and there's always something for him to moan about. I don't think you'll enjoy working with him as much as you have on the farm,' she warned.

I tried to smile. Nothing will be better than working at the farm I thought.

After dinner I saw Maisie. It was very brief. She was going to the infirmary for a check up. She was with a nurse so we couldn't talk properly.

27 February 1931

Mrs Jenkins was supposed to come and see me in February to give me a review. On Sunday March begins, I wonder why she hasn't come. No-one has said anything and I haven't heard of anyone else going for their assessments either. I must ask. I also haven't heard from Cousin Clifford although I did see Mrs Skilton this morning. She asked me if I had any news. I said 'No' and she told me that she hasn't heard anymore either. Everything seems to have gone very quiet since the new Medical Superintendent arrived.

At dinner time I stayed with the Flynns. It was my last day helping on the farm. Mrs Flynn had baked a big rabbit pie especially and all the farmhands came to say goodbye to me. Mr Flynn offered them all a glass of Irish whiskey but told them they could only have one because they had to go back and work afterwards. Donald handed me a gift, it was wrapped in brown paper and tied with string. Everyone went quiet while they waited for me to open it. Inside it was a photograph of me at the Village Show in the arena with my pot-bellied pig. I didn't know that it had been taken. I was very pleased and said thank you to everybody. They all clapped and started singing... *'For he's a jolly good fellow.'* I felt very proud of myself but very sad that I had to leave the farm. At least I can come back and help on some Saturday mornings when there's not a trip.

28 February 1931

We were supposed to go on a bus trip with Albert today to a place called Wisley Gardens but it has been cancelled. There's still some snow and ice on the ground and it's very cold. Silas told us that it's being rearranged for another Saturday in the spring.

'It'll be better then, more flowers will be in bloom and the weather should be much warmer for us all,' he said.

After dinner Silas took us over to the Nag's Head Inn. We had only been there once since Mrs Juett left. Stanley and Lionel also came. Edward wasn't allowed to come.

'We don't want him to have one of his mad episodes in public, it wouldn't look very good,' Silas said.

Whilst we were sitting inside Silas asked us to remember to call him Mr Greenwood when he's working on the ward.

'It's very important to me that I can show an air of discipline to my colleagues, particularly when there are new superiors about.'

We all laughed and said... 'Yes, Mr Greenwood.'

Tonight there's a concert in the Main Hall. A military band is coming over from Aldershot with a couple of singers.

'They play all the war songs, you'll like that Tommy,' he said with a grin.

1 March 1931

When I was walking around the grounds this morning I saw Maisie. She was with a very well dressed lady who was wearing a dark red coat.

'This is my cousin Suzanne who I'm going to live with at the end of the month,' she said.

We shook hands and I introduced myself.

'Hello, I'm Tommy, Maisie's friend.'

Suzanne said that Maisie had told her everything about me, how I sit under the tree and write things down all the time.

'I hear that you're interested in looking after pigs, we have a pig farm near us, you'll have to come and visit some time.' She said quite assertively.

Maisie smiled. She turned to Suzanne and asked...'When Tommy is free from here can he come and live with us too?'

I felt a bit embarrassed. Not because of what Maisie had said but because I was there to hear it. Suzanne didn't answer. She just smiled and then turned to me.

'Are you Maisie's boyfriend?'

'Yes,' I replied.

Maisie said... 'Yes, Tommy is my boyfriend, I love him very much and I want to be with him forever.'

I felt quite overwhelmed by the conversation and I think that Maisie noticed. She took my hand and held it tight against her chest. Suzanne frowned and then smiled.

'I think Maisie and I need to have a long chat about everything,' she said with a gasp.

After they'd gone I just sat down and pondered everything. Maisie will be gone from here in a few weeks time but I still don't know what's happening to me. I think I need to get some answers quick and I'm going to ask if I can speak to Miss Rance tomorrow.

2 March 1931

Despicable is the word I found in my dictionary today. It describes the man in the stores. He's everything that Mrs Flynn said he was. His name is Mr Brisbane and he's very a short man with a pitted red face, he has patchy black hair, wears spectacles that are crooked and he's very rude. He kept referring to me as 'the imbecile'. That's a word that I've only ever heard Mr Horlock use before. I don't think that they're supposed to say that word. He made me move some heavy boxes around and then move them back again and all for no reason. When the bell went for dinner, he wouldn't let me go.

'Finish that first!' he demanded.

When I got to the Dining Hall I was told off for being late and my dinner was cold. When I got back afterwards he was asleep in his chair. I just sat opposite him until it was 3 o'clock and it was time to go. He didn't even notice that I had come back and I certainly wasn't going to wake him.

When I got back to the ward I asked Nurse Applejack why I hadn't had my assessment with Mrs Jenkins in February.

'I've been waiting for months to see her again and nothing has happened,' I said.

'Don't ask me, no-one tells me anything anymore,' she snapped.

Lionel suggested that I should walk over to the reception in the morning on my way to the stores.

'Just walk in and ask Miss Rance to see her yourself, don't be afraid, it's your life they're playing with.'

I agreed and said that I would. Now I worry. I worry a lot!

3 March 1931

Well I did it. I just walked in; Miss Rance was by the door and asked me why I was on my own. I told her that I was very worried about a few things and that I wanted to talk to someone. I told her that I thought that she was the only person I could talk to. As my Uncle Charlie would have said, I was trying to 'butter her up.'

'Does Nurse Applejack or any of the attendant's know that you have come to see me this morning?' she asked.

'No, I stopped by on my way to the stores on the spur of the moment, I will tell them about it when I get back, I promise,' I replied.

Miss Rance told me to sit down and said that she would give me five minutes of her time.

'So what do you want talk to me about?' she asked.

I told her that I was expecting an important assessment by Mrs Jenkins in February but she never came and that I really need to know more about what's happening. Miss Rance told me that the new Medical Superintendent is making a lot of big changes. One of those changes is that all assessments are now being carried out in-house.

'He wants to use our own staff and has already brought some new people in to assist. He will not be using Mr Stevenson, Dr Barnes or Mrs Jenkins anymore. He won't be using anyone from outside at all.'

I felt very shocked and realised that this news was very bad for me. She told me that the Medical Superintendent is arranging for all patients to be reassessed over the coming months.

'There are about 1,400 of you altogether and you will all be seen in alphabetical order, so yours shouldn't be too long. You will receive an appointment note soon,' she said.

On the way to the stores I realised that Maisie would be one of the first to be seen as her surname is Albright. She's expecting to leave by the end of March so I hope that she's not going to be affected by it all.

When I got to the stores Mr Brisbane was waiting for me.

'You're three minutes late, not good enough and why didn't you come back to me to work after dinner yesterday you insolent little imbecile,' he shouted.

I told him that I did come back but he was asleep all afternoon.

'I never sleep so don't lie to me, do not ever lie to me!' he shouted.

I wasn't lying and I knew that I was telling the truth. He then told me to move some boxes, the same boxes as yesterday.

'I'm expecting a delivery of cleaning materials this afternoon and we need more room,' he said.

I have now decided that I do not like Mr Brisbane.

6 March 1931

Nurse Primrose was talking to me about some of the other nurses
and why the Medical Superintendent is getting lots of trainees in.

'We're very short on all the wards and in the infirmary. The
younger ones need more experience but they never stay very long.
By the time that they're trained up they go and get themselves in the
family way and have to leave,' she said.

She also told me that Nurse Montague is one of the seven nurses
who had been given notice to leave recently because of her
condition.

'She was a very good friend and a fine nurse. I will miss her,' she
added.

I will miss her too. She's the nurse who risked getting into trouble
when she sneaked me into to the infirmary to see Maisie on
Christmas Day.

The last few days in the stores haven't been any better but at least
Mr Brisbane has left me alone. He's been busy sifting through loads
of old newspapers and all I've had to do is make him cups of tea all
day.

10 March 1931

Since around last Thursday, the awful pain I had a few months
ago all down my right side has started to come back. I don't know
what's causing it but the discomfort is immense and it's been
keeping me awake during the last few nights. This morning I could
hardly bend my knee enough to pull on my boot, my ankle was very
swollen and my boot would hardly fit; it was a bit of a struggle. It's
been very hard for me to walk. My shoulder also hurts and I feel
great anxiety in my chest. It feels very tight and I worry. Lionel
thinks that I should go back to see the doctor but I don't want to be
put in the infirmary again, sometimes they do some very strange
things to people in there, they experiment and do other unspeakable
things. I remember that the last time I had these pains I was given a
special diet but I only stayed on it for a few weeks because the cooks
kept changing over in the Dining Hall and they didn't know what I

should have been eating. Tomorrow I shall go and see Missy Hope in the scullery. Perhaps she could remind them what I should be having for my dinners. I think there's still a special list pinned up somewhere by the serving hatch of who should be eating what. Lionel thinks that my pains might have come back because I'm missing the outside air as I'm not helping at the farm any more. I'm not sure but the stores are very damp and claustrophobic and the pains have started again since I've been working over there. This morning Mr Brisbane gave me a pencil and a ruler and told me draw some straight columns in his new ledger books. At least I could sit down and I don't think he noticed that I wasn't walking properly. This afternoon he fell asleep so I just sat in the corner and read his *Times* newspaper but it was very cold.

11 March 1931

Last night I showed my swollen knee and ankle to Nurse Primrose. She laughed and said it looks like I've got an old man's disease. She took me to the side room about an hour before 'lights out' and wrapped a cold wet towel around my knee. She then went outside and brought in a bowl of very cold water and told me to soak my foot. It was freezing and I could feel my foot tingling. She told me that her father had very bad arthritis so she understands how much it can hurt and what she can do to help. She asked me if my mother or father have arthritis.

'No, my mother hasn't and I'm still not sure who my father is. My Aunt Betty has it though; she's had to use a walking cane since she was very young although she disguises it with an umbrella now.'

She told me that I need to rest for a few days.

'Don't worry, you won't need to go to the infirmary, you can rest in the ward, I will get you dispensation so that you won't have to work in the stores for the next few days as well,' she said.

I was quite pleased with that but I think I would rather not have all the pain and swelling. It also means that I won't be able to come out into the grounds for awhile. A doctor is coming to see me later to give me his opinion.

20 March 1931

It's been a long few days and I've been very bored. I like Lionel a lot but spending every day in the ward with him can be quite tiresome. His jokes stop being funny after a while. There has also been Nurse Applejack to worry about. She seems to have changed a little but since she got her new Sister's uniform she just marches up and down the ward looking very proud and doesn't shout as much as she used to. Lionel told me that she's been asked to help train some of the new nurses that we saw Albert bring in the other day

'I suppose she's been told to amend her ways,' he said with a grin.

Tomorrow we have a trip to Worthing and because I'm better now Mr Randall has told me that I'm allowed to go but on Monday I have to go back to work in the stores.

22 March 1931

Yesterday we set off for Worthing at 9 o'clock. On the way I put my head out of the window and my cap blew off. I was very upset and I thought that it was going to ruin my day. Uncle Charlie gave me the cap on my 21st birthday. It was the last thing he ever got for me. When we arrived in Worthing I told Albert what had happened and he said that if I could remember where it was it had blown off, he would slow the bus down on the way back to see if we could find it.

'It might be nearly dark by then so I wouldn't hold out much hope,' he said.

The weather was very grey and windy but at least there wasn't any rain. Mr Randall came with us, the first time he'd been out on a trip for awhile. Silas told us that Mr Randall knew a very attractive woman who had moved to Worthing from Knaphill and that he was hoping to see her. He did find her but then found out that she had just got married a few weeks ago.

'I think he had a bit of a shock when he met her new husband as well,' he laughed.

On the way back the bus started swerving all over the place and there was a lot of commotion. Edward had smuggled a bucket of crabs on to the bus and the bucket had fallen over. The crabs were running all over the floor and everyone was laughing. Albert had to stop so that Silas and Mr Randall could catch them and throw them all out of the door. We then went on for another couple of miles and then Albert stopped the bus again near some woods so that we could all get out for a pee. Edward wanted to do his number twos and fell down a ditch and stung his bottom on some nettles. It was very funny and he had to lie on the floor of the bus on his tummy until the stinging stopped. I noticed that the sun was starting to set and I recognised where we were. It was the place where I thought my cap had blown off. Albert slowed down but told me that it would be like looking for a needle in a haystack. Just then we saw two small boys about five years old sitting on a farm gate, one of them was wearing my cap, it was too big for him. Albert got out of the bus and explained to the boys what had happened and whose cap it was. I saw him give the boy who was wearing my cap some money and then shake his hand. When Albert gave me my cap he said... 'Right, that's threepence you owe me.'

I was very thankful and felt very lucky that I had got it back.

23 March 1931

Today I had to go back and work in the stores. Mr Brisbane wasn't very happy and seemed very abrupt. He called me a skiver and said that there was a backlog of work to do.

'It's your fault it hasn't been done yet,' he snapped.

I think that someone else could have helped him while I was away but I don't think anyone had thought of that.

At dinner time I went to the farm to see Donald. I wanted to explain why I haven't been able to go help on Saturdays. Donald told me that he knew I had been having problems walking. Missy Hope had told him that I'd been in to see her about my food diet. I also told him about the trip to Worthing and what had happened with Edward on the way back. He laughed.

'Just make sure you're here this coming Saturday, we'll have some fun,' he said.

25 March 1931

After dinner I saw Maisie and we had the chance for a quick chat. She told me that Angela Reeves had been allowed back into her ward.

'She's in the bed opposite mine. It's all very unnerving. She just sits there and stares at me all the time.'

I asked her why she has been able to go back there and she told me that the Medical Superintendent has exonerated Angela of any blame because she was in the care of Miss Maunders when the attack took place.

'She had a review last week and he has given her the benefit of the doubt.'

Maisie is upset and very worried that Angela may attack her again.

'I simply can't sleep at night but hopefully I only have a few days to go.'

I had nearly forgotten that Maisie was leaving at the end of the month. She told me that there had been a delay because the Medical Superintendent wants to see her for a new assessment first.

'I've been told that the date will probably be the 5th April now which is Easter Sunday,' she said.

I couldn't answer. I didn't want to appear to be selfish but I genuinely feel pleased for her. I know that I will miss her so much and that a big hole will be left in my heart when she leaves.

26 March 1931

Today I received a letter from Cousin Clifford. It was very short and he has apologised for not coming to see me. The baby has been ill with gastroenteritis and he and Gloria have been very worried although it does say that little Amanda Louise is better now. I wonder when Cousin Clifford will come and visit again. Perhaps I should write back to him and ask.

27 March 1931

I had just got to the stores when Mr Randall came in behind me.

'Come with me Tommy, you have a visitor,' he said.

He took me over to the reception and there was a gentleman standing in the door way. When he turned round I noticed that it was George O'Leary, the man who had come to see me about a year ago.

'Hello, young Thomas. How are you?' he asked.

'Fine, I think,' I replied.

He then suggested that as it was a bright and sunny morning we could go for a walk down towards the bottom field.

'There are some benches down there and it's very quiet, it'll be an ideal place for us to sit and talk,' he said.

When we got there he asked me if I had seen Cousin Clifford recently.

'No, but I did receive a short letter from him yesterday telling me that Amanda Louise had been ill which is why he hasn't been here to visit for awhile,' I replied.

Mr O'Leary paused and then looked very thoughtful.

'The reason I'm here is to tell you some truth, I know that you will be shocked by what I'm about to tell you but you are old enough now to be told everything.'

I wondered what he was going to say and I felt very apprehensive.

'Just sit and listen and I will explain everything,' he said.

Cousin Clifford is not your cousin. He's actually your older half brother. You mother is not your mother. Your Aunt Betty is your real mother. As for me, I am most definitely your father.'

I felt aghast and very confused.

'Would you like me to tell you all that again?'

'Yes,' I replied.

Afterwards there was a long silence and we just sat there looking at each other.

'So you <u>are</u> my father!'

'Oh yes, most definitely, most definitely, yes,' he replied.

'It all happened when Betty's husband went off to Europe on business and he was away for quite a long time. Betty and I had a bit of a fling and she fell in the family way. Just before he came back it was decided that Marion, that's Betty's sister, the lady you call Mother, should look after the baby as her own. Betty paid her a handsome sum but Marion squandered it very quickly and ended going back to work on the streets. It all had to remain a secret because if Betty's husband had found out there would have been hell to pay. He was actually a very violent man. The other complication was that I was married myself and already had three other children of my own.'

I had to sit still and ponder and take everything in that he was telling me. I then rather abruptly asked him if he was really telling me the truth.

'Oh yes, most definitely yes,' he replied.

I then asked him if Cousin Clifford knew about all this.

'He was too young to understand what was going on at first but he became quite inquisitive himself about a year ago and Betty spilt the beans. She contacted me and I think that you know the rest now.'

Just then Mr Randall came over with Miss Rance. Mr O'Leary turned to me and told me that he had spoken to them earlier and informed them what he was going to speak to me about.

'I need to be sure that you'll be alright after I leave. It's my priority now to get you out of here,' he said.

Today has been very unsettling for me. I have some answers now that I have been looking for but the news that Mother is not my mother has very much shocked me and I don't really know what to think anymore. I feel confused.

29 March 1931

Sometimes I just love sitting out in the rain. If there's no wind the trees keep me dry, even in winter. The sound of the rain in the woods is one of the most wonderful sounds I know; it's just nature and me and it provides the perfect background for my thoughts. It is spring now and the birds are singing with their beautiful voices. Today I needed to sit down and reflect. Think about Maisie leaving, think about what Mr O'Leary said. I suppose I ought to call him Father now. There's been so much to absorb and I think that some things will be changing very soon.

Yesterday I went to help at the farm. It was Mr Flynn's birthday, he was fifty years old, I think. When we had finished with the cows and pigs we went back to Rose Cottage and he got very drunk. He started dancing on the kitchen table and it collapsed and he knocked us all flying. Mrs Flynn poured a bucket of water over him. We all laughed. I think I needed that; I needed a bit of a laugh, I needed to be with friends.

30 March 1931

Mr Randall came into the ward just after breakfast and told us that all the attendants were called over to see Dr Aitken at the crack of dawn this morning. They were told that all release assessments as well as the annual interviews were going to be delayed for around two months because all the current policies are being revised.

'It means anyone who was hoping to go home over the next few weeks will be disappointed, he said.

No-one is expecting to leave from our ward yet but then I thought of Maisie, this news will mean that she will have to stay in the asylum for another few weeks at least. That's good news for me but I don't think it will be for her. I will try to talk to her. I know she can't wait to leave, especially now that Angela is back in her ward. This is all very bad news. Very, very bad news!

31 March 1931

Last night I was talking to Nurse Primrose about the visit I had from George O'Leary, I told her that I was very pleased now that I know who my father is but very shocked to find out that my mother is my aunty and my aunty is my mother. Nurse Primrose looked very confused so I tried to explain it all like Mr O'Leary did to me. She then mentioned my arthritis.

'See I told you, I told you it could be hereditary. You told me that your Aunt Betty has had it since she was very young and now that you've found out that she's really your mother that explains everything,' she said.

Nurse Primrose was starting to ask me lots and lots of questions and I was beginning to wish that I hadn't told her anything.

Today I found out that next week I will be working with the Water Man. Most of the work will be outside. I have not enjoyed my time in the stores with Mr Brisbane at all so I do look forward to the change although I wish I was still helping Donald and the others at the farm instead.

2 April 1931

I saw Donald this morning, he asked me if I would be about to help at the farm on Saturday.

'We've just had our first batch of piglets and we could do with an extra pair of hands,' he said.

I told him that I would be there on Saturday as soon as I could after breakfast.

This afternoon on the way back from the stores I saw Maisie. She was just about to tell me why she was still here when I stopped her and told her that I already knew the reason. She told me that she was very disappointed.

'It's not fair that they can cancel an important thing like that. It feels like the Medical Superintendent is playing games with my life.'

She told me that she had given Katherine a note to pass to me with her cousin, Suzanne's address in Wrecclesham so that I could write to her.

'Never mind, I can tell you it myself now but obviously you won't need it just yet,' she said.

There seemed to be a lot of people milling around us so I couldn't say everything that I wanted to say but Maisie told me that Angela was still giving her problems.

'She keeps trying to provoke and goad me into doing something that I might regret. I've complained about her but no-one seems to care.'

I wasn't sure what to say but I told her to be careful, I asked her to promise me that she would stay safe. I so wanted to tell Maisie about my recent visit from George O'Leary but that will have to wait until another day.

4 April 1931

Today is Easter Saturday and this morning at the farm with Donald and the others was great fun. I enjoyed feeding and washing down all the new piglets. Sixty-two of them had been born over the last few days and without any problems. Mr Hampton was there, I hadn't seen him for quite a long time. He told me that he didn't know about the patients' new working rotations but said that he wondered why he hadn't seen my smiling face at the farm for a while.

Donald laughed and said... 'What do you mean, smiling face? Tommy never smiles!'

'That's what I meant,' Mr Hampton said. I smiled.

Later this afternoon Albert is coming to collect three of us from each of the convalescence wards and we're being taken to see a show which is being put on by the staff and patients at Broadmoor. Albert said that he would stop off at the Royal Military Academy at Sandhurst on the way so that we can eat our sandwiches by the lake and feed the ducks.

'Who knows, you might see some marching soldiers too,' he said.

It'll be the first time that I've been in the bus with female patients on board but I don't think Maisie will be coming, I'm sure she would have said something me when I saw her on Thursday.

5 April 1931

George O'Leary came to see me again today. He asked me if I was alright and if I had come to terms with everything that he told me when he came on 27th March last. It's very difficult to suddenly start referring to someone as Father when you don't really know them but I promised him that I would try. He told me that he has three grown up children between twenty-seven and thirty years old.

'There was a fourth child, a boy called Daniel, but he died in a drowning accident, dragged down by a heavy current and caught in weed in the River Blackwater when he was just fourteen.'

I asked him about the others, one is a girl called Laney, who helps in his butcher shop, and the others are two boys, well fully grown men now who are away in the army.

'You'll be very proud of them and I'm sure that you'll all get on well.'

I asked him if they knew about me and he told me that they know everything.

'I always tell the truth. I told them why you were sent here. It was very wrong that you were brought here and I have always been disgusted by your mother and your Aunt Marion's actions. He told me that he had given Miss Rance notice that he will now be my appropriate relative.

'I know I can't get you out yet, they have to issue an official release document for that to happen but I promise that you will be free from here by the summer,' he said enthusiastically.

I think that he wants me to go and live with him and his family in Frimley Green but that will mean that I won't be able to work back here on the farm. Everything seems to be getting very complicated but now at least it looks like I might at last be getting out.

6 April 1931

Today was my first day with the Head Water Man. He's called Mr Armstrong, he's quite old but very cheerful. This morning he took me up to the top of the water tower; it holds nearly 3,000 gallons that comes up from a well underneath. The water well is over 880 feet deep. There's a great view of the village and you can see Woking and Guildford from up there. He then showed me the reservoir, I had walked past it many times before, sometimes it has water and sometimes it doesn't. We then went to the pump house just inside the grounds by the canal.

'There was a time when we pumped water into the asylum from the canal but that's what caused all the typhoid. Now we use the same pumps to get rid of our sewage back into it,' he said.

He told me that my main jobs will be to measure the water levels and to check that all the pumps are working properly each day.

7 April 1931

Today Mr Armstrong showed me where all the shafts and tunnels are. The entrances and shaft covers are all padlocked.

'They're not all registered on the maps and can be very dangerous, I can't let you go down in them - I have a little helper called Joseph to do that. He goes down once a month to check for blockages and always comes back out covered in shit. He has a special hose in the pump house to clean himself up.' He told me.

Mr Armstrong took me to the corner of the bottom field and pulled back the branches of a gorse bush.

'Some years ago they started digging a tunnel here but it stops just this side of the canal. People say that they were going to use it to take bodies from the mortuary through to the cemetery but it was always going to be too small. I think it eventually developed a leak which is why they stopped digging,' he said.

He then told me that most of the blockages in the sewerage tunnel were caused by animals.

'There are plenty of rats down there but they actually help keep the tunnels and pipes clear. Quite often fish, usually grass carp swim in from the canal and get caught, we've even found weasels and the odd beaver down there,' he said.

He then told me about a time a few years ago when they found the body of a man who had been missing from the asylum for nearly three years.

'His body was perfectly preserved in shit, as you can imagine, it was the worst blockage we've ever had,' he added.

When I got back to the ward I told all the others about it and Lionel remembered.

'The man went missing the very first day he arrived and no-one ever saw him again until the day he was found dead. There was a horrid smell about the place for quite a few days and raw sewage was running back up into the ablutions. They had to get help from outside, there were lots of workmen and fire engines, we all had to stay inside for a good week,' he said.

8 April 1931

Today I met Joseph. He looked very familiar. He then explained that he used to work at the nursery at the bottom of the hill on the other side of the village at a place called Whitfield. I then remembered that we went for a walk down there one day and that he was the boy who showed us around with a lady called Mrs Bundy.

'I've been working here for nearly a year now,' he said.

He asked me if I knew Lionel.

'He used to help me catch the rats but I think that they made him ill,' he said.

I told him that Lionel is fine now but he has to stay in the ward most of the time.

'He's not allowed to work anymore but he does come out with us on trips.'

Just then Mr Armstrong came over and said that he'd just been up at the farm and had been talking to Mr Luscombe about me.

'It appears that they're missing you up there young Tommy. They're finding it very hard to teach some of the other patients. Some of them think that they're only there to stroke the animals.'

I couldn't help smiling and I think Mr Armstrong noticed that.

'Don't be so smug,' he said and then laughed sort of unexpectedly.

10 April 1931

Today I received a note from Miss Rance. It confirms that George O'Leary is now my appropriate relative. Inside the envelope was another slip of paper which says that I have a review assessment with the Medical Superintendent at 10 o'clock on Monday 13th April. I think that this is the assessment I should have had with Mrs Jenkins in February. I know I shouldn't worry but I do worry. Nothing has happened for quite a while which they can use against me. I've kept my head low and have tried not to show any signs of mania or anything melancholy although there have been days and nights when I've felt down and sad. I also know that my speech is alright now. Everyone has said that there's been a great improvement.

12 April 1931

Last night there was a performance in the Main Hall by a magician called The Greek Gorgon and he kept making things disappear. He also put a lady in a long box and then cut her in half with a saw. There was no blood and then he made her whole again. She stood up and waved to us all. No-one could tell how he did that. He then shouted out to us and asked if any of us would like to disappear. I looked over to Nurse Applejack. Eventually a lady from the village put her hand up. The magician placed a big blue shroud with yellow stars over her. Suddenly, there was a big bang, a puff of smoke and he pulled the shroud away. She was gone. Everyone clapped and then he shouted out... 'Look behind you!'

The lady was stood behind us at the back of the hall and everyone clapped again. Edward, Stanley, Lionel and I spent most of this morning trying to work out how he managed to do that.

'It's magic, just magic!' Edward said.

Lionel laughed.

'It was clever but no more than a just piece of trickery to fool us all,' he said.

I was hoping to see Maisie today so that I could find out what is happening with her. It's been raining so perhaps she didn't want to come out. Its ten days now since I last saw her.

13 April 1931

Today I had my assessment with Dr Aitken. There was another man in the office but I don't think that they told me his name. Miss Rance was taking notes. Nurse Applejack was sitting just behind me. Everything seems a bit blurred now but I can still hear Dr Aitken's voice inside my head. I need to get it out!

'I am Dr Aitken and you will address me as Sir at all times and you will only speak to me when I ask you to speak to me. Do you understand?'

'Yes,' I replied.

'Yes what?'

'Yes Sir!' I answered.

I knew then that this was going to be a very difficult day for me and I felt my heart pounding hard inside my chest.

'Just to make sure that I have the right person sat in front of me I need you to tell me who you are. Are you Thomas Compton of 49b, Whatley Avenue, Raynes Park?' he asked.

'I used to live there but my family lost the house when my Uncle Charlie died just after I came here,' I said.

'I just wanted to know the address and you must remember to call me Sir when I speak to you,' he snapped

He then looked over to Miss Rance and I saw her whisper something in his ear.

'What is your date of birth?' he asked.

'It's 9th August, Sir.'

'WHAT YEAR?'

I had to think, I felt myself becoming very frightened and nervous by him. I hesitated.

'It's err 1904, Sir,' I answered.

'You were sent here with a speech impediment and adolescent development problems. Do you think that there's been any improvement in yourself?' he asked.

I told him that I felt there was.

'I can speak much better now and I feel very grown up. Working at the farm has helped me a lot Sir,' I said.

He then asked me to leave the room and wait outside. It felt like I was sat there for an eternity. I was watching the big clock on the wall. After twenty-seven minutes Miss Rance poked her head around the door and asked me to go back in.

'I've been reading your notes and it seems like you have had quite a few other issues since you have been here, can you tell me about them and what you think has caused them?' he asked.

I looked at Miss Rance and then around to Nurse Applejack but she just looked down into her lap.

'ANSWER ME!' he shouted.

'I'm not sure, what you're asking Sir, I know that I have been accused of mania and being melancholy and even being delusional before but they're all exaggerations and made up stories to make me look bad, Sir,' I said.

'How can be attacking Sister Applejack not be mania? It's all here in black and white. How can talking to dead people not be delusional? It's all here in black and white. How can spending nights on end crying your eyes out over nothing not be melancholy? It's all here in black in white.'

I couldn't believe what I was hearing and I told him that it was all lies, all made up lies. He paused. I then saw Miss Rance lean over and whisper something again. He then asked me to leave the office for a second time. This time I was outside in the waiting room for over an hour. When I went back into the room it was full of pipe and cigarette smoke. I could hardly see or breathe.

'Sit down Compton,' he ordered.

'Right, now tell me this, how do you see yourself in the future, if you walked out of here tomorrow, what would you do?' he asked.

'I would see myself working on a farm, probably with pigs and earning an honest living, Sir.'

He told me that he had received a comprehensive report from Mr Luscombe, the Farm Bailiff.

'It's in contrast to everything else I have here about you, he's obviously seen the best and brought that out of you, he can't praise you enough and I like that.'

'Miss Rance has told me that your family circumstances have also changed and that you've only recently been told who your father and real mother is. Is that correct?' he asked.

'Yes Sir,' I replied.

'I currently have 1,463 patients under my management at this institution. We are badly overcrowded and only 12% of those are fit for release. You should be one of those but I need to be sure that you don't get sent back as soon as I let you out. My decision is that you will stay here for a further twelve weeks. I will issue you with a provisional release date which will be one Sunday in July. How do you feel about that?' he asked.

'I think that's fair and I'm very pleased with that Sir,' I replied.

He then turned to Miss Rance and asked her to write to my father to inform him of the outcome of the assessment.

'Right, be off with you Compton and don't let me down,' he said.

Today I think has been the hardest day for me since I've been here but at last, at last perhaps now I can see an end to it all.

15 April 1931

When I was on the way to meet Mr Armstrong this morning I could hear someone calling my name. It was Katherine from Maisie's ward. She was calling me from inside one of female airing courts.

'Tommy, Tommy, I've been looking out for you,' she shouted.

I went over to talk more quietly and she told me that Maisie had suffered a breakdown late on Sunday evening.

'It was Angela, she had been taunting Maisie with her eyes for a number of days and was being very mean to her without actually saying anything, well you know, she has that way about her.'

I asked Katherine if she could tell me more and she said that she thinks Maisie might have worked herself into a frenzy just to get away from her.

'She's in an isolation room now where Angela can't get to her. I think that Maisie might have done it all on purpose, she was paranoid and very worried that Angela might attack her again, even without that Miss Maunders here,' she said.

I know Maisie was also disappointed that her release had been delayed.

'This won't help her; this will hold things up even more,' I said.

I thanked Katherine for telling me and she said that she would look out for me on other days if she has any further news.

16 April 1931

This afternoon Stanley told us that he would be leaving on Sunday. He had received notice from the Medical Superintendent this morning who has signed his release certificate.

'I'll be staying with my sister in Bisley permanently but they're letting me come back to the asylum once a week to help out the tailor and the cobbler, just to give me something worthwhile to do until I can find proper work outside,' he said.

We all gathered around, patted him on the back and shook his hand. Stanley has always been very popular with us even though he's a bit odd looking. Edward didn't know that Stanley once tried to shoot himself dead which is why the top part of his head is missing and why he always wears a big hat when we go out on trips. Stanley overheard our conversation and took Edward to one side.

'Now let me tell you the proper version,' he said.

We all laughed. We'd all heard the same story so many times that we knew it wasn't going to be any different to what Edward had already been told. I will miss Stanley. He's always been a good friend.

17 April 1931

Today Mr Armstrong took me on to the canal towpath and showed me where the sewage comes out. There are two ducts, one near the basin and one further along towards the Bagshot Road Bridge. A barge was berthed along the bank and a man was sorting out his fishing rod while his wife hung up some washing in the trees.

'Come on, I know them, let's go and say "Hello", we should be alright for a cup of tea,' Mr Armstrong said.

The man invited us on board and we climbed down a couple of steps.

'Welcome to my galley,' he said.

His wife then came down and gave us some biscuits.

'Let me get the pot on the stove and make you all a brew,' she said.

Mr Armstrong had known the man and his wife for about twenty years.

'They come through twice a year, towards Hampshire in the spring and back towards London in the autumn,' he said.

I noticed that the barge didn't have any cargo. Most carry logs or coal but this one was empty.

'It won't be when they come back in the autumn; you see that big empty space over there, it will be full with cages of Christmas turkeys the next time I see them,' he added.

When we got back into the grounds Mr Armstrong opened up one of the shafts, the water was flowing very fast and I could see lumps of raw sewage floating on top.

'Yes that's all going into the canal; you won't want to be eating any fish from there tonight,' he laughed.

18 April 1931

There are some new people in Mr Mycroft's old cottage now. I was going to say 'Hello' but they didn't look very friendly. The man had ginger hair and steely grey eyes and just stood and glared at me. The woman, his wife, I think looked at me very strangely. I heard children's voices coming from inside. There was lots of swearing. It was all very unsettling.

Mr Armstrong was talking to me about Mr Mycroft the other day. It seems that they have known each other for a long time. He told me that Mr Mycroft thought that he could live in the cottage forever.

'He hasn't done any real work for years and everyone was turning a blind eye. When the new Medical Superintendent arrived, that was obviously going to change. There are a few others who will be looking over their shoulders as well but poor old Mycroft was an easy target for him to start with,' he confided.

Tonight there's a Spring Ball in the Main Hall and some high up people from the village have been invited.

19 April 1931

This morning after breakfast I went for my normal Sunday morning walk. Unusually, there were pigs out in the grounds; I could see some in a herd moving down towards the East Lodge Gate. I ran towards the farm, there was no-one there but I noticed that the gates had been opened; the pigs must have been let out on purpose. I ran over and banged on the door of Rose Cottage and shouted for Donald and Mr Flynn. An upstairs window flew opened and Mr Flynn popped his head out.

'Tommy, what do you want?'

He seemed very sleepy eyed and I shouted... 'Look, look someone has let all the pigs out.'

I heard him call Donald and Mrs Flynn. They all ran out and were hurriedly getting changed into their farm clothes at the same time. Mrs Flynn started to wind up the hand klaxon and then some more farmhands and attendants ran over. Luckily most of the new born piglets were still in the pens with their mothers and appeared to be oblivious of all the fuss. The pigs which had escaped were all working their way down to the bottom field. We managed to get a few back and then we noticed people coming out of the chapel. They all came over to help and started running after the pigs as well. Even Parson Jaggs joined in. It was very funny seeing him running around in his white frock and waving his crook. By the time we got all the pigs in, everyone had missed dinner. Most of the attendants were also with us so they knew the reason why.

'Don't worry. I'll sort dinner out, make sure that you're all back here in an hour,' Mrs Flynn said.

Later, on the way back to Rose Cottage I could smell fresh meat and rosemary cooking. The Flynns had put a small deer on a spit and it was coming along very well. There were some big pots of vegetables hanging up over a fire and Missy Hope was sitting at the outside table peeling potatoes, Donald was helping. One of the store men had brought over lots of beer and wine and a man from the village had brought in some of his homemade punch. It turned out to be a very fine afternoon. Mr Horlock came over and said that at around midnight last night he had chased some boys off.

'It was probably them horrible little bastards who opened the gates,' he said.

21 April 1931

One of the new men in the ward set fire to himself last night. He just stood there laughing at himself while he was ablaze. Nurse Primrose and two night attendants doused him down with buckets of water and then Harry Horlock came but by then the fire was already out. The man had only arrived last Sunday and no-one really knows him yet, we don't even know his name. The doctors came and rushed

278

him off to the infirmary. His face and hands were all burnt. The attendants took us all over to the Recreation Hall so that Mr Horlock and the firemen could clear the dormitory of smoke. The dawn chorus had just started and we were let back in just as it was getting light. There was a black circle on the charred floor where the man had been standing. Mr Randall came in and roped it off.

'We need some new floorboards put down, it isn't safe,' he warned.

22 April 1931

Maisie's friend Katherine called me over this morning. She was stood in the female airing court eating an apple. She told me that Maisie is still in an isolation room. The nurses have given her some medicines to help keep her relaxed.

'She's very feeble now. She's been calling out for her father and has not really been making any sense at all,' she said.

I worry for Maisie, it wasn't long ago that her hopes were high and she was looking forward to leaving here. Everything seems to have gone wrong and I think it's all to do with what's happened with Angela. That horrible bitch has spoiled everything for her.

23 April 1931

The man who set fire to himself on Monday night has died. His name was Basil Mullins and he was fifty-six years old. Mr Armstrong told me that he saw the body being taken out through the bottom gate in the hearse this morning. He told me that when there's a burial down at the cemetery the bodies are taken out this way and always just before dawn to keep the spectacle away from the locals.

'It's a quick route round into the Lye and then through to Cemetery Pales,' he said. 'It doesn't take too long!'

Mr Armstrong asked me if I knew how to catch rats and I told him that Lionel had shown me once. There's a problem with rats from the sewer getting into the Fruit and Vegetable Store and he wants me to help him lay some traps; 'proper traps.' They've had to throw a lot of good food away because they've found droppings in the stores.

'The Medical Superintendent is very angry about it and wants a full enquiry, he doesn't want to hear of any rats around the grounds anymore but he's got no hope with that,' Mr Armstrong said with a smile.

Today I caught four rats.

25 April 1931

Today we were supposed to be going on a trip to Frensham Ponds but Albert's bus had broken down so we couldn't go. Edward was very disappointed. He had been there before when his brother was still alive and wanted to take his toy yacht. This afternoon I played football with some men from another ward and a couple of boys from the village. It wasn't a proper game and the ball wasn't blown up properly. It was very hard to kick and it hurt my toes. After all the running around I felt all my joints beginning to ache again, so I stopped.

Tonight the doctors and nurses are putting on a show called *Pictures of Lilly* in the Main Hall. Mr Randall said that they will be singing lots of songs that we wouldn't have heard before.

'They wrote all the songs especially for the show themselves,' he said.

26 April 1931

When I was walking near the porter's West Gate Lodge this morning someone driving a brown Morris automobile tooted its horn at me. When I looked over to see who it was, it was Maisie's Uncle Sylvester. Her cousin Suzanne was sat in the front passenger seat, she must have recognised me. Another lady was on the back seat who I didn't know. They must have been to visit Maisie. I do hope she's well. I must look out for Katherine now to find out if there's any more news.

After dinner Silas took some of us for a walk around the village. We were going to go to Embleton's but it was closed. Everywhere was closed, even the beer houses. When we got back into the grounds Edward tried to jump up on one of the horses but he fell and hurt his arm. Silas told him off. I'd never heard Silas shout before. He just seemed to roar at Edward like a lion. I think that he must have thought he could get into trouble if one of us got hurt whilst he's in charge.

27 April 1931

This is my last week helping Mr Armstrong. In fairness I've quite enjoyed working with him. Next week I'm supposed to go and work with the carpenters and woodmen for a month but Mr Luscombe is trying to get me back at the farm until I leave in July.
'The other patients don't do much more than just stroke the animals and are no help at all and we have a very busy time coming up what with the pigs due to farrow again soon,' he said.
This morning I saw Donald, he's very worried and he thinks that he's got Missy Hope in the family way. He's asked me not to tell anyone. He hasn't even told his mother yet and is still trying to pluck up the courage. I wished him luck. Naughty Donald!
This afternoon I found an old black cat caught in one of Mr Armstrong's traps. It was full of mange and looked like it was going blind. I called Mr Armstrong over and he said that it needed putting out of its misery. He hadn't seen it before so didn't know who it belonged to. He took it over to the reservoir and held it under the water until it drowned. I took it from him and buried it under a cluster of bluebells in the woods near my tree. It was very sad but I think Mr Armstrong did the right thing.

28 April 1931

Today I saw Mr Mycroft walking his dog through the grounds. He told me that he has now settled in at his new lodgings in the Broadway and that the lady there cooks him a hearty breakfast every day. He told me that he had read some more articles in the newspapers about Maisie's Uncle Sylvester. Apparently he's been in the Winchester assizes accused of colluding to procure paintings on the cheap from other artists and trying to sell them at a handsome profit to galleries in London.

'Someone's caught up with him at last. It's probably because the Albright girl hasn't been painting very much lately and he still needed a source of income,' he reckoned.

I asked if I could see the articles but he thinks that he's thrown them away.

'It was a good few weeks ago,' he muttered.

Today I had to wade out into the middle of the reservoir with a measuring stick. I was wearing special boots but the water wasn't very high. Mr Armstrong said that unless it rains very hard over the next few days the reservoir will be as dry as a bone by this time next week.

'Fortunately there's a sufficient supply to keep us going in the water tower,' he said.

29 April 1931

I saw Katherine this morning and asked about Maisie. She told me that she was being kept in the isolation room and is in still very much in the same condition. 'They're trying to keep her sedated most of the time. I've been allowed to go and see her for a few minutes each day but I don't think that Maisie realises I'm there,' she said.

She told me that she thinks that it's all very unfair.

'They should take Angela away so that Maisie can come back into the ward and live normally.'

I agreed. It does appear that Angela has a knack of getting away with things. Katherine told me that Angela has now started bullying one of the other patients because she has a birthmark on her face.

'She's being very mean and nasty to her.'

I asked Katherine if she knew that Maisie had some visitors on Sunday last.

'Yes, I saw them arrive, they didn't stay long. I think that it was Maisie's uncle and cousin. I heard someone say that the other lady used to be Maisie's art teacher.'

I asked Katherine if Maisie was awake and if she spoke to them but she didn't know.

'Probably not which was why they left so soon after arriving,' she said.

30 April 1931

Mr Armstrong told me that he always calls the last day of April the last day of spring.

'Look around you, all the daffodils and narcissus have shrivelled, that's a fair sign that summer's on its way,' he said.

I don't know when the seasons are supposed to start and end. I just go by the weather and try and tell by how warm or cold it is. Summer is my favourite season but the autumn has the best colours.

On Saturday there's a big May Fayre in the grounds. Men have come in from the village and are helping the woodmen erect big white tents on the cricket field. Children will be dancing around the Maypole and the Asylum Band will be playing. Mrs Flynn told me that she's making some rabbit and game pies especially and that she'll be selling them to the village folk.

'It's a chance for me to make some extra pennies,' she said.

I wonder if Donald has told her and Mr Flynn about what he's done to Missy Hope yet!

3 May 1931

I was just about to go for my usual Sunday morning walk when Mr Randall came into the ward and told me that I had visitors waiting for me at the reception. I wasn't expecting anyone so was rather curious. He gave me a wry look but didn't say anymore. I felt very apprehensive walking over and wondered if it could be Mr George O'Leary, my father again. When I got there I could see that it was Cousin Clifford. Sitting in the waiting room was Mother and Aunt Betty. I felt shocked and aghast and didn't know what to say.

'Hello Thomas, how are you today?' Aunt Betty asked.

Mother stood up and came over and gave me a hug.

'I understand someone has been here to see you and has told you a few things about us,' she said.

At that point Miss Rance told us that we could go and sit in her office so that the other visitors wouldn't have to hear our conversation. Aunt Betty then gave me a hug.

'I'm so sorry Thomas. I knew that this would all have to come out one day but when you were born we did what we thought was right and for the right reasons. We had your welfare and your future to consider.'

I asked her about George O'Leary and she confirmed that he is my father. 'I am your mother, your mother is your aunty and Clifford is your half brother. Is that what George told you?' she asked.

'Yes,' I replied.

The conversation seemed to stop while everyone drew their breath. I was surprised by how grown up I felt. I even felt that I was in command of the whole conversation. I then asked Aunt Betty what had happened to her husband. She told me that when he came back from Europe he was struck down by a fever.

'He had nine brothers; some were gangsters so we had to keep the secret going. The whole thing was very complicated and we panicked a bit if I'm honest. Becoming pregnant by a man who is not your husband is very dishonourable and John would have killed me and your father if he'd found out,' she said.

I assumed then that John was her husband and that he must have since died.

'Yes, he died but I told him the truth about everything when I knew he was on his death bed. It was too late for him to tell anyone else. He just sat up and gasped one last breath and then was gone as soon as I told him. I did love him though,' she murmured.

I looked over towards Mother. Of course I now know that she's not my mother at all but she was very quiet. It's Mother who has lied to me all of my life and then I thought about Uncle Charlie. Did he know? I had to ask Mother that question.

'Yes, he knew everything, he had to and he was the one person who could help us and he gave us somewhere to live and helped me keep the secret. It was only when Clifford became suspicious about things a year or so ago that everything came out.'

Clifford then stood up and apologised to me. He told me that Gloria had accidentally listened to a couple of conversations between

Mother and Aunt Betty, they didn't realise that she was in the same room and was listening.

'She told me that she had heard them mention certain things and that's the day when a few unanswered questions about you began to add up. Look how much more you look like your Aunt Betty, you don't have your mother's looks at all,' he said.

Everything was becoming very confusing again and I was starting to forget exactly who was who. Aunt Betty then asked me what I thought of George O'Leary when I met him. I told her that I thought he was a fine gentleman.

'If he's my father, then I'm very proud,' I said.

She then told me how she met him and how a secret affair had carried on while her husband John was away.

'It was love but it was also a very deceitful act. I was so ashamed when I fell pregnant and I was very grateful to my sister Marion, the woman who you call Mother for helping me out but she had all sorts of her own problems. You must know by now what those were,' she said.

Oh yes, I do. Clifford then asked me if George O'Leary had managed to confirm a discharge date for me. I told him that it should be one Sunday in July. He asked me where I was going to live.

'It can't be with him, he has another family you know,' he said.

I told everyone that I would like to live in Knaphill so that I can carry on working here as a farmhand with the pigs although I was still waiting for someone to tell me what was happening. Clifford reminded me that George O'Leary is my appropriate relative now.

'He's the one who should be talking to the Medical Superintendent to arrange things for you now,' he added.

After they had all left, Miss Rance made me sit down for awhile and arranged for a servant to pour me some tea. Today has been very hard and it's the first time that I've ever heard Aunt Betty mention her husband John. John Turner. I asked Miss Rance if she knew what might be happening with my accommodation when I leave here in July. She said that she would try to find out and get a message to me as soon as she could.

'The Medical Superintendent is always changing things around so I'm not always sure what is happening around this place sometimes,' she said.

I didn't really like the sound of that!

7 May 1931

Incessant is a word I've picked out of the dictionary to describe the rain that we've had since Monday. It's rained very hard and only stopped this morning just after breakfast. I'm helping back at the farm now and I feel privileged and happy. I'm very pleased that Mr Luscombe has managed to persuade the Medical Superintendent that he needed me back. There's lots of work to do. The pig pens are very over-crowded and some of the older pigs are being taken for slaughter earlier than usual. It is very sad to see them go. Donald told me that it's another reason why we had to get rid of the pot-bellies to market.

'We need the room and it's always the Middle Whites which make the money, that's what keeps the Chief Clerk happy,' he said.

8 May 1931

This morning I saw Mr Flynn talking to a very fat solemn looking man outside Rose Cottage. The man had a big red spotty face and was wearing a brown dust jacket. Donald told me that he was the Head Mortuary Attendant.

'He's been helping out at the slaughterhouse. No-one's died at the asylum for a couple of weeks so he's had no new bodies to cut up for post mortems. He quite often helps out if he can.'

Later I heard the man talking but I couldn't understand what he was saying, even Mr Flynn was scratching his head; I don't think that he could understand him either. After he'd gone Donald told me that the man's name is Johnny Cut-Throat. He comes from a place called South Shields up in the north.

'His real name is Jonathan Cutler. Cut-Throat is just a silly nickname we've always had for him,' he said.

I smiled and then we both laughed. I think Mr Flynn heard what we were talking about. He laughed as well and then told us to get on with our work.

After dinner Donald told me that Missy Hope is going to live with him at Rose Cottage until they can find some accommodation of their own. His mother was very shocked and horrified when he told her that Missy was going to have a baby but he made me laugh.

'My mother asked me if I was sure that it was mine. No, it's Missy Hope's,' he had told her.

That comment tickled me pink and has made me smile to myself all day. Donald's mother has told him that he must get married as soon as possible. I think he's already been to see the vicar at a church in St. Johns with Missy Hope in tow.

9 May 1931

Today has been a beautiful day of sunshine and it's probably the warmest day of the year so far.

On the way back from the farm I saw Katherine. She told me that Maisie is still in isolation but is at last making some progress and is sitting up in bed and taking food. The nurse has told her that Maisie should be back in the ward next week. Katherine also mentioned that Angela had attacked a night attendant with a mop on Wednesday just before lights out. She said that she had made 'friends' with the mop which had been left behind by one of the ancillary workers and got very angry when the attendant tried to take it away. Angela was then put in restraints and marched off to the refractory where she has been ever since. The attendant who is quite new was left with a bad scratch mark down one side of her face. I asked Katherine if she thought that Angela may now be locked away permanently but she wasn't sure.

'You must remember that Angela is very devious and has a knack of always getting away with things,' she said.

I hope this is at last the start of some better news for Maisie.

10 May 1931

I've noticed that Lionel has been cutting himself again. Mr Randall has already taken some razors off him but he's found some sharp pieces of metal from somewhere and has got some very deep cuts all down his left arm. There's been blood all over his sheets and I've heard Nurse Applejack tell him off quite a few times. I think it's something to do with a letter he received from his wife on Tuesday last. He's been quite quiet and has not said anything. He's also been banging things around and very heavy on his feet. I want to ask him if he's alright but when he's like this, it's best not to say anything.

This afternoon I saw Mrs Skilton. She doesn't work on Sundays but she had been to the Recreation Hall to help some of the female patients with their arts and crafts.

'We're putting some of them up for sale in the village next week,' she said.

She then asked me if I had heard anymore about my accommodation when I leave. I told her that I expected to be let out of here in July. I told her all about what had happened with George O'Leary and how he told me that he was my father and what had happened with Mother and Aunt Betty. She asked me to say it her twice because she couldn't believe what I was telling her.

'It's true, it's so very true,' I told her.

She then told me that she still has a spare room in her house and that I would be welcome to stay there although a reasonable weekly rent payment would be necessary. I told her that I wasn't sure if I could pay and she said that if I could get a proper job at the farm with Mr Luscombe that would suffice.

'Don't worry; I'll look after you Tommy,' she said with a smile.

I then told her that George O'Leary, my father had suggested that I could go and live with him in Frimley Green but there would be complications because he has his own family. Mrs Skilton said that she would speak to Miss Rance.

'It may also be a good idea if you can put me in touch with your father, let's try and sort this muddle out once and for all.'

I feel very grateful to Mrs Skilton. She's always been very kind to me.

13 May 1931

Things are starting to get back to normal today after a few days of bad weather. Mr Luscombe said that it's been very unseasonal. Yesterday there was a big hail storm and we all got soaked and battered even though we sheltered under the tree at the corner of the farm. The hail stones were nearly as big as golf balls and they hurt when they hit my head. We spent the rest of the morning drying out at Rose Cottage. Mrs Flynn kept making a fuss of me because I was sat in her scullery in just my pants and stockings while she ironed my overalls dry and lit a fire. Donald just changed into another pair of his own farming clothes. When we got back over the road the sun came out and it got very hot. My overalls were still a bit damp and the sun made a lot of steam come off. Mr Flynn and Donald joked that I was on fire and that they would get Mr Horlock to come and put me out. My trousers made me feel very uncomfortable for the rest of the day and I couldn't wait to go back to the ward to get changed.

14 May 1931

A very happy looking Katherine called to me this morning. She told me that Maisie is back in her bed on the ward.

'She's very quiet and seems very thin but at least she's back,' Katherine said.

This is good news but I do fear for Maisie. She has always been very thin so if Katherine thinks that she's got thinner I wonder if she might be ill. Katherine said that she'll try and bring her out for a walk, probably on Sunday morning. She'll leave me and Maisie to chat why she goes off somewhere to read a book. I thanked Katherine, I don't know what I would have done if she wasn't about to give me all the news.

15 May 1931

I like Fridays. Everyone always seems to be a lot more cheerful, especially at the farm. Mr Flynn always whistles on a Friday and

Donald tries to sing. It's also usually Mrs Flynn's early finish in the Bursar's office so she comes over to help in the afternoon and brings us drinks.

Unfortunately we still have to send the older pigs off to slaughter and some have had to go to the slaughterhouse in the village. It's been a record year for farrowing and this morning I counted eighty-seven piglets. They're taking up a lot of space as well as a lot of time to look after although most of the younger ones are still feeding off the sows.

Tomorrow we're going to the pictures in Woking to see two cowboy films. Mr Randall has arranged it with Albert, I think that all the men are going from our ward except one of the new patients who is nearly blind and is very old. Lionel thinks that the old man has just been sent here to die. It's the first real conversation Lionel has had with anyone since he got the letter from his wife and started cutting himself again. I do hope he's getting better now.

17 May 1931

Yesterday at the cinema it was very hot and smokey. It was hard to breathe. The reel kept stopping and everyone kept cheering. It ruined the film. I can't remember that much about it now but I liked the bit when the cavalry charged into the town to rescue a lady from the top window of a burning saloon after she had been tied up by a masked cowboy. It reminded me of a story I'd read in one of the books Mr Mycroft had given me. When we came out I was so glad that I could breathe properly again. All the smoke in there was making feel sick and I've already decided that I never want to go back. It was a horrible place and I couldn't enjoy the films. I didn't want to tell Mr Randall because I knew how hard he had worked to arrange the outing for us.

Katherine brought Maisie up into the woods. I had been sitting here for about two hours hoping that I would see her. They came just before the dinner bell was due to go off which meant that we didn't have a lot of time to talk. Katherine then went away and sat under another tree. Maisie was very quiet and tearful. At first it seemed like she didn't want to say anything. She then apologised for not being able to see me. I told her that it was obviously not her fault. She took my hand and then told me that she has been having lots of fits over the last few months. The Medical Superintendent has told her uncle that she needs to stay at the asylum a bit longer for further treatment.

'They told my family a couple of weeks ago when I was in isolation. I was hoping to be out of here by now. It looks like you'll be gone long before me and I won't know what to do then, she whispered.

I clutched her hand as tight as I could. I noticed that she had a hanky in her sleeve so I pulled it out and wiped away a tear that was running down the side of her face. She then told me that she was worried that Angela could be back in her ward in the next few days.

'She's making my life a living hell,' she said quite angrily.

Just then the bell went for dinner. I could see Katherine walking over towards us out of the corner of my eye. Maisie then squeezed my hand as hard as she could. We looked into each other's eyes and then she gave me a quick kiss on the cheek and then ran off towards Katherine. She then turned and waved as they walked away towards the ward. She smiled but her face looked gaunt and sad. I felt a lump come into my throat. I wanted to hold her more closely and kiss her properly but there wasn't time. I needed to tell her how much I love her, how deep for her my feelings really are.

18 May 1931

When I got to the farm at 9 o'clock this morning, there was no-one there. I looked across to Rose Cottage and noticed that all the curtains were still drawn which was very unusual. I decided to wait by the gate and hoped that someone else would come along. It felt very eerie. After about twenty minutes Mrs Horlock came waddling over from the North Lodge and asked me if I was Tommy.

'Yes, I am, we've met and spoken before,' I said.

'Don't worry boy, my memory is not what it used to be. Anyway, you need to go back to the ward, the Flynn's had a bit of an upset in the early hours and have now gone back to bed for the rest of the morning,' she said.

291

I asked her what was wrong but she said that it would be more respectful for me to ask them myself.

'Be tactful though,' she warned.

I was both curious and worried but decided that I would go back to the farm after dinner. Hopefully I would find out everything then.

After dinner when I returned to the farm Mr Flynn was out watering down the pigs. He looked very tired.

'Hello, Tommy, I suppose you've heard our news by now,' he said.

I told him that I hadn't. I said that Mrs Horlock had advised me to go back to my ward this morning and then come back to the farm after dinner. He then told me that Missy Hope had fallen down the stairs last night and lost her baby.

'She hasn't been living with us very long and got confused in the dark when she was trying to find her way to the toilet. There was a terrible mess. She will be in hospital for quite a few days or even weeks and young Donald is inconsolable.'

I told him that I was sorry to hear about what had happened and asked if there was anything I could do.

'Just be here and help me with the pigs, that'll be enough.'

I detected an upset in his voice which I'll never forget. Mr Flynn was close to tears. He told me that Mrs Flynn and Donald had gone back to the hospital.

'They won't be home now until they can be sure that the poor girl will live,' he said.

It was only when he said that that I realised how awful things were. It made me think that perhaps its days like today we do need a God?

19 May 1931

Yesterday evening Parson Jaggs came into the ward to do his weekly bedside rounds. He came over to me and said that I looked very troubled. I always feel uncomfortable in his presence but I felt that I needed to tell him that I feared for Missy Hope and now wished that there was a God. He wasn't aware what had happened to Missy so I had to explain to him who she was.

'Hope Harrison, the scullery maid, she used to be a patient and then came back to the asylum to work, we sometimes call her Missy Hope, she now lives with Mr and Mrs Flynn at Rose Cottage,' I said.

He paused and then looked very disapprovingly at me.

'A child out of wedlock is the devil's work. Losing it is God's intervention,' he said.

Even Lionel looked across in disbelief. I thought that Parson Jaggs was supposed to show compassion but I became very shocked and angry by what he had said. This was a time when I was beginning to think that there actually is a God but he has spoiled it for me now. Lionel advised me to go and talk to a vicar in the village when I get the chance. He thinks that Parson Jaggs and Nurse Applejack are responsible for taking any belief I may have had in God away.

'They're just hypocrites. Personally I'm not sure what I believe in anymore but what I do know is that whatever I believe, it should always be my choice and not something that has been influenced by the right or wrong opinions of others,' Lionel said.

I think he's right. In fact, I know he's right!

21 May 1931

Edward absconded from the asylum yesterday. He was brought back this morning after a lady had found him hiding in her coal house in St John's. Mr Randall and some of other attendants had been out all night looking for him but were happy when a policeman brought him back to the reception at about 11 o'clock. Edward told us that the lady made him have a good scrub in a big tin bath and then gave him breakfast. When she found out he was from the asylum she ran out of her house and into the road when she saw the policeman riding by on his bicycle.

'I was looking for the railway station but got a bit lost after I slipped through a hole in the railings just before dinner time. I think I turned left when I should have turned right,' he said.

Edward was nineteen years old yesterday and told us that he wanted to go home and open his birthday presents but I think he's forgotten where he actually lives.

22 May 1931

I saw Mrs Skilton today and she told me that she's been to see Miss Rance. She said that I will have to attend an interview with the Medical Superintendent in July before I leave.

'Your father and I will be invited. The plan is that you will stay with me from Monday to Friday so that you can carry on working at the farm and that you stay with your father in Frimley Green at weekends. Miss Rance is writing to your father in the hope that he will agree to the proposal. Nothing can happen unless he agrees because he is your appropriate relative.'

I liked what she was telling me and I thanked her for all her help. But now I must think of Maisie and decide how best to break my latest news. It seems that even with good news there are still so many complications.

25 May 1931

Today is the Spring Bank Holiday and I only had to help on the farm for a couple of hours this morning. Donald was back at work and he told me that Missy Hope is now out of danger but she has to stay in hospital for at least another week. He also told me that last night there was a big argument at home with his mother. The Medical Superintendent has found out that Missy had moved into Rose Cottage without his permission and is asking to see Mr Flynn so that he can explain all the events.

'When Missy comes out of hospital she'll probably be going back to live in Queens Road, I will move with her if I can, I don't want to be without her now. I don't want her to be all alone,' Donald said.

This afternoon there was a Spring Fayre on the cricket field. Lots of people from the village came and they were buying vegetables and fruit from our farm. Mrs Woolston was selling crafts from a stall in the corner under a tree and I noticed Katherine was helping so I went over to talk. Katherine told me that Maisie was still feeling quite weak and wanted to stay back in the ward. 'She's got her nose in a big book but she'll be fine and you'll be able to see her again soon,' she said.

26 May 1931

Last night I dreamt that I had slept with Maisie. It was the most beautiful dream. We were lying naked on a bed in a seaside hotel and the moonlight was shining into the room through a crack in the curtains. The promenade was down below our window and we could hear the waves dragging the shingle back into the sea from the beach with every turn. The bright moon meant that we could look into each other's eyes and see our smiles. At last we were free and alone together. Everything was very tender and I felt Maisie slowly running her fingers up and down my spine. She gently turned me over and our bodies entwined. Our tongues pressed deep into each other's mouths as we kissed and then I felt some pain, then a shudder and a wonderful feeling I have never felt before. Did this now mean that we were lovers? The moment didn't last very long and it seemed to be suspended in time. I didn't want the dream to end. I wanted to dream it all over again and again but the light of dawn and sound of all the other patients getting out of their beds woke me up. I must tell Maisie about my dream. I wonder now if she may have had this dream as well!

27 May 1931

This morning Nurse Applejack came and took Edward to see the Medical Superintendent about running away the other day. Edward's mother had come to see him as well and she promised that she will try and get him out of here as soon as she could. Edward has been told that if he tries to abscond again he will be put in the refractory ward or even high security. I'm very worried for him now because I think he may try it again. He's very obsessed with getting out of here but he doesn't plan it very well. He doesn't even know where he's going to go if he gets free.

This afternoon I've been cradling one of the newborn piglets. Its mother has rejected it and it needs to be hand fed. It's a lively little thing and it made my arm ache while I struggled to keep it still. Donald told me not to give it a name or make a pet out of it.

'You'll only be upset if it dies,' he said.

I don't think that it will die, it's very strong and it takes the milk very well but not from its mother.

28 May 1931

Yesterday I spent a long time talking to Silas Greenwood. He asked me if I was looking forward to leaving here in July. I told him that I was still very anxious about everything despite what Mrs Skilton had said. I don't think that I'll be really comfortable with it all until I'm walking through the gate with my bag over my shoulder. I mentioned what Parson Jaggs had said when he was doing his rounds in the ward the other evening, Silas was quite shocked. I told him that I had been trying to understand in my own mind if there really is a God and that I think Parson Jaggs is the person who is stopping me from doing that. Silas suggested that I could go to the Baptist Church in Knaphill with him on Sunday morning and that I might find the answers I'm looking for in there.

'I don't go every week because I prefer to drive around in my new car on my days off but if I can, I'll get permission for you to come with me if you like,' he said.

I agreed and wondered if that meant I would also be lucky enough to have a ride in his Bugatti!

29 May 1931

Nurse Primrose was back on duty in our ward last night. She told me that she's been working in the refractory where Angela Reeves is being kept. I immediately asked her how long she would be staying there and she said that patients should only stay there for a maximum of four weeks but there are exceptions.

'It's then for the Medical Superintendent to decide what happens next. Most but not all end up going back to their original ward.'

She told me that she has been trying to befriend Angela.

'It's part of the process of getting her to calm down.'

Angela had told her that her father was an American chap who ran off when he saw that she had been born with a deformity. Her mother believed in the occult and thought that she had given birth to the devil's daughter. She later died in a workhouse while Angela was sent to an orphanage. While she was there she was repeatedly picked upon and bullied. She had always dreamt that one day she would be a proud mother with a baby of her own. It never happened.

'I don't think that Angela realises that it needs a man to help get her in the family way. I think that's the real cause of all her problems,' Nurse Primrose reckoned.

I asked her if Angela would stop attacking people if she went back to her ward.

'Who knows? Who really knows? But please don't tell anyone that we've had this conversation.'

So now I worry about poor Maisie again, I worry that she may not be safe at all.

31 May 1931

This morning Silas took me and three other patients to the Baptist Church. We walked there so I was very disappointed that I didn't have a chance to ride in his Bugatti. Perhaps there were too many of us and I think that it only has two seats. I was a bit confused because I was sure that one of the other patients was a doctor, the one with a squeaky voice who had examined me before. When we got to the church it was a quaint little place with two arched shaped windows at the front either side of a big wooden door. Above the door was a small stained-glass circular window which was very unusual. When we got inside I recognised some of the people from the village. They come to the asylum to give out presents on Christmas Day. The vicar is one of them although Silas told me that they call him a minister at this church. Everyone was very friendly and the minister didn't shout at everyone like Parson Jaggs would. He told us that we must try to see God in our own way, in our own light; God is about choice and embracing your own beliefs. I understood that and I think that's what I've been trying to do lately. I asked Silas if he could take me there again. He seemed quite pleased that the trip had been worthwhile for me but was in a rush so that he could meet Mr Randall and some other friends at the beer house.

After dinner I spoke to Lionel and I told him about the patient who I thought was actually a doctor.

'That'll be Nigel Brownbill-Smith, he's not a qualified doctor but they do let him do some medical work. He was transferred here from another asylum somewhere up in London where he had been sent after getting into trouble with the police. He was training to be a doctor but was surgically castrated and then went a bit mad afterwards. He has his own room here in the same block where Anton is and although he's a patient, they treat him like a member of staff,' he said with a chuckle.

I didn't know what Lionel meant by 'surgically castrated' but it sounded quite nasty so I chose not to ask him anymore questions.

3 June 1931

When Katherine calls me I know it's either good news or bad news. Today she called me over and told me that Maisie had suffered another fit last night. She was restrained and given some medicine.

'She's sitting up now but is not allowed to leave the ward,' she said.

I asked her if it was all to do with not being able to leave the asylum as expected or if she was still calling out for her father. Katherine told me that Maisie is very confused.

'It doesn't help with her knowing that Angela could be coming back into the ward and that could happen by the end of the week.'

Katherine put her hand on my shoulder and told me that she is very worried about her.

'Her health and mind appear to be ebbing and I don't think that the nurses are helping in the way that they should. I'm very worried about Maisie now,' she whispered.

I too am worried but I don't know what to do. I need to see Maisie so that we can talk. Perhaps I could perk her up a little, but how?

4 June 1931

Today when we had finished feeding the pigs Mr Luscombe asked Mr Flynn, Donald and me to go and help Mr Armstrong. There'd been a tunnel collapse in the eastern corner of the bottom field and he was worried that it could cause more problems with the sewers. When we got there some men from the village were helping Mr Armstrong and Joseph dig it out.

'This one's a very long tunnel and it's supposed to lead all the way to the church at St John's, it gets smaller as you go. They say that it was originally built by monks but we use it to dump all the shit in the canal these days,' Mr Armstrong said.

One of the men from the village told us that people used to be able to walk through the tunnel until they came to a place called The Hermitage.

'It starts to get narrower about there; I don't think the monks ever finished it,' he said.

We did what we could to get all the debris out but Mr Armstrong told us that he would have to get a few men with some special machinery to finish the job but that won't be until next week.

'I'll have to tell the cooks not to feed you lot any spinach until after then,' he said.

Donald told me that Mr Armstrong was joking but I still didn't understand what he meant.

5 June 1931

When I was working at the farm this morning there was a man in a black gown standing by the gate, I heard him shout... 'Young man, young man!'

He was beckoning at me so I walked over.

'Do you remember me from last Sunday, Mr Greenwood said that I should come and introduce myself. I'm John Crosby and I am the Minister from the Baptist Church in Knaphill,' he said.

It was only then that I remembered him but I felt very apprehensive. I wasn't sure what he was going to say next.

'Don't worry, I'm not here to ram the name of God down your throat, I'm just here to help you find him. Be at peace with yourself and you will,' he said.

Before he left he told me that he hoped to see me at the church again and promised that he was always available if I ever needed to talk.

'Don't worry, I won't force anything on you, I'm just here to listen and to support you if you ever need that vital nudge in whatever direction you choose,' he said.

I was quite astounded by his kind words. At last I felt that I had found someone who really understands me and the way I think about God. I'm happy now. In just a few days I have found that there could really be a God. I just need to see him now. If Mr Crosby is right, God is here with me all the time but I need God himself to prove it. I need to know that he's here in my own mind!

9 June 1931

Lots of men with machinery came to help Mr Armstrong finish mending the collapsed tunnel today. Mr Flynn thinks that they're going to build a new shaft which will need to have a metal grill over it.

'It will be the easiest way,' he said.

I've been looking out for Katherine again today. I need to know how Maisie is but I haven't seen her yet and I'm now beginning to worry. It's been a long time since I last saw her. With summer here now each day is too long!

12 June 1931

After breakfast I was called to see Miss Rance in the reception. She explained that she had been talking to Mrs Skilton about my release from the asylum.

'I've written to your father Mr George O'Leary and I still await his reply,' she said.

She then told me that Mrs Skilton would accommodate me during the week from a Sunday evening until a Friday evening. I would then catch a train to Ash Vale at weekends and walk along to where my father lives in Frimley Green.

'I'm arranging a meeting with your father and Mrs Skilton in this office at 10 o'clock on Wednesday 1st July and if all is well, you will leave here on the Sunday after but your father must be here and in full agreement with this,' she warned.

She then asked me if I understood everything and I said 'Yes!'

I now need to tell Maisie everything. We should be leaving the asylum around about the same time. We need to make plans so that we can see each other once we are both free of this place. I will look for Katherine and see if there's any more news.

Mr Randall had been to the Chief Clerk and Attendant's office and brought back a postcard he had received from Mr Elliott in New York. Mr Elliott had arrived safely on his first voyage after going back to sea. On the postcard he asks Mr Randall 'How's that Tommy?' I liked that and felt very privileged that he's thought about me while he's been in America.

Mr Randall told us that the Medical Superintendent has appointed a new Chief Attendant and he will be here from next Monday. He's apparently very strict and has been told to make sure that some very big changes are made.

'He's coming here to crack a whip and none of us are very happy about it. I was hoping to get promoted into the job myself but the Medical Superintendent thinks that my discipline record isn't good enough. I don't think I have a future here anymore so I might have to leave,' he said.

13 June 1931

Today has been very hot. Mr Randall took Edward and me down to Pirbright along the canal. We sat and ate sandwiches and watched a man and his son fishing. Mr Randall seemed to know them very well and so they chatted for a long time. Edward started talking to me about football. He's hoping that he'll be able to go and see a game at Fulham when the new season starts in August. He's expecting to be allowed out of the asylum soon as well but it all depends on his behaviour. When we left the canal Mr Randall took us to a hotel at the railway station. He told me that this is where I'll be catching the train when I go to stay with my father at weekends. Mr Randall didn't have much money but Edward had enough so we sat on a bench outside the hotel and drank cider. I think Mr Randall got a bit tipsy and he was still very angry about what the Medical Superintendent had said to him yesterday.

'I'm just trying to get it all off my chest,' he said and then burped very loudly.

A lady in a big white floppy hat who was sitting near us turned around a looked at him very disapprovingly and Edward sniggered. I hid behind my glass.

14 June 1931

Silas asked me if I would like to go to the church with him again this morning. It was very awkward because I wanted to walk around the grounds and look for Maisie or Katherine. In the end he persuaded me to go but while I was in the church all I could think about was Maisie and getting back into the grounds to see if I could find her. When I got back I walked around but didn't see either of them.

Today has been another very hot day and this evening I have sat under my tree until the sun started to go red. There's a breeze now. My heart is aching for Maisie so much. I love her so. I need to see her. I need to be with her but still, I have no further news.

15 June 1931

When I was going back to the ward at dinner time I saw Nurse Applejack walking towards the reception with Miss Rance. Nurse Applejack was smiling which was very odd and also very unusual. In the ward there was lots of commotion and Mr Randall and a new nurse were trying to calm everyone down. Lionel, Edward and some of the other patients were banging their boots against their bedsteads and cheering. Another man was dancing around in circles looking very happy. When the noise stopped Lionel told me that Nurse Applejack had just been in and told everyone that she was leaving on

Friday to go and work at an asylum in London so that she can be closer to her family.

'It's such excellent news isn't it?' he shouted.

All the others started singing again and Mr Randall just sat down smiling at us. Just then the door flew open and Nurse Applejack walked in. Everything suddenly went quiet. I think that she knew what was going on and asked to speak with Mr Randall and the new nurse in the side room. When she came out she didn't look very happy and Mr Randall looked a bit embarrassed. The new nurse looked like she'd been crying and scurried off very quickly down the stairs.

18 June 1931

Missy Hope has been dismissed from her job in the scullery because she fell in the family way. Mr Flynn has been given a warning by the Medical Superintendent about allowing her to stay at Rose Cottage without his permission and Donald has left the farm to go and live with Hope in Queens Road.

'He won't be back, he got very angry, it was me who told him to leave, I didn't want him staying here and making things worse for his mother,' Mr Flynn said.

This is very bad news, I regard Donald as one of my best friends now and I will miss working with him at the farm. Mr Flynn gave me the number of the house in Queens Road and said that I could go and visit him there when I'm free. I'm almost counting down the days now but I still have some doubts as I don't think Miss Rance has heard from my father yet. She said that she would tell me when there's any further news but again, everything has gone very quiet.

19 June 1931

At last I saw Katherine today. She told me that Maisie has been receiving some special treatment in the day ward at the infirmary.

'I think that the doctors are experimenting with her.'

I asked her what the treatment was but she didn't know. She said that Maisie doesn't really want to talk about it.

303

'She comes back into the ward with a hop, skip and a jump and seems very happy but in the evenings she starts muttering about her father. She's also very frustrated that she wasn't able to leave here when she expected to and then becomes very melancholy just before the lights go out. The nurse has been tending to her every night and given her something to help her sleep.'

I asked Katherine if Maisie had mentioned me.

'Oh, all the time, she never stops talking about you.'

I was pleased to hear that but all I want now is to see her again. Katherine told me that she hoped that Maisie would get better soon and everything would go back to normal. She warned me that she thinks that Maisie's changed. Changed quite a lot!

'She's certainly a lot more restless these days and always seems very troubled.'

I asked Katherine if Angela Reeves had been allowed back in her ward yet.

'No, not yet but that's another thing that must be worrying Maisie.'

20 June 1931

Last night after tea there was much rejoicing in the ward, Nurse Applejack was gone and everyone was singing and dancing. The new nurse looked quite confused. Mr Randall was trying to get everyone to quieten down but no-one was taking any notice. It all went on for an hour until the Medical Superintendent came in with the new Chief Attendant and Miss Rance.

'I've never heard such a song and dance, what's it all about?' he asked.

Everyone went very quiet and looked around at each other. No-one said anything until Lionel spoke up.

'It's because Nurse Applejack, sorry, Sister Applejack has left at last, she won't be here to cast her evil spells on us anymore. We're glad to see the back of the fat nigger bitch,' he shouted.

The Medical Superintendent ordered Mr Randall and the new Chief Attendant to restrain Lionel and take him to the side room.

'There will be no more of it, no more disrespect, no more insulting my staff. In return I promise you that there will be no more abuse if that's what's been happening around here,' he said.

This morning Lionel was allowed back in the ward.

'I had to give the Medical Superintendent a report of everything that I was accusing Nurse Applejack of doing. Miss Rance wrote it all down for him. You and some of the others will be asked to do the same. I've told him everything that I know about the bitch,' he whispered.

I wonder now if I might get myself into trouble if I am asked to say anything. Whilst I'm glad she's gone I now worry about what else might happen. I don't need any more ~~fucking~~ complications in my life!

21 June 1931

Today has been a very good day. After breakfast Silas came for me and one of the new patients called Martyn and took us both to the Baptist Church. As we walked along Silas was telling us about his Bugatti. Next Sunday he's driving it to Brighton and is taking his new lady friend. I asked him when I could have a ride and he just laughed.

'The passenger seat is just for ladies,' he said.

When we got to the church everyone was very friendly and looked very pleased to see us. We sat three rows from the front and the Minister, Mr Crosby waved to us before he begun the service. He started mumbling something and I thought that I would just wait for the first hymn. I like looking at the windows when I'm in a chapel but there isn't many in the Baptist Church. It's very tiny in there compared to the asylum's chapel. When the hymn started it was very joyous and everyone sung it loudly. I joined in too.

Summer suns are glowing over land and sea
happy light is flowing bountiful and free.

It reminded me of Maisie. As we were singing it, Silas kept nudging me in the arm and winking. He did it three times before I realised that he wanted me to turn and look over my shoulder. When I turned, I saw Maisie in the pews four rows behind with a nurse and a female attendant. She smiled brightly and I felt my heart grow warm. When we left the chapel we had some time to talk as we all walked back to the asylum together. Maisie told me that because she keeps blacking out she's not allowed to be left unattended anymore. She showed me a bruise on her forehead.

'I got this when I fell against the bedstead on Wednesday when I passed out,' she said.

I asked her if she would ever get better but she seemed to hesitate before she could answer.

'I don't know, I'm having treatment and it feels wonderful until it stops and then I become all melancholy. I just want to get out of the asylum and be myself, who I really am, an artist with a husband called Thomas or Tommy but so much is in the way, there are so many things stopping me and it just isn't very fair.'

I wanted to squeeze her hand and give her a hug but Silas and all the others were with us. I was already aware that they had heard most of our conversation. I think Silas is very good friends with the lady attendant and I wondered if it was her that he was taking to Brighton in his Bugatti next Sunday. When we got back into the asylum I said goodbye to Maisie at the North Lodge Gate. I wanted to kiss her but I wasn't allowed. I had to settle for just a smile and a wave and I felt very frustrated but also very happy that I had been able to speak to her after such a long time.

Silas asked me to show him the pig farm and asked me what I knew about all the pigs. I told him that Donald was the one who taught me everything but he's left now and things on the farm aren't the same. While we were there, Silas told me that Mr Randall had mentioned that I was very fond of Maisie.

'I will try and arrange for you both to meet at the Baptist Church again in a couple of weeks,' he said.

I thanked him very much because I was aware that he shouldn't really be encouraging male and female patients to see each other. Now I long to see her again but I wish that today we could have be alone together so that we could have talked properly, cuddled and had a kiss. A proper kiss!

23 June 1931

Mr Flynn is very angry lately and has been snapping at everyone. I don't think he means it but he seems to have changed a lot since Donald left the farm. He hasn't got a replacement farmhand yet and there's still all the work to do. He told me that he's asked Donald to come back and he's thinking about it but there's a lot of anger about since Missy Hope got pregnant, lost the baby and then had to leave. There's some sickness among the cows and Mr Hampton has been at the farm and down to the Sparvell field to check them all for disease. There's no news if he's found anything yet but they're not producing enough milk. The last thing Mr Luscombe will want is for milk to be bought in from Hilltop Place again.

24 June 1931

I saw Miss Rance today and she told me that she has still not had a reply from my father to her letter about the meeting. The meeting is supposed to be next Wednesday 1st July. I am now very worried. Miss Rance asked me if I had heard anything from anyone else which I thought was quite odd because all letters and visitors have to go through her to be vetted first. She then explained that she'd been away on holiday for a few days so may have missed something. I told her that I hadn't heard from a soul. I hadn't even seen Mrs Skilton since our last conversation. Miss Rance told me not to worry and said that she would write another letter to my father just in case the last one had got lost by the Royal Mail.

I think Lionel noticed that there was something wrong with me today because he kept asking if I was alright. He doesn't normally bother but today I do feel very melancholy and he must have noticed. Lionel is a very good friend but he has plenty of his own problems so I didn't really want to bother him with all my silly little troubles.

25 June 1931

Martyn Bosworth, the new patient was allowed to leave the asylum this afternoon just after dinner. A very smart rotund lady came for him who had travelled all the way down to Brookwood from Scotland by train. He'd only been in our ward for two weeks but had a second medical assessment yesterday. Mr Randall told us that the Medical Superintendent thinks that he should never have been sent here in the first place.

'Apparently, there's nothing wrong with him,' he said.

It made me think back to when I was first sent here. I know I couldn't speak very well but there wasn't really much wrong with me either and I've had to stay, it's been nearly two years now. Lionel told me to stay quiet and not say anything.

'You don't want to bring any unnecessary attention to yourself,' he warned.

I think he's right but I'm still also wondering why my father hasn't responded to Miss Rance's letter yet. I worry.

26 June 1931

I had a long conversation with Mr Randall today. He reckoned that I must be counting the days now until I get out on Sunday 5th July. I told him that I am but I have serious worries about my father not replying to Miss Rance's letter and not visiting again recently. I'm beginning to fear the worst and I worry that he will not be at the meeting with the Medical Superintendent and Mrs Skilton next Wednesday. I asked Mr Randall if he knew what would happen if my father didn't come.

'If he doesn't come to the meeting and sign the release authority papers you won't be able to leave. Mrs Skilton won't be able to do that on her own because she's not your appropriate relative. If you didn't have any relatives at all then perhaps she could,' he remarked.

I pondered for a moment and asked if I could get Cousin Clifford to become my appropriate relative again.

'You could but remember that there's no provision for you to be accommodated where he lives so he probably wouldn't be in a position to sign for your release now anyway. Now that you've told me that your Aunt Betty is your real mother, perhaps she can help, and she must owe you at least that after everything that's happened to you,' he suggested.

I told him that I also have Maisie to think about.

'Don't worry about her. Just get yourself out of here first. If her family are agreeable you can come and visit her every week. Before you know it, she'll be out as well,' he said.

Mr Randall has always been a man of good advice even though I did think that he was a bit of a scoundrel when I first met him.

27 June 1931

This afternoon we are going on a trip to Stonehenge and Salisbury. Mr Randall told me that its Albert's last day with the bus before he retires. Mr Randall isn't coming but told me that Silas and one of the new attendants will be looking after us.

'Make sure that Albert doesn't drink too much while you're down there, he needs to get you all back safe and I know what he's like when he's had a tipple,' he said. 'I'm glad I'll be in the bar up the road where I can just fall over on home soil,' he laughed.

I've been watching the squirrels this morning. There seems to be more greys than brown ones now. The greys have longer bodies and look much stronger. They always get to the food first and are quicker getting back up the tree.

29 June 1931

I couldn't go to the Baptist Church yesterday because Silas wasn't around to take me. He was driving down to Brighton. I just stayed in the grounds and walked around hoping to see Maisie or even Katherine. Neither of them was about and I felt myself becoming upset and very anxious.

The good news today is that Donald has decided to come back and work on the farm. Mr Flynn seems happier again and has been whistling while he works. I like it when he whistles, Ha-ha, it seems to cheer us all up. It's a real tonic!

30 June 1931

Tomorrow is Wednesday. I wonder if my father will attend the meeting. I wonder if he has received the second letter from Miss Rance.

2 July 1931

He didn't come. Mr Randall made sure that I was dressed in my Sunday best and was looking smart. I was wearing the suit that used to belong to Donald that I wore to his mother's wedding when she married Mr Flynn. It was 10 o'clock and we walked across to the reception. Mrs Skilton and her husband were already there. Miss Rance was looking very pensive. There was no sign of George O'Leary, the man I now know to be my father. Miss Rance was checking the train timetable to see if he would be late but I remembered that he always cycled over from Frimley Green on his delivery bike. Everything was very quiet while we waited, just the clock ticking, ticking - tick - tock - ticking - tick - tock and then chiming every fifteen minutes. A quarter past ten. Half Past ten. A quarter to eleven. 11 o'clock DING and then tick - tock - ticking until Miss Rance stood up.

'Would anyone like a nice cup of tea?' she asked.

The silence was broken but now I felt in my heart of hearts that my father wasn't ever coming to get me out of this place. Mrs Skilton came over from the other side of the room and sat beside me and put her hand on my shoulder. At that moment I felt myself beginning to weep. I think I was trembling, either with emotion or anger, I can't remember which. She offered me her handkerchief. It was then I that I realised perhaps I might never get out of this place. When it reached 12 o'clock mid day Miss Rance sent for Mr Randall. He came over with the new nurse and they took me back to the ward. I changed back into my normal clothes and just lay on my bed for the rest of the day. Lionel winked at me but I think he knew that I didn't want to talk. He must have guessed what had happened. I then stayed awake all night and watched the stars passing by the crack in the drapes; Nurse Primrose hadn't drawn them together properly. The next thing I knew, it was this morning, the dawn chorus and another day in this place. I won't be leaving here on Sunday. I don't think that I will ever be leaving here!

BOOK THREE

5 July 1931

The last few days had already been very difficult for me when just after breakfast this morning the new nurse told me that I had a visitor waiting in the reception to see me. It was a lady. She told me to get changed and said that she would take me over. The new nurse is very black and has a funny sounding name that I can't pronounce. I don't even know how to write it down. All I know is that is begins with O and ends with a U. When I got to the waiting room at the reception Miss Rance was there.

'This lady has come by train from Frimley and has something to say to you. Don't worry, I'll be here with Nurse O-----u. This lovely lady has promised me that she will stop talking if you begin to get upset,' she said.

I still didn't know who the lady was but she was quite tall and had a stern face and straight grey hair.

'Hello young Thomas, or is it Tommy they call you in here?' she asked.

I told her that I'm always called Tommy by my friends.

'Have you got any friends?'

I told her that I have lots of friends, some are patients and others are people who work here like Donald, Silas and Mr Randall.

'Have you guessed who I am yet?'

'No,' I replied.

There was a moment of hesitation and then she smiled but then her expression went back to stern again. In fact she looked quite cross and I began to worry.

'I'm the wife of Mr George O'Leary. Mary O'Leary. I'm also the mother of all his children except for you Tommy it seems.'

'I'll be frank, it was me who stopped your father from coming here on Wednesday, I wanted to meet you myself and have a say in the matter, after all I have three grown up children of my own, two boys and a girl. Yes, they are all grow up now but this, this is a matter of principle and I need to be involved.

'Did you know that we lost another son?' she asked. 'He drowned.'

'Yes I remember Mr O'Leary telling me this when he came to visit on the 5th of April last.' I replied.

Then you'll understand that I don't think it's right and proper for me to embrace a child who is not my own. You're not mine, you're not a normal sort of boy either and why should I take you in and treat you as my own? I've a marriage and a family to consider and I will not pay for that old bugger's past misdemeanours even though, like a fool, I stand by him every inch today,' she squealed.

Her voice was getting louder and Miss Rance stopped the conversation. She asked the new nurse to take me back to the ward and said that she would send for me later. Everything felt very awkward but at least I now know why my father didn't come on Wednesday. I don't think that everything is his fault, I don't think that it's his wife's either. She already has her own family to consider even though all her children are grown up just like me. I think that she doesn't want me to stay with them because I'm in the asylum and I think that she has made my father bow down to her opinion about the situation.

6 July 1931

Last night I had a very vivid dream. I dreamt that I was standing on my own in the Recreation Hall. Maisie's painting which is called *Angels Descending* was hanging on the wall. Somehow I was able to step into the painting and walk among the angels. There was a bright light. Maisie was already there standing inside her own brush strokes. The angels were gliding in and out between some tall stone columns that were holding up the sky. The floor was black and white and looked like a life-size chess board. I stepped across on the black squares left and right until I reached where Maisie was standing. Just as I got to her the light got even brighter and then everything disappeared. Suddenly I was lying on the floor back in the Recreation Hall. When I awoke I could remember everything about the dream and I wondered if it was a sign. I wondered if it was a sign of what would become of us.

7 July 1931

I keep thinking about what happened on Sunday when Mrs O'Leary came to see me. I now wonder why she came. I think that she wanted to explain but wasn't very good at it. My father should have come as well but now I think that he's just a gutless coward. I think that everything was cancelled for me because I'm from the asylum and they don't want other people to know where I might have suddenly appeared from. There's a thing called stigma that Mrs Skilton was telling me about. I wonder if that's got something to do with it. I wonder if that's why my father has decided that he doesn't want me now.

I'm trying to get a message to Maisie to let her know that I'm still here. For all she knows I left here on Sunday and she might think that she'll never see me again. I've been looking out for Katherine or for anyone else that knows her. Perhaps Nurse Primrose could help me get a message to her when I see her tonight.

8 July 1931

Mrs Skilton came by the farm to see me this morning. Mr Flynn let me go off to the cricket field so I could talk privately with her. She told me how sorry she was about how things went on Sunday when Mrs O'Leary came but still thinks that something can be done.

'Your father only needs to sign your release document and you can still come to live at my house. You're welcome to stay with us at weekends as well and your father can visit you whenever he wants.'

'Would you like me to talk to Miss Rance again?' she asked.

I told her that I would and I thanked her for giving me some fresh hope. I'm sure that my father will oblige when he finds out how simple it is. I'll be happier staying at Mrs Skilton's house all the time now anyway particularly after meeting his wife. I felt that she didn't like me because of who I am and she wasn't very friendly. Mrs Skilton said that if need be she will go and visit my father and his wife to explain what can be done, even if the Medical Superintendent or Miss Rance can't.

'It should be easy. I don't understand why there are so many silly complications,' she said quite angrily.

I thanked her again for her trouble and she told me that she would come back to see me again in a couple days time when hopefully she has more news. I also thanked Mr Flynn for giving us the time to talk.

I still haven't seen Maisie or Katherine to tell them that I'm still here. Nurse Primrose was sick yesterday and the new night nurse doesn't want to talk to anyone.

9 July 1931

Lionel has been inconsolable today. I think that today is one of the anniversaries with his wife, either a wedding anniversary or a birthday, I'm not sure, he hasn't been very clear. He's been mumbling about how hurt he is, how he did everything for her, how he worshiped the ground that she walked on only to have it all thrown back in his face. Lionel has told me things about her before, about how she used to sleep with other men and women behind his back. How he still loved her and forgave her, though it wasn't enough. She turned everything against him which is how and why he ended up here. When Lionel gets like this I fear for him. I fear that he becomes suicidal and may harm himself. He already cuts himself with pieces of metal and is always having to be bandaged by the nurse.

'This is what women do to you,' he always says.

He told me later that he has received a letter from his wife and that she's coming to see him on Sunday. She wants a thing called a divorce which will allow her to go off and marry another man.

'I won't allow it, despite everything I still want her, I want to be able to leave this forsaken place and go back to her, because I still love her!' he said.

At times like this I don't know what to say to Lionel. I know he has syphilis so I just nod and agree with him and I hope that's the reaction he's expecting. I listen to him because he's my friend. I always listen to him because he always listens to me. He's always there for me when I talk about Maisie.

10 July 1931

Mr Randall has told me to make the most of my time sitting up here in the woods. New high fencing is being put up around the airing courts to make everything more secure.

'The Medical Superintendent doesn't want patients wandering around the grounds on their own anymore, even when they're just on their way to work. He's being very strict about it, an attendant will always be needed to escort a patient in future, it's all going to be changing some time at the beginning of August,' he warned.

I now worry because my time alone here is what's been keeping me sane. Being made to stay in the airing court will mean that I'm with other people all the time. I won't be able to write things down. My valuable personal time will be lost. I'll feel really hopeless and won't be able to do anything except to listen to other people's nonsense and all of that would really drive me MAD!

I really do need to get out of here - but how? I do hope Mrs Skilton will be able to pull a few strings but how long do I have to keep clutching at straws? How many more times will my hopes get dashed?

11 July 1931

This morning in the ablutions I stared at myself in the mirror. Normally I just shave, wash and ignore myself then carry on. This time it was different. There was a voice in my head telling me to STOP! It was challenging me to look at myself differently and stop being this lost soul that I sometimes think I am. The voice was a guiding voice, not religious or anything of any authority. It was calm and sincere, warm and friendly. It was like the voice of someone I once knew but is no longer here. It wasn't the voice of a dead person either; it was different which is what I couldn't understand.

That moment in front of the mirror has been bothering me all day and now I don't really know what to think. Was it my imagination?

316

Or, was it something real? I don't know but I must carry on looking for the answer if I'm ever to see an end to this.

I've been looking out for Maisie or anyone who knows her so that they can tell her I'm still here. I haven't seen Katherine or anyone from Maisie's ward for days now. Not even an attendant or a nurse. There's no news of Maisie at all and I worry.

12 July 1931

Edward is a very lucky man. He's been allowed to leave the asylum today. He didn't even know that he was going. His mother wants him back home, she feels that she can look after him properly now. Edward came back into the ward to collect his things, we all gave him a hug and wished him well. I felt anger inside me. I felt jealous because I had been betrayed by my own father; indeed my whole family has betrayed me. There's a word for it but I can't find it in my dictionary. Edward leaving has made me think about everything again and again and I'm becoming very angry now. Really ~~fucking~~ angry!

13 July 1931

Mrs Skilton came by the farm this morning. She told me that she had been to see Miss Rance on Friday afternoon last. Miss Rance has finally had word from my father and he's agreed to come and sign my release papers. I'll be staying at Mrs Skilton's house and will be able to visit my father one Sunday a month.

'His wife has kindly agreed to this,' she said.

'Miss Rance has also spoken to Mr Luscombe and you'll be working full time hours at the farm so that you can pay your way,' she added.

At last this is the news I've been waiting for. I asked Mrs Skilton if she knew when this would all happen.

'Tuesday 4th August, the day after the Summer Bank Holiday, you should be able to leave and come to me the following Sunday,' she said.

I now look forward to then but I've heard this sort of thing before. Can I trust my father to attend the meeting and sign the papers? How can I be sure that something else might happen and stop me from leaving here?

14 July 1931

Just before it got dark yesterday there was a lot of commotion outside in the grounds. The new Head Attendant came into the ward and did a role call to make sure we were all inside. We were. Nurse Primrose and a new trainee nurse were told to make sure that no-one left their sight. Outside on the forecourt the asylum lorry came round and I saw Silas and Mr Randall jump in the back with lots of attendants from the other wards. It sped off towards the Bagshot Road exit at great speed. Nurse Primrose wasn't sure what had happened.

'It must be something very serious because I've never seen the attendants behave like this before,' she said.

All the patients were very excitable and it took Nurse Primrose a long time to get everyone off to sleep. At about 2 o'clock I heard voices outside. The asylum lorry had come back and dropped all the attendants off. They were chatting but I couldn't make out what they were actually talking about.

Silas and Mr Randall were missing at breakfast time and a new attendant was watching over us. Lionel asked him what had happened last night but he didn't know.

'I came on duty at 6 o'clock this morning and was given a message that Mr Randall and Mr Greenwood would not be signing in until nine. I don't know why,' he said.

Lionel had worked out that there must have been some trouble in one of the female wards.

'All the men are accounted for but some of the women patients looked quite distraught and upset when I saw them on the way to breakfast this morning,' he said.

We don't normally see any of the female patients at breakfast time so it did make me wonder.

Later at the farm Donald and his mother asked me if I knew what had happened last night.

'No, I was going to ask you, I thought you'd all know,' I said, but they didn't.

When I was washing the pigs down I began to worry that something might have happened to Maisie but then I felt that I was being stupid. I shouldn't think like that, surely someone would have said something to me if it had.

15 July 1931

I saw Mr Randall this morning and he looked very strangely at me. It felt like he was ignoring me. The new attendant came over and told me to get on with my breakfast.

'Get on with it! All the others have nearly finished theirs,' he said.

At that moment I felt a pit in my stomach. A voice was saying something in my head but I couldn't make out exactly what. I felt dizzy and rushed back up to the ward to lie down. Silas came in and told me that it was nearly time for me to go to the farm but I didn't feel well.

'Don't worry, I'll get a message over to Mr Flynn and tell him that you won't be working today because you're ill,' he said.

I must have slept for at least two hours. Just after 11 o'clock Mr Randall came in and asked me if I was alright.

'You probably just need some fresh air, come on, put your boots back on, let's go for a walk.'

This was very unusual and I began to worry. Now I began to sense that something very bad had happened. We went and sat on the logs on the edge of the woods.

'It's about Maisie isn't it?' I asked.

'Yes, I'm afraid so,' he replied.

He looked at me and I could see a tear in his eye. He started to tremble. I'd never seen him do that before.

'She never stood a chance; the poor sweet lass never stood a chance,' he said.

I wanted to say something back but I couldn't get any words out. He put his arm around me.

'She's dead, the poor sweet lass is dead.'

I went to ask him - How? Why? But still there were no words. My body suddenly went cold and I felt all fuzzy, dizzy.

'Take some deep breaths; I need to tell you what has happened to the poor girl.'

There was about a minute's silence where I just kept looking at the ground and then he told me.

'She got out on Monday night. The window was left open in the ablutions and she slid down the diagonal rainwater pipe and made good her escape. We wouldn't have known but there was an accident down at the railway station involving the 20.05 hours Waterloo to Southampton Docks. Someone had been hit and smashed to pieces. The constabulary contacted the Medical Superintendent when they found a note on the body linking it to the asylum. We were all called down there immediately to assist the railwaymen. The driver of the engine was in a right old state and the passengers were getting annoyed with us because they had a boat to catch to the Americas. The incident made them late. I didn't care for them toffs, if they missed their boat then I'm glad,' he said.

I still couldn't say anything. It was a lot to take in.

'Tommy boy, I'm very sorry for you, I know that you were fond off that poor sweet lass and I don't know what else to say. I think that you should go back to the ward now and lay down in the side room to get some rest. Take in what I've told you. I know it won't be easy but I felt it was only right that I should be the one to tell you before you heard it from anyone else.'

Just then I found some stamina to ask a question. Was it an accident or did she mean to get killed by the train? I asked.

'As I said the constabulary found a note on her, people quite often leave a note if they want to kill themselves,' he said.

I breathed in deeply and then wondered if it was because she thought that I had already left the asylum when I hadn't, or was it because of Angela Reeves? I know that she was supposed to be going back into Maisie's ward but I hadn't heard a thing. Now I am left to think about it all and I don't know what to do. Everything hurts inside so much.

17 July 1931

The sky is grey and everything else is black. All I want is my Maisie back...

19 July 1931

Yesterday evening I walked over to the mortuary. Mr Cutler and another man were outside smoking.

'Can I help you lad?' He asked. He was difficult to understand.

'Yes, I've come to see Maisie. I would like to see Maisie!'

He laughed. 'I can't let you do that and what was she to you anyway?'

'She was my girlfriend, my lover, my future wife!'

I felt myself nearly crying when I said that but I knew I had to say to him what I did. The other man who was with him walked away. I don't think he wanted to be involved in the conversation. Mr Cutler sat me down on the step.

'Look, even if I wanted to show you I couldn't. They brought the girl back in three separate hessian sacks, she's all in bits. It looks like her face was taken off the front of her head by the impact of the engine and other bits of her young body are still missing. My guess is that the foxes have had them by now. Anyway, she stinks of rotten meat and shit.'

I asked him why he was telling me all of this.

'Look, you asked if you could see her dead body and I'm telling you why you can't,' he snapped.

Walking back I didn't really know how to feel. Everything is still a mixture of emotions. I don't want to live without Maisie. I can't see how I can move on and live my life without her. I miss her so much and I still need to know why she died. I do hope that it wasn't because of me.

21 July 1931

Today has been Maisie's funeral. They took her from the mortuary just before dawn. She's been buried in the churchyard near Tilford Green. I wasn't allowed to go but Mr Randall passed me a scribbled message from her cousin.

'Maisie loved you with all her heart,' it says.

There were no further entries.

14482006R00183

Printed in Great Britain
by Amazon.co.uk, Ltd.,
Marston Gate.